Schism

Coming soon

Prey for the Soulless

Just Us

Dream Kill

Schism

K.R. Lugo

iUniverse, Inc.
Bloomington

Schism

iUniverse books may be ordered through booksellers or by contacting:

iUniverse
1663 Liberty Drive
Bloomington, IN 47403
www.iuniverse.com
1-800-Authors (1-800-288-4677)

ISBN: 978-1-4620-9353-3 (sc)
ISBN: 978-1-4620-9354-0 (hc)
ISBN: 978-1-4620-9355-7 (e)

Library of Congress Control Number: 2011963231

Printed in the United States of America

iUniverse rev. date: 01/31/2012

For Alisa, Virginia, and Robert—welcome aboard a nutty ride.

Acknowledgments

With loving gratitude to those who furnished me with everything needed to make this creation remotely possible.

Alisa Hurst, my truest partner in what we call this crazy life of ours, for never wavering in her belief in me, selflessly sacrificing endless hours, no doubt, assisting me during the dark times to make this all possible.

Virginia Lugo, perhaps the most devoted mother on the planet, for persevering and tolerating my incessant babbling during the creation of this book. Her job is not an easy one.

Robert Lugo, just a great father by every definition, for passing the receiver over to my mother when I was about to complain about something. He always makes me laugh.

Chapter 1

The light hazel eyes that reflected from the perfectly polished mirror were those of a woman who had seen far too many things in her life, terrible things that would forever alter the course of anyone's life. She licked her dry lips, causing her dimpled cheeks to elongate, as she continued to stare with unblinking eyes into the glass. She then leaned slightly forward to get a closer view of her facial features, not wanting to make any detectable errors that might make her appear even slightly clownish; ran a light coat of red lipstick over the contours of her pouty mouth; and then carefully blotted them on a folded-up piece of tissue paper by gently pressing her lips together. Once she had finished applying the final touches of makeup to her face, smiling to verify that she had correctly rouged her high cheek bones, the woman reached down and pulled each of the lilac spaghetti straps over her shapely porcelain shoulders. She then meticulously dabbed at the hair clips that held up her thick brunette mane and stood up from the chair that rested in front of the vanity once she was completely satisfied that her physical appearance was immaculate. She ran her hands over her ample breasts and down her tiny waist to smooth the material of the dress over her voluptuous body, shaking her hips ever so slightly.

The sound of the elevator doors opening from outside the room and down the hall reached her ears. Seconds later two voices—those of a man and a woman, probably a husband and wife—could be heard arguing as they walked down the hallway toward her room. They stopped right outside the door, each of their voices rising in the heat of the moment as words continued to be exchanged.

The woman inside the room remained unmoving as she listened intently to the subject of the conversation just outside the door. *Typical*, she thought as she pressed her tiny hands into fists. She blinked with deliberate slowness, wishing they would either kill each other or just do the courteous thing and be quiet. No one wanted to listen to their nonsense. She certainly didn't. She dabbed at her hair again for effect. "We don't need any interruptions, do we, baby?" the woman asked in a seductive whisper.

The sound of a door slamming shut across the hall echoed throughout the floor, followed by a man cursing loudly and kicking the door.

Silence.

Then the familiar mechanical sound of the elevator doors emerged once again.

"Finally, we have some privacy again, my love," the woman whispered. "People can be so very rude." She then used the mirror to look over her right shoulder in order to see the results of her unfortunate but very necessary actions. She frowned from the sight, wondering why everyone she ever cared for always left so selfishly. Like shadows during daybreak, they just vanished without a trace or explanation. No one, especially men, ever put her first. It just wasn't fair. But she always forgave them, regardless of their trespasses and betrayals. Blessed by God, she had been born with a heart of gold. If they couldn't see that—well—that was just their loss.

Sprawled out across the king-size mattress, hands and feet tied with leather straps to each of the four corners of the canopied bed that was prominently displayed by the posh hotel in pamphlets to lure visitors, lay the lifeless body of the man who had unwittingly approached his future murderess in the bar downstairs. Had he been alive to see the fate of how his life had ended, Samuel Smith might have found the surrounding circumstances somewhat amusing, if not downright hilarious. Samuel had always been a loving and faithful husband, never straying from his devotion to Marcia in thought or deed, but when he saw the stunning woman sitting alone in a booth in a dark, obscure corner of the bar, something almost primal had awakened within him, drawing him to her like a moth to a flame. The woman was flawless in appearance, and she exuded a sexuality that defied explanation, which was coupled with an aura of unidentifiable mystery, even a modicum of danger. He was powerless to resist her. He didn't know, and never would understand, why he felt overwhelmed with the desire to speak with her, to touch her, to be devoured by her, but the impulse could not be ignored or suppressed.

Arousing even more intrigue, the woman did nothing but sit alone in the shadows and daintily sip at a glass of red wine. She did not speak or move a single muscle other than those required to lift the crystal and drink from it as she stared off into the abyss.

If he had not been an out-of-town visitor, venturing out beyond the borders of the safety of his own hometown and to a distant city only because his company had sent him to attend a business conference, Samuel would have sprinted outside and driven off in his car as fast as the wheels would spin the first moment he had coveted anyone other than his beloved wife. Instead, since he opted to violate his own moral conscience by mustering up a misplaced version of courage he did not previously realize he possessed, shamelessly choosing to flirt with a woman who was physically out of his league, the dead body of Samuel Smith would eventually be found tied to a foreign bed in a thick pool of his own blood. Both corners of his mouth had been slashed up to the ears. A large knife was jutting out from his bare chest, and his severed genitals were floating in a jar of formaldehyde that rested on a nearby nightstand. His eyes had been meticulously sewn open with purple thread so he and those who found him could see and understand that all was not lost, because all men could be saved and sent into the realm of loving bliss. Sometimes people just had to be coaxed into seeing with their own eyes, so she had made certain those helped by her would see the error of their ways. None could escape or deny the incontrovertible truth, an absolute she had received in a biblical vision.

The woman walked over to the bed where her latest love lay and looked down at him with an almost quizzical expression. *He's so quiet,* she thought, tilting her head and wrinkling her nose from the metallic scent that was emanating from the massive amount of blood that saturated the linen. She then leaned down and ran her hand lovingly over his balding head with a sense of compassion for his plight. "You poor little man," she whispered, shaking her head ever so slightly as she peered down at the slain tool salesman. She caressed his cheek with the back of her hand, paused on the chin, and then pulled it away. "You have no one to blame but yourself and the weakness of your own flesh. The essence of this necessary act shall cleanse and give you a rebirth to make you worthy of my daughter." She then reached out to the nightstand that was located next to the bed and plucked a single rose from the bouquet he had bought for her in a pathetic demonstration of chivalrous romanticism and slid the stem between his two mangled lips. "For you, my misguided prince. Farewell, for I love you, if only briefly."

The sound of the door from across the hall being opened came again. A woman's voice was apologizing for acting like a jealous schoolgirl, immediately followed the sound of the door being shut. Seconds later the hum of the elevator summoned into operation sprang back to life.

When all fell silent once again, the woman stepped across the lush carpet and retrieved her designer purse, which was resting on a nearby chair. She removed an expertly handcrafted doll and smoothed out the blonde hair that cascaded over its head, cooing softly. Tears began to pool in the woman's eyes as she looked down at the perfect child she had constructed with her own hands and had loved since she'd willed the girl to life. "Shhh, Wendy," the woman breathed as she straightened out the doll's dress. She then walked back over to the bed. "I know, Wendy, but we need to take care of him, love him. He should not be alone. No one should ever be alone, not ever." She brought the doll up to her right ear and listened intently. Then she nodded her head in understanding. "Yes, sweetheart. Please do not fret over such minuscule matters.

Of course, I'll tell your sisters that you love and miss them." The woman moved the doll away and looked down at it with nothing but love filling her eyes. She then brought the doll up to her chest and hugged it with all her might, twisting her body as she did so. "I love you so much, Wendy." The woman then adjusted the doll's arms in the outstretched position and placed it facedown over Samuel's neck, providing the image that Wendy was hugging him tightly, like a lover who cannot bear to be separated from the one she adores beyond all else.

The woman, content that she was doing the right thing, the proper thing, walked over and picked up the purse, secretly wishing she could take Wendy with her. The others would understand, she thought. It was the natural course of all things, the inevitable conclusion for all those who matured into womanhood. *I will find them all a man to guide, to love, with whom to grow old.* She dabbed at her moist eyes with a silk handkerchief, careful not to smear her mascara, ashamed at herself for feeling a scintilla of jealously because Wendy had found a man to love her, and for her to love over the course of eternity. She then walked over to the front door, placed her hand on the brass knob, and started to turn it when she heard a voice call out to her from behind. She turned and smiled. "You're welcome, Wendy," the woman said. "Good-bye, my beloved daughter. I shall hold you in my heart forever." She opened the door and headed toward the elevator doors, happy that she had married off another one of her treasured babies.

After the elevator doors closed in front of her, finding the shimmy of the floor as she descended down the shaft slightly unnerving, she rocked her head to the melodic voice of Karen Carpenter singing about an ascending balloon. She then began to hum along with the music.

When the doors opened with a muffled mechanical clatter to the downstairs lobby, where dozens of visitors and employees were either busy scurrying about or reclining on plush chairs and couches, the woman nonchalantly stepped out and walked across the beautifully polished marble floor. She put on a false smile for all of the testosterone-driven men who looked upon her body with evil lust in their eyes and in their black hearts. *Pigs!* she cursed silently.

A large fountain was located in the center of the large room. The focus of it was a perfectly sculpted unicorn with the right foreleg raised. A constant stream of water flowed from the mythical equine's three-foot horn.

A young man of perhaps twenty years old approached her, obviously an employee of the hotel, and bowed slightly at the waist. When he stood completely upright he found it impossible to look away from the most penetrating eyes he had ever seen. They reminded him of those of a cat. Even the pupils seemed to vertically elongate. "Excuse me, miss, but may I be of service?" the young man asked in a voice that seemed overly polite. He reached out to take her purse, but she quickly pulled it out of his reach, clutched it against her chest, and shook her head. Her features suddenly took on a strained look, almost as if she were afraid for her safety. Taken aback by the woman's physical reaction, hoping no one had seen the obvious rejection, he grimaced slightly and took a step back. "I'm sorry, miss. I meant no harm. I work for the hotel as a bellhop, so I thought I would offer to help you, nothing more." He made certain to keep his voice soft and caring.

There was something in the tenor of the young man's voice that caused the woman to relax. She let her hands fall to her sides, still holding the strap of the purse tightly in her hand, and looked directly into the dark brown eyes of the employee. She measured the veracity of his words against the honesty of the eyes that looked at her. She didn't move for several seconds; she only stared at the patient bellhop.

And then a thought occurred to her.

She smiled from her innate matchmaking abilities. *He would be the ideal husband for my Jenny*, she thought.

The bellhop furrowed his brows, wondering why the woman would not speak to him. "Are you all right, miss?" he asked, concern crossing his young features. He looked over his shoulder in search of the desk clerk. "I can call you a doctor, if you're feeling ill."

The woman shook her head and held out a free hand. "Oh, no, that will not be necessary," she said. "I'm perfectly fine. I'm not very familiar with the city. And I'm extremely cautious of people."

The bellhop smiled in response to the reasonable explanation for her behavior and gladly accepted her hand. He blushed slightly when he felt her slowly run a thumb over the soft area between his index finger and thumb, and then he swallowed hard to clear his throat before daring to speak. "Perhaps, if you would like, I might be allowed to give you a tour of our city," he said, his voice cracking from nerves. It was obvious that an older woman of such astounding quality would never give someone like him the time of day. He half expected the ultimate humiliation that she would burst out laughing right in front of him, to his face.

"I think I would enjoy that very much," the woman said, releasing his clammy hand. Always on the prowl, she could smell the nervousness dripping from his pores. "As a matter of fact, I know I would like that very much." She peered at the expensive watch fastened around her petite wrist and nodded slowly. "So, when would you like our date to occur?"

"Our date?" the bellhop asked, the shock in his voice evident to anyone within hearing distance. He ran his tongue over his suddenly parched lips.

"Well, of course, silly," she said, giggling. "You are asking me out, are you not?" She offered a couple of flirtatious flutters of her long lashes. "Please correct me if I've misconstrued your intentions." She placed a single hand over her chest to feign embarrassment.

Afraid that he was going to inadvertently sabotage the situation, the bellhop searched his mind for the best line he knew to recover from such an unexpected change of fortune. He was speechless. All he trusted himself to do was smile dumbly and nod his head.

"Shall we say dinner tonight?" she asked. "After dinner, then perhaps you can escort me through the city and show me all of the wonderful sights."

The young bellhop, surprised beyond belief at his good luck, continued to smile and nod his head. "It would be an honor, miss," he finally managed to choke out.

"What time do you get off work?" she asked.

"Six," he replied.

"Six is just fine," she said. "How about I pick you up, then?"

"Okay," he said numbly, barely hearing her.

"So, what is your name?" she asked.

"Billy … I mean, William Preston," he replied.

"William, huh?" she repeated, licking her lips seductively. "I like that name. So very regal by nature." She leaned over and kissed him on the cheek, pausing ever so slightly with her moist lips pressed against his skin for sexual effect. "My name is Verona Capulet, William." The heat radiating off his skin spoke volumes to her. *Yes, he will be most perfect for my Jenny, and she will adore him, just as it was meant to be,* she thought, biting on her lower lip.

"It's a true pleasure to meet you, Miss Capulet," Billy said, wondering if the words sounded as stupid to her as they did to him. He knew that he was playing in a game that was so far out of his league that all he could do was fumble around and try not to appear like too much of a geek. The fact that he was a twenty-year-old virgin was embarrassing enough, leaving him about as much game with women as a diapered monkey playing chess.

"No, the pleasure is all mine, William," Verona said. "And, please, call me Verona. My mother was Mrs. Capulet."

"Okay," William said, inwardly chastising himself for acting like such a lame.

"Well, I have several appointments to make before our date, so I better take care of business so that we can concentrate on us," Verona said. She looked at her watch again. "Shall we say right here at six?"

"Okay," William replied, mechanically nodding his head up and down as if a ventriloquist had a hand shoved up his back and was controlling his every move.

"Perfect," Verona said.

"Uh-huh," Billy mumbled incoherently.

"Good-bye, William," Verona said. "Until tonight. It shall be an evening you shall never forget. I promise." She then turned and walked toward the exit of the hotel, the sound of her stiletto heels clicking against the marble floor, echoing throughout the area.

Still uncertain that he wasn't asleep and having one of those sex dreams that everyone was always talking about, Billy watched the most beautiful woman he'd ever seen walk away. He couldn't help but to admire the sensual way in which she sashayed as she gracefully traversed the floor. The perfect shape of her calves and the muscles when they contracted with each step sent shock waves through his nether region.

And then she turned to wave back at him just as she was about to walk through the front doors, smiling, her green eyes penetrating him even at such a great distance. He waved back, content with the fact that he knew it was real and not some sort of wishful thought.

And then she was gone.

Billy had not taken more than two steps when several of his fellow bellhops ran over to ask him about what they had just witnessed. They had heard stories about Billy's alleged magnetism for women of all ages, all of which were secretly started and spread by him, but now they had seen firsthand the evidence to support the story that Billy was the hotel stud and that no woman could resist or refuse him.

Jeb, a pimple-faced bully with anger issues and a proclivity for fighting, was the first coworker to reach him. Still wheezing from breathing in fumes from disinfectant bottles, he exhaled deeply and slapped Billy on the back. "Man, Billy, we saw that hooker babe hit on you," Jeb choked out. "Man, what did she say? Are ya gonna hit that or what?"

Several of the other hotel employees were now standing next to Jeb, waiting in anticipation for the answer to the question. A janitor pushing a mop bucket across the floor looked at the small squad of gossiping misfits as he passed by and raised a judgmental eyebrow when he overheard the first question. He had never understood why any of his moronic colleagues believed a single word that dripped from the kid's mouth. Anyone who had ever had a conscious thought could see the kid was nothing more than a bullshit artist, and not a very good one. But as he walked by whistling, trying to ignore the string of nonsense and mind his business, he shrugged his shoulders. Perhaps he'd been wrong. Either that or none of the hotel's crew had a functioning brain.

Grateful for the distance he had put between himself and the gaggle of horny young men, the janitor headed toward the restrooms. The voices were already fading from earshot.

Billy didn't immediately answer the question. Instead, trying to act like an experienced playboy and womanizer, he looked at each of his friends and smiled devilishly. He moved his hips back and forth. The others leaned toward him in anticipation, waiting as patiently as they could for him to speak.

Petie, a scrawny asthmatic, opened his eyes wide and burst out laughing from the sexual display. He didn't need to hear the answer, because Billy's body language said everything. "I knew it; I knew it," Petie chirped as he pretended to spank himself on the butt.

The others joined in on the fun and began to jump around like village idiots.

"You're all a bunch of lousy perverts!" a girl from behind the check-in desk called out to them. "You should be ashamed of yourselves."

Jeb turned to the girl and smiled. "You're just jealous is all, Harriot, because no one wants to do you," he said venomously.

"Do me?" Harriot blurted out in a tone of utter disgust. "What in the world would ever make you little pervs think I'd want to be done?"

Jeb put his hands on the back of his head and gyrated his pelvis. "Oh, we all know what you hookers want, baby. I bet you're a little freak in the sack."

The others laughed even harder from the antics.

"You're a pig!" Harriot yelled. She looked around the room and shook her head at the ridiculous display.

"Eat me," Jeb said, grinning.

"No thanks, girlfriend, I choke on small bones," Harriot said, lifting her chin in defiance. "Especially when they're microscopic." She held up a single pinky finger.

Jeb stopped moving immediately and lowered his hands to his sides. His mouth fell agape.

The other men fell silent seconds after Harriot hurled the insult, eyes darting back and forth, and then burst out laughing so loud that everyone in the lobby stopped what they were doing and stared at the flock of young men.

Petie giggled under his breath. He looked at Harriot and then at Jeb. "Oh, man, she burned you like a cheap match," Petie said. "That was cold, dude. She completely disrespected your joint."

Jeb moved forward and punched Petie in the shoulder. His face twisted into a combination of anger and humiliation. "Shut up, man, or I'll knock your head off," Jeb spat. He then squared off as if ready for an attack.

"Hey, man, don't get all crazy on me," Petie said, moving away, rubbing at the sore spot on his shoulder. "I didn't say nothin'." He pointed at Harriot, who was staring at them with a smirk on her face. "She's the one who capped on you."

Jeb started to walk toward her but was stopped when Billy grabbed him by the arm. Enraged, Jeb spun on his heels and pulled his arm loose. He glared at the other man. "Don't touch me, dude," Jeb growled.

"What's the matter with you?" Billy asked. "Not at work."

"Screw that!" Jeb spat.

"Mellow out, or we'll all get fired," Billy warned, his features pinching from the prospect of being unemployed.

The magnitude of the words struck each of the men with such a profound sense of concern that everyone fell into a somber silence. No longer were the words and actions of their colleagues remotely humorous.

Petie rubbed his hands together, nervous from the idea of losing another job. He knew his mom would kill him if he lost this one for acting like the same kind of moron she had always accused him of being. He peered at the others, cringing inwardly. "Billy's right," Petie muttered, stuffing his hands deep into his pockets, lowering his head. "I can't afford to lose my job, not when my mom needs help with her rent." He turned to walk away and get back to work.

"Where you goin', Petie?" Jeb asked in a belligerent tone. "What, are ya afraid of the boss, punk?"

Petie craned his head around and frowned at Jeb. "I'm afraid of losing my paycheck, dude," Petie replied, shrugging his shoulders. "Some of us have responsibilities and can't risk losing our job."

"I think you're just scared," Jeb said. He looked over at the others for support, but none of them would meet his mean-spirited stare. Jeb recognized the submissive faces and thought them all weak for buckling under the idea of losing what he thought was a lousy job. He turned his attention back to Petie. "What, you don't deny it?"

Petie waved him off. "Whatever, Jeb," Petie said. "Sometimes you can be such an ass, you know that?" He then left without saying another word.

Jeb spun around to the others and smiled crookedly, chuckling sinisterly. "What a stinking weenie," he commented.

The others looked at him with disgust and shook their heads.

"What?" Jeb asked, surprised by their collective reaction.

"You know what?" Billy said. "Petie's right. You're an asshole." Without saying anything further, grumbling under his breath, he walked away.

"Jerk," the others grunted loudly and walked away, leaving the perplexed Jeb staring after them with his mouth open.

The moment Verona stepped outside the hotel and into the warmth of the late morning, she stretched out her arms and smiled brightly from the prospect of finding a new husband for another one of her daughters. She raised her face skyward. The sun that caressed her perfectly sculpted features felt as if a thousand angels had reached down from the heavens with cherubic fingers to lovingly stroke her skin.

The people who were casually walking down the sidewalk stopped in their tracks when they saw the beautiful woman, wondering what could possibly be so interesting, and looked up into the sky. Finding nothing, and feeling silly for blindly mimicking her, they shook their heads and continued down the path.

Appeased by the warming of her face, Verona turned left and walked toward a distant traffic light, where dozens of pedestrians impatiently awaited the green light to cross the street. Not wanting to accidentally be touched or bumped into, she kept as close as possible to the storefronts that lined the street as she made haste to her office.

Cars of every make and design filled the street in bumper-to-bumper traffic. The drivers, growing impatient and hostile when progress down the avenue was nearly nonexistent, honked their horns and yelled obscenities out the windows.

As Verona was crossing the street, she raised her purse to her ear and leaned down, making certain to keep her eyes focused on her chosen path. "What's that, sweetheart?" Verona asked, concern filling her voice. Unable to hear the muffled voice from inside, she opened the purse and glanced inside to get a clear view of the perfectly handcrafted doll she had affectionately named Jenny only seconds after she had birthed her. "I've told you before, you must speak up so Mommy can hear you." She moved out of the normal path of people when she reached the end of the street and stopped next to a building. "Yes, Jenny. I understand. But you must be a good girl and be patient with Mommy." She then reached down into the purse and stroked the long blonde hair of her daughter. "Mommy loves you. Yes, we'll talk about this a little later. Yes, I have to get to work right now. No, you're going to make me late." Verona looked down the street and then focused back on Jenny. "Stop it!" She then closed the purse.

Worried over the general welfare of people in his hometown, having noticed the peculiar woman who stood near an open doorway seemingly talking to herself, an overweight man stepped over and made to introduce himself and offer his assistance.

"Excuse me, miss, but ..." he began, but he was startled into silence when the woman yelped in fear and quickly made for an escape. Once he understood that he had scared her, realizing that he had only antagonized the situation, he called after her, offering his help. She neither answered nor looked back.

With the purse clutched tightly against her chest, grossly panicked over being accosted by a complete stranger, Verona picked up her pace into what would have looked like a practiced power walk to the casual observer.

"Oh, Jenny, that was so close," Verona squeaked. "Did you see the wicked lust in that man's eyes? Oh, my goodness, he would have raped us both if we hadn't gotten away from his filthy paws. I could smell it on him." She quickly rounded the corner, her place of work now within eyesight, the only place of refuge where she felt completely safe, excepting her own pristine home. "We're almost there, baby, so hold on." She could hear Jenny's frightened screams. "Don't you worry, honey. Mommy will protect you."

When Verona entered the powerful law firm of Hanson & Hanson, the legal secretary stood up from behind the desk and smiled widely. "Good morning, Miss Hanson," the secretary said. She looked over at the ten-foot grandfather clock to verify the time. "The board of directors is waiting for you in the conference room."

Once she had walked into the private domain where she reigned supreme above all others, Jillian Hanson, daughter of Zachariah Hanson, a rich industrialist and cutthroat lawyer, was transformed into her father's chiseled legacy of iron-fisted rule. Similar to previous heirs of powerful men and women, Jillian's destiny was mapped out by the elder Hanson only seconds after learning that his wife was carrying his heir apparent inside her belly. From the moment Jillian was capable of speech and cognizance, Zachariah had indoctrinated her with one fundamental principle: losing was for losers. And if she wanted her father to love her, truly love her, then she would follow in his footsteps without question and conquer all obstacles that were foolish enough to test a Hanson's resolve. She was Daddy's little girl, forever and ever. When his wife had attempted to protest, espousing her motherly concerns that he was warping his own daughter in order to fit into his own perverse concept of family values and loyalty, he had called in several favors to rectify the undesirable interference. One week later to the day of the telephone call, Emily Hanson was forcefully committed to a mental hospital, where she lived in four-point restraints until the accumulation of high doses of medication finally claimed her life. Immediately following the death of Zachariah Hanson, who was erroneously suspected of succumbing to a long struggle with leukemia, Jillian had learned during the reading of the will that she had inherited everything from her father's massive estate, to the absolute exclusion of his own brothers. Thus, with a single stroke of a pen, Jillian Hanson had become a multibillionaire, the richest woman in the world, and well beyond the borders of reproach.

"Thank you, Miss Gardner," Jillian said, her voice strong and confident. "I appreciate all that you've done."

"You're very welcome, Miss Hanson," she replied. She picked up the receiver. "Shall I notify the board that you're on your way up to see them?"

Jillian shook her head. "No, thank you," she said. "That won't be necessary. I will just surprise them." She headed for the elevator doors.

"As you please," Miss Gardner said, setting the receiver back on the cradle. She stared after the woman, who walked with purpose in her stride.

The moment Jillian entered the luxuriously decorated conference room, an air of superiority filled the entire area. She made no formal introduction or greeting. Regardless of the fact that she had summoned the board of directors to meet her in the main room, she made no apology for her tardiness. As far as she was concerned, they were there to serve her interest, and if one of them didn't like it, he or she could leave the property and collect a severance check later in the week.

The members remained absolutely quiet as they watched the daughter of their former founder stand unmoving just inside the open door.

With eyes of a jungle predator, she just stared with methodically slow, shifting eyes as she gazed upon each face, measuring each individually for any sign of weakness.

Her behavior reminded them of a panther preparing to strike at its intended prey. When she still had not uttered a single syllable after nearly five minutes, the board members began to move about uneasily. Although they considered the female version of Zachariah brilliant, there was something deeply disturbing about her mannerisms. Some were genuinely afraid of her.

Always preferring to have people fear her rather than love her, Jillian ruled her life at work like a queen who lorded over the realm in which she was born to control. She was well aware of the inevitable fact that she had corporate enemies, particularly within the legal community, not that she actually cared what they tried to do or what they thought about her. She would crush anyone who was asinine enough to stand in the way of her objective. The more combative the challenger, the more vicious she would gladly become, thriving as she traversed the path to another's ultimate destruction and destitution. She simply referred to it as her "thing" when asked why she was such a coldhearted bitch.

Content that she had made her point of projecting dominance over the subordinates when they demonstrated signs of slinking down in the chairs, Jillian hugged the purse that held her beloved daughter inside against her chest and took a seat at the head of the long table. Gifted with a photographic memory, she had no real use for notes, written or otherwise, so rarely did anyone ever see her carry a briefcase.

To those seated at the table, who had stacks of paper to guide them through arguments, the fact that Jillian needed no such crutch to effectuate her averments was exceedingly intimidating.

Although expertly trained in corporate law and finance by her father, she preferred to practice criminal law. Prosecutors silently wished she would return to arguing in the civil world and leave them to use the public defender's office as cannon fodder for their own means. The minute the district attorney learned that she had become a defendant's lawyer, be it by retainer or pro bono, it was only a matter of minutes before a call was made to her office for the purpose of entering into plea negotiations. She was too smart, ambitious, well connected, and wealthy to beat. It was an irrefutable truth that was proved every time one of her cases went to trial. Jillian Hanson never lost a trial, and the district attorney refused to have his office embarrassed further by trying to alter the fact.

"So, what is the status of the antitrust case?" Jillian asked. She looked over to the lead counsel she had put in charge.

Nathanial Brooks opened the brief he had prepared for the meeting and began to peruse the pages, a slight frown creasing his features as he searched for the best answer.

Jillian huffed slightly and shook her head with impatience. "It's not a trick question, Nate," she said, "so close the paperwork and just give me a quick synopsis. Is the government willing to accept the proposed offer of a fine and no felony charges?"

Nate reluctantly closed the brief and peered up from the brown cover. "We're still in the middle of negotiating, but I think the government will settle only on the premise that Mr. Piper serve at least two years in a federal correctional center, possibly a camp."

"I see," Jillian offered, a shadow covering her features. She then narrowed her eyes. "And you find that acceptable, do you?"

"Miss Hanson, I think the situation is amicable enough to ..." the woman who was sitting second chair to Nate on the case began, opening her own drafted brief.

Jillian craned her head around and glared with deadly eyes at the woman. "I do not believe I was speaking to you, Heather," Jillian interrupted, her voice low and coarse. She looked at the woman's brief and shook her head in disappointment. "Our clients pay us obscene amounts of money to keep them out of prison, not to make deals for minimum time, so the day I cannot crush a government puke who graduated from some obscure community college is the day I shoot myself in the damn head."

Heather lowered her eyes, wishing she could crawl under the massive table and remain there until the meeting had concluded. "I apologize for inadvertently diminishing this firm's ability," Heather said, her voice submissive.

"Don't be sorry, Heather, just don't do it," Jillian said. "I handpicked all of you for your incredible skills and intelligence, so never believe we are not legal immortals." She turned her attention back to Nate. "Have you filed a suppression motion?"

Nate shook his head. "Not as of yet," he replied, looking at a booklet of papers resting in front of him. "I've been researching the case law and believe Heather and I have completed enough briefing to draft up an effective motion."

Jillian reached out and tapped the intercom button that sat on the table.

"Yes," a voice answered. "May I help you?"

"Yes, Michelle," Jillian replied. "This is Jillian."

"Hello, Miss Hanson," Michelle said. "What can I do for you?"

Jillian looked at her legal crew with smiling eyes. "Would you please send Brad in and tell him to bring me the Sherman Act motion."

"Of course, Miss Hanson," Michelle said.

"Thank you, Michelle," Jillian said. She then depressed the button and waited with professional patience for her personal hatchet man to show up.

No one uttered a single word.

Less than two minutes later a knock came from the door.

After hearing the familiar voice of his employer summon for him to enter, Brad Renfro opened the door and walked directly over to where Jillian sat. He set a stack of stapled documents on the table. "This is the motion you requested, Miss Hanson," he announced.

Jillian looked up at her personal paralegal and grinned. "Thank you, Brad," she said. "Did you find any errors or misrepresentations?"

"Not one," Brad replied, adamant. "I thoroughly Shepardized the decisional law germane to the issue of prosecutorial misconduct and reached the conclusion handed down by the Supremes that bad faith is not an element under any circumstances. At best the government must assert an unqualified statement." He nodded his head in affirmation. "Your brief is perfect."

"Thank you, Brad. I appreciate the vote of confidence," Jillian said.

"It's my pleasure, Miss Hanson," Brad said. "Is there anything else you need me to do before I go back to my desk?"

"No, this is fine," Jillian replied as she picked up the documents and rapped them on the top of the table. "Thank you."

No one said anything until after Brad had left the conference room and closed the door behind him.

Nate was the first to sit up, followed by Heather, and look over to where Jillian was separating multiple copies. "What is that?" Nate asked, unnerving apprehension dripping from his voice. He glanced over to where Heather was biting back on her lower lip, probably wondering if he was about to become removed from the case, and then back to Jillian. Surprises made him extremely uncomfortable. In his experience, nothing good ever came from the unknown or unexpected.

Jillian held up the papers and looked at the two attorneys assigned to the Piper case. "Since I rather predicted there would be a problem with getting the government to submit to zero prison time, as stubborn as the US attorneys always seem to be in their blindness, I took it upon myself to draft up a motion to quash the warrant on the home of Harold Piper's mistress," Jillian said. She tossed a copy to both Nate and Heather, who picked them up.

"I wasn't aware that a suppression motion was filed by this office," Nate said, dumbfounded. He looked at Heather for her input, but she merely shrugged her shoulders.

"It hasn't been filed, not yet," Jillian said. "I want you to personally take that to the US attorney and give it to him. I want you to tell him to read it right there. Do not leave until you are certain he's read it." Jillian steepled her fingers together. "Tell him that he has one hour to accept the no-prison deal, or I shall personally file that in the court. Just tell him that it's a professional courtesy before his case is obliterated, along with any future ambition to run for political office."

Heather shifted uncomfortably in her chair as she read the document.

Jillian noticed the woman's discomfort immediately, grinning malevolently. "Is there something wrong, Heather?" Jillian asked.

"How did you learn that one of the federal agents perjured himself on the search warrant?" Heather asked. "I mean, if that is true—"

"Oh, it's true," Jillian interrupted. "It's damn true, and I can easily prove it, if the prosecution does not bend to my will. As far as how I came into possession of the knowledge, that does not concern any of you. I have my own, external sources."

"I would feel a lot better if I knew the source, Miss Hanson," Heather said, cringing.

Jillian smiled and tilted her head. "I understand your dilemma, Heather," Jillian said, her voice soft, almost tender. "You're off the case."

Heather looked horrified. "B-B-B ..." Heather stuttered, words failing her.

"But nothing," Jillian said. "Please leave the room."

Unable to summon the courage to protest her summary removal, Heather stood up and did as ordered. She held her head in shame.

After Heather had closed the door, Jillian turned to Nate. "Pick a new second chair, Mr. Brooks," she directed apathetically.

"Uh, I will need a little time to ..." Nate began, eyes wide, stunned by the summary expulsion.

"Choose now, or I'll replace you myself for indecision," Jillian warned. She was no longer smiling. Her voice was as sharp as a razor, her eyes chilling.

Without any further hesitation, Nate pointed a finger across the table. "Carl will serve as an excellent second chair on the case," Nate announced. "He's already fairly familiar with the case and the players."

Carl gritted his teeth and glared at Nate for dragging him into his mess.

"Great decision," Jillian said. "This meeting is officially adjourned." She stood up and motioned for the board members to leave the room.

One by one, without speaking, holding their heads slightly bowed, the twelve men and women filed out the door. Every one of them wondered if any of them would see Heather Lasko the following day.

Chapter 2

T he longer Billy Preston found himself waiting for the woman to show up, for what he had come to believe would be a memorable night of carnal delight with a far more experienced lover, the more he was beginning to feel like an absolute fool for daring to think such a thing. It was starting to become humiliating for him to have friends nearby. Harriot had already left from work nearly thirty minutes earlier, making sure to cruelly tease Billy for being so pathetically stupid on the way out the door. Jeb was quickly losing what remained of his patience by waiting for a woman he now highly doubted ever intended to return to the hotel, least of all to pick up a lowly employee who was one step above a toilet cleaner. Only Petie held on to faith that Billy was indeed a babe magnet, harboring no doubts whatsoever about the stranger's intent to bed his best friend. She would show. He was sure of it. She had to.

Billy looked down at his knockoff wristwatch for the tenth time in as many minutes and grimaced from the late hour. If she stood him up, there was no doubt in his mind that he would become the new butt of every joke in the hotel, especially since he had flagrantly boasted about the expectations for the evening. Harriot would unquestionably see to that, while enjoying every single second of emasculating him.

Although most of the employees adored her and thought she was a real sweetheart, there was a mean streak in her that ran red.

He'd seen it on more than one occasion. He would have to quit his job, maybe even leave the city, at least the immediate area, if the humiliation became too much for him to bear.

Silently he cursed himself for spouting off at the mouth; he couldn't believe he could be so idiotic as to repeat history so quickly. He had been in the city less than nine months. *Stupid! Stupid! Stupid!* Billy thought as he looked up at the hotel doors. She was now forty-five minutes late. *She's not coming. I'm just going to get burned.*

"Don't you worry none, Billy," Petie chirped, enthusiastically nodding his head up and down like a bobble toy. "She'll be here. I just know it. She probably just had to go get some vitamins or something like that."

Billy conjured up a face of confidence he did not feel and gave a quick nod of his head to affirm what his friend had just said to him. "Yeah, you may be right about that, Petie-man," Billy said, the tone of his voice lacking a degree of conviction. "She probably wanted to get one of those energy drinks."

Petie slapped his leg and laughed aloud. "That's it, I bet!" he said, smiling broadly. "I just know that's what those ritzy hookers do. I see it on the TV all the time. They're all total freaks in the sack."

Jeb rolled his eyes and slapped himself on the forehead with an open hand. "Jeez, dude, what are you, completely brain dead?" he stated, completely flabbergasted. His voice was one of annoyance. "The only action Billy's gonna get is if he decides to pull on his vine like a spider monkey in a banana tree." He looked around the open area and grunted his disbelief. "I can't believe I waited around this long for something that was never gonna happen. This just sucks!" He glared at Billy with critical eyes. "You are so full of crap, dude. I'm so out of here." He then turned to leave but was stopped in midstride when Petie grabbed him roughly by the arm and spun him around.

"Hey, man, how about showing some respect for our main dude?" Petie spat, squeezing Jeb's arm as tight as his scrawny appendage could manage.

Angry about being touched by the dweeb, Jeb yanked his arm

free of the smaller man's grasp and then pushed him away with a hard shove. "Get off me, lame," he growled. "Don't make me homicide you, because I will!"

Without concern for himself, Billy stepped between the two men and held his hands up to each of their chests. "Will the two of you knock it off?" he said sternly. "You're acting like a couple of stupid kids in the playground."

"Hell, I don't need this crap," Jeb said, rolling his eyes and shaking his head at the whole situation.

Petie lifted his chin and smiled at Jeb in defiance. "Then leave, why don't you?" he said. "No one wants you here anyway." He shifted his eyes to look at Billy, his features expressing undeniable admiration. "Ain't that right, Billy?" He nodded his head. "None of us like him anyhow."

"Man, dude, you're like some sort of chick in love," Jeb said, smiling crookedly. "What, are you like in total love with the dude? You're friggin' disgusting."

"Screw you, butt wipe," Petie said. "Billy's my ace-deuce, and you know it."

"That's enough!" Billy said, his voice angry. "Both of you just shut the hell up and shake hands."

Jeb held up his hands and shook his head. "I'm history, Billy," he said. "I'll see you and freak boy tomorrow." He turned to walk away and was annoyed even further when he bumped into a teenage boy dressed in bicycle spandex shorts, who was just standing in front of him for seemingly no particular reason. "Now what in the hell do you want?"

The pubescent held out a piece of paper, frowning, and pulled his head down into his shoulders as if expecting to be punched in the face at any given moment. "Sorry for interrupting you guys, but I was told to give this to a guy by the name William," the delivery boy said. His hand trembled ever so slightly as he continued to hold out the piece of paper in hope that it would be accepted without question or argument.

"Is that right?" Jeb asked in a slight snarl. "So who gave it to you, bicycle boy?"

"Is your name William?" the boy asked, his voice a slight tremble.

"Maybe," Jeb said. He snatched the piece of paper from out of the boy's hand, narrowing his eyes at the youth as a tactic to intimidate.

"Hey, you can't take that," the boy complained, perking up. "I could get fired."

"Shut up, asshole," Jeb said. "Now, who gave this to you?"

The boy started to move to take the paper back but then quickly changed his mind when he saw the look on the other person's face. He decided it was prudent to just simply answer the question. Nothing was worth getting beaten up for, certainly not a lousy letter. "Some dude who looked like that butler on *Batman* gave me fifty bucks to pass it over to some guy by the name of William," the boy replied. "He said he worked here in the hotel." He licked his lips nervously. "I didn't ask any questions. I just wanted to make a fast fifty bucks, that's all. It's from someone called something like Corona. The name was really strange. Never heard it before, at least not that I remember. It was kind of pretty."

Billy stepped forward and quickly snatched the paper from out between Jeb's fingers. "Are you sure it wasn't Verona?" he asked. He unfolded the note and began to read the brief message that was scrawled across it.

"Yeah," the boy replied, figuring he'd just met William, "that's the name. Verona. Kind of nice, don't you think?" When no one bothered to offer a comment, he shrugged his shoulders and silently walked off in search of the bicycle he had chained outside, hoping that no one had stolen it.

After having finished reading the note, Billy held up the small piece of paper and whooped in glee. "So, I'm not getting any, huh?" he piped, waving the paper in front of Jeb's face. "I don't think so, dude." He took the upper two corners of the note between the index fingers and thumbs of his hands and held it up so Jeb could read the writing. "In your face, Jebster!"

Petie threw several shadow punches in victory. "Ha, in your face, Jeb!" he cried out, jubilant. "You don't know nothin', nothin' at all."

"Whatever, lame," Jeb mumbled under his breath, his patience for Petie's irritating antics quickly dwindling with each passing second, now nearly reaching the end of its tether. He gave a short sweep of the hand and walked away, having lost all interest. The last thing he wanted to do was lose his job for getting into a physical altercation at work, especially for punching out the one employee everyone, including the manager, seemed to like, unlike himself. Jeb knew without one scintilla of doubt that none of his fellow coworkers would shed a bitter tear if he were to be seen in the unemployment line, collecting free state cheese. As quiet as he kept the truth, though he complained incessantly, Jeb genuinely liked his job. "I'll see you idiots tomorrow." He waved to them as he walked away.

Petie laughed at Jeb's ultimate defeat and pointed an accusing finger at the man's back. "You don't have to get all pissy for losing," he teased, sticking his tongue out at the man.

Jeb stopped dead in his tracks the moment he heard the sarcastic words spew from Petie's mouth. He considered simply turning around, taking the few steps needed to be standing directly in front of the mouthy little pest, a rodent he could easily smash like a bug, and knocking him smooth out with a right hook to the jaw. Instead, reaching deep down and exercising every ounce of self-control he could muster, he hunched up his shoulders and headed directly for the exit with haste. He silently prayed Petie would keep his mouth shut until after he was out of earshot.

The moment Billy saw that Petie was about to open his mouth again, undoubtedly prepared to say something even more asinine, words that would certainly cause him to get beaten within an inch of his 120-pound life, Billy slapped him on the back of the head and then glared at him with eyes of warning when Petie craned his head around to look at him.

Wincing more from hurt feelings than actual pain, Petie rubbed the spot where he'd just been struck and bit down on his lower lip.

"What was that for, homey?" he asked, continuing to rub his head. "I was just sticking up for you."

Billy shook his head. *Damn, he's as dumb as a sack of wig hair,* Billy thought. "No," he replied. "You were about to be used as a human mop on the floor, dummy, and Jeb was going to be the janitor."

Petie frowned from the insult and then lowered his eyes. "I thought you said it wasn't right to call me dumb, Billy," Petie muttered miserably. He slowly lifted his eyes to meet those of his best friend. "You said it's mean."

Billy sighed heavily, unable to shake the guilt gnawing at him for the hurtful words he had hurled only seconds ago. He smiled apologetically. "You're right, buddy," he said, draping his arm over the other man's shoulder. "I shouldn't say such mean things. Of course you're not dumb. I'm really sorry, okay?" He pulled the smaller man against him tightly. "Are we okay?"

Petie cheered right up and smiled brightly. "Oh, that's okay, Billy," Petie chirped happily. "Sometimes I have to be reminded that I talk too much." He playfully punched Billy in the arm.

"So, does that mean you forgive me?" Billy asked, even though he already knew the answer to the question. He then punched his friend back in kind.

Without speaking a single word, Petie bobbed his head up and down excitedly.

"Glad to hear it, P-man," Billy said, holding up the note delivered to him by the spandex boy.

"So what does the letter say, Billy?" Petie asked, narrowing his eyes in curiosity. "Is she going to come and pick you up?"

"Actually, no," Billy replied. "It says a car is going to be sent to pick me up and bring me to where she is waiting for me."

"What car?" Petie asked, not comprehending why she would send a car and not come herself. "So who's coming?"

"I'm not real sure," Billy replied, furrowing his brow. "I'm just supposed to go outside and wait on the corner over by the bench until the car comes to pick me up."

"Well, that's kind of weird," Petie muttered, crinkling his nose as if he smelled something bad. "But I guess that's how those fancy-schmancy women are, huh?"

Billy thought about what Petie had said and grunted inwardly. It was rather strange, Billy thought, wondering why she would even bother with sending a car if she wasn't willing to do as she had said by coming to pick him up. But a woman such as herself was probably very busy. He was unsure as to whether he should be offended or flattered about receiving such a clandestine message. It was definitely unexpected. Nonetheless, in spite of the wave of mixed emotions, he couldn't help but to be excited over the whole cloak-and-dagger circumstance that was usually reserved strictly for the movies. The woman was quickly proving to be more of a mystery than he had first suspected.

Intrigued by her course of action in writing the note in the first place, Billy decided to waste no further time and tucked the stationery safely away in the front pocket of his pants. He then headed out the front door of the hotel lobby.

Admiring his friend's moxie from the ever increasing distance, Petie held a single thumb out and pointed it straight into the air. He waited for Billy to turn around and wave good-bye, but neither scenario took place. Billy simply disappeared through the doors as he left the massive structure. The speed of his steps indicated a man on a mission.

Although it was beginning to grow dark from the lateness of the hour, accompanied by a cold bite to the wind that mercilessly blew in from the south, a few people were still walking along the outer sidewalks that lined the streets. The traffic that was once congested and hostile had become sparse and peacefully quiet.

It was a beautiful evening, one that people cherished when opting to go out for a nightly romantic stroll.

The second Billy stepped outside he lifted his face to the night sky, breathed in heavily, and stretched his arms outward like a bird spreading its wings. It was his favorite time of the day, just after twilight, and the faint scent of moisture in the air only added to his immense pleasure. The atmosphere smelled of cleanliness, the same kind of aroma that alerted a person's nose that it was going to rain in the very near future. The few people who had chosen to brave the coolness of the weather started to walk past the uniformed hotel employee, but then they stopped and mimicked the young man. They wondered what the young man could possibly find so fascinating overhead and searched the sky momentarily, squinting their eyes in desperation to locate the object evidently so interesting. After only a few seconds of pointless stargazing, deciding there was nothing at all to see, they huffed angrily and shook their head in annoyance, believing the boy was either playing a childish prank at their apparent expense or was a complete moron for wasting time by staring up at nothing.

Ignoring the chastising expressions on the faces of those passing by along the sidewalk, Billy turned his head to the right and immediately noticed an elderly woman sitting alone. He then made his way toward the lonely bench located on the curb without further hesitation.

When the old woman saw the young man approach, she looked up and offered a broken-toothed smile. She quickly picked up the small pile of newspapers that had been haphazardly strewn across the hard surface and stacked them neatly on her lap. She then gently patted them as if they were a beloved pet. In spite of the old and tattered appearance of her clothes, which were akin to the garments of a long-fated homeless person, the warmth and compassionate nature emanating from her was undeniable. Her smile never wavered in the slightest.

Filled with empathy for the old woman, who was obviously all alone in the world, Billy stood over her for several seconds before returning her smile. He couldn't help but to wonder how people could find the unfortunate virtually invisible. They were all people, only differentiated by an affliction of tragic events and circumstances.

She continued to smile, her eyes bright and oddly clear.

"Hello," Billy greeted, maintaining a permanent smile.

"Good evening," the old woman reciprocated, tilting her head slightly.

"May I sit next to you?" Billy asked, his voice soft and polite. He was afraid of doing anything that might startle the old woman.

The old woman smiled even wider, grateful for the company, even if only for a brief moment in time, and patted the loose planks beside her. "Of course you can, young man," she said. "It's a free country."

"Thank you very much," Billy said. He then sat down on the badly worn and faded bus stop bench and gazed into the sky. "Nice night, huh?"

The old woman turned her ancient head and peered at the young person sitting next to her with a curious eye. "It's pretty enough, I suppose, but it's a little chilly for this old girl's tired bones," she said. She held out a fingerless gloved hand. "My name is Maude, Maude Clemens. My friends just call me Ma."

Billy reached out and took a firm hold of her gnarled fingers, sympathy coursing through him when he found that her emaciated hand was nearly frozen, and shook her hand. "I'm Billy, Ma, Billy Preston, and it's my pleasure to meet you," he said sincerely.

"Aren't you a polite little charmer," Ma said, releasing his hand. "It's rare these days that anyone, particularly a person as young as yourself, would treat someone like me with—with any semblance of common courtesy or respect. Most people would have just walked past me when they saw me sitting here, and just looked for somewhere else to sit while waiting for the bus. We're not to be seen or heard, like phantoms in the dark corners of the forgotten alleyways." Her smile faded momentarily as she thought about the past abuses she had suffered at the hands of those who would prefer her to slink off and die in obscurity.

Cringing from the woman's self-deprecating opinion, Billy wondered how someone obviously educated could find herself in such a dire situation. Although the face that now looked back at him was heavily marked by lines of anguish and disappointment, a certain dignity remained behind the sagging folds of flesh that had laid claim to a quiet beauty that had once existed before the ravages of abuse and time had usurped her youth. He struggled to find his voice. "I … I don't think everyone is like that," he stammered, his voice wispy and lacking conviction.

Ma reached out and patted his hand in an almost grandmotherly fashion. "Neither do I, Billy," she said. "At least not anymore." She nodded her head. "You've brought some joy to an old woman's heart, young man, and I thank you for that fact. You're a very special person, so don't you dare ever let anyone tell you different."

Billy opened his mouth and started to engage the old woman in further conversation, but he fell silent when a black limousine silently pulled up alongside the curb and came to a sudden stop. The old woman audibly gasped in awe of the luxurious automobile, while Billy sat absolutely motionless. His eyes remained focused on the gas-guzzling vision that idled before him.

"That is some kind of car," the old woman uttered. "It must cost well over a million dollars."

The incongruent sound of a vacuum filled the air, and then the back door of the car opened with a slight whoosh.

"Lordy, I've never seen nothing like that," the old woman said. She dabbed at her hair as if she expected royalty to emerge from behind the cab.

There was a slight crackle of the sound from a speaker, followed by a high-pitched, tinny voice. "Mr. Billy Preston, please enter the vehicle," a voice announced.

The old woman turned and looked at Billy in shock, her mouth slightly agape. "Didn't you say your name was Billy?" she asked, unable to bring herself to stop gawking. "Lordy, all that's good and decent."

Billy silently nodded his head, numb.

The synthetic crackle repeated. "Please enter the automobile, Mr. Preston," the alien voice said again. "Ms. Capulet is waiting for your arrival, and I assure you that she is not a patient woman. We have a schedule, so I urge you to make haste. You shall not be asked again."

The old woman wrinkled her ancient brow and stared at the limousine. "Capulet?" she mumbled, turning to Billy. "And are you suppose to be Mr. Montague?" She nudged him to wake him from an obvious stupor.

Billy blinked several times and then shook his head ever so slightly as if he were trying to shake away dizziness. "Excuse me," he breathed. He turned to the old woman and smiled. "I'm sorry, I didn't hear you."

The old woman chuckled and slapped him on the knee. "You better get going and get in the car before it drives off and leaves you here with me," she said, the tone of her voice betraying the words she had just spoken. "I doubt you want to spend such a beautiful night with an old wrinkle puss like me."

Billy looked at her with eyes brimming full of compassion for the old woman he'd just met. A sense of guilt, coupled by a degree of shame, gnawed at him. He didn't want to just abandon and leave her in the cold, all alone. "I'll stay here with you, if you want me to, Ma," Billy said, sincerely.

She looked at him with a curious glint in her eye and then smiled. "And why would you do that, Billy?" she asked, monumentally touched by his words.

Billy reached out and took her hand into his own. "Because we all need a friend," he replied, gently squeezing her emaciated fingers so as not to hurt her, "and I want you to know that I am your friend."

Maude sniffed back tears as she looked into the face of the first person who had shown her genuine affection for longer than she could actually remember, or ever dare admit. "My young friend, thank you," she said, wiping tears away with the back of her free hand. "I am truly touched by your gesture."

Billy furrowed his brow. "For what?" he asked, uncomprehending.

"It's people like you that give me reason to believe there are still good ones in the world," she said. "Just when I was about to lose all hope, you come along, sit next to me, and give me reason to believe in people again." She squeezed his hand to reinforce the level of gratitude she truly felt. "And I love you for that, child."

"Thank you, Ma," Billy stammered, slightly embarrassed. "That's nice of you to say, but I cannot just ..." He paused, turned and looked at the car, and then looked back at her.

"Please, go," she said. "Go have some fun, enough for the two of us." She smiled. "You're young. The whole world is right at your fingertips, so reach out and snatch it to claim as your own."

Billy sat up from the bench. "Are you sure?" he asked.

"Yep," she replied, waving him off. "Go."

Billy reached into his back pocket and withdrew a tattered wallet. He retrieved a card from the hotel with his name on the back and one of the three twenty-dollar bills he'd stashed from his last paycheck. He then held one out to her.

"What's this?" she asked, frowning slightly, not reaching out for the offered item.

"Just a little something for you from a friend," Billy said. "Please take it. I want you to have it."

"I don't want your money," she said.

"I know," Billy replied simply. "I want you to have it, along with the address of the place where I work." He paused. "If you wouldn't mind, I'd like to talk to you some more."

"Why?" she asked.

"I like you, and you're nice to talk to," Billy said. "And I'd feel better if I knew you were okay."

"So this is for you, is that right?" she asked, her mouth beginning to form a grin.

"Absolutely," Billy said. "It's a selfish gesture, nothing less or more than that. Just call me self-centered." He set the things on the bench and walked toward the car.

"Have a nice time, Billy," she said. "I'll talk to you soon."

He reluctantly peered back one last time to see if the old woman he'd come to affectionately know as Ma had changed her mind about having him for company, only to watch her slowly shake her head with a genuine smile plastered on her weathered face. Billy then climbed into the back of the stretch limousine.

The same peculiar sound of air, like that of a tire going flat, came again.

And then the heavy car door shut, immediately followed by a sharp click of it being locked.

Momentarily startled by the unexpected confinement behind the driver's cab, Billy looked around the expensively furnished area for any means of escape, if such became necessary. There appeared to be none. In fact, the back of the limousine seemed to have been built like a fortress, allowing no one entrance or exit. And he was hopelessly trapped inside.

Fear increasing, he pressed the intercom button on the console, to no avail. After a second attempt to get the driver's attention failed, Billy laid down on his back, pulled his legs back, and was about to kick at the darkly tinted side window in hope of breaking the glass when the partition began to slowly descend. Taken by surprise, hoping for the best, he quickly sat up and looked forward.

Smiling brightly, with a small microphone held only inches away from her mouth, Jillian was peering back at him through the rectangular opening. "Now, you weren't going to try and wreck my car, were you, William?" the tinny voice asked. "I must warn you that all you would accomplish is a broken foot or ankle. The glass is quite impenetrable. It is both bulletproof and shatterproof. Quite expensive, in fact."

Contrary to the obvious fun the woman he knew as Verona Capulet was having with him, Billy was not remotely amused. "I don't like being treated disrespectfully, like some sort of chew toy," he said, his voice tight. Although he would never admit such a thing to anyone, let alone a woman he was intent on impressing with his overt manliness, the whole situation was scaring him badly. He looked out the window and saw Ma standing up from the bench, the newspapers still held in her lap. She was eyeing the car with suspicion, moving her body side to side as if trying to get a clearer view.

Jillian recognized the vast difference in the demeanor of the young man she had met earlier in the day, and she couldn't help but to let her imagination take a firm hold of her thoughts by wondering if he had somehow decided to reject her for another woman. The provocative concept was too much for her to either grasp or accept. The one thing Jillian would absolutely not tolerate was betrayal, especially that of a worthless, adulterous man whose sole motivation in life was to pillage and rape the innocent women of the earth. And her daughter deserved far better than some treacherous, cheating bastard. *I'll teach you a lesson you'll never forget, you damn ingrate,* Jillian thought. *You're just like him, like them, like all of them!* She ground her teeth together. *And I don't think I like you anymore!*

When Billy refocused his attention on the woman who was supposed to be his date for the night, the features of her face were completely stoic, almost mannequin-like, an expression evincing an absolute absence of feeling. Her eyes sent shivers down his spine, rendering him momentarily speechless. They held him like those of a snake. Mentally unable to avert his eyes from the dead stare, he grappled for the right words to say. He didn't know what he had done to cause her to become so cold toward him, but somehow, instinctively, he knew he had to say something. Anything.

Jillian looked down at the passenger seat, where Jenny was safely strapped onto the leather upholstery. She reached out and stroked her hair, smiling lovingly at her daughter. Jenny looked absolutely stunning. Jillian had taken painstaking measures to prepare her baby for the big day when fixing her hair and picking out a custom-tailored dress that was made of the purest silk. The diamond dust she had sprinkled in her hair lighted up the entire front seat of the huge limousine. "I'm so sorry, baby, but he's no good for you," she said, her voice soothing, motherly. She nodded. "Yes, of course he shall pay for his transgressions, sweetheart. Mommy promises."

Billy leaned forward and tried to see who she was talking to but then sat back when Jillian jerked her head to the right and glared at him. "Excuse me, Verona, but who are you talking to?" he asked, his voice slightly trembling. "I mean, I don't see anyone in the seat next to you."

"Quiet, you … you awful reprobate!" Jillian spat, her face twisting into a snarl. "My name is not Verona."

Confused by the revelation, Billy furrowed his brow and pursed his lips nervously. "I don't understand," he said. "Why would you lie to me?" He paused in an attempt to contemplate his dilemma. "What do you want from me?"

"Nothing ... now," Jillian said. "At least not until the purifying process of ablution has transpired."

"If you want an apology, I'm sorry," Billy said, losing his composure. He tried the door handle and found that it was securely locked.

"Well, that is a start, I suppose," Jillian whispered. The rage on her face only seconds ago slackened just enough to be noticeable. She then reached out to the dashboard, pressed the control button that raised the partition, and then stepped on the accelerator.

The car floated away from the curb like a stealth giant and raced down the street in one smooth movement.

As Billy watched the solid pane that separated him from the cab of the car rise, comparing it to the feel of being forever sealed up in a crypt, he lunged forward and thrust his fingers through the porthole in an attempt to stop the partition from completing its journey upward. He then tried to push the panel back down with all the leverage and strength he could muster, but all he could manage to do was slow the seemingly inevitable progress. It would not be denied from accomplishing its quest, no matter what he struggled to do in prevention of being deprived of freedom.

"I wouldn't do that if I were you," Jillian said, her voice one of utter amusement. "I'd pull your little piggies out."

Committed to fight for his release from the rolling prison, Billy ignored Jillian's words of warning, even after he felt the pressure begin to mount against his digits, and continued to fight against the ascension of the door that somehow seemed destined to seal his fate. He would have none of it.

And then he howled in pain.

The sound of bones crunching like a bundle of dry sticks filled the car. Too late to pull them free, his fingers were crushed in the mechanical maw of the divider.

"I tried to warn you, silly," Jillian chastised as she flipped a nearby toggle switch that lowered the panel a half an inch. "You can't possibly think that that's the first time someone has tried that pointless stunt. I thought you were at least a little smarter than that, William." She sighed again. "Perhaps I should reevaluate the magnitude of your mental prowess and acuity."

The second there was enough room to free himself, Billy slid his mangled hands from the unforgiving contraption and cradled them against his chest. He wept softly, rocking back and forth on the plush leather seat. He thought of his mother and all the times she had tended his injuries when he was a child. He wished she were with him now. She always had a way of making everything better.

And then the panel shut with a snap.

"Please, God, help me," Billy cried. The pain of his broken fingers was nearly unbearable.

The ring of a tiny bell sounded, followed by the blinking of a small red light overhead. Billy looked up with tear-filled eyes, wondering what could be happening now and what the madwoman was doing. Then he heard something that sounded like a small gas leak. Seconds later his head began to swim, lightheaded. His vision grew blurry, and the throbbing in his fingers dulled. All muscle control and strength left his body as he slumped over and crumpled onto the seat in an unconscious heap of human body parts. His last thoughts before hitting the floor were those of his sister. He missed her.

Always vigilant, born to be a control freak and never taking anything for granted, Jillian watched the man in the back of the limousine over a closed-circuit television screen that was mounted on the dashboard. For the life of her, she could not understand why he was being so difficult. After all, what was he clinging to? she wondered. He worked as a glorified houseboy for a hotel, making a mere pittance, and she was offering him everything a man could ever want. It must be that infernal chromosome. All the hairy beasts ever did was beat their chests and act like perfect apes. They pick, they scratch, they burp, and they fart. Now that she really thought about it, weighing the pros against the cons, Jillian concluded that all men in general were disgusting. No wonder women turned to lesbianism.

The thoughts continued to course through her mind as she maintained a watch on the screen, so when she witnessed Billy succumb to the overwhelming flood of nitrous oxide she let out a small sigh of relief. At least he would no longer hurt himself by practicing acts in futility. Jillian always found it amusing that men believed they were in charge of the world. They may be at the controls, but women were life's navigators.

She craned her head and looked down at her patient Jenny, shaking her head. "Men," Jillian breathed. "Aren't they a pickle, Jen?" She then laughed. "Oh you're so right, sweetheart. We do need to help them. If not women, then who? Am I correct?" She laughed again when she heard the response.

Like a black wraith in the night, the stretch limousine weaved in and out of the light traffic and headed southbound on the freeway, its designation known only to the beautiful woman driving the dark beast.

The first thing Billy saw when he awoke from his chemical-induced sleep was the eerie flicker of light that reflected from off the ceiling above. He slowly blinked his eyes as full consciousness began to take its hold. He looked again, though his vision was still being affected from the drug, preventing him from accomplishing proper focus. Some sort of image seemed to be painted on a white background. The harder he strained to see the picture, the more difficult it seemed to become. His head ached slightly, but the pain seemed to ebb as he mentally shook away the cobwebs struggling to cling to his mind. He made an attempt to shift his body and found that his limbs would not obey his brain's demand. All he could manage to do was shift his eyes and blink his lids as he helplessly continued to stare up at the mural that was beginning to take shape. Tears began to well in his eyes. *Oh, God, what has she done to me?* Billy wondered, fear gripping him with a cold, merciless stranglehold. *Where am I?* He tried to move again, but to no avail. Not even a twitch of muscle occurred below the neck. Petrified beyond anything he previously thought possible, completely paralyzed, he wondered if she had somehow, in some maniacal way, removed his head from his body because he could feel nothing at all, not even the sound of his own heartbeat. His eyes nervously darted back and forth, seeing very little. Stainless steel bars appeared to run parallel to his prone body. They reflected that same disturbing flicker of light that had caught his peripheral vision on the left. He thought he saw a large dresser on the right side, along with a table that supported what appeared to be a pitcher of some sort. Somehow the domestic appearance of the furniture only added to his already escalating fear. Billy began to sob within his own mind.

"Rise and shine," the voice of Jillian echoed somewhere beyond his field of vision. "We can't have you sleeping all day long, now, can we?"

The soft sound of a motor began to purr to life. The bed jiggled as the gears started to catch and turn, causing one half of the bed to incline.

Frozen in position, Billy's eyes looked on in horror as the surrounding environment came within his vision. It was beyond anything he could have ever imagined. It was at that moment when he realized the woman, whoever she called herself, was certifiably insane.

Hundreds of stump-like candles had been spread throughout a room that was five times larger than his apartment, all burning brightly. The scent of jasmine filled the air. Posed in sitting positions, legs twisted to straddle each of the cylindrical objects that flickered with its golden life of timeless illumination, hundreds of dolls of every color, size, and shape were meticulously dressed in what appeared to be matching bridesmaid dresses of deep purple and situated to face the man of the hour, their future brother-in-law. Unable to turn away from the abominable scene, Billy felt the cold blackness of their eyes drill into his own. Their unmoving, forever smiling mouths, which would never offer a single word of kindness or condolence, only seemed to mock him and his predicament, creating an even more macabre aura than the sick one already enveloping the room.

"Aren't they just beautiful, William?" Jillian asked, the tone of her voice denoting unadulterated adoration. "They are my beloved daughters, and I love them the way only a mother can."

Billy shifted his eyes to where he believed the voice emanated, then mewled silently within his throat when he saw Jillian step out from behind the shadows of a doorway that had been lined with an arc of long-stemmed roses. *Oh, my God!* Billy thought. *I'm not going to leave here alive. She really is crazy.*

Standing in the doorway, dressed in the same matching dress as the hundreds of dolls that lined the shelves, tables, and floor, Jillian smiled brightly. Cradled lovingly in the crook of her arm, she held a doll dressed all in white and was gently running a tender hand over its veiled head. She looked about the room, her eyes floating across the porcelain faces of her beloved family, and cooed like a mother playing with her baby. The hundreds of timeless smiles, all colored red, remained frozen as they stared upon the beautiful bride to be. "It's all for you, daughter Jenny," Jillian whispered into the doll's ear.

Billy watched on in utter horror. The magnitude of the insanity transpiring in his presence tested the barriers of his own. He thought he would lose his mind, feeling himself begin to slip away into the realm of his captor's sick game.

Jillian stepped farther into the room and focused her undivided attention on the man she had secured to the mental ward bed. She smiled at him and then took another step. "Hello, William, my wonderful William," Jillian breathed as she continued to stroke the top of Jenny's silk-covered head. "Isn't she beautiful?" She lowered her eyes and shuddered, feeling nearly overwhelmed by her child's beauty. "We've decided to forgive you—to give you another chance."

Horrified by the implication, Billy averted his eyes from the ghastly sight that defied any sane explanation. Jillian noticed his reaction almost immediately.

"Oh, yes, William, she is almost too pretty to look at for very long," Jillian said. "Sort of like looking into the sun." She then moved over to a wooden podium located at the foot of the bed and set Jenny down on a miniature chair she had personally constructed for the special occasion. A Bible was resting to the right of the tiny piece of furniture. "You're a very lucky man to have my daughter's hand in marriage, William." She meticulously arranged Jenny's wedding dress to make certain that nothing was out of place. "You should start to call me Mom, dear William." She turned around and grinned. "Yes … Mom. I like that."

Billy felt his grip on reality slip away into the abyss as he watched the crazy woman slide open a hidden drawer and remove a dark piece of rolled-up cloth. She then took out three small jars and set them on top of the stained wood. Unable to pull his eyes away from the woman who looked as if she were merely going about a daily routine, Billy audibly mewled in terror when he watched her unroll the cloth, pick up two large scalpels and hold them up to the flickering candlelight.

Hearing the noise coming from her soon to be son-in-law, Jillian looked at him and shook her head. "Always the little scamp, aren't we, William?" she asked, the undercurrent of her voice snide, severe. "Well, we shall remedy that flaw in your unacceptable behavior, not that I don't find it endearing on occasion."

She pulled off the sheet that was covering Billy, exposing his naked form, and tossed the sheet on the floor. She then set one of the scalpels between his feet, while keeping the other one firmly gripped in her hand. "In order to make you worthy of Jenny, I must first sever the offending instruments of man's destruction. I will try to make it fast to spare you any indignity." Without saying anything further, Jillian took a firm hold of his scrotum and penis, pulled on them as hard as she could, and then removed them with near surgical precision. Billy grunted out in agony as blood poured from the gaping wound, soaking the mattress, and dripped onto the carpeted floor like a crimson waterfall. With the same methodical slicing, her face remaining completely stoic, never revealing the slightest empathy for the man who was being systematically butchered while firmly awake and aware, Jillian cut out his eyes and tongue, the former for the sin of visually lusting after the female body, the later for speaking the evil thoughts that he harbored for all her sisters and daughters of the world.

The daughters of Jillian, like all those other times in the past, remained mute and unmoving as they watched their mother wash away the sins of their future brother and cleanse him of all his former iniquities, none daring to ever contemplate the temptation of casting judgment. He had become their family, embraced by all their hearts.

Mesmerized by the thick flow of the sinister liquid that had been corrupted by the temptation of a diseased world, Jillian stared in fascination as the sins of the boy she now considered a son slowed to a mere trickle, then ceased. The curse from which Adam had failed to spare Eve had been rectified, freeing William from eternal condemnation and thereby sanctifying her child's marriage to a man for all time.

As Billy felt his eyes flutter for the last time, the agonizing pain that had been mercilessly inflicted upon him on multiple occasions sent him into shock, and coldness blanketed him as life drained from his body. He was tired, so very tired, and now just wanted to slip off into nothingness, where the specter of the grim reaper could rise up and wrap its cloaked arms around him. Tears rolled down his cheeks. *Why did this happen to me?* he wondered as he continued to fade away into a darkness his physical body could no longer see. I never hurt anyone.

His last thoughts were of his mother as he died in the mysterious room filled with candles and hideous-looking dolls. He finally understood why so many men were deathly afraid of them, thought them evil. He hated them with every fiber of his being. Always had. Never trust a doll!

Chapter 3

It had been thirty years since Benita Ravenez had fled the communist soil of her native Cuba, forced to wave good-bye to her loving husband. Despite her pleas to join her, he had chosen to stay behind so the tiny raft they had worked so hard and long to build would not disappear into the unforgiving waters of the ocean from the weight of far too much human cargo. Weeping as she watched the devoted face of the man she had known all her life slowly fade into the horizon, she and her two babies drifted toward freedom and away from the totalitarian tentacles of a murderous dictator. She knew there would never be another man to fill the endless void in her heart that increased with each nautical inch.

Alphonse Ravenez had risked everything for his family.

Although he had unequivocally promised Benita that night on the beach, under the shadows of the new moon, that he would join them within six months, taking a solemn oath that he would not be thwarted, she knew that his selfless act of love would carry a heavy price, and that their eyes would never again meet.

Two weeks later her suspicions were realized when Benita Ravenez received a long-distance phone call at her aunt's house in Florida. She knew it came from her homeland even before the telephone was handed over to her. With shaking hands, she lifted the receiver to her ear and reluctantly listened to the words, which informed her that her husband had been arrested on charges of treason and subterfuge. Alphonse Ravenez was summarily shot in the head on that same day. His last thoughts were those of his wife and his children.

In spite of the passage of years, never taking another man into her life because she had never fallen out of love for her deceased husband, Benita still suffered the same pain from her loss as if she had just received the news of her husband's execution. No matter how many friends and family members urged her to move on with her life, trying to convince her that Alphonse would want her to meet a nice man and remarry, Benita refused to listen to what she considered to be nothing more than sacrilegious advice.

Although she had waved farewell to the man nearly three decades earlier, Benita could remember every line in his face, every nuance that told her how he was feeling, and the way he looked at her when he didn't think she was watching him. For everyone else life had moved forward. But for Benita it was still June 1, the day when her heart died. It was the moment she had lost her soulmate, with whom to share a freedom that carried very little value without him. Not a day passed when she did not think of her beloved, or light a candle for his eternal soul.

Thoughts of Alphonse were running through Benita's mind as she pushed the cleaning cart down the luxurious hallway of one of the city's most lavish hotels. She was headed toward the room of the rather lengthy trek when she came to the door that held a Do Not Disturb sign hanging from the golden handle for the past two days. Although it was not entirely unusual for people to remain in their rooms for several days at a stretch, it was unheard of that no one in the room would at least order room service in that length of time. Even the most amorous of honeymooners had to eat between bouts of lovemaking throughout the course of the day.

She started to simply saunter past the locked door but then paused to listen for any sign of life on the opposite side. There was none, not even a whisper.

A man and presumably his wife stepped out of the elevator located in the direction from which Benita had just come. The man gave the woman a playful swat on her backside just as she took her first step on the floor, causing her to jump and laugh in response. Benita watched the couple stop at the first door on the right, disabusing her of the idea that perhaps they were the tenants of the room before which she stood. The man retrieved a key card from the inside pocket of his coat and slid it into the slot of the door. The two lovers then disappeared behind closed quarters.

The surrounding area once again fell silent.

Benita pressed her ear against the door.

Nothing.

She furrowed her brow. Having worked in the hotel for years, Benita had a keen sense for things that were awry. Concerned for the guest's health and safety, she removed the master key card from her shirt pocket and slid it into the door. The door clicked open with an audible snap. She extracted the card and returned it to the safety of her pocket. Then she stuck her head through the opening of the door and looked around. Nervous, the hairs on the back of her neck standing on end, she cleared her throat. "Hello," Benita called out. "Room service." She paused momentarily to wait for an answer. "Sir, is everything okay?"

Nothing. All was quiet.

She opened the door a little wider and started to enter the room but then stopped when the foul odor of decay assaulted her nose. She threw her hands over her nose and mouth, cringing from the offensive stench, and reluctantly crossed the threshold. She stopped after several feet, the odor nearly overpowering, and called out again. "Hello. Sir." She scanned the room for any sign of life. "Room service."

Nothing.

Although every ounce of intuition screamed out for her to leave and simply call the police, Benita continued to journey deeper into the hotel room. She stopped when she came to the bedroom door and gently rapped on it. "Excuse me, sir," she began, "room service." Preferring to avoid walking into an embarrassing situation, she knocked again, this time much louder than before. "Room service!"

The odor was thick and unyielding.

Again nothing.

Benita placed her hand on the handle of the door and turned it until the familiar click reached her ears. She then pushed the door halfway open and stuck her head through the opening. The stench of death struck her in the face with the force of a putrid hurricane, causing her to violently gag. Bile rose halfway up the length of her throat, the taste of the acidic substance burning like liquid fire. Her eyes began to water. She covered her nose and mouth with a single hand and mewled into the palm. She searched the immediate area with a careful eye. Everything appeared to be in proper order. And then her vision came to rest on the bed, where she saw a figure that appeared to be someone fast asleep.

Believing she had inadvertently walked into the very situation she had tried to avoid, Benita started to step back. "Oh, please excuse me, sir," she whispered, apologetic. The thick stench seemed to coat her tongue when she opened her mouth to speak. Feeling her stomach lurch, she stopped moving. *Oh, God,* she thought as she began to heave. She covered her mouth again. Unable to stop the inevitable, she bent over and vomited on the richly carpeted floor.

A female coworker knocked on the door and entered the room. "Good lord, Benita, what is that smell?" she asked, wrinkling up her nose, waving her hands around in the air. She then walked over to where Benita was wiping the residual puke from her face. "God Almighty, Benita, you should air this place out. It smells like a dead dog." She walked toward the bed and then screamed at the top of her lungs when she saw the decomposing body of Samuel Smith smiling upward with a wilted, dead flower hanging from his mutilated mouth.

When the police arrived ten minutes later, Benita and her coworker were sitting huddled together on the floor outside the room where they had the misfortune of discovering the body. Terrified, both trembled in the other's arms, neither caring that Benita still had part of her last meal spread across the front of her shirt. Several officers had tried to speak with the women, but they were far too distraught to hear anyone speak, let alone composed enough to answer any questions about what they had found. So rather than press the women, no doubt compounding their trauma, they decided it would be prudent to tend to their immediate needs and just wait for the homicide detective to show up. None wanted to make matters worse.

Fifteen minutes after the first officers had arrived at the scene of the crime, which was already being labeled by the hotel employees as the slaughter room, Homicide Detective Bob Harris stepped out of the elevator and made his way to the crowd of officers standing out in the hallway.

At twenty-five years old, endowed with boyish features that made him appear even younger, Detective Harris was the youngest homicide detective in the precinct's history. Having graduated at the top of his class, he surpassed all others' previous achievements with relative ease.

Detective Harris was the department's golden child, especially to those local politicians who took it upon themselves to boast about the percentage of solved cases over the airwaves in comparison to other cities in the country. What the self-promoting supposed public servants didn't say was that they personally had absolutely nothing to do with it, or admit the undeniable fact that it was basically only one man who was responsible for making such stellar statistics possible. In the realm of forensic science and criminal behavior, there were very few others who could match his ability to unravel the conundrums of evidence, both tangible and intangible, which was why the FBI had tried to lure him away with the promise of access to the country's best laboratories and personnel.

But to everyone's surprise, Detective Harris had summarily declined the offer, preferring to work exclusively in the field of homicide because it was the only aspect of crime that held his interest for more than thirty seconds. He found the aspects of mentally hunting the ultimate predator on earth as a challenging and worthwhile endeavor, something to test his skill. And the serial killer was his most treasured adversary, his first love ever since he was a child, and was the reason he was so obsessive in striving to become a detective.

And it was not the senseless taking of human life that drove him. It was the prospect of the hunt.

Without bothering to make a formal introduction, Harris walked up to a lieutenant, a slightly older man by the name of Tim or Tom something or other, who was scribbling down notes, and gave a quick nod of the head. "Have you locked the place down?" he asked, his tone one strictly of business.

"Yes, sir," the lieutenant replied. "It's tighter than a drum."

"And the employees?" he asked.

The lieutenant flipped to the front page of his notes and quickly perused the page. "As a matter of fact, detective," he began, "they're downstairs in the lobby."

"Perfect," he said.

The moment the officers, who were still hovering near the emotionally traumatized women, recognized the detective they straightened up and nodded their heads with respect. Every officer in the department was familiar with the man's accomplishments. And all had heard the not-so-veiled rumors that he was about as spooky as anyone could be, even for a cop.

Detective Harris pulled out a stick of gum and meticulously unwrapped it. He took painstaking measures so that the foil was not damaged, then folded it into a tiny triangle. He smiled. "So, officers, what do we have?" Harris asked, his voice monotone, denoting no emotion whatsoever. He then slid the stick of gum into his mouth. Grape flavor was his favorite, but he simply referred to it only as purple.

An officer on the left moved forward a half inch and spoke up first. "A murder, sir," he said. "It looks like a pretty bad one. The body is ..." He paused momentarily, swallowing hard, and then finished. "Well, it's pretty tore up, sir."

"Is that right, Officer?" Harris asked in the same flat voice.

"It is, sir," the other officer replied, grimly nodding his head. "It's an awful thing for any man to see."

"How so?" Harris asked, cocking his head to the right. "Please …
explain."

Conscious of the two traumatized women sitting no more than a
few feet away, the officers looked down, shuffled their feet uneasily,
and then peered back up. No one wanted to describe the details in
front of them. It just seemed cruel.

"Perhaps it would be best for us to step inside, sir," the first
officer said, motioning toward the door.

"Why?" Harris asked.

The officer looked down at the women again, sympathetic to
their plight.

"We just think it would be better, sir," a second officer said.

Harris peered down at the huddled women, studying them
carefully, as if he had just fastened the top of a petri dish over
a specimen in the laboratory. "And who might these people be,
Officer?" Harris asked, the tone of his voice dry and unfeeling.

The officers exchanged befuddled glances, disbelieving the level
of apathy being displayed by the detective.

"Uh, sir, they are the employees who found the body," the first
officer said uneasily, finding it repugnant that he had to actually
explain the obvious. He didn't quite understand the reason, but the
detective was actually starting to give him a severe case of the goose
bumps. He had seen some of his child's action figures demonstrate
more emotion.

"I see," Harris said. He looked down at the women again, his
face expressionless. "That must have been terrible for you." He then
wrinkled his nose when the smell of puke reached his nostrils.

Benita lifted her chin, raising a tear-stained face, and bit down
on her lip. "I can't believe someone could do that to another human
being," Benita said through gasps. "It … It's just horrible, horrible
and godless."

Harris raised a single eyebrow when he heard the religious
analogy and exhaled with exasperation. "Yeah, well, I'll stick to the
earthbound," Harris said. He looked up at the stunned officers and
rolled his eyes. "If you don't mind, I'd prefer to field the scene of the

crime alone, without any interruptions or distractions." It was meant as a statement, not a question.

The officers lifted their hands in surrender.

"Be our guest," the first officer said. "I doubt any of us are in a big hurry to go back in there. At least I'm not." He looked down at the women again. "Don't you want to question the employees, so they can go home? You know, take the witnesses statements while their memories are fresh."

Harris blew and popped a bubble with the gum. "And what exactly do you think they witnessed, Officer?" Harris asked, then resumed chewing.

"They found the body," he replied.

"Yes, you already said that," Harris said, his voice emanating annoyance. "My question is whether they actually saw anything or anyone."

The officers furrowed their brows.

Harris snapped his fingers loudly at the women. "Excuse me, ladies, but did you see anything or anyone suspicious on the floor?" Harris asked in a no nonsense tone of voice. "You know, like something peculiar or out of the ordinary?"

Benita shook her head. "No, we didn't see anything," she replied.

Harris placed his hands on his hips and stared at the officers. "You see, they didn't see a damn thing, so let them go home for now," he said. "Get their addresses and phone numbers, and I'll interview them later." Without offering any further explanation, he turned and entered the hotel room, stopping just inside the door to take a quick scan.

After the detective had walked into the room, the officers kneeled down and helped the two women to their feet. Benita and her coworker clung to their arms as if they were life preservers tossed their way.

The first officer held Benita firmly against his chest and looked helplessly at the other officer. He shook his head in amazement. "I don't know about you, Gary, but that dude is about the creepiest friggin' thing I've come across in my life," he said. "Something just ain't right about him, not by a long shot."

The officer supporting the other woman, who was still sniffling back tears, nodded his head in affirmation. "I heard some of the rumors about him but never really thought any of them were true," Gary said. "Now that I actually met the dude, they were being kind." He shook as if suddenly struck by a blast of cold air. "That dude scared the shit out of me. I mean, he's fright night material. When he looked at me with those dead friggin' eyes, I damn near crapped my pants."

The officers then assisted the women to the elevators at the far end of the hallway, neither speaking nor making eye contact until they reached downstairs.

Standing just past the threshold of the room, Harris looked around at the other members of the department and shook his head morosely. *Idiots*, he thought, believing each and every one of them was either actually or potentially destroying evidence because of their incalculable incompetence. "Everybody, get out!" he ordered. "Get out right this minute!"

Everyone inside the room, officers and forensic members alike, stopped moving and turned to the sound of the order. Those senior officers who were territorial about their cases glared at the arrogance of the much younger man spouting demands. Although each of those investigating the crime scene immediately recognized the belligerent man, none appreciated the rude and dismissive manner he used to bark orders. A longtime lieutenant approached the detective with his hand held out. Harris merely looked at the offered appendage as if it was a bacteria-infested rodent that had just been fished from out of the local sewer. He neither spoke nor smiled.

"Hey, Detective Harris," the lieutenant announced, determined to withhold judgment on the much younger man's pompous attitude. "I'm Lieutenant Miller. I'm in charge of the crime scene. I'm pleased to do whatever I can to get to the bottom of what happened." He lowered his arm when it became apparent that it was not going to be accepted.

"Correction, lieutenant, you *were* in charge," Harris said, his tone flat and not open for debate. "You and your people may leave now. I have been assigned to take over this case by our superiors, so your assistance will no longer be required." He attempted to walk past the lieutenant, then stopped when he felt the man's hand press firmly against his chest and push him back a few inches.

"I don't know who the hell you think you are, Mister, but I won't be treated like some kind of punk," the lieutenant spat. "I was working on cases when you were home sucking on your mother's tit." He curled his lip into a snarl. "You will respect me and my entire team, do you understand me?"

Emotionless and unfazed by the lieutenant's attempt to physically intimidate him, Harris slowly lowered his eyes to the man's calloused hand, raised them even slower, and then grinned in a manner that denoted no humor. "You will take your ape paw away from my person right this second, or I shall reciprocate a hundredfold," Harris said. "I will not be molested by you or anyone else from your gang of neophytes." He then brushed the lieutenant's hand off his chest and set to straightening out his shirt. "I think it's best that we both forget this unfortunate chain of events and move forward with the business at hand, don't you agree?" He stared with unblinking eyes, waiting for the only plausible answer.

Miller had seen the eyes of career criminals and cold-blooded murderers on more occasions than he cared to count. He had arrested them and been instrumental in securing their convictions for the atrocities they had committed against the state and the people of his city. From what he gleaned in those that looked upon him with icy indifference, the lieutenant believed Detective Harris's were of the same nature. Not only were they the eyes of a predator, they held an intelligence, a brilliance, that penetrated his own far deeper than the last man he'd helped onto death row. Harris was not only dead serious with his stern warning, the lieutenant believed, but he would carry out the promised threat. *The man is not just arrogant*, he thought, *he's genuinely insane*. Miller licked his lips, grateful for the presence of witnesses.

"Do we have a problem, Lieutenant?" Harris asked, unflinching. "I require an answer from you."

"No, sir, no problem," he replied. He looked at the members of his team, who were watching the two of them in stunned silence. He then twirled his index finger in the air. "Let's wrap it up and let the detective conduct his business, people."

Without uttering a single word in protest or bothering to question his motive, the other members, who had watched the scenario take place, quickly gathered up their equipment, and could barely contain their enthusiasm to follow the lieutenant out the door. All of them, man and woman alike, were thankful for the break and for the distance which they were being allowed to put between themselves and the man rumored to have some sort of blood fetish.

"I'd appreciate it if one of your people left me one of their forensic bags so I can conduct a few tests, if necessary," Harris said in a monotone voice. "I'll make certain to return it before the day is through." He looked directly at the lieutenant with the same dead stare he gave to everyone, and tilted his head to the side. "I would like to take some samples and run a few tests."

The lieutenant nodded his head numbly. At that moment he would have gladly given the man anything he wanted if it meant speeding up his departure. The detective thoroughly gave him the creeps. "That's no problem, Detective," he said. He turned to the youngest of the members, a man in his middle twenties, and pointed at him. "Mikey, would you please leave your bag for the detective?" The tone of his voice left no doubt that the question was a demand, not a simple request.

"Of course, sir," Mikey said without hesitation. "Whatever the detective wants, lieutenant." He set the bag on the ground and then looked at the detective. "You can get it back to me whenever you want, sir. I'm in no real hurry. I have another bag in the car." He started to head for the door.

"Hang on for a minute, Mikey," the lieutenant said, holding up a hand. He turned and looked at the detective for several seconds before speaking. "If you don't mind, Detective, I'll wait out in the hallway for you to finish." He paused. "After all, I still have some responsibility over the crime scene."

The detective offered a smile that chilled the lieutenant to the bone. "Of course, I don't mind," Harris replied. "I hope I can call if I need assistance." He looked at his wristwatch. "I will need approximately a half hour to conduct the preliminary."

"Take all the time you need, Detective," the lieutenant said. "I'll be just outside the door. I'll keep my team in the building until you are ready to recall us."

"That will be perfect," Harris said. He then looked at the other man. "Thank you for letting me borrow your equipment, Mikey. I understand how possessive and territorial people can become over their property."

"No problem," Mikey replied as he disappeared around the corner.

When the last of the crew had left the room, Detective Harris slowly walked over to the door and shut it with a gentle push of the hand.

Silence filled the air, the kind that only death could provide.

He placed his forehead against the door, relishing the peaceful solitude that always accompanied privacy, and inhaled deeply. The smell of blood was intoxicating, bringing him close to experiencing what he surmised to be the precipice of nirvana. Sighing in pleasure, a smile creased his lips as he thought about licking the salty essence. A few seconds later he shook himself from out of his self-imposed trance and removed his head from the hard surface of the door. Always fastidious about his physical appearance, he ran two hands over his clothes to straighten them out, turned around, and then walked over to where the victim had been abandoned to dwell in the land of eternal sleep.

When the remains of Samuel Smith came into full view of his anticipated vision, Detective Harris found that he had finally discovered an artist that few could ever fully grasp, let alone value the magnitude of what lay before him. Only a true connoisseur could appreciate the magnificence of it all.

Fascinated and mesmerized by the lethal wounds that had been inflicted on the body of the man, whose name meant nothing, oblivious to the stench of the rotting decay that floated upon the air currents within the room, Detective Harris enthusiastically removed a pair of surgical gloves from his pocket, snapped them on, and kneeled beside the bed. He was smiling. It was the most beautiful sight he had ever seen. Although he could do nothing but admire the precision utilized in the castration process, it was the symbolism of the doll left behind to straddle the victim's neck that held his interest the most.

He removed an ink pen from the front pocket of his shirt and used it to lift the doll's hair so he could get a clearer look at its face. There was no doubt that it was handcrafted with a loving hand. The detail was far too perfect to have been created with anything less. "Hello, beautiful," Harris whispered as he ran the pen down the length of its long neck. "Someone loved you very much, so why would you be left behind, I wonder." He then studied the stem of the wilted rose. Working down the length of it, his attention came to focus on the incisions made on both sides of the mouth. What are you trying to tell me? He licked his lips.

Curious, thriving on the quest to learn the psychological implications involved, he scanned the surrounding area of the room in search of a clue, and anything inadvertently left behind that might provide a scintilla of insight into the killer's mind. *Finally, a worthy opponent,* Harris thought.

Other than the mutilated body and bloodstained bed, everything else in the room appeared to be in proper order. Nothing seemed to be out of place, and there was no evidence whatsoever to believe a struggle had taken place. *Curious,* Harris thought. He then stood up and began to walk about the room until he came to the vanity that supported a half dozen extinguished candles. He picked one of them up and sniffed at it several times. The scent was familiar to him, but he couldn't quite place it. He then pulled out a chair that was positioned in front of the vanity and sat down to clear his mind for a couple of minutes, where he looked into the reflection and over his shoulder so he could concentrate on the body. He blinked his eyes slowly several times as he delved deeply into his own mind. It took him only a few minutes to realize the tactic that usually proved highly useful was producing no fruit, so he stood up and walked over to where Mikey had set the medical bag down. He picked it up and stepped over to the bed.

"Well, Mr. John Doe, let's see what some forensics will reveal," Harris said, opening the bag of medical instruments. He held up a swab kit and smiled. "Shall we begin with the undignified procedure, sir?" Without saying anything further, Detective Harris started his evidentiary investigation.

Thirty minutes later, Harris zipped up the bag. He was finished with his preliminary work. To his great satisfaction, other than the sample of blood he had extracted with a certain degree of belief that it would reveal the man was in fact drugged, there was not one shred of physical evidence to link anyone to the man's murder. No fingerprints, no DNA, and no apparent motive. The only evidence that appeared to exist external to the crime itself was a doll that was undoubtedly untraceable. Of course, as was standard operating procedure, he would ask the usual questions of the hotel's employees and conduct a thorough investigation into each of their background. But he knew it would lead absolutely nowhere. The only possible way anyone would have anything of value to offer would be more from fluke rather than a mistake on the part of the killer. Whoever had murdered the man did so with meticulous tenacity. The murder was executed with a precision Harris himself would incorporate into the act if he were to decide to take human life. Although there was nothing to support the conclusion, Harris intuitively knew that Mr. John Doe was not the first to be killed by the unknown perpetrator and would certainly not be the last. The skill was just too honed for either a simple amateur or novice, one for which he had complete respect.

When Harris finally opened the door that led to the outside hallway he was not at all surprised to find Lieutenant Miller standing against the wall with arms crossed over his chest. He looked to be less than pleased with having to wait for the whole half hour.

Frowning, he pushed himself away from the wall and looked at the detective with tired eyes.

Harris set the bag on the floor and then brushed at a piece of invisible lint on his pants.

"So, what do you think, Detective?" Miller asked. "Is that a total creep show or what?" He paused momentarily, expecting a response. When none was forthcoming he began to feel uncomfortable with the silence, especially since all the man did was stare at him with unblinking eyes. Nervous, he cleared his throat. "We must be dealing with some kind of freak, don't you think?"

Had Harris harbored any respect for the lieutenant's level of intelligence, he might have been offended enough to verbally lash out at the man for his complete lack of insight into the mind of a genius. Like most errors made by people in general, the man was myopically focusing his attention on the human factor and the emotional impact all deaths have on the human being, because it served as a constant reminder of man's frailties and inevitable mortality. Detective Harris did not suffer from such trivial weaknesses because the body was merely the canvas, a bi-product of the masterpiece left behind for those who recognize creative brilliance, over which to swoon.

The lieutenant shifted his feet uneasily when the man continued to remain mute. "Well, aren't you going to say anything?" he asked.

"I don't think the term creep show is a justified response to serve as an explanation, Lieutenant Miller," Harris said matter-of-factly. "Further, I find the description of 'freak' rather offensive." He exhaled deeply. "I'm fairly certain my colleagues would agree with me wholeheartedly."

"You must be joking," the lieutenant said, amazed.

"I assure you, I do not joke," Harris said, his voice flat. "I am a staunch professional at all times."

"But you can't be ignorant to what all the others say about ..." he began, but then he let the sentence trail off, not feeling comfortable with finishing it.

Harris smiled in understanding, nodding his head. "Ah, you

mean how everyone thinks I'm some kind of heartless vampire, or something to that effect," Harris said in the same bland tone.

"Yeah, something like that," the lieutenant said uneasily. "You know how people talk. And quite frankly, detective, you kind of give me the creeps."

Harris let out a genuine chuckle and shook his head. "Unlike most of the people I have to work with on a daily basis, I like you, Miller," Harris said. "At least you have enough gumption to speak your mind." He paused, enjoying the exchange. "That is, most of it."

Deciding the man wasn't nearly as bad as the circulating rumors, the lieutenant shrugged his shoulders. Years ago there had been a lot of negative things said about himself, so he thought it fair to give the guy a break and just focus on the work at hand. "Is it clear for my people to return to the room and process the scene?" he asked.

"Yes, they may return," Harris said. "I've finished with my preliminary investigation and evaluation. However, I would like to interview any potential witnesses while I'm here. That is, if there are any emotionally stable to speak to."

"Of course, Detective," the lieutenant said. "I've questioned a few of the employees." He removed a pad of paper from his shirt pocket and flipped it open. "If you would like to conduct your own independent interrogations, I'd be happy to provide the names."

Harris took out his own pad of paper and a pen. "I'd appreciate that, Lieutenant," Harris said. He dabbed the tip of the pen on his tongue. "Go ahead and give me their names."

"The first person I interviewed was a Peter Robinson, the second a Jeb Cartwright, and the third was a girl by the name of Harriot Mills," the lieutenant said. "The manager was out of town at the time, and we're still trying to locate a Billy Preston. According to the hotel records, all of them were working on the day in question. Each of them said basically the same thing, that there was nothing strange or out of the ordinary. It was just the usual day at work, no weirdos or anything that aroused the slightest attention. Although, I'd still like to talk with this Preston kid."

"Do you suspect him to have any additional knowledge or to

be involved with the murder?" Harris asked. Even though he didn't question the man's ability to conduct something as simple as an interview, Harris was well aware of the fact that people usually knew a lot more than they realized. Sometimes the most innocuous thing to them was the one piece of information that often broke open a case and led to an immediate arrest. The manner in which the questions were asked was the most critical aspect of any interrogation.

"Not really, but I am curious as to why he's gone AWOL just days after such a heinous murder in the hotel," the lieutenant said. "It's probably just a coincidence, but none of his friends seem to know where he is and why he hasn't showed up at work." He shrugged his shoulders. "I'd feel more comfortable with labeling him as a person of interest at this time, if you know what I mean."

"I see," Harris said. The one thing the detective definitely didn't believe in was coincidence. There was always a reason for something, even if it wasn't a rational one. What he did believe in was that people were unpredictable, particularly the young ones. He then looked over at the bag he'd set down on the floor and picked it up. "Would you please tell Mikey that I'm taking his bag with me? I collected some blood and DNA samples and would prefer to keep them from potential contamination. I will get it back to him as soon as I can secure the evidence."

"I will tell him personally the moment he gets back on the floor, Detective," the lieutenant said. "I promise." He reached out with a hand. "It's been a pleasure working with you, Detective Harris."

Harris shuffled his feet uneasily and looked at the offered hand with discomfort. Suffering from an acute phobia of coming into contact with germs, completely averse to the unsavory prospect of anyone touching him with bare skin, particularly since he was well aware of how people in general lacked the proper practice of personal hygiene throughout the course of the day, the detective reluctantly accepted the man's hand and quickly shook it. He then released it and wiped his own on the leg of his pants. "I agree," he muttered.

The lieutenant watched the man with curious eyes. "Please, since we're going to work together on this, just call me Miller," he said.

"If that's your preference," Harris said.

"It is," the lieutenant replied.

"As you please, Miller," Harris said. He turned to leave. "I think I'll go down to the lobby and question the employees you mentioned." Without saying anything further, Harris walked toward the stairwell.

The lieutenant stared after him for several seconds. *Strange fellow,* Miller thought as he watched the man disappear behind the door that led to the stairs. He then walked back into the room to use the phone so he could call down to the lobby and contact the team members, who were no doubt none too happy with being treated as second-string benchwarmers.

It only took the first three words to fall from Jeb's mouth for Harris to conclude that he detested the bipedal creature. If the detective had ever harbored any doubts as to the concept of retroactive abortion, a theory in which he had often found pleasurable, there definitely was no reason to hold on to them any longer.

The man who called himself by the short name of Jeb was the poster child for it. He had little intelligence. Misanthropic at heart, Harris found it difficult to believe that people such as Jeb had an actual purpose for being and was genuinely offended that he was allowed to suck up his oxygen.

His patience waned with every passing second. He found Petie equally annoying but was able to tolerate the man and get through the interview with him because at least he was born with a good and gentle heart.

Harris pinched the bridge of his nose for the fifth time in ten minutes. He felt a headache beginning to raise its ugly head in the back of his brain, and cursed himself for leaving a bottle of aspirin in the car. *Why couldn't the killer have gotten this idiot?* he wondered, enjoying the idea of zipping the irritant up in a body bag. "Look, I'm going to ask you this one more time, so try and concentrate," Harris said, the tone of his voice exuding exasperation. "Do you have any idea why your friend has not come in to work? It's a simple enough question."

Jeb pulled out a cigarette and went to light it with the strike of a single match. "I told you that he has his own reasons," Jeb said. "I don't give a fat crap what he does."

Harris slapped the match out of his hand and the cigarette out of his mouth. He'd had enough of the man's ridiculous antics.

"Hey, dude, what's your damage?" Jeb protested. He kneeled down to retrieve the cigarette but was blocked by a dress shoe that smashed down on it. "Shit, man, that was my last smoke."

Harris grabbed him by the collar and yanked him upright. "I've just about had enough of your nonsense," Harris spat. "One more sideways comment from you, and I'm going to arrest your worthless carcass for interference with an officer's duties, maybe felony obstruction."

Jeb held up his hands in surrender. "Hey, easy, Kojak, I'm cooperating," Jeb mumbled nervously. The last time he'd gone to jail several of the other prisoners had beaten him up bad enough to send him to the infirmary, so he was in no hurry to suffer a repeat performance. "I already told you that he was going on some sort of a date with some rich cougar on the prowl for some young tube meat. That's all I know. I never saw the bitch, because some stupid kid with queer pants gave him a note. I don't even know if Billy was telling the truth because I didn't read the note. The dude tells a lot of friggin' stories, and most of them are just crap." He furrowed his brow. "Go ask that idiot Petie. He's on Billy's leg constantly."

"I already did," Harris said. "He said about the same thing."

"Well, there ya go," Jeb said. "I left before Petie. Harriot was here, but she left way before any of us."

"Yes, I know," Harris said. "That's what she said."

"So what do ya want from me, man?" Jeb asked. "I don't know nothing."

"That's 'anything,'" Harris corrected.

"Huh?" Jeb looked at him in confusion.

Harris released him and shook his head. "Never mind," he said, feeling nothing but disgust for the man. "I hope you understand how serious this is?"

"Yeah, I get it," Jeb replied, fixing his collar. "It has to do with that dead dude upstairs. That's really messed up, but it has nothing to do with me."

Chalking up the man's indifferent response to the murder of an innocent man to generation excrement and the overall youth of the day, Harris just stared at the loathsome hood with revulsion. *What has happened to people?* he wondered. Even though he felt very little, if anything, for the victim, it just seemed unnatural for others to share in his apathy. Sympathizing with a victim had no bearing on how well he did his job. Personal feelings were irrelevant. In fact, from personal observation of his colleagues, it often interfered with professionalism and the ability to competently do the job. "So that's how you feel, is it?" Harris asked, exhaling deeply, tired of speaking with him.

"Uh, yeah, pretty much," Jeb replied, shrugging his shoulders. "I didn't know the dude, so why would I care."

"I guess you wouldn't," Harris said, his tone one of defeat. He removed a card from his wallet and held it out to the man. "Take this. If you think of anything else, I want you to give me a call, all right?"

Jeb took the card and shook his head. "Yeah, sure thing, dude," Jeb said. He slid the card into his back pocket.

With the medical bag clutched tightly in his hands, Detective Harris turned around and headed out the door of the hotel. He was looking forward to spending the next twelve hours alone in the sanitized environment that could be found and enjoyed only in the comfort of the laboratory.

Chapter 4

T he sun had just cleared the outline of the distant horizon when the dark limousine surreptitiously pulled alongside the curb and parked. The engine continued to idle with perfect precision. The gentle vibrations that coursed through the five-ton automobile offered very little comfort as Jillian gazed out the heavily tinted bulletproof window.

She drummed her exquisitely manicured fingers on her well-tanned knee and stared at the field of tombstones and white crosses scattering the grounds like tiny gray and white soldiers from days better left in the residual memories of the forgotten past. Bitterly, always loathing the beginning of each month, the same sense of revulsion in which she harbored every time the monthly visit to her father's crypt came due raised its insidious head. She silently cursed the memory of him under her breath every single time she remembered the monstrous condition Zachariah Hanson had attached to her if she desired to receive the whole of his vast estate, a written codicil demanding memorial fealty that required his only daughter to visit his grave on the first day of every month until she could be buried in the adjoining sarcophagus on his right for all eternity.

The thought of resting next to the man who had been responsible for murdering her own mother and victimizing her over the period of half her life made her want to retch. Nonetheless, since she was a true Hanson in flesh and bone, after every specialist in the field of trusts and wills could find no legal loophole in which to challenge such a condition, Jillian eventually exercised reason and acquiesced to the demand by doing as the small army of lawyers had advised. It was, after all, a multibillion dollar estate that reached across the circumference of the globe with financial tentacles that seemed to have no monetary end.

In one fell swoop, Jillian Hanson had become one of the richest and most powerful women the planet had ever known. She did what she wanted, when she wanted, to whomever she wanted, and for whatever reason that struck her fancy. There was no doubt in anyone's mind that she was the true heir to the Hanson fortune and the lineal offspring of Zachariah Hanson, particularly those who had the misfortune of angering either one of the two people.

As time passed, many came to believe that Jillian was actually more intelligent and cutthroat than her own father, because she genuinely appeared to take an immense amount of pleasure in accumulating what she referred to as corporate fodder. Of course, Jillian was well aware of what everyone thought about her, not that any of their obtuse opinions carried any weight whatsoever. If she desired to hear any of their opinions, on little more than a fleeting whim, she could easily force one out of any one of them. The bottom line was that each and every one of them feared her, just as her father had come to fear her in the last seconds of his life.

She smiled from the memory of watching his widened eyes stare back at her in terror as she injected a syringe full of liquid nicotine into a small tube snaking out of the intravenous bag that dangled almost precariously only a few feet from his paralyzed body. It was a priceless moment in time for her, a defining one that represented how the student had become the master, especially after she had apologized to the dying tyrant for no longer loving his own wicked creation. The soft death rattle that escaped Zachariah's treacherous lips was the sweetest music Jillian had ever heard in her life, for it was the sound of a final conquest, resulting in a freedom she had longed for since a long ago birthday party that had stripped her of every human dignity.

Jillian looked at the watch that was fastened around her tiny wrist and groaned audibly when she saw the time. It was already getting late, and a mountain of paperwork was still waiting for her back at the office. *What a life,* she thought. Although most of the drivers she had used in the past would never dare contact her from the cab, she didn't place such a Draconian demand on the man now at the wheel. Excepting the one currently stationed in the front of the limousine, any break in proper etiquette by an employee would never be tolerated. True to the blood that ran through her veins, Jillian would leave when the mood moved her, never before, especially not in response to an inappropriate urging or interruption from an ill-mannered, ill-bred minion who failed to recognize his or her station in the pyramidal food chain of modern society.

No one told Jillian Hanson what to do.

No one. Ever.

Jillian suddenly stopped rapping her nails on her shapely leg and sighed deeply. She looked down at her hands, well aware that continuing to procrastinate would only prove detrimental to her already depressed state of mind, which would only compound the level of humiliation for which the unsavory spectacle of traipsing up the hillside would invariably bring down on her. *Well, I guess I might as well get this over with,* Jillian thought, wishing she could kill her father on the first of every month rather than serve his last sadistic whim.

She looked back out the window and then chuckled at the irony that always seemed to surround the landscape of a cemetery. It was one of the few places on earth where people came to pay tribute to those they utterly despised, symbolizing a true landmark for hypocrisy. Contrary to the actual and true thoughts and feelings of the supposed mourners endowed with plenty of audacity to show up, those in attendance would speak only nice words for the recently deceased. They would quote quaint little platitudes about the departed while shedding crocodile tears, when in fact most of them were glad the person stuffed away in a wooden crate was indeed dead and on the way into the cold, dark ground, silently hoping that it was a long and painful death.

Jillian firmly believed that most of the people who made an appearance at a funeral did so only to make certain the object of their dissatisfaction and hatred was indeed worm food, and would no longer be able to breathe even more poison than already coursed through the circulatory system that made up their daily lives. Jillian herself had nearly choked on her own words when she referred to Zachariah Hanson as a loving husband and father. She would have preferred to pay each pretended mourner handsomely to take off their pants and defecate on the monster's grave. When Jillian looked around at the dozens of faces feigning sorrow for her creature of a father, she wished there was a way she could arrange to have them all tossed into the afterlife with him and quickly sealed up in a box of concrete for all time. There was no doubt in her mind, contrary to the tears being shed for the despicable man, that most of them, if not all, were secretly grateful that the land pirate had raided his last business, his last soul.

But in the end, like most things in a vacuous, plastic life, the appearance of propriety and civility prevailed over honesty. Such had become the world in which people now lived and breathed.

Jillian reached out and pressed the intercom button located on the console. "Ferguson, I'm ready to visit my father's resting place," Jillian announced, the tone of her voice denoting a scintilla of dread.

"Very well, Miss Hanson," came the slight crackle of Ferguson's voice over the speaker. "If you would be so kind, Miss Hanson, please wait for an old man's assistance. I shall do my best and hurry to be at your door in just one moment."

Jillian tittered from the old man's words. "Thank you, Ferguson," Jillian said, her voice unusually affectionate. "I'll wait for you and your much-anticipated help with my door, clustered with adoration and appreciation."

"It's my pleasure, Miss Hanson," Ferguson said. The tone of his voice was both deep and highly professional.

"Please, Ferguson, I've told you countless times that you need not stand on such formality with me when we're alone," Jillian said, exasperated. "I've asked you on numerous occasions to please call me Jillian."

Ferguson cleared his throat. "I do apologize, Miss Hanson, but I am far too old and cantankerous to change my decrepit ways," Ferguson said.

"Did you just attempt to make a joke, Ferguson?" Jillian asked, surprise evident in the tone of the question. She laughed softly.

"I did at that," Ferguson replied in the same stoic tone. "You shall always be Miss Hanson to me. I ask only that you please respect my manner and do not deprive me of such a time-honored tradition."

"As you wish, Ferguson," Jillian said. "I meant no disrespect, my dear man. I deeply apologize if I have caused you umbrage."

"Thank you, Miss Hanson," Ferguson said. The static of the intercom suddenly went dead over the speaker.

No more than five seconds later the rear door of the car was opened in a methodically slow manner. An elderly gentleman dressed immaculately in black stood no more than three feet away, smiling down at the woman he had been instrumental in helping raise from the time she was a baby. Almost grandfatherly, with a left hand positioned behind the small of his back, Ferguson held the other out to her. Jillian looked up into the weathered, leathery face of one of the only people she had ever sincerely loved. She gladly accepted the outstretched hand that had often been used to wipe away the many tears of her childhood.

Ferguson McIntyre, a descendant from a proud family of men who had devoted their lives to butle, had worked for the Hanson family long before Jillian had been born, and was the one person who had dared to stand up to her father on more than one occasion. Although born and cultured to be subservient to the master of the house, Ferguson McIntyre had instantly fallen in love with the green-eyed baby girl he had brought home from the hospital and was almost obsessively protective over the tiny bundle of joy he had helped bring into womanhood.

"With all due respect to your father, Miss Hanson, I do not understand why Mr. Hanson would place such a ridiculously morbid condition in a codicil to his will," Ferguson said as he helped her out of the car. "It just seems so ..." He paused in search of a proper word. "Shall we say, grotesque."

Jillian smiled and gently patted Ferguson on the back of his liver-spotted hand. "What can I say, Ferguson, it's Daddy's way of punishing me," Jillian said, contempt filling her voice. "He wishes to haunt me from beyond the grave like some sort of malevolent ghoul, to remind me that he is ..." Jillian's voice trailed off as the memories of what he'd done to her surfaced, causing her to blanch and tremble as if suddenly hit by a gust of freezing wind. Tears welled up in her eyes.

Instinctively, Ferguson took the petite woman into his arms and hugged her tightly. "Sssh, child," Ferguson cooed as he tenderly rocked her back and forth, swaying like a willow tree in a gentle breeze, trying to fend off his own tears. "It's okay, Miss Hanson. It's all right. He cannot hurt you anymore. I am here for you, my dearest child. I will always be here for you, where no one can harm you ever again."

Embarrassed by the demonstration of momentary weakness and vulnerability, Jillian sniffed back tears and straightened herself up, then quickly wiped away the moisture that still remained on her cheeks and in her eyes. "Please forgive my foolish behavior, Ferguson," Jillian said, forcing herself to regain control over the slight quiver that lingered in her voice. "You must think me hopelessly pathetic."

Ferguson reached out with a single finger and wiped away a single runaway teardrop that clung to her delicate chin. "Not at all, Miss Hanson," Ferguson replied. "In fact, if I might be so bold and take the liberty, it is reassuring to see you cry. The release of such emotion is very cathartic for the soul."

"You are too good to me, Ferguson," Jillian said. She quickly fixed her clothes and gathered her composure.

"It is my pleasure, Miss Hanson," Ferguson said. "You are like my own ..." Suddenly self-conscious over the unintended disclosure of personal feelings for the young woman, Ferguson let the words trail off. He licked his lips, uneasy. A sense of shame for the possibility of being perceived as unprofessional touched him.

Surprise covered Jillian's face. In all the years she had known Ferguson she had never known him to display such overt emotion. He was the epitome of staunch professionalism, a true credit to the traditional values instilled in him since birth. "Own what?" Jillian asked, the tenor of the question exuding interest, coupled with a hint of teasing humor."I'd like you to finish the sentence."

Flustered by the query of his employer, Ferguson averted his eyes and pretended to look at something fascinating lying on the ground. He then pushed the toe of his shoe across the pavement, nudging a few stones around on the street. "I'm quite certain you understand, Miss Hanson," Ferguson mumbled under his breath, the usual confidence in his voice all but nonexistent. "You are a very intelligent woman, even more intuitive, I suspect, so please do not order me to answer."

Aware that she had inadvertently brought shame on her best and most cherished friend, Jillian thought it prudent to change the subject before she did irrevocable damage to their existing relationship. "Please forgive my adolescent silliness, Ferguson," Jillian said softly. "I shall not broach the subject again, if that's acceptable to you"

Thankful for the gratuitous reprieve, Ferguson stood erect and nodded his head proudly. "It is, Miss Hanson," Ferguson said. He then smiled. "Oh, good grief, I almost forgot your present." Without explaining further, he walked back over to the front of the car and removed a dark satchel from inside the cab of the limousine. He held it out to the woman he had always thought of as his own daughter. "When I saw it in the window of the store I knew you would simply love it."

"What did you do, Ferguson?" Jillian asked, her voice squeaking ever so slightly. The animated joy that covered her face in getting an unexpected gift brought an immediate smile to the old man's face. She accepted the package and opened it for a quick peek, then squealed in delight when she saw what was inside.

"I hope you like it," Ferguson said, struggling to contain his own glee. "It made me think of you." His smile grew as he watched the full grown woman revert back to a childhood that had been cut short. "Isn't it a beauty?"

Jillian looked up at him with unadulterated happiness. The expression on her face reminded him of the time she was just a little girl in pigtails. "Like it?" Jillian asked, bewildered, swooning. "I love it!" She then reached into the bag and pulled out a perfectly handcrafted doll with fiery red hair that ran down the length of the torso. She held it against her chest as she shifted her feet in what would have been described as a type of slow dance by a casual observer.

Ferguson smiled like a proud father. Tears welled up in his eyes. Making Jillian happy was perhaps the only pleasure left in what little time remained in his life. "I'm so glad you like her, Miss Hanson," Ferguson said. He craned his head and looked in the direction of the crypt that was located at the top of the hillside. "I thought you might like to have a little company when you visit your father's grave. I understand that you do not wish for me to join you. However, I also know how you do not like going up there alone, with no one to speak to or lean on, if need be."

Jillian draped a single arm over his shoulder and kissed him on the cheek. "I love you, Ferguson," Jillian said. "I wish you could have been my father." Jillian pulled away and looked into the tired eyes of the man she'd known all her life, the only man who had stayed awake all night in her bedroom to protect her from the nightmares that plagued her as a young girl and the monsters that lived in both the closet and under the bed.

"That is a beautiful dream, Miss Hanson," Ferguson said. He remembered fondly all of the nights he had spent sitting in the old rocking chair, often reading children's stories until the tiny girl fell asleep. He treasured every memory beyond anything else in the world, though selfishly grateful for her fears because they provided him the opportunity to spend time with a daughter he would never have the fortune of claiming as his own.

And then, to his unimaginable horror, a despicable crime for which he would never be able to seek or attain absolution from because of such inexcusable, blind ignorance, even though it was not evidenced until years later, following the death of her father, Ferguson McIntyre discovered the identity of the real beast who had committed unconscionable violations against his own child during countless late-night visitations to the bedroom of little Miss Hanson.

Jillian lifted the doll into the air, admiring the magnificent radiance of her new daughter's hair in the morning sunlight. "I shall name you Roxanne," Jillian said, twirling merrily in a tight circle.

Ferguson watched her, grateful that he was able to bring a glimmer of happiness into her life on such an otherwise dreary day. He was familiar as to how Jillian dreaded the demand on her.

And then Jillian stopped spinning. She looked down at her watch. A slight shadow of gloom masked her facial features. She exhaled softly and then looked up the hill. She had nearly forgotten why she had come in the first place. Almost. When her eyes met those of Ferguson, there was a noticeable wound opening behind the green windows that looked back at him, clearly expressing a pain no one else would ever be able to fathom, least of all a man. It was a brief countenance that demonstrated both the depth and type of torment that only an innocent child sinned upon by a parent could unknowingly withstand, while simultaneously attempting to reconcile it by denying that the offense had ever happened.

"Miss Hanson, with your permission, I shall be honored to escort you up the hill," Ferguson said.

Jillian looked at him and smiled weakly. "I truly appreciate that, Ferguson, but I realize that you want to go up and visit that monster about as much as I do," Jillian said. She then looked at the doll held lovingly in her hands and shook her head. "No, I think Roxanne and I are quite capable of handling this alone."

"As you wish," Ferguson said, bowing his head ever so slightly. "I shall remain here and await your return." He then stepped over to the front door, turned around with his hands placed over one another and stood facing the lush landscape.

With the prized gift held safely in her arms, Jillian walked across the grounds of the cemetery and up the meticulously manicured hill that led directly to the family crypt. Dozens of expertly cut topiary were spread out everywhere to the right and left of the path she traveled. The serenity of the posh greenery that had been created only seemed to add to the abomination that was her father, fabricating an illusion that mocked her with malevolent intent that threatened to drive her into an abyss of madness. So much love and detail had been provided by the artists to engender a Utopian environment, serving as a complete contradiction to the man that it was designed to represent, that Jillian wanted to burn every perfectly trimmed branch and leaf until nothing was left but a charred and barren wasteland.

Still struggling with his own demons and a series of conflicting emotions, Ferguson dutifully stood by the car and watched Jillian slowly trek up the hill with the doll clutched tightly against her bosom. She turned around to look down at him from the hill several times to reassure herself that he had not abandoned her to the evil clutches of her dead father, and then she waved when he merely nodded his head in the same professionally endearing manner that had always made her feel safe and secure. Regardless of the fact that Ferguson completely understood the reasons why Jillian refused to allow him to accompany her to the monster's grave site, there was nothing preventing him from hoping that she would one day come to realize that accepting help, particularly from him, was not weakness. Some things were just so despicably unspeakable that no one should have to face them alone, not when there were loved ones willing and capable of carrying at least a small portion of the burden.

When Jillian reached the top of the hillside and found herself standing less than ten feet away from the door that led to the family of corpses that had come and gone long before her, she removed a small chain from around her neck and daintily held it up to the light. A single golden key glittered in the sunlight as it dangled at the end of the serpentine links. She then looked at Roxanne and smiled adoringly. "It's such a beautiful key, isn't it, Roxanne?" Jillian asked as she studied the tooled surface of its machined teeth, finding the incongruity of its purpose unsettling. "It's just terrible that it loosens the shackles of the devil himself." She tilted her head to the side. "What is it, sweetheart?" She brought Roxanne up to her ear and then giggled. "Oh, yes, you are so right." She then stepped forward, inserted the key into the lock and carefully twisted it to the right until she heard the familiar click of the lock. Leaning forward, she pushed the heavy door open.

Descending into what Jillian would have gladly described as the belly of hell itself, the concrete steps that led into the chilled darkness below slowly vanished from eyesight after the first dozen steps. Although the chamber had been fully equipped with a system that would allow for the lights to remain on twenty-four hours a day, along with a lifetime retainer for daily maintenance of the structure, Jillian had refused to allow the incestuous beast the comfort of being bathed in any kind of light. As far as she was concerned, his soul was the kind that should forever dwell in the pit of total and complete blackness, an empty vacuum not so dissimilar to the rancid organ that beat within the cavity of his chest. The smell of dust long settled along the walls and floors filled her nose with the staleness of an unexplored mine shaft. She clutched Roxanne even tighter to her chest, fearful of the monsters that always lurked in the corners of the shadows of pitch, stalking and waiting to snatch girls away so that they could commit horrific acts of violence against them.

"Don't you worry, sweetheart, Mommy will protect you from all the bad things and awful men in the world," Jillian said, her voice trembling slightly. She wondered if the usurpers of innocence awaited their arrival downstairs. "I'm just glad we're together." She then reached out and flicked the small switch on the wall, bringing a flood of light into the area. Tears filled her eyes, squinting against the glare. "Daddy can't touch you, Roxanne, not anymore." She suddenly wished she hadn't been quite so hasty in dismissing Ferguson's offer to accompany her.

The steps that led down into the main chamber went down

into the earth exactly thirty feet before they curved to the left. The whitewashed walls that ran down into the bunker-like burial vault had become faded with time and no longer appeared sanitized to the naked eye. Jillian had forbidden anyone from entering the tomb to clean. Similar to the belief about her father living in eternal darkness, she thought it only suitable that he should also be condemned to live in the same type of filth he had visited up her young body and soul.

Bent on fulfilling the terms of the obligatory event, gathering up the same sort of courageous inner strength she had utilized to survive the emotional and physical torment Zachariah Hanson had inflicted upon her on a near daily basis over a period of years, Jillian inhaled deeply and grudgingly took the first of many steps that would guide her into the womb, where the seed of evil awaited her inevitable return.

She clutched Roxanne against her bosom with all the strength she could muster, though consciously careful so as not to harm the new addition to her lovely family, and then looked down into her arms when she felt a frightened shiver within her motherly embrace. "Shhh, baby," Jillian said soothingly, leaning over and gently planting a loving kiss on the forehead of Roxanne. Having consoled the child, she continued to move down the cold corridor with slow, calculated steps, counting out each one in her head. "I know, sweetheart, I know." She paused. "I don't like it here either, but everything is going to be just fine. Just watch and see. We need to visit for only a few minutes." Jillian lowered her eyes to her new baby girl. "Yes, I know. I'm scared, too."

Somewhere behind her, perhaps near the entrance of the Hanson pantheon, the sound of something scurrying across the dust-covered ground echoed throughout the chamber. The hairs on the back of Jillian's neck began to stand on end. She stopped where she stood and craned her neck around to look up at the open door but had already rounded the corner, so the doorway was no longer within her field of vision. She considered walking back up the stairs to investigate the matter, but whatever nuisance had made the scratching noise suddenly ceased. Probably just local vermin, she told herself in order to calm her own frayed nerves. All fell eerily quiet. The only sounds that seemed to exist on the planet were the heavy ones of her own nervous breath and the soft mewling coming from Roxanne's lips, both of which were on the verge of being drowned out by the pounding of her own heart. She waited for the sound to resume, hoping to find any excuse to vacate the premises.

Nothing.

Jillian was tempted to call out to no one in particular in a feeble ploy to assuage her own gripping terror, but opted instead to exercise self-restraint and common sense. She remained unmoving for several minutes, deciding that it would be better to be patient and wait for the pretended intruder to make the first mistake.

After the passage of several minutes, content that whatever she had heard was truly nothing more than a harmless visitation from one of the species indigenous to the immediate area, Jillian renewed her journey down the desolate path until she arrived at the main chamber of the crypt.

Similar to the design of an Egyptian tomb erected for a revered pharaoh, sparing no expense on funerary materials, a grand sarcophagus constructed of solid gold rested in the center of an immense room that was larger than most people's home. A magnificent life-size funerary mask of Zachariah Hanson, accompanied with two ten-carat diamonds set in the sockets for eyes, adorned the top of the near priceless structure. The floor was made of pure obsidian. The ceiling was covered with a pristine depiction of the Egyptian zodiac that had been procured from the temple of Hathor at Dendera. Located on three of the walls inside the burial chamber were elemental images to each of its mythological counterparts. On the left was the sky goddess Nut. On the right was the land god Geb. And situated directly between the god and goddess, a representation of perfect balance, was the god Shu, the personification of the Duat, which was etched on the wall opposite the entrance. The wall of the entrance had a depiction of the god Anubis performing the last funerary rite, "Opening of the Mouth," before the body was to be entombed. Incongruent to the design of the ancient architecture that enveloped the entire area was a state of the art surveillance camera that loomed overhead like a bird of prey in the far left corner of the sepulcher. A small speaker was positioned less than two feet away.

Cringing inwardly when she heard the infernal contraption rotate its black head on a stainless steel neck as it followed her every movement, Jillian cursed her father for all his evil deeds. Even in death, from well beyond the grave that rested no more than a few leaps away, the parental abomination still haunted her with his all seeing eye, the same perverted one he had used to study her as he lurked in the shadows of her bedroom, preying on her untainted innocence with unnatural lust.

All she wanted to do was scream out for him to just leave her alone and cease to exist, but the Eye of Ra had been set upon her from the edge of his private domain, and any outburst that could be construed as irrational behavior might bring adverse consequences from those who still remained loyal to the elder Hanson, and anonymous under the provisions of the last will and testament.

Regardless of all the immense wealth and power at Jillian's disposal, Zachariah Hanson still managed to exert unyielding control over the massive fortune while harboring many secrets. Desperate to overcome the mounting anxiety that threatened to conquer her sense of logic, Jillian pressed Roxanne against the side of her face and moved toward the rectangular container that glittered brilliantly under the lights. Knees trembling and growing weak, she could taste the bile that rose up in her throat with every closing step. It was the same flavor she experienced every time a new month approached, and it never seemed to diminish no matter how many times the act was repeated.

When she finally reached the side of the sarcophagus, she placed her hands on the lid and looked down at the golden mask that was an immaculate portrayal of her father's face. No tears of love were welling from her eyes, only the cold, stoic expression of a woman who had seen and experienced far too much pain to feel empathy for anyone, least of all for her heartless victimizer.

"Hello, Father," Jillian said, the tone of her voice icy and indifferent. She shifted her gaze up to the camera that continued to examine her every move. "I'm here, Father, just as you demanded from your loving daughter." She looked at her watch, wishing the time would pass faster than the second hand advertised. The slight feeling of nausea rose in her stomach and then subsided. While maintaining a straight face, she looked around at the doors of the other family members' tombs, which were all encased in the bedrock walls. *Poor bastards,* she thought. *Who would want to spend eternity in the presence of an incestuous pedophile? Talk about eternal damnation here on earth.* She was grateful to know that her mother had been spared the indignity of having to be laid to rest next to the man she had once called husband. Jillian suspected Ferguson had a hand with making the arrangement for her mother to be cremated and have her ashes spread out into the waters of the Mediterranean Sea. The last thing Emily Hanson would have ever wanted was to be buried with the man who had orchestrated her premeditated murder and the rape of her daughter. Suddenly feeling the stress of the day's event taking its toll on her body, Jillian leaned over the tomb, closed her eyes, and unintentionally drifted off into a deep sleep, reminiscing over the last memory she had of her mother.

It had started out as one of the most joyous days in young Jillian's life. To her initial chagrin, Ferguson had been sent on a series of family errands to Europe by her father, so she took the new birthday toys she had received during the party earlier that day up to her bedroom, where she planned on playing alone until Ferguson returned from whatever chore her father had ordered him to perform. Although she had been angry with her father for sending her best friend away on her birthday, it was okay because Daddy was always being mean and bossing people around. Emily Hanson, her mother, had tried to defend her husband's actions, informing the young girl that her father was a very important man and that it was his job to tell people what to do. But Jillian didn't care. He was still mean to everyone, always yelling and sending people away, most of whom were always very nice to her when they came to visit. In spite of her stubbornness, Jillian had learned several years earlier, at her fifth birthday party, that it was usually better to just do what Daddy said and not argue with him at all. Broken arms and black eyes were no fun.

Whenever Jillian would become overly petulant and start to anger her father, she would invariably receive the covert signal from her mother to quiet down. It was always a surreptitious sign that consisted of a single finger placed against the lips. Jillian usually complied with the secret code, but sometimes she just got overly excited and lost control. Her failure to harness the childish antics was dealt with by Zachariah swiftly, often with brutality. Even though Jillian was well aware and had grown relatively accustomed to the physical beatings her father had delivered as forms of punishment, it wasn't until the late afternoon following the gala of her tenth birthday party when she learned what the loss of true innocence entailed.

Jillian was sitting on the floor playing with a box of dolls Ferguson had gifted to her on each of the previous birthdays over the past five years when her father staggered through the open door dressed in only a pair of boxer shorts. Although Jillian had seen her daddy in his underwear several times before, he had never come into her bedroom dressed in such a manner. She looked at him with a puzzled expression, wondering if he was sick. She thought he looked kind of funny. "Hi, Daddy," she greeted, holding out two of the dolls that were gripped in each of her tiny hands. "Do you want to play with me?" When he didn't answer, she furrowed her little brow. Concern covered her face as she squeezed her lips together tightly. "Are you okay, Daddy? You look kinda different, like you're feeling icky or something."

Zachariah stepped farther into the room and shut the door behind him. He didn't utter a single word. His eyes never strayed from the young girl, who sat Indian style on the shag bouncing the figures across the floor to imitate walking. "You're my big girl, aren't you, Jilly?" Zachariah asked in a husky voice. He then licked his lips, savoring the moment of ogling his own child.

Jillian smiled affectionately. She liked being called a big girl. It made her feel all grown-up, like her mom. "Yes, Daddy," she replied, smiling brightly, trusting. She freed the dolls and held up both hands with the fingers splayed apart. "I'm this old. I'm almost like a woman."

"Yes ... yes, you are, Jilly," Zachariah breathed, nodding his head, then licking his lips once again. "And you know what that means, don't you?"

Jillian looked at her father with an intense appearance of deep concentration and then lowered her hands in futility. The answer did not rest in her hands. Confounded, she shook her head. She suddenly turned sad. "No, Daddy," she replied, the tenor of her voice denoting disappointment from her lack of ability to figure out such a tricky question. "I'm really sorry, Daddy, but I don't know."

Zachariah walked over to where Jillian sat, and he pulled his penis from out of the shorts and pointed it at her. "I want you to touch it, Jilly," Zachariah said, shaking the stiffening member at her.

Jillian recoiled in horror and scooted away. "No, Daddy!" Jillian cried out, shaking her head adamantly. "I don't want to do that. I won't do it, and you can't make me. It ain't right to do that."

"You'll do what your father says, or you'll be severely punished for disobedience," Zachariah warned. He moved closer to her. "Now do what I say and touch it."

"No!" Jillian screamed. "Go away and leave me alone."

Zachariah began to stroke himself as he stared down at his daughter with incestuous lust. "You'll do exactly what I say, Jilly, or I'll take away all of your dolls and throw them in the Dumpster. You'll never see any of them ever again." He glared down at her. "I'll burn them in the fireplace until there's nothing left for you to love."

Jillian stood up to her full four feet, clenching her fists together in fury, and glowered at the object of her anger. "You leave my babies alone, you mean old bastard!" Jillian screamed in rage, her whole body shaking in fury. She pointed a tiny finger at the door.

"Now you get out of here, you disgusting sicko, or I'll tell Mommy what you did. I'll tell everyone, even Ferguson." She stared at him with eyes far older than their years. "I hate your stinking, mean, old guts!"

Filled with a rage he had never experienced, coupled with a foreboding fear that he would be exposed to the outside world, Zachariah balled up a fist and punched the defiant girl squarely in the face with all his might.

The sixty pound girl went flying back nearly ten feet, barely able to hang onto consciousness. The pain was so terrible that she thought her head was going to explode at any given second. Gasping for air, there was something wrong with her nose, because she couldn't breathe very well. A wet stickiness dripped from her face. She opened her mouth to cry out for help when she suddenly felt herself being lifted up off the ground and hurled through time and space. She wondered if she had died, if her daddy had finally killed her. Jillian's thoughts were disjointed, swimming in a current of dizziness, and then she felt herself land on a soft surface that allowed her small form to bounce. At first she thought she was in fact dead and had fallen on top of a fluffy cloud in heaven, but then she felt her clothes being torn away, the sound of fabric being ripped apart reverberating in her ears. Stripped of all her clothes, unable to fight off such a rabid attack, the worst part soon followed when her legs were forcibly spread. A loud pop filled her ears, immediately followed by an excruciating pain radiating in her left leg. The sound of her father's grunting echoed in her ear, and the stench of alcohol filled her nostrils just as an unimaginable pain pierced through her body. Jillian shrieked at the top of her lungs.

"What in God's name are you doing?" Emily yelled from the doorway, appalled by the horrendous sight.

Zachariah turned his head and stared daggers at his wife of fifteen years. "Get the hell out of here, bitch!" Zachariah spat, snarling like a feral dog. "I'm busy, so don't you dare interrupt me or you'll pay too."

"You're a monster!" Emily screamed. She then ran at the man

raping her only living daughter with both fists raised over her head. "I'll kill you, you evil son of a bitch. I swear to God I'll kill you."

Zachariah waited until Emily got within a couple of feet of the bed before he savagely lashed out with a single leg as hard as he could. The kick landed solidly on her chin with a loud crack, stopping her cold in her tracks. Without making a single yelp of either surprise or pain, Emily Hanson fell to the floor in a crumpled, unmoving heap. Blood began to puddle beneath her shattered jaw.

Jillian was reaching desperately out for her mother, who was lying on the floor like a broken marionette whose strings had just been cut, when the painful sound of high-pitched feedback emanating from the speaker system inside the chamber awakened her with a start.

Breathing heavily from the shock of the nightmarish memory, Jillian's eyes sprang open as wide as saucers. She sat up and looked around in fright. A thick coat of perspiration covered the features of her strained face.

"Is everything all right, Miss Hanson?" an unfamiliar voice asked through the static of the speaker. "Are you in need of assistance, perhaps medical attention?" The voice paused, waiting for an answer. "A team of personnel can be summoned immediately, if you are not feeling quite up to acceptable standards. Our monitors indicate that you are suffering from a rapid heartbeat, potentially resultant in the abnormal elevation of blood pressure you are experiencing at the moment."

Jillian stood up and moved her gaze over at the cycloptic buzzard that spied on her with its reflective lens. Self-conscious of her disheveled appearance, she wiped the moisture from her face. "I assure you that such shall not be necessary," Jillian said in a tone that was unquestionably firm. "I have been billing over a hundred hours a week at the office and just succumbed to the weariness that accompanies such a heavy workload and schedule, nothing more than that."

"Yes, of course, Miss Hanson," the voice said in a sanitized tone. "The conglomerate is fully aware of your immeasurable contribution and expertise in leading the entity into new worldly frontiers germane to business and financial domination over all competitors, both actual and potential. You, Miss Hanson, are far too valuable to risk losing to unnecessary infirmities. Are you certain that you do not require medical attention?"

"Yes, thank you, I am quite sure," Jillian replied, tightening her grip on Roxanne. "I am merely tired, nothing more. It is nothing a good night's sleep will not cure."

"Very well, then," the voice said. "Deference shall be rendered to your opinion on the matter."

"Thank you," Jillian said.

"You are quite welcome, Miss Hanson," the voice said. "The conglomerate truly cares for you and your well-being, and it is always a pleasure to see the daughter of our great founder and visionary to the future."

Revulsion filled every molecule of Jillian's body when she heard the verbal praise and reverence attached to the man who had molested her for years. Cognizant of the advanced technology monitoring the room, even though she looked into the camera's eye with the hint of a smile touching the corners of her mouth, inside Jillian felt as if she were about to become violently ill. *How would everyone feel if they knew the man they worshipped like some sort of demigod was no better than a common child molester wasting away in a protective custody prison cell?* Jillian wondered as she lifted a single hand and waved at the camera.

"Until next month, Miss Hanson," the voice said.

Jillian nodded her head and slowly lowered her hand, the nausea continuing to cling with her. "Yes, until next month," she repeated mechanically. Taking painstaking measures to retain complete control over the emotional roller coaster that raced through her veins like an errant gremlin on the rampage, Jillian turned around and headed toward the flight of stairs that would lead her out of Zachariah's realm of iniquity and into the fresh air above ground, thus paroling her from the stifling confines of the subterranean dungeon. The sound of the metal vulture twisting on its perch as it followed her out of the chamber was similar to that of a recalcitrant student scratching a chalkboard.

The second Jillian stepped out into the sunlight and felt the familiar breeze caress her face, she let out an involuntary exhalation of relief. Fresh air had never smelled so wonderfully pure, a pleasurable satisfaction that was only outmatched by the warmth that reached down from the sun and kissed her chilled face.

Momentarily content with merely standing stationary as the universe's elements saturated her with its life-sustaining essence, Jillian closed her eyes and held Roxanne against her cheek. "I told you Mommy would keep you safe from the bad man, baby girl," Jillian cooed. She then giggled from the response. "Yes, Roxanne, I completely agree with you. You are such a smart little girl."

After securing the door, she quickly began to walk away from the massive structure that harbored one of the most destructive men in history.

Ferguson pushed away from the limousine and smiled widely when he saw Jillian suddenly appear from behind a row of trees that encircled the burial vault.

When Jillian arrived at the limousine, the features of her face now appearing far more strained than when she had left only twenty minutes earlier, Ferguson smiled sympathetically and draped an arm over her shoulders. She was clinging to the doll almost ferociously as she allowed herself to be held by the trusted and adored butler now turned personal driver. He wished there was something within his power to take away all the pain that pummeled her on a daily basis. The fact that there was nothing he could do only added to the guilt that had riddled him for all the years he had lived in blind ignorance of what was taking place right under his own nose, and his failure to protect the child from her own father. Her pain would forever serve as a constant reminder of the inexcusable neglect for the child of the only woman he had ever fallen in love with.

"I hate coming to this place, Ferguson," Jillian said in little more than a whisper. "He was such an awful human being, and I can't get past anything." She looked up into his weathered face with the eyes of a child. "I will never be able to move on, to have a real life, to just be."

Ferguson stroked the back of her head and then opened the car door. "You've had a terrible day, Miss Ferguson," Ferguson said, then saw the hurt on her face. "I mean—Miss Jillian." He offered a lopsided grin.

Jillian smiled through the pain. "Close enough, Ferguson," Jillian said. "I'll take it."

Ferguson then helped her into the back of the limousine. "I'm pleased to hear it. Let's say we get you home."

"As wonderful as that sounds, Ferguson, I must return to the office," Jillian said. She was less than cheerful about the prospect. "I have a lot of work waiting for me. I'm late enough."

Ferguson sighed heavily. "As you wish," Ferguson said.

"Thank you," Jillian said.

"It is my pleasure," Ferguson said. He then closed the armored door. *My poor little lamb,* he thought as he headed to the front of the car. He knew it was going to be a long drive back to the office.

Chapter 5

eeling the humiliating sting of being summarily removed from one of the largest antitrust lawsuit cases in recent history, an immense liability tort of such epic proportions that the compensatory and exemplary damages would easily reach into the billions, Heather Lasko sat behind her desk with a numb expression plastered across her face. Just the prestige alone for arguing such a case would have placed her on the litigator's map, right next to those recognized in the field of law as the kings of the courtroom. Often sleep deprived, she had devoted nearly every waking hour for the past twenty months on the case. She had personally conducted hundreds of depositions and had read thousands of pages of discovery directly and indirectly germane to the client's ultimate defense and countersuit. Although she understood that Jillian Hanson was the senior partner of the firm and could whimsically do whatever she wanted without even the slightest concern of ever being questioned, Heather found it impossible to comprehend why she had been so rashly singled out and plucked from the team. And then expeditiously replaced after having proved her worth to the firm and the case on at least a dozen separate occasions.

Not only had she been unfairly treated in front of the other associates, but she now wondered if she was about to become just another unemployed lawyer collecting a pittance for a severance package while chasing ambulances. Whatever the amount, it certainly would never cover the living expenses and lavish lifestyle to which she had grown accustomed.

Even though it lasted for only a glimpse of a second, there was more than enough time for Heather to notice the meekly clandestine expressions of sympathy on each face when Jillian had seen fit to drop the gavel on her career. It was as clear as the blinking cursor on the computer screen flashing in front of her that her lifetime of work and dedication to the cause was in danger of being permanently flushed down the proverbial toilet.

There was not an attorney on record whose career had survived after being discharged from the firm of Hanson & Hanson, which served as a major deterrent for those legal climbers from daring to conjure up the guts to undermine the firm. It was rumored among the staff of lawyers that half of its former employees ended up swallowing a bullet or dangling from the end of a rope.

Not unlike most of the predecessors who had willingly sacrificed everything to walk the same halls with some of the greatest legal minds in the country, decades before she had even been born, Heather had given up her husband and custody of her children to pursue a life of power, wealth, and prestige. But now it appeared that all that bloodletting had been for naught, and she did not understand the reason for her cataclysmic fall from grace.

For hours she had watched people pass in front of her office window, no doubt scurrying about with a single-mindedness to tend to the daily grind that demanded all of their undivided attention. The fact that the firm's employees scrambled throughout the building like a variety of mice trapped in an elaborate maze for some sort of lab experiment didn't surprise her in the least because it was the normal routine. However, the inference drawn from no one daring to look her way or even bothering to offer a single wave of greeting as she sat alone in her office spoke volumes. When combined with the fact that her telephone had not rung even once, it only compounded the fear that her life as she had previously known it was about to come to a crashing halt. Both the actions and inactions of those she had often considered friends openly expressed each of their realization and acceptance that Heather Lasko, the estrogenic dynamo, had been transformed into an ephemeral neuron of the cerebral cortex, soon to be eulogized as a deceased alter ego of the sovereignty for which they had pledged their life's blood, sweat and tears.

While wondering what she would do if the worst thing imaginable did come to pass, Heather slowly pulled out the drawer of the imported desk and looked at what might be the only form of peaceful sanctuary left to someone who had been tossed aside by the power that defined her ultimate destiny. She laid her hand over the cold steel of the Colt .38 caliber handgun and considered the idea of writing a brief memorandum to memorialize her last act as a high-priced lawyer. Regardless of the circumstances, Heather Lasko was first and foremost a conscientious advocate in favor of full disclosure. She started to reach out for a pad of stationery and a pen when the buzzer of the office intercom erupted into unexpected life.

She jumped in the chair.

"Excuse me, Miss Lasko, this is Brad Renfro," he announced in a friendly enough tone of voice. "I apologize for the interruption, but may I borrow a few moments of your time to discuss a matter?"

"Yes, Brad," Heather said uneasily, dreading the next words that might slip from his lips. "What can I do for you?" Subconsciously, afraid of her plans somehow being discovered, she snatched her hand back and slid the drawer shut with a deliberate slowness that made no sound at all.

"I'm calling to give you a heads-up on a meeting scheduled for today," Brad said, his voice now businesslike. "I would have had a memo forwarded, but the news was just sent to my desk."

"One moment, please, Brad," Heather said. She quickly went to work on the keyboard of the computer to check on her calendar for the week. Nothing. "I'm sorry, Brad, but my docket shows that my schedule has been, uh, well, completely nullified as of yesterday."

"Ah," a short pause, "yes, of course, Miss Lasko. I understand your misapprehension," Brad said, his voice almost soothing. "The trust case is not the issue to be discussed, Miss Lasko. It is something external to the normal procedures here at Hanson & Hanson. I suspect a peripheral endeavor of some sort."

Heather's hands began to tremble uncontrollably, her mouth suddenly becoming bone dry. *Oh, my God, it's over,* she thought. *It's really over for me and all my dreams.* Tears welled up in her eyes. "I … it's not?" She stammered, not really wanting to hear the answer for fear of the finality it would bring if in fact it did involve the case, and Brad was simply baiting her so that he could slap her down with a cruel joke.

"No, I assure you that the meeting is relatively unrelated," Brad replied matter-of-factly.

"Relatively?" she queried.

"Yes," he replied. "Relatively."

"May I ask with whom is this surprise meeting?" Heather asked, barely able to keep the nervousness from invading her voice.

"Yes, of course, you may," Brad replied.

Silence.

"Hello?" Heather asked after several seconds had passed with no answer or elaboration. She coughed a couple of times to prod some sort of response, but none was forthcoming. "Are you there, Brad?"

"Yes, of course, I'm here," Brad replied mechanically.

"Well?" Heather asked.

"Well what?" Brad queried in return, his voice denoting a sense of confusion.

"Who am I meeting?" Heather asked, her attitude toward the man's obvious elusiveness now becoming slightly peevish.

"Oh, you want the name," Brad said. The sound of embarrassed chuckling resounded over the small speaker. "I apologize for my obtuseness, Miss Lasko, but I thought it was implied as to whom you were to see."

"No need," Heather said.

"Miss Hanson wishes to speak with you in her office," Brad said. He then paused. "Let's say in fifteen minutes, shall we, Miss Lasko?"

"I'll be up there in five, Brad," Heather said.

"That will not be necessary, Miss Lasko," Brad said firmly. "I'll be down in five minutes to fetch and escort you upstairs, so please remain in your office and wait for me. Miss Hanson is running a little late today, so timeliness is of the gravest essence."

"Brad, I assure you that I can just ..." Heather began, but the line of the system went dead before she had the chance to finish the rest of the sentence.

Exactly five minutes later, not a second past, Brad Renfro opened the door to Heather's office and stuck his head through the opening. The smile on his face was as plastic as a child's action figure. He looked around the small office as if searching for something hidden away in one of the nearby corners. "Are you ready, Miss Lasko?" he asked in a tone that matched his toothy grin. Phony.

Standing up from the chair she had sat in for the past five years, quickly brushing her hands over her designer business suit, Heather picked up a pen and legal pad. "Yes, I'm ready, Brad," she replied uneasily, maintaining a posture of quiet pomp that contradicted the tone of her voice.

Brad pointed at the materials she had just picked up and shook his head. "Neither of those items will be necessary today, Miss Lasko," he said. "There will be no dictation or briefing." He then began to wave his hands to motion for her to hurry.

Heather eyed him suspiciously and reluctantly set the items back down on the desk. Of course, why would I need to take notes of me getting the hook by her majesty? she asked herself as she maneuvered around the desk. "So, do you know what this is about Brad?" she asked, keeping a critical eye focused on him in hope that he would disclose something through inadvertent body language. "I mean, it's not like I have a vast itinerary or anything on my list of things to do."

Brad pushed the door open wider and stepped aside to allow her plenty of room to pass unhindered. "I'm afraid that I cannot comment on the subject matter, Miss Lasko," Brad replied dryly. "It was one of Miss Hanson's instructions." He then swished a hand toward the elevator that led to Jillian's private office on the thirteenth floor. "If you will please follow me into the elevator, then I am quite certain you will have the opportunity to obtain all the answers you require."

Agitated with all the cryptic platitudes that stank of obfuscation, ignoring the awkward stares coming from everyone on the floor, who suddenly stopped moving as if watching a car accident occur in slow motion, Heather turned and faced Brad. She looked directly into his eyes.

The brown, calculating orbs that stared back at her offered no emotional response whatsoever. It was as if they were those of a reptile preparing to devour its prey in one swallow, not so dissimilar to those of Jillian Hanson. It then occurred to her that the two of them would fit nicely into the consanguineous fold as brother and sister. Both seemed to be entirely predatory by nature. Heather then realized that the idea of them sharing a bloodline was unusually disturbing, though not completely sure as to why.

"Am I being fired, Brad?" Heather asked. "If so, then please grant me the professional courtesy and just tell me right now, right here. I'd prefer not to go in blind."

Brad continued to gaze at her with the same bland expression that seemed to be permanently affixed to his physical features, as if what she wanted, like her very existence, did not matter in the least. "I do apologize, Miss Lasko, but I am not at liberty to discuss the topic," he said in a monotone. He looked about the room and narrowed his eyes critically at those who saw fit to shirk their responsibilities by wasting precious time in gawking at a personal event that clearly held no social applicability for any of them that was germane to their daily business.

Feeling the glare of the man who most of those working in the building believed to be the hatchet man for their boss, even though his official position in the firm was that of a paralegal, each of the employees immediately shifted his or her visual and audio attention to other stimuli and walked away in haste. For reasons unknown to any of them, Brad Renfro gave most of the attorneys the creeps, and all of them were grateful that he rarely made an appearance downstairs, among the mere mortals forever exiled to dwell on the fifth floor.

Finally deciding to accept the man's refusal to engage her in conversation about the unscheduled meeting upstairs, Heather sighed in defeat and swept her hand toward the elevator door. "Very well, Brad," she said. "By all means, please lead the way to the queen's realm."

"Excellent," Brad said. He looked down at his watch and then frowned slightly. "We risk running behind schedule if we do not move posthaste, Miss Lasko, so please keep up." Without saying anything further, he pulled out a security card and hustled over to the doors.

When the elevator doors parted in the middle on the designated floor, two heavily armed security guards stepped forward to meet Brad and the visitor close in tow. A third man, dressed in an expensively tailored three-piece suit, remained down the hall. He held his right hand poised just inside the left side of the double-breasted pinstripe. Heather thought each of them looked like three wanted members of the former German police commonly known as the Gestapo. Silently, Brad stepped out with his arms held over his head, while the man on the left used a small handheld device to sweep him for weapons. After he finished the quick check he nodded his approval at Brad and motioned for him to step aside.

Frightened by such excessive security measures, wondering why such would ever be deemed remotely necessary, Heather took a single step back from the two intimidating figures that looked at her like a pair of fascist cyborgs.

The second guard on the right moved forward and held a hand out toward her. "Please, Miss Lasko, step out of the elevator so we can conduct a noninvasive search of your person," he said, resting his other hand on the butt of what appeared to be some kind of futuristic machine gun.

"It's all right, Heather," Brad said calmly, motioning with his hands. They're not going to hurt you. I promise. It's just a security provision that was implemented several years ago, following an incident."

"I understand that precautions must be taken, but this ..." She turned her head side to side, "... this goes way beyond what's normal," Heather said through a quivering mouth. "I mean, this is a law office, not a presidential bunker or Air Force One."

"I understand and can appreciate your trepidation, Heather, but I assure you that such measures are indeed necessary," Brad said. "We live in the real world, and just because you may only think someone is after you does not mean they aren't, am I correct?" He smiled in the same contrived manner he had downstairs.

"In other words, better safe than sorry," Heather muttered, uncomfortable with the whole concept for justification of such communist tactics.

"Precisely," Brad replied, smiling and nodding his head. "It is not a safe world these days, and all precautions must be exercised."

"Do you realize how insane that actually sounds?" Heather asked, feeling less fearful, though the lack of trust remained the same. "You will have order, but at what cost? Do you really believe that personal freedoms must be destroyed in order to save a perception that is not absolute?"

"Yes, Miss Lasko, I certainly do," Brad replied, motioning for her to step out and hold up her hands. "I did not create the conditions of the world we now live in, but we can adapt to them, wouldn't you agree?"

"No, I do not," Heather replied. "Infringement diminishes the quality of life for everyone, leaving nothing to pursue or dream for."

"Then you opt for the potential of anarchy and chaos?" Brad asked.

"I suppose, if it means freedom to choose such," Heather replied. "All government is evil. The larger the government the greater the evil. Whether you agree or not, it is an axiom beyond dispute."

Consternation still jerking on the hairs on the back of her head while she kept a watchful eye on the two men garbed in black uniforms, Heather stepped out of the elevator with her arms held high in the air to allow the first guard to slowly run the wand over her petite frame.

"She's clean," the second guard announced once the sweep had been completed. He then turned his head to the man down the hallway and nodded his head. The man quickly nodded back and whispered into a small device that was attached to the lapel of his suit. Less than three seconds later he motioned for them to return to their original positions. Without offering any words of explanation whatsoever, the two security guards retook their designated posts on either side of the elevator. The man down the hall did nothing but stand in the center of the walkway, staring after the pair of visitors like some sort of cathedral gargoyle.

"Shall we proceed, Miss Lasko?" Brad said.

"Uh, yeah, sure," Heather said uneasily.

The whole situation was creeping her out. She couldn't help but to wonder from which military surplus cult the firm had found the three spooky men. The cloned sheep Dolly came to mind. A slight shiver ran down her spine from the mere thought of people being cloned for the purpose of policing the populace.

"Wonderful," Brad said, gesturing toward the hallway that trailed away from the suited sentinel. "If you will please continue to follow me, we shall arrive in just a skip of a heartbeat." He chuckled softly under his breath from his attempt at humor and then quickly fell silent when Heather didn't join in on the joke.

Incongruent to the ostentatious architecture and furnishings of the monumental edifice, the door that led to the personal office of Jillian Hanson was made of simple construction. Devoid of any semblance of flamboyance, a modest sign signifying that it was in fact the office of Jillian Hanson read only her name, absent any hint of an elaborate title proclaiming any executive importance. Fascinated by the simplicity of the plaque attached to the wood, Heather was unaware that Brad had already opened the door and was standing to the side, waiting patiently for her to step past the threshold.

"If I may offer you a scintilla of advice for this momentous occasion, Miss Lasko," Brad offered politely, his voice unusually soft. He then smiled sincerely.

Heather nodded her head. "Of course," she said, furrowing her brow. It was the first time the man had actually sounded like an actual human being, and not some brainwashed facsimile. "I'd be grateful for anything you have to say that might prove helpful."

Brad's features softened considerably. "That's great to hear," he said, relief filling the words. "Please do not react in a peculiar manner to anything you may see or hear because it could possibly hurt Miss Hanson's feelings or make her feel self-conscious. She is a very private person and does not accept many visitors. In fact, you are one of the very few who have ever been summoned by her to this office. I do not know the particulars or the underlying reasons, but you should be honored that you have merited her attention, good or bad. She is an incredibly impressive woman, but with brilliance comes, shall we say, certain idiosyncrasies and eccentricities."

"I understand, Mr. Renfro," Heather said, though she was actually more confused now than she had been just a few minutes earlier. "No matter what the reason, you have my word that I shall treat her with the kind of respect a woman of her station has unquestionably earned and deserves."

"Thank you, Miss Lasko," Brad said, exhaling as if a huge burden had been lifted from his shoulders. He started to walk down the way he had come but was stopped short when Heather grabbed a tight hold of his arm. He looked down at her hand. "Was there something else, Miss Lasko?"

"Aren't you joining us?" Heather asked, suddenly nervous from the prospect of being abandoned by the man.

"Oh, no, Miss Lasko, not this time," Brad said, shaking his head adamantly. "Miss Hanson was very specific and quite clear when she said that she wished to see you alone." He reached over and gently slipped her hand from off his arm. "I assure you that everything will be fine. Just be sure to heed my advice. If you do, I believe you will find Miss Hanson to be full of surprises."

Brad Renfro then left in the same direction from which they had come.

After Heather watched Brad disappear, she exhaled deeply. All of a sudden the entire area seemed to be larger than life.

"Please close the door behind you, Miss Lasko," a voice sounded from a speaker resting on a lone desk located at the opposite side of the room, centered between two large doors. The decor of the room was sparse, almost as if it had been intentionally designed to be void of all feeling and warmth. It was reminiscent of a sanitized hospital room for those patients who required to be quarantined under the direst of circumstances. "Please slide the bolt closed as well. We here at Hanson and Hanson are extremely security conscientious."

Remembering the words of caution she had been provided only moments ago, Heather did exactly as instructed by the faceless box intent on delivering orders. She had never felt so alone or vulnerable, and the sound of the bolt clicking solidly in place only exacerbated the sense that she had just obligingly locked herself away from the world.

Dread filled her as she started to walk toward the desk, but then she stopped dead in her tracks when the door on the left suddenly opened unexpectedly. Fear pulled at her. At that moment it would not have shocked her in the least if some quasi-Nazi in jackboots not so miraculously moved out from behind the doorway and mowed her down with a submachine gun similar to the ones the uniformed spooks around the corner were carrying. Talk about being fired— literally, Heather mused, in spite of the brewing anxiety threatening to boil over. She then chuckled softly at her own silliness.

"Care to let me in on what's so funny, Miss Lasko?" Jillian asked as she walked into the room. She then stopped and eyeballed the summoned visitor with a glint of curiosity. "I've always enjoyed a good joke."

"I apologize, Miss Hanson," Heather said, her voice cracking slightly. "I didn't mean to be rude or disrespectful." She didn't know why, but the woman standing no more than ten feet away from her was far more intimidating alone than when in a populated area, like the boardroom. Heather thought her to be downright scary. "I mean …" She lowered her eyes submissively.

Smiling in a friendly manner, Jillian walked over to where Heather stood and rested a single hand on the woman's shoulder. "Miss Lasko, I assure you that there is no reason for you to be nervous," Jillian said. "I did not call you to my office to hand you walking papers, if that is what you think."

Surprised by the revelation, certain that she had been only seconds from being blackballed from the legal community, Heather lifted her chin and looked at Jillian with a perplexed expression. Of all the words that could have been uttered from her employer, she would never have expected the ones that were just said. "You're not firing me?" she asked, unable to hide either the relief or surprise emanating from the tone of her voice. "Are you serious?"

Jillian shook her head, grinning mildly. "Of course, not, my dear girl," Jillian replied. "What would ever lead you to believe I would do such a thing to such a prominent attorney in my employ?"

Heather licked her lips nervously, eyes darting about. "Well …" she stammered. "You seemed to be fairly upset with me when you arbitrarily removed me from the biggest case of my career."

Jillian smiled knowingly. "Ah, yes, of course," she said as if she had just experienced an epiphany. "Miss Lasko, you must not read too much into things." Jillian raised a single eyebrow, finding the girl relatively amusing. "I can promise you from vast experience that it will drive you crazy. For example, do you think I'm ignorant as to how people in general perceive me?" She paused and studied the girl's body language. "I can pretty much guarantee you that I am more than aware of everyone's opinion. The difference is that I don't give a donkey's sphincter what anyone actually thinks, not really. After all, in all truth and honesty, what difference does it really make?"

"So no one's opinion of you matters at all?" Heather asked.

"Not one hoot of them," Jillian replied.

"What about charity people and those kinds of groups?" Heather asked, even though she knew it was an underhanded cheap shot.

"Not really," Jillian replied, shrugging her shoulders in complete apathy. "Would anyone like me any less if I was poor?" She shook her head. "No, I think not. The only difference would be a lesser form of hypocrisy, because then I would not possess anything they would want themselves. I compare the behavior of such financial whores to those who celebrate Christmas with exuberance and pass out a bunch of presents." Jillian held up a single finger. "Now I ask you, does the individual day of supposed benevolence and gift giving absolve the person or make up for the other 364 days when that same person is an ass?"

Heather furrowed her brow in concentration, momentarily biting down on her lower lips as she contemplated the most intuitive, profound answer without subjecting herself to absolute commitment. "I suppose it would greatly depend on what you mean by ass," she said, then smiled at her innate ability to hedge a position.

Jillian smiled appreciatively and then chuckled softly. "You see, Miss Lasko, you're exercising your gift to practice words of art," she said, enjoying the exchange of words. "Put the lawyer's hat to the side and answer the question in absolute terms." Jillian noticed the discomfort on the younger woman's face and sighed deeply. "I apologize, for I have a tendency to digress, Miss Lasko."

Heather looked at her boss with a strange expression on her face. It was abundantly clear to her that Jillian Hanson was a far more complicated person than she had ever dared to anticipate. "That is perfectly fine, Miss Hanson," she said in a faraway voice. "I understand."

Jillian waved the comment off with a sweeping gesture of her hand. "Please, at least when we're alone, call me Jillian," she said. "To be completely honest, I detest being called by my last name. It makes me feel old."

"Only if you will agree to call me Heather," she said, feeling far more comfortable with the woman now that they were on a first name basis.

"Is that an ultimatum?" Jillian asked, narrowing her eyes.

Heather smiled devilishly. "I think so," she said.

"Done," Jillian said, nodding her head approvingly. "Heather it is." She looked around the sparsely furnished room and then frowned. "I guess there is nowhere to sit and talk in here, is there?"

"No, not really," Heather agreed. "It's kind of cramped."

"Shall we go into my office, then?" Jillian asked.

Heather looked around the room a second time. "This isn't your office?" she asked.

"Good heavens, no," Jillian replied. She turned around and started to return from where she had entered. "If you will please follow me, Heather, we can get down to some business. I have something of grave importance I want you to do for me, if you have the stomach for it." Jillian disappeared behind the door, giggling happily.

The transformation of the decor came as one of the biggest surprises Heather could have ever expected when she took a step of faith and obediently followed Jillian into the room. She exhaled deeply at the wondrous splendor that filled the penthouse office.

The immaculate design of the room was one of Roman art deco in appearance. The highly polished floors were constructed of Italian marble, and the priceless artifacts and paintings that were either mounted on the walls or rested almost lazily atop antique tables had been expertly crafted with gifted and loving hands. A sunken swimming pool in the shape of a teardrop was located on the left of the great room, with two Roman pillars situated on either side of the shimmering steps that lead down into its watery warmth, and was set aglow by the sun's rays, which gleamed down through a monolithic skylight that stretched across half the distance of the ceiling. Incongruent to the picturesque furnishings displayed, a game room area with a couple of pinball machines, a pool table, and other assorted video equipment was set up on the right, along with a ten-foot-wide-screen plasma television, refrigerator, and complete wet bar. A small kitchen was set off to the right of the refrigerator.

Heather gasped, amazed. As far as she could tell, it was every man's dream room.

"It's amazing what sort of luxuries money can buy, wouldn't you agree, Miss ... I mean, Heather?" Jillian asked. The tone of her voice was distant, reminiscent. "Unfortunately, none of it provides any true substance to an otherwise vacuous life." She turned and moved her eyes across the area. "Nonetheless, even though wealth cannot purchase happiness, it can lease the sort of misery one may desire." She looked at Heather and smiled.

Heather eyed the woman curiously and tilted her head, fascinated. "Isn't that a simple statement for you to make because you have such wealth, Miss Hanson?" she asked. "The poor may disagree with you."

"Perhaps," Jillian said, nodding her head affirmatively, "but what many people fail to realize, even those endowed with great finance, is that the rich become slaves to the money and lose all sense of personal freedom. Eventually this causes the person to become incapable of balancing objectivity between the normal and abnormal because the events of their lives are dictated by self-indulgence and paranoia."

"If it is all so horrible, then why don't they just give the money away?" Heather asked. "That would cure the dilemma you posit, wouldn't it?"

"They cannot bring themselves to give anything away," Jillian said, "at least not an amount that would not be simply deducted from taxes."

"Why not?" Heather asked. "I mean, if money is the root of all evil, then why not dispose of it?"

"Because it is the only thing that defines them as an individual," Jillian replied. "They have nothing else in their life. All the relationships they supposedly have and share are mirror images of themselves. With very few exceptions, each of them is self-destructive, a perverse version of symbiosis that is more akin to a sickened nest of suicidal parasites with unquenchable thirsts."

Heather gaped at her, repulsed by what she had just heard. "No offense," she said, cringing inwardly from the imagery the explanation produced, "but that is insane."

"Yes, it is," Jillian said simply. "Are you still envious of the rich and powerful?"

"I … I'm not quite as sure, but I wouldn't mind giving it a try," Heather said, grinning. "After all, perhaps it would not have such a negative effect on me."

"Perhaps," Jillian stated.

"So you think I could be corrupted so easily?" Heather asked. "You don't think I would be any different?"

"I think 'easily' is an incorrect term," Jillian said. "But yes, in one form or another, you would acquiesce and succumb to the inevitable."

"No offense," Heather said, "but you didn't."

Jillian looked at the woman with a dead stare. "You have no idea what I've done," she said.

Heather eyed Jillian curiously and tilted her head to the side. "So you are a sellout, too, like all the others you've condemned," she said, more heatedly than intended. It then occurred to her that Jillian could infer the words as a direct attack and insult on her character, and she would have given anything at that moment to rescind the words.

Jillian stared at the woman for several seconds with a blank expression and then slowly smiled. "I like you, Heather," she said gently, choosing her words carefully. "In spite of the fact that I could toss you and your entire career like a Caesar salad, permanently foreclosing any chance for you to become an important figure in the courtroom, you remained true to yourself, stood your ground and spoke your mind." She paused to methodically study the girl with whom she felt an instant rapport. "I'm quite impressed with you, Heather, and that is not an easy task to accomplish, not with a cynical bitch such as myself. It has been my experience that such a person is usually very trustworthy and honest. I assure you that it is a rare quality in these times, rare indeed." She squeezed her lips together and rolled her eyes upward as if suddenly faced with an irreconcilable dilemma, then relaxed. "Hmmm, let's see." Demonstrating a behavior similar to that of an obsessive-compulsive, she turned on her four-inch heels and resumed walking toward a desk that was positioned in the far right corner. She continued to hum to herself as if no one else was present in the immediate vicinity.

More confused than ever by the peculiar antics of the woman who was known throughout the world, while ignoring several unmarked doors on the right that were secured by padlocks, Heather followed Jillian in silence. She remembered and was thankful for the advice Brad had given her just before he'd left for downstairs.

Jillian stepped around the desk and slid down into the soft leather of the chair. She leaned back, pressing her back against the twenty-four-carat gold initials embossed onto the supple hide, and motioned for Heather to take a seat opposite the desk.

Heather sat down, crossed her legs, and leveled an even gaze at the woman she had taken painstaking measures to emulate.

"Do you have any idea as to why I summoned you to my office, Heather?" Jillian asked.

Heather shifted uncomfortably in the chair. "Well, at first I thought I was going to be discharged from the firm," Heather replied. "The way everyone in the office was acting led me to believe that I was going to …"

"You should not have inferred anything from the drones downstairs," Jillian interrupted. "I can assure you that no one stationed below this floor is ever furnished with foreknowledge of any action I intend to initiate. Even Mr. Renfro, my right-hand man, is often kept in the dark as to unilateral decisions involving the future of this firm. It's my firm, and I shall do as I see fit in order to ensure its future." Jillian leaned forward and placed her elbows firmly on the table. "You don't question my authority to do as I please, do you?" The levity Jillian had demonstrated only minutes earlier had completely evaporated. She was all business.

Heather shook her head. "No, of course not, I would never imply otherwise," Heather replied. "The firm and its resources are yours to do with as you please."

Jillian resumed her relaxed position and smiled. "You could not have provided a more perfect answer, Heather," Jillian said. She opened the lower right drawer, removed a brown accordion folder filled with paperwork and set it on top of the desk. "So, what do you think about criminal law?" She pushed the materials across the desk.

"I don't understand," Heather said, looking down at the folder with caution. "I'm a civil advocate, not a criminal lawyer."

"I'm aware of your legal background," Jillian said. "I've reviewed your work since you arrived and have found it nothing short of brilliant."

"Then why would you remove me from the antitrust case?" Heather asked, her voice rising in pitch. "I devoted a great deal of my life to that case, and you just dismissed me like a first-year law student."

"I apologize if you feel wronged by what I did, but it was necessary in order to accommodate my plan to divert your expertise to better use," Jillian said.

"What could be better than a multibillion dollar lawsuit?" Heather asked. "I can't imagine anything more important in the legal world than being directly involved in such a huge case. I mean, just the publicity alone would catapult a career into the stratosphere."

"I think you're being myopic, Heather," Jillian said. "And what happens when the case loses its luster in the press and falls to the wayside? People in our line of work have very short memories, sometimes exceeding short. Any seasoned veteran in our field is well aware that one favorable verdict does not define the attorney."

"But certainly you must admit that it couldn't hurt my career," Heather said. "Don't you think the fact that I am no longer working on the case functions as a detriment to my credibility as a competent lawyer? People will talk. Speculation will probably settle on lack of confidence by this office in my ability to litigate the case."

"So you are concerned about what people will think or say about you and your legal savvy, is that correct?" Jillian asked.

"Well, of course," Heather replied. She paused. "Are you referring to criminal law?"

"Yes, I am," Jillian replied. "Both trial and appellate. I think you will find it a lot more fast-paced and exciting. Besides, I think your skills as a litigator can be put to better use as a criminal defense lawyer."

"Don't you think this will appear to be a demotion?" Heather asked. "Criminal defense lawyers are perceived as bottom-feeders in the field. No offense, but I don't have the immovable foundation or earthly omnipotence at your disposal, Miss Hanson, and I cannot afford to be crippled before I even being to jog."

Jillian smiled broadly. "Not even if you were to be personally named by me as a junior partner of this firm," she said.

Stunned, Heather blinked her eyes in silent disbelief. "What— what?" Heather stammered, unsure as to whether she had heard the woman correctly. "I … I'm sorry, but I don't think I heard you right."

"Oh, yes, you heard me correctly," Jillian said. "This firm has never had a partner outside the name of Hanson. You, Heather, will be the first partner, albeit junior, this firm has ever appointed. If you accept the terms proffered, I shall contact the local television stations, senators, congressmen, even the president, and announce this fact to everyone on the planet. In just a fraction of a minute, you will be recognized as a legal partner to the most powerful conglomerate in the world."

"I don't understand," Heather said. "Why would you do such a thing for me?"

"What makes you think I'm doing it for you?" Jillian stated. "After all, it's my chattel to do with what I wish, am I right?" She lowered her eyes to the folder resting in front of her. "If you wish to accept my offer, then by all means pick up that folder and take responsibility for the case." Jillian craned her head around and peered at the stack of banker boxes to her right. "Take those as well."

"What is it?" Heather asked.

"Does it really matter?" Jillian asked, grinning. She knew the woman was far too hungry for wealth and fame to ever pass up such an offer, deliberately choosing to remain blind to any ulterior motive and hidden agenda.

Heather inhaled deeply, looked over at the boxes, and then shook her head. "No, it doesn't," she replied.

"That's my girl," Jillian said happily. She stood up and extended a hand toward the new recruit. "Welcome to the team, Miss Lasko.

I think you are going to find your new title very empowering, and we are going to accomplish a great many things together."

Still reeling from the unexpected news and sudden elevation of status, Heather stood on weak legs and slid her trembling hand into Jillian's for two feminine pumps of unified sisterhood. "I don't know what to say, Miss Lasko," she said as she felt Jillian's grasp release her hand.

Jillian waved a single finger in the air like a metronome. "Now that we're sisters in arms, you must call me Jillian," she said warmly. "And the only thing you need to say is that you accept the position." Jillian looked down at the folder. "All you need to do is pick up that case file."

"That's it?" Heather asked, licking her lips in anticipation. The thought that she was about to become immortalized as a family member of Hanson & Hanson was almost more than she could bear.

"Yes, that's it," Jillian replied. She leveled her eyes at Heather. "Pick up that folder and accept the case to seal our alliance, Heather."

"Do you mind if I ask whether it is a trial or appellate case?" Heather asked, lowering her eyes to the curious file of documents.

Jillian smiled devilishly, shrugging her shoulders. "It could be potentially both, perhaps only the former, but probably neither if all goes as intended," Jillian replied cryptically. "One hedged is properly guarded, don't you agree?"

"A riddle, huh?" Heather asked, unable to keep a curious tone out of her voice. "I'm more than a little intrigued."

"Then pick up the documents," Jillian said.

"What sort of case is it?" Heather asked, licking her lips.

"Can't say," Jillian replied.

"Can't or won't?" Heather asked, prodding for more of an answer.

"Either," Jillian replied.

"And the client?" Heather asked.

"Not until you accept," Jillian replied. Jillian stared at her with unmoving eyes. "Don't make the same mistake your father made, Heather, by passing on an opportunity that will forever change your life. I will not make this offer again, ever, to you."

"What do you know about my father?" Heather asked, surprised by the avenue in which the conversation had been taken.

"Everything, my dear," Jillian replied. "I have a great many resources and can find anything and anyone I desire. Nothing and no one can stand in my way or, if you accept my offer, our way."

Without further delay, feeling the sting of being reminded of the failure her father had become, which had resulted in him taking his own life by jumping off the same building in which he had tirelessly worked for twenty years, Heather snatched up the folder and opened it. The name of the client written across the top of the cover sheet stole every ounce of breath that was in her lungs only seconds earlier. She looked up at Jillian with wide eyes, her mouth slightly agape. It exceeded anything she could have ever imagined. Jillian merely stood watching her with a stoic expression, nodding her head to confirm the fact that everything enclosed in the materials was indeed accurate and mysteriously true.

Chapter 6

It was barely past 8:00 p.m., and Jeb was already flying higher than a Chinese box kite on New Year's Day. The alcohol that tainted his hedonistic breath with every spew of laughter smelled like a fetid brewery on a hot summer afternoon. Dressed only in a pair of skintight superhero underwear, with rivulets of perspiration dripping from his near naked body, he was screaming at the surrounding crowd and twirling the shirt he had just torn off as he continued to dance badly on top of a dilapidated table that refused to remain stationary.

A large metallic tub filled with ice and plain white-labeled cans, which read only that it was beer, rested in a corner of the untidy living room, next to an empty keg of the same brand of hobo elixir. Spread out across several mirrors on a nearby counter were several lines of the worst quality of methamphetamine in the neighborhood. A collection of cracked and stained bowls filled with pills of every assorted color was resting on a heavily worn-out recliner.

Standing at the far end of the room with a sour expression on his face, Petie watched the orgiastic masses of men and women jump into the air in rhythm to the heavy metal music that was blasting from the set of speakers screwed against the wall. Sweat stained and under the influence of every type of narcotic the host was willing to provide for free, Petie had started to lose interest in the festivities after he was sexually grabbed by one of the men who had swallowed a handful of Ecstasy. Petie had always enjoyed a good party, but things were getting out of control. He and Jeb had originally invited just a small group of people from work, but somehow word had gotten out that a party was being held in the neighborhood, and people neither one of them had ever seen before started to show up by the bunch.

Harriot, quickly becoming disgusted by the unacceptable change of ambiance, without saying a single word to anyone, even the host, had left after the first couple of troublemakers took it upon themselves to crash the private soiree, an unfortunate scenario that had made Petie incredibly upset because he had been hoping to enjoy at least one dance with her.

Jeb's unwavering assurance that he could convince her to attend was the only reason Petie had agreed to hold the party at his apartment.

Although he would never admit it to anyone, least of all to Jeb, as embarrassed as the fact made him feel, he had always carried a secret torch for Harriot. Even the sound of her name made him smile. Innately shy, Petie had made several feeble attempts to ask her out on a date, but the results always ended the same: tongue-tied. Failing miserably, those around him poking fun at him, a flood of incoherent, stuttering words would fall from his lips, followed by a quick retreat to the bathroom, where he would vomit from an overly nervous stomach. Luckily, even though most of his colleagues had long ago grown suspicious, particularly Jeb, he'd been able to convince everyone who worked at the hotel that he was merely suffering from the effects of drinking far too much alcohol the night before.

The crowd of people continued to grow. Most of the uninvited strangers, having rudely taken it upon themselves to walk into the tiny apartment and act as if they owned the place, wasted no time in emptying out the refrigerator and breaking property. The men looked as if they were nothing more than a gang of tattooed, needle junkie freaks, who had escorted what appeared to be a disease-ravaged coven of concubines that had somehow escaped from a remote leper colony and still bore the plague of festering cold sores that peppered their woefully emaciated bodies.

Petie began to grow agitated and terribly worried over his own personal safety, especially since the Typhoid Martys that had thought fit to bring the infectious incubators appeared no healthier than their female counterparts. Another disturbing factor was that each of the party crashers seemed to know one another, having called one another by first name the moment a new face appeared. But Petie failed to recognize a single one of them. Deathly afraid of contracting some sort of incurable virus, a phobia that had afflicted him since childhood, every time one of the enthusiasts accidentally bumped into him and rubbed their bare skin against his own he ran into the bathroom to scrub the area.

Drenched in sweat and shirtless, Jeb clumsily climbed down from the table and staggered over to where Petie was standing alone against the far wall. It was obvious that he was doing everything possible to keep plenty of distance between himself and the motley crew that was slowly destroying the small apartment and all the furniture he had worked so hard to buy with his modest income. Jeb smiled and laid an unsteady hand on Petie's shoulder. His breath smelled like that of a well-used septic tank. Repulsed from the stench emanating from the open orifice, Petie shied away as Jeb leaned in closer to his friend. Petie felt his stomach flip-flop, threatening to spill the meal he had eaten only a few hours earlier.

"Great party, huh?" Jeb asked in a slurred voice, wobbling on his feet to and fro, eyes half-lidded. He smacked his lips together, craned his head around, and took inventory of the mounting guests. "Isn't this great! The party of the year, homeboy, maybe even the century." Jeb licked his parched lips, grunting like a wild animal. When Petie didn't respond, Jeb shifted his drunken attention back on his friend and furrowed his brow. "Hey—hey, dude, what's bummin' you out, man? You should go hit on one of the hoodrats and tear off a good piece for yourself, homey. You're the host here and should get some from each of them, like a little head at least, dontcha think? I sure do, homeboy."

Petie took a second glance around the room, trying to force himself to digest the thought of actually touching any of the women willingly, and cringed inwardly. *I might as well lick one of those damn Ebola monkeys,* he thought. *I miss Harriot.* He then looked at Jeb and shook his head. "Naw, that's all right, Jeb," Petie said. "They're not my type, if you know what I mean."

Jeb narrowed his bloodshot eyes and directed them into the now sober ones of Petie. "How—how come?" he asked, slightly swaying back and forth on unsteady legs. He then lifted the corner of his lip into a snarl. "Are you gay, P-man? Is that what you are? You know, a big take it in the rear until there's only fear as the pecker disappears." Jeb snickered under his breath. "You like it up the old poop chute, ain't that right, homey, dontcha know me."

Before Petie actually realized or thought about what he was doing, the smirk on Jeb's face mocking both him and his manhood being more than he could stand, he lashed out and punched Jeb squarely in the mouth, dropping the man to his knees with a single blow.

Everyone in the room suddenly stopped what they were doing and focused their attention on the two men none of them had actually met or knew personally.

Slightly bent over, bracing his weight with a single hand that was firmly planted on the floor for balance, Jeb rubbed at his jaw and shook his head as if trying to clear the dizziness from his thoughts. The searing pain that radiated from his mouth had an immediate sobering effect. The physical attack had caught him completely by surprise. Prior to the incident, Jeb would have never thought Petie capable of such a thing. He chuckled to himself.

In anticipation, expecting the other man to retaliate, certain that he was about to take the beating of his life, Petie took a couple of steps back and prepared to defend himself to the best of his limited ability by taking a traditional boxer's stance. He held his fists at the ready.

Someone had turned off the music that was blasting throughout the small area, sending the room into utter silence.

Jeb looked up at Petie and grinned through bloodstained teeth. He then chuckled louder when he saw Petie tense up and lift the corner of his lip in what was assumed to be some sort of aggressive snarl.

No one spoke a single word.

Jeb ran a single finger across his busted lip and then looked at the trickle of blood that had colored it a dark red. "Not too bad of a clip, P-man," he said, smiling. He licked the blood away, enjoying the metallic warmth. "I've felt weaker ones. It takes a pretty good one to take me off my feet, even with no warning."

Petie clenched his jaw and tightened his fists until the knuckles turned to a bloodless pale. "I got more for you, too," he said, his voice dead serious, licking his lips. "I know you can kick my ass, but no one is going to call me a queer or a punk, Jebster, not even you. I can't let that go."

Jeb chuckled again. "No, I guess you didn't like it that much at all, did you?" he asked, still rubbing his sore jaw.

"No, I didn't," Petie replied. "You shouldn't have said something like that to me. I thought we were better than that, you know."

"Probably," Jeb admitted, "but now what do I do, homeboy." Jeb smiled. "You know I gotta come get some, dontcha? I just can't punk out and let you dis me in front of everyone. It's nothin' personal, nothin' at all."

Petie took another step back and motioned with his hands for him to stand up. "Yeah, I know," he said. "So stop talking about it and come get some."

Jeb smiled widely at Petie, impressed with the smaller man's moxie, and nodded his head. "All right, homeboy," he said. "You got heart, P-man, I'll give you that, but I'm going to stomp a mud hole in you."

"Get to stompin' me, then," Petie said.

In spite of the amount of drugs and alcohol Jeb had consumed over the past few hours, the speed in which Jeb moved was incredibly fast and unpredictably coordinated when he rose to his feet. Petie stepped forward and threw a roundhouse hook aimed directly at the man's head as hard as he could, but Jeb expertly ducked beneath it and struck a wicked punch into Petie's midsection that sent him spitting and sputtering to the floor.

"Put some boot to his sorry ass," someone yelled from inside the crowd of people that was enjoying the spectacle. "Bust his sorry ass up!"

While poised in a tripod position, wheezing from the incredible force of the blow that had knocked the air out of his lungs, Petie held one hand against his stomach and looked up with pinched features. He could barely breathe. The pain that wracked him was reminiscent from the third grade when Sally Huntington had kicked him in the balls for grabbing her butt in front of all his friends. Squinting his eyes, Petie awaited the knockout blow that would consist of either a hard kick to the ribs, a sadistic move Jeb was notorious for, or a downward crushing blow to the side of the face that would render him unconscious. Instead, to the spectator's disappointment, Jeb simply offered a crooked grin and an outstretched hand in a bizarre display of unified friendship. Petie scrutinized the other man with a slightly distrustful expression on his face, wondering if it was some sort of trick to obtain a better angle to strike. He had never known Jeb to act fair in anything, least of all a fight.

"Come on, dude, put some boot to his sorry ass," the voice said again. "Don't get weak. Don't bitch out, man!"

Jeb craned his head around and quickly surveyed the faces of all the guests, who were staring back at him, hoping to identify the one that had been disrespectful enough to open his mouth about something that didn't concern him. "Did someone say something?" he asked, the tone of his voice menacing, challenging. When no one had anything to say in response, he shook his head in disgust. "Yeah, I didn't think so." He then turned back to Petie. "We square, homeboy?"

Petie accepted the hand and stood up. "Yeah, we're good," he replied, rubbing his sore stomach. "You didn't have to hit me so hard. I damn near tossed my friggin' cookies."

"Hell, you're one to talk," Jeb said in a firm tone of voice. "You damn near knocked out one of my teeth. I didn't know you could actually fight, let alone hit that hard."

"To be honest, neither did I," Petie said.

Now that the excitement of the fight was clearly over, and the two men had obviously put the whole incident behind them, the music was once again set at a clamorous level, and everyone in attendance resumed dancing with unbridled sexuality in rhythm to its beat.

Jeb draped an arm over Petie's thin shoulders and guided him into the crowd of inebriated, libido driven performers whose only interest was to defile their own bodies. "Come on, bro, we gotta find you a hoodrat to bang like a drum," he said, as they walked over to a waif-like brunette that was busy trying to harmonize the incongruent act of leaping into the air while guzzling a generic can of beer.

"Uh, that's not really necessary," Petie said uneasily. "I'm fine, homeboy. Just give me a beer, and I'll be a-okay. You can call me cool breeze, homey."

"Nonsense, P-man," Jeb said, patting him on the arm. "You're my bro, so I gotta get you laid proper like. You're the host of this little shindig, right?"

Petie groaned aloud. "Don't remind me," he said, rolling his eyes. "I just want everybody to get out of here and go away so I can go get some sleep. I'm exhausted and don't feel real good. It's my stomach."

After the girl had finished draining the last of the gold liquid that was splashing around inside the aluminum cylinder, she wiped away the residual suds that sloppily ran down her chin with the back of her heavily scarred hand. She then burped loudly and looked at the two men who had just invaded her personal space. She belched again, louder. "Yeah, what the hell do the two of you want?" she asked in what could have easily been perceived as a truck driver tone of voice. "I'm a little busy and don't want to listen to a bunch of man garbage, if you know what I mean."

Jeb lifted his hands in mock surrender. "Relax, sweetheart," he said, smiling. "My friend here thinks you're the bomb and would like to spend a little private time with you." He elbowed Petie when he felt him shift from anxiety.

"The bomb, huh?" she repeated, as if the words were completely foreign to her. She then smiled, exposing two unnaturally gapped rows of tiny black teeth that resembled decomposing fragments of Good-n-Plenty.

Petie cringed from the mere thought of putting his mouth anywhere near the woman's rotting maw. His stomach twisted in knots and heaved in turmoil. The taste of bile touched the back of his tongue.

"Oh, yeah, baby," Jeb said, squeezing Petie's arm. "My main man just told me how much he'd like to hit that over and over again until there's nothin' left to hit."

She lifted the corners of her chapped lips and made the same grisly smile. "Like our own private party, is that it?" She whispered softly, batting eyelids that drooped lazily over two milky, bloodshot orbs that refused to focus.

"Exactly," Jeb replied. "You can take his bedroom and get down to some serious business."

The brunette shifted her gaze from Jeb to Petie, then back again. "Are we talkin' about both of you or what?" she asked, licking her lips in what she believed would be seductive enough to seal the deal with the two men. "I mean, I'm game for both at the same time or one after the other, like a tag-team. It's all the same to me, as long as I get somethin' out of it." She winked a lazy eye. "You know what I mean?"

"I hear you," Jeb said, nodding his head, "but it will be just him for now. I'll bring my own girl in on the action, if that's all right with you, honey?"

"The more the merrier, I say," the girl said. Without any warning as to what she was going to do, the brunette moved forward and aggressively grabbed Petie firmly by the crotch and squeezed. "I guess your equipment is good enough to get the job done." The tone of her voice was acutely vulgar. "Of course, I prefer there to be a bit more, but you'll do." She then released him and took a step back.

Shocked by the appalling act, turning several shades of red, Petie jumped back and stared at the girl in utter disgust. Jeb removed his arm from around his shoulder and laughed uproariously. It was one of the funniest things he'd seen in a long time, and Petie's overreaction to the girl's pawing only added to the hilarity of the entire situation.

Petie glared at him.

"Oh, you got a live one here, P-man," Jeb said, slapping him on the back with gusto. "She's gonna be one hellava a she-demon in the sack, a real succubus under the sheets, if you know what I mean."

Petie looked at the girl and then at Jeb. *The two of them are a match made in hell,* he thought. He focused on Jeb. "Don't you think we should go out and try to find Billy?" Petie asked, grasping for any reason to distance himself from the situation. He had never wanted to change a subject so badly in all his life. "He's been gone for a few, and that isn't like him. He never disappears without saying something to someone, and I think something's wrong. He might be in trouble."

"Oh, come on, P-man, you're bummin' me out with all that crap," Jeb said, impatient. "Billy's a big boy and can take care of himself. I'm sure he's just fine. He's probably shacked up somewhere with that rich chick he hooked up with at the hotel." He exhaled deeply. "Hell, if I snatched her up, I'd do the same damn thing."

Petie thought about what Jeb said for several seconds, before shaking his head. He knew Billy better than anyone and didn't think that was it at all. Something was definitely wrong. He could feel it deep down in his gut. "I don't think so, Jeb," he said. "He would've at least called to let me know." He paused. "And there's no way in the world he would skip out on work because he needs his job."

Jeb groaned outwardly, tired of the conversation and his friend's unwelcome tactics. "What, are you his friggin' mother or something, dude?" He said angrily, his voice growing strained.

"Well, no," Petie replied, shrugging his shoulders. "But I am his friend. I just think that if something is …"

Jeb held up a single hand, warning him to drop it. "Look, P-man," he began, "I don't want to hear anything more about Billy or your feelings, all right? You're starting to piss me off with all this worry nonsense. He's fine."

"Fine," Petie huffed. "I still think you're wrong."

"How about I agree to go out and help you look for him tomorrow," Jeb said reluctantly. "Would that shut you up for now?" He stared at Petie with a bland expression.

"Yeah," Petie replied sourly. He paused. "I guess that would be okay."

"Good," Jeb said, breathing a sigh of much-needed relief. "Now why don't you take this thing in the back and use her to help take your mind off of Billy."

"Hey, wait a minute," the brunette interrupted. "What else is in it for me?"

"Huh?" Petie asked.

"I said, what else is in it for me?" she asked.

"Oh, come on," Jeb said. "Give me a break."

"If you want it to be good, then you gotta give me something else," she said.

Jeb shifted his gaze over to the girl and exhaled loudly, his patience running extremely thin. The entire evening was quickly becoming far more complicated than he preferred. The only thing on his mind, and that held his interest at the moment, was to do dope, drink a bucket full of booze, and screw a local whore. "What in the hell are you talking about, hooker?" he asked, growing annoyed with the whole scene. "What, are you trying to negotiate some sort of payment plan or something?"

"Maybe," she replied, thrusting her jaw forward. "A girl's gotta survive, and I got certain things I like, things you gotta give up if you want to have a yummy taste of some of this sweet meat."

Petie grimaced from the girl's delusional description of herself in the same sort of way that any young man would if he had just been deliberately French-kissed by his own maternal grandmother.

"What do you want?" Jeb asked, suspicious.

"How about some uncut go-go juice," she replied, running her discolored tongue over cracked lips in a seductively hungry manner. "You now, some Ecstasy and coke mixed in a cocktail to make things a little more interesting and intense for all of us."

"I think that can be arranged easy enough," Jeb said, smiling crookedly. "I have a separate stash in the back bedroom, some real hard-core stuff that will get you off like never before, like a coronary."

The girl's eyes widened in famished anticipation as she nodded her head. "Lead the way, boys," she said. "I'm gonna blow your socks off; you just watch and see."

"Follow me," Jeb said. He took several steps toward the short hallway that led to the back bedroom before realizing that Petie wasn't coming with them. He turned around and narrowed his eyes. "What's up, P-man? Aren't you coming with us?"

"Naw, I don't think so," Petie replied, still unable to suppress the revulsion he felt for the female fleabag, whose sole motivation for pimping off her own flesh was to obtain a collection of illicit narcotics. "I'm just not into it tonight." He looked at Jeb with steady eyes. "I think I'm just going to grab a beer, sit back, and listen to some tunes. You know, just watch everyone dance and relax."

"I'm not going to do her with you, if that's what you think," Jeb said. "I'll get my own bag whore. I'm just going to pinch some off for her, that's all."

"Yeah, I know, but that's not it," Petie said, trying to keep himself from looking her way.

Jeb lifted a hand and started to protest but then decided to choke back on an unnecessary verbal attack and simply accept the fact that Petie was not remotely comfortable with sexual arrangements made with a total stranger. "Are you sure you don't want to give her a good hard poke and ride, homeboy?" he asked, even though he was almost certain Petie would not budge or change his mind about having sex with the local gutter snipe. Of course, with standards about as low as one could possibly hold for oneself, Jeb was more than willing and able to lie down with just about anything that had even the slightest hint of a life sign. Jeb was all about quantity, not quality, and prided himself on being the epitome of a generation that was morally bankrupt in a modern society of reprobates disguising themselves as both the entitled elitists and underappreciated paradigms of misplaced virtue. He was trisexual. And would try anything.

"Hey, wait just a damn second," she spat angrily. "We made a deal, and I want my damn dope. Don't either of you even think about trying to burn me because I'll raise holy hell if you try."

"Don't get your panties all in a knot, girlfriend," Jeb said, rolling his eyes. "No one is going to burn your nasty ass, so just mellow out. There's just been a swap." He then looked back at Petie. "Are ya sure, homey?"

"Yeah, I'm sure," Petie replied, relieved that Jeb was not going to actually press the whole issue.

"Hey, you just can't disrespect me and call me names, not if you expect me to do you, dude," she complained. "I'm not some hooker who takes money to screw. I do a guy because I want to, not because he pays me money."

"If you don't like it, kick rocks," Jeb said, shrugging his shoulders. "I'll just go snatch up one of the other hoodrats and give her what I was going to give you. It makes no big difference to me as long as I bust one."

Afraid that she was about to lose some easy action to score a bag, biting her lower lip, the brunette shook her head. "No, it's cool, dude," she said. "Whatever you say is fine with me."

She then walked up to Jeb and began to kiss him on the neck. "I'm sorry, baby, okay? I promise to make it up to you."

Jeb looked at Petie with a curious grin. "You mind if I take a stab at her?" he asked, chuckling from the expression covering his friend's face.

"Naw, dude, I don't mind one bit," Petie replied evenly. "Go ahead, knock yourself out." He shook his head to make absolutely certain that there was no possibility of misconstruing the meaning behind the words. "Feel free to do whatever you want with her. I'm more than happy to just kick back."

"Cool," Jeb said as he watched Petie turn and head toward the large tub filled with cans of beer.

"Are you about done messing around with that loser?" she asked as she reached down and took a firm hold of Jeb's crotch. "Now that's a little better." She smiled at him. "My name is Marcia, Marcia Walker."

"I don't care what your name is, hooker," Jeb said. He then slapped her on the butt, causing her to wince a little in pain. "Can you hum?"

She furrowed her brow. "Can I what?" she asked, confused by the question. She stared at him, waiting for an explanation.

"Never mind," Jeb said. "We'll find out soon enough, so don't bother talking. All I need you to do is follow me in the bedroom and take off your clothes."

"I still get to get loaded, right?" she asked, eyeing him carefully.

"Yeah, that's the deal, homegirl," Jeb replied. He then draped an arm over her skinny shoulders and walked her down the narrow hallway.

Grateful for not having to be the one to join the scab-covered girl in the same bed, Petie watched the two people disappear down the small corridor. Relief coursed through every molecule of his being. He would definitely have to throw out his mattress, maybe the entire bed, because he was never going to lie on anything the girl had crawled into bare naked. A shiver streaked down his spine from just the idea of it. He took a long, hard swallow of the cold liquid and drained what was left in the plain-labeled can in an attempt to quell the revulsion swimming through his mind.

When the alcohol failed to provide the necessary relief so desperately sought, Petie tossed the empty container in the metal trash bin and left the apartment. In spite of what Jeb had promised to him about searching for Billy the next day, Petie decided to go out into the dark of night and search for his best friend. He turned his head around one last time to look back at the debauchery taking place inside the walls of his once treasured sanctuary and shook his head in sadness, knowing it would never again feel the same as it did before everyone had defiled his home. *You can all go to hell!* Petie thought. As far as he was concerned, the ungodly congregation of unwashed masses ransacking his tiny castle, including Jeb and the disease-ridden floozy, could burn the whole place to the ground until nothing but a few ashes was left.

Jeb had just rolled off the latest conquest and onto his back, staring up at the ceiling, when the girl began to demand another thick line of the high-grade cocaine. He tilted his head to the side and then shook in the negative.

"Come on, you cheap bastard," the brunette spat as she rose to her knees. She looked down at Jeb with a scornful expression, her lips curled up into a snarl. "I took care of you, so the least you can do is take care of me proper like." She then began to run her hand down his body with the tip of one of her gnarled fingers. "Come on, baby, I'll make you feel even better if you give me a little to sprinkle on it." She reached out and started to fondle him.

"I think you've hoovered enough of my dope, you dead fish," Jeb grumbled. "I would've been better off using a damn blow-up doll to get off." He chuckled loudly. "It would have been a lot cheaper, far less noisy and a whole lot better to talk to. You're conversation sucks even worse than your ability to screw."

"If you don't give me more, you lousy prick, I swear I'll tell everyone you couldn't get it up and that it's puny," the brunette threatened, wrinkling her nose. "Yeah, you piece of crap, that's exactly what I'll do."

Jeb smiled cruelly. "Like I give a flying shit what you tell all those losers out there," he said, chuckling from the emptiness of the threat. "You're just some guttersnipe who can't screw for shit. Hell, I've seen bloated catfish floating belly up in the water move more. I thought you were legally dead."

"I swear I'll do it," she said, leaning forward to show that she was dead serious. She glared at him. "I swear I will."

"Go ahead," Jeb said, rolling his eyes. "I couldn't care less about anything you do, or who you do, skank."

"Last chance," she said, the tone of her voice wavering from the confidence it had held only seconds earlier. "I'm warning you. You better give me some more dope, pal, or there's gonna be trouble."

Jeb placed a foot on her chest and shoved her off the bed with relative ease. She hit the floor with a dull thud, which was immediately followed by a sharp yelp from a combination of pain and surprise. Jeb laughed out loud. "Get lost, ho' bag," he said. "I'm done with your nasty ass, anyway. All you are is a lousy sperm receptacle, as far as I'm concerned, a blown out one that has been ridden far too much."

The girl jumped to her feet and glared down at the man who had just pushed her onto the ground like a piece of garbage. Her hands were held firmly on bony hips. "Hey, you can't treat me like that!" She yelled angrily. "I'm a human being, you lousy prick, and I've got feelings, god dammit, like everyone else."

Jeb leaned back and placed his hands behind his head. He continued to look at her. "Okay, and ..." he began, deliberately letting the words trail off for the desired effect of conveying his disdain for the girl.

"And nothing, you prick," she said. "You just can't treat people like garbage. It's mean and not right."

"Watch me," Jeb said, feigning a yawn. "Besides, stupid, you are garbage, real nasty stuff that needs one of those heavy-duty Hefty bags like you see on television."

The girl moved forward and raised her hand to slap Jeb in the face but then stopped when she saw an instant change in his demeanor. He was no longer smiling. All semblance of affability went completely void. Alarms warning her of potential danger rang out by the dozen. She lowered her hand and took two steps away from the bed.

"You're not as dumb as you look, sweetheart," Jeb said, his voice icy.

"Well, we might as well be friends, huh?" she stated uneasily.

Jeb smirked and rolled across the bed, setting his feet on the floor. He then opened a small drawer of a nearby nightstand and removed a small baggie filled with a white powder. When he looked up into the greedy face of the girl watching his every move with hungry eyes, it took all of his strength not to just spit on her. "Look, I'll give you just a little more to get you going, but that's it," Jeb said as he opened the plastic satchel and sprinkled the illicit substance on a small mirror resting on top of the stand. He quickly tossed the baggie in the drawer and set a razor blade next to the tiny pile of powder. He then pointed at the dope that was awaiting her attention. "Go ahead, homegirl. I have no doubts that you know exactly what to do with it."

Similar to the behavior of a hyena pouncing on a wounded gazelle, the girl dropped to her knees and began to enthusiastically chop at the cocaine with the blade. She then formed a perfectly straight rail. "I need a tooter," she said, her voice anxious.

"I think there's one in the drawer," Jeb said as he stretched his arms skyward. "If you'll just take a second to—"

"Aw, screw it," the girl blurted out. "I don't need one." She then bent over, twisted her nose to the left, smashed the nostril against the glass and snorted as hard as she could while dragging her face over the line of drugs.

"Jeez, girl," Jeb said, disgusted by the dope fiendish behavior displayed by the addict. "No one's gonna steal it."

She lifted her head, coughed a couple of times, and smiled widely. "Now I can function better," she said.

Jeb was about to offer an additional insult to the girl when he heard an explosion of screams erupt from the opposite side of the closed door, followed by a loud crash of something either being thrown against the wall or the floor. Forgetting all about the man she had just had sex with, the girl had barely enough time to turn her head and look behind her when the door came flying open. She let out a scream at the sight of a group of heavily armed police officers rushing into the small bedroom, yelling at the top of their lungs for everyone in the room to get down. Seconds later she found herself being wrestled to the ground by a man nearly three times her size. She cried out when she felt her arms being twisted behind her back at an unnatural angle.

"Get off me, you fat piece of crap!" The girl screamed as she felt her face being smashed into the carpet. "You're breaking my damn arm, you Nazi bastard."

The moment Jeb saw the first dark figure dressed in police attire he threw the drawer open and tried to swallow what dope remained in the baggie but was knocked backward by two police officers and dragged to the ground before he could lay a single hand on the contraband that would send him straight to prison.

While forced to lie facedown on the floor, struggling desperately to free himself from the two men who were pressing their knees on the back of his neck and the middle of his back, Jeb turned his head to look at the girl, but the bed blocked his view of her. *You better not say a damn thing, you stinkin' bitch!* he thought when he felt the cold steel of the handcuffs fastened over his wrists. He was then yanked up to his feet by the arms.

The girl was already on her feet and being searched by a female deputy.

"I didn't do nothin'," the girl screamed. "I don't even live here." She looked at Jeb and shook her head. "It's not my dope. It's his. He tricked me into getting high so he could rape me. I'm a victim."

"Shut up, you friggin' skank!" Jeb yelled, fighting against the two officers who continued to hold on to his arms. "I didn't rape no one, you damn lying whore. You're just a bag whore who gives it away for next to nothin'."

"I swear to God he raped me," the girl yelled. "He forced me in here, fed me that stuff that made me dizzy and raped me." She looked over at the female deputy with tears streaming down her face. Her chin quivered for the desired effect of incurring sympathy. "I want to make a deal. I'll testify against him and say that it's his dope and swear he raped me. I'll sign anything you want."

The female officer rolled her eyes and shook her head from the girl's audacity. "What, do I look stupid?" she asked.

The girl feigned ignorance. "Huh, no, of course not," she said. "I just want what's fair and to see the prosecutor to make a deal."

The officer smiled. "So, you've been through this before, is that it?" she muttered.

"No, I've never been in trouble before," the girl said.

"Yeah, right," she said. "You're practically a virgin."

"But it's his dope," the girl said.

"Shut up, you stupid bitch!" Jeb yelled. "You're burying both of us."

"See what I mean, Officer," the girl said. "See how violent he is. I was in fear for my life if I didn't go along."

"I'm going to strangle you to friggin' death!" Jeb hollered.

The officer holding Jeb by the right arm shook him roughly. "Shut up, both of you," he ordered. "You're giving me a friggin' headache. You and your little girlfriend are in deep shit, so I want you to be quiet."

"That hoodrat piece of crap rat fink bitch isn't my girlfriend," Jeb said, offended.

"Whatever," the officer said. "It's not important, so listen up." He cleared his throat. "The two of you idiots have the right to remain silent. If you choose to ignore that right, then anything you say can and will be used against you in a court of law. You have the right to an attorney. If you cannot afford an attorney, one will be provided to you by the state, free of charge." He paused long enough to look at each of the suspects. "Do you understand these rights I have read to you?"

"Yeah," the girl replied. "Can I make a deal now?"

The officer ignored her and looked at Jeb. "How about you, stud? You understand?" he asked. "It's not rocket science."

"Yeah, I understand," Jeb replied. "I want my lawyer."

The officer smiled broadly. "That's a good decision, kid, because you're going to need one, a pretty damn good one if you want a snowball's chance in hell," the officer said. He looked over at the female deputy. "You got her, Margie?"

"Yeah, I'll take her out to the car and put her in the backseat," she said. "I'll be back in a minute." She then tugged on the prisoner. "Come on, virginal princess, it's time to go for a ride to your new home."

"What about my deal?" the girl asked.

"Why don't you do everyone a big favor and just shut the hell up," she said, feeling her patience with the drug fiend begin to wane. "You should just listen to your little boyfriend and do what he said before you get some nightstick therapy." Without saying anything further, the officer escorted the girl out of the room.

The officers tightened their grip on Jeb's arm. "You're next, kid, so don't give us any lip," the officer said as he pulled Jeb along. "I'd prefer not to add a charge of assault on a peace officer."

Jeb nodded his head in understanding. The last thing in the world he needed at the moment was another charge to go with the drugs. "I'm not going to cause you guys any problems," Jeb assured the officer. "I don't want any trouble."

"That's smart of you," the officer said. "You have a few more brain cells than your little girlfriend."

"She's not my girlfriend, and I didn't rape her," Jeb said, his voice tight from being worried about getting charged for a sex crime.

Jeb had been to jail on more than a few occasions and was well aware of the politics that occurred behind the bars. Although county jail could be brutal for someone charged for rape, prison was absolutely lethal if someone learned of the crime. No one could hide a sex crime for very long because one of the yard shot callers would either approach the new arrival or have one of his underlings do so within a couple of days and ask to see the man's paperwork in order to verify the reason for being in prison. Normally the person of interest would have a few days to produce the paperwork. Failure to do so would usually result in a stabbing, depending on the level of the prison and the mentality of the inmates.

The officer pulled Jeb up short as they walked across the empty living room of the small apartment. Everyone who had been partying in the immediate area only ten minutes earlier had been either chased off by the police or arrested.

"If you're worried about getting charged for a rape, kid, I wouldn't lose much sleep," the officer said. "I don't believe her for a second, and I know Officer Danforth didn't either."

Jeb exhaled deeply. The stress of having to go through the system with a rape charge evaporated. He'd rather risk getting killed by a shank than lockup in protective custody. He was too proud to allow himself to be treated like a punk by the other prisoners. "So, no rape?" he asked.

The officer shook his head. "No rape, just drugs," the officer replied. "You're still looking at a few years in prison."

The other officer groaned outwardly and tugged at his prisoner. "If the two of you are done chatting, can we get this guy to the jail so I can get home to my wife?" the second officer said tiredly. "Angie is on the verge of divorcing my ass."

"Keep your pants on, Frank," the officer said. "We're gonna get there soon enough." He chuckled loudly. "Besides, you don't even like your wife."

"I do too," Frank said. "I love my wife."

"Yeah, well, she doesn't like you very much," the officer said.

Forced into silence, lost for any words in response because even Frank didn't believe his wife liked him very much, he merely shrugged his shoulders and pulled on Jeb's arm.

The three men, one of them definitely less enthusiastic over where he was going compared to the two men walking alongside him, exited the apartment and walked toward a squad car that was parked in front of the residence. No one said anything further.

The neighbors standing around outside watched in silence.

Chapter 7

It was 2:00 a.m.

Struck by another acute bout of insomnia, a condition from which he had suffered since early childhood, Detective Harris gave up with trying to get some much-needed sleep.

Instead, unable to get the finer details out of his mind, he climbed out of bed and got dressed. Although it usually took nearly all of his inner strength to force himself to take even the slightest break from studying the evidence pertaining to an ongoing investigation and step outside the realm of the job that defined him as a person, Harris only returned home after being ordered by a superior officer to take a break and get some rest. He had tried to argue the point, asserting that he was perfectly fine and didn't require sleep for at least another twenty hours, but then acquiesced when provided the choice of either going home willingly or taking a temporary suspension if he refused the former. Without a puzzle or riddle to solve, life carried very little meaning for him. So, when all was said and done, leaving only one plausible avenue to take, Detective Harris opted to be reasonable and settle for a brief recess rather than forced stagnation.

However, after failing to relax enough to actually fall asleep, there was only one way for him to quell the obsession that tugged on his overactive mind. He would have to sneak into the laboratory and continue his work.

Mesmerized by the contents of the glass jar, Harris slowly turned it in his hands and studied the severed genitals sealed inside. *Why would the perpetrator castrate the victim?* he wondered, narrowing his eyes and admiring the efficiency of the skill utilized. He stared at it as if expecting the organ to scream out an answer. He then set the specimen jar down on the stainless steel table and peered up at the clock on the wall. It was just after 4:00 a.m., leaving him at least three more hours before the morning crew would begin to show up for work.

He then moved to the right and picked up the clipboard that held the results of any forensic evidence that was lifted at the scene of the crime. Contrary to most of the cases in which he was involved, nothing was found. Nothing at all: no prints, no DNA. The body had been thoroughly checked and swabbed for any body fluids and foreign residue. There was not a single strand of anything that would lend a clue to the investigation. He flipped to page two and reviewed the particulars of the doll and the results of the panoply of test that were run in search of evidentiary material that could lead to a suspect. Amazingly enough, the doll was completely clean. *How unusually bizarre,* Harris thought, smiling. He had always appreciated a fastidious murderer. It made things far more challenging, not to mention interesting. He turned to page three and quickly perused the document that read off the information obtained pertaining to the rose that was found on the victim, and exhaled deeply. Other than a common variety of rose that could be purchased from an endless list of florist shops or personally grown in someone's garden, there was nothing of consequence discovered. It was as useless as the other objects. He set the clipboard on the table and smiled.

"So now the game begins," Harris muttered. Without giving the paperwork a second thought, he reached out and picked up the evidence bag that contained the doll. "Hmmm. What's your name, sweetheart?" He shifted the bag around in his hand, methodically studying the exquisite details of the face and fingers. "Someone put an awful lot of love into you, didn't they?"

"I certainly hope the doll isn't actually responding," Lieutenant

Miller said. He was leaning against the wall, watching the detective with a curious eye.

Detective Harris set the doll on the table and slowly turned around to face the man with the familiar voice. "I wish she would," he replied. "I imagine she has a number of interesting tales to tell."

"I didn't realize that speaking to evidence was a new method for conducting a murder investigation," Miller said. "Of course, someone on the outside looking in could see it as a form of insanity. The craziness of homicide." He moved away from the wall and offered a crooked grin.

"Is there something I may do for you, lieutenant?" Harris asked as he removed a pair of latex gloves.

Miller ignored the question. "I thought you were supposed to go home and get some sleep, Detective," Miller said.

"Where did you hear that?" Harris asked, tossing the gloves in the wastebasket. "Are you following me?"

"Not at all," Miller said. "Your reputation as an obsessive-compulsion precedes you, so I left a message at the desk to contact me if you were seen entering the premises."

"Why?" Harris asked.

"I figured you'd ignore orders and come back to work, so I wanted to know when," Miller replied. "They say you're like some sort of evil genius, and that you can actually get into the head of the psychopaths who murder people for seemingly no rational reason."

"Who says that?" Harris asked.

"You know, people in our line of work," Miller said. "I may not like most of them, but that doesn't preclude listening to what they have to say, especially when it's everyone in the department." He walked into the laboratory. "Most of them believe you have some severely broken toys upstairs, but that doesn't really matter if you're good at your job. From what I've gathered, the consensus is you are the absolute best."

"I'm just doing my job," Harris said.

"Perhaps," Miller said. "If you're concerned, I assure you that I'm not going to say a damn thing to the chief or captain. Quite frankly,

I think both of them are boobs lacking any true insight." He walked over to a box and plucked a pair of gloves from it.

Harris watched with a critical eye as the lieutenant wandered into the laboratory and snapped on a pair of gloves. "What makes you think I care whether either one of them learns of my alleged insubordination?" Harris asked. "I'm my own man and do as I please, if it means getting the job done."

Miller looked at him with smiling eyes. "I never meant to imply anything otherwise," he said in a voice that lacked any real emotion. He licked his lips and looked about the desolate laboratory. Everyone, including the most devoted technicians, had left hours ago. He shook his head, amazed by the man's tenacity to work around the clock without a break. "But it is after midnight—well after—and you're basically off the clock and yet here you are. You don't have to be Steven Hawking to figure it out."

Harris stared at him with dead eyes, quickly tiring of the man's incessant ramblings, which were interrupting his work. "What is it that you want, Lieutenant?" Harris asked, his voice tight and impatient.

"Are you working on the hotel victim?" Miller asked.

"You would not ask me that question unless you already knew the answer," Harris said, maintaining a stoic position.

"Is that yes?" Miller asked.

"That is affirmative," Harris replied. "Now what is it you want? I have a lot of work to do if I want to beat the time line for when these type of cases attract ice."

"I want to help," Miller said, stepping closer to Harris.

"No," Harris said, his tone adamant.

"Why?" Miller asked.

"I work alone, always have," Harris replied. "I don't need help and definitely don't want any."

"Then perhaps I can just observe," Miller said.

Harris clucked his tongue, watching the man. "You're not going to leave me alone until I agree to let you get involved, are you?" Harris asked.

"I'm already involved," Miller stated, his voice matter-of-fact. "I am merely requesting to be brought into the inner circle." He smiled in a friendly manner and then added, "And no, I'm not going to leave you alone."

Harris sighed heavily, shaking his head from the aggravation of the whole situation that he couldn't discourage the man. "Oh, very well, then," Harris breathed. "I can't sit here all night discussing the finer details germane to the privacy of techniques utilized, so you might as well join me so we can move forward." He picked up the bag that contained the doll and handed it to Miller. "Tell me what you see."

Miller passed the item back and forth in his hands as he looked it over with a careful eye. "I see a doll that was probably made somewhere in the Netherlands region, maybe Holland or Sweden," Miller said. "I'd say around sixty, perhaps seventy, years ago, maybe longer but not much. Definitely twentieth century craftsmanship."

"You got all that from looking at the doll through the bag?" Harris asked, dubious as to the accuracy of the man's statements.

"Yeah," Miller replied.

"How can you be so certain?" Harris asked. "I didn't see anything on the paperwork."

"My mother has collected specialty dolls like this since she was five years old, and I have bought one for her birthday every year since I was eighteen years old," Miller said. "A lot of them were done through the mail service." He turned the doll upside down and looked at the bottom of its feet, searching for initials of the maker. "I recognize the style of craftsmanship, very unique."

"Interesting," Harris commented. "Is it expensive?"

"Yes, very much so," Miller replied.

"How much?" Harris asked, curious.

"I would say this particular doll would run a collector about eight grand," Miller replied.

"Eight thousand dollars," Harris said, unable to hide the shock in his voice. "Dolls can be that expensive?"

"Yeah," Miller replied. "I've seen some well over fifty thousand dollars." He continued to look at the feet. "I would say someone is missing this particular one a lot."

"What are you looking at?" Harris asked.

"Initials," Miller replied. "A lot of these collector dolls carry the initials of its maker on the bottom of their feet. However, this one doesn't seem to have them, which I find extremely curious."

"Can it be traced without them?" Harris asked.

"I believe so, but it will be far more difficult," Miller replied. "I'm afraid my knowledge of foreign items such as this is limited. The easiest way is to take it to a collector for an appraisal as to the background on it. Every doll has a history." He set the doll down. "I think I know someone who can help."

"Who is that?" Harris asked.

"Why, my mom, of course," Miller replied. "She is the best and only expert I know of who knows just about everything on this subject." He smiled lamely, shrugging his shoulders when he saw the expression on Harris's face.

Impressed with the unexpected expertise and knowledge of the lieutenant, Harris nodded his head in respect. It was only on a very rare occasion when someone actually stepped from out of the box of orthodox thought and made a genuine contribution. It had been the detective's experience that most people were capable only of one-dimensional, linear thought, which lacked any semblance of creativity outside their own myopic biases. Harris looked at the clock on the wall to check the time. To his great disappointment, it was still far too early to knock on anyone's door to ask questions about a doll.

Miller could see that Harris was troubled about something that he either didn't feel comfortable talking about or was still trying to figure out. "Something on your mind?" Miller asked, peering down where the doll rested and clucked his tongue, uncomfortable with the silence.

"I'm missing something," Harris said.

"Like what?" Miller asked. He picked up the clipboard and perused the writings with a studious eye. "This appears to be standard."

"The crime scene and the victim are just too sanitized," Harris said. "I can't believe this is the killer's first rodeo, so to speak." He pinched the bridge of his nose. The first signs of a headache raised its ugly head, causing pressure on his sinuses and eyes. "The whole thing was just far too immaculate."

Miller set the clipboard down and looked at Harris with narrowed eyes. He licked his lips, not liking what the man was trying not to say. "You think there are more victims?" Miller asked, his voice slightly nervous from the thought.

"I didn't say that," Harris replied, evading a direct answer.

"No, you didn't, but I also didn't hear a denial," Miller said. "Without confirming, how many would you say there might be?"

"Theoretically, I'd say there could be many," Harris replied. He then paused. "Even worse, I'd say there are going to be a lot more. Whoever killed our victim did it methodically slow and is highly intelligent." He looked at Miller with a level eye. "Don't you find it curious that there were no defensive wounds whatsoever?"

"Perhaps he was chemically subdued first," Miller said. "You know, drugged. It happens all the time."

"The toxicology report does not evidence anything in his system," Harris said. "Although there are substances that can slide past the tests, there is nothing in the evidence to support it. Besides, if some sort of drug was utilized to render the victim helpless, that would only further support my position that the killer is not only intelligent but also educated, because it would mean a working knowledge of drugs and so forth. Calculate that knowledge into the fact that the physical trauma inflicted upon the body was done with efficient precision, and that makes for a very dangerous and elusive person."

"You don't think it's going to stop, do you?" Miller asked.

"No, I don't," Harris replied. "In fact, I think the killer's appetite will only increase."

"Why?" Miller asked, his voice a little harder.

"Because the killer is now confident enough to leave the body for someone to find," Harris replied. "Don't you find that just a little more than interesting? It's a major shift in modus operandi."

"Only if there are earlier ones," Miller said. "Your theory lacks substance if this is in fact the first."

"It's not," Harris replied, adamant.

"You can't know that," Miller said.

"But I do," Harris said. "I am as certain about that as I am that I'm standing here talking to you."

"And you believe the murders will continue?" Miller asked.

"Absolutely," Harris replied.

"Why?" Miller asked.

"Because I would keep killing," Harris replied. The tone of his voice was emotionless, almost robotic, as he stared down at the doll and smiled cruelly. "The doll is somehow the center of the case, the nucleus, and symbolizes the underlying reasons for the actions taken against those who fall victim to the killer's thought process." He blinked his eyes slowly several times before looking up at the lieutenant. The smile on his mouth slowly faded, then died away completely, leaving only an expression of bland indifference.

Miller felt the hair on the back of his neck prickle as he listened to the monotone words spill from the lips of a man who seemed nearly as psychotic as the person they were now hunting. He searched his mind for something to say in response but could not find a single syllable. *Do I really want to introduce this nut to my mother?* he wondered. *He's friggin' insane.* Miller averted his eyes and looked up at the clock. *I have to find some sort of excuse to get out of here,* he thought.

"Is something wrong?" Harris asked.

"No," Miller replied. Overly nervous, he unintentionally answered a little too quickly. He checked his watch. "I just remembered that my mom has an early appointment with my dentist."

Harris studied the lieutenant with a knowingly critical eye and smiled. "I see," he said. "So what time is this appointment, if I may be so bold as to ask?"

"Early," Miller replied uneasily, hoping his actions were not too transparent. "I think she said about eightish." He looked at his watch again.

"What do you say about meeting at the station around noon to discuss our next move?" Harris asked. "That should give you plenty of time to finish your personal business and query your mother about the doll."

"You don't want to be there when I ask about the details?" Miller asked.

"I don't see how that would provide any real difference to the investigation, Lieutenant," Harris replied. "She would probably be far more relaxed if it is just the two of you, without the third wheel. Although the reasons for it elude me, I seem to have a tendency to make some people nervous." He shrugged his shoulders.

"So does this mean you're going to keep me in the loop, sort of like us working in a joint investigative effort?" Miller asked.

"At least for now," Harris replied simply.

"But you might dump me later?" Miller asked, incredulous over the man's arrogance.

"You've contributed to this case so far and have proven to be an asset," Harris replied. "The moment you are no longer useful our relationship will be terminated. I don't waste valuable time on liabilities, actual or potential."

"You don't mince words, do you?" Miller asked, not bothering to hide his annoyance with the man.

"No, I see no point in being diplomatic," Harris replied. "My job doesn't require it. In fact, I find that the so-called political correctness nonsense does nothing but interfere and obstruct my ability to conduct a thorough case study. I'm not one of those two-faced politicians who manipulate language to avoid offending people. I'm not running for office. If someone gets offended, then that is their problem, not mine. The people I hunt down don't ascribe to the flavor of the day, so neither do I." He looked around the laboratory. "Our job is relatively straightforward. We collect evidence and follow the bread crumbs until we reach the final destination as to where they lead, nothing more."

"And the murders of the innocent people you investigate, they mean nothing to you?" Miller asked.

"They are merely the by-product of the criminal act," Harris replied. "I don't allow myself to become emotionally invested."

"What of the families and the victim's loved ones?" Miller asked.

"What of them?" Harris asked in a monotone voice, maintaining an even gaze at the lieutenant.

"Surely they must have some sort of profound effect on you," Miller said, amazed that the man could honestly hold to the position of absolute indifference to the world around him and the people living in it.

"Why must that be?" Harris asked. "Why would I care about the inner turmoil or suffering of a total stranger?"

"How can it be otherwise?" Miller asked, slowly shaking his head. He didn't believe anyone could be as cold-blooded as Harris was making himself out to be. It must be some sort of mind game.

"How can it not be, Lieutenant?" Harris asked. "It has been my experience over the years that people are extremely judgmental and even more hypocritical. We are constantly bombarded with images of people weeping and speaking aloud over the atrocities that occur each and every day. However, they really don't care because they're far too self-absorbed and egocentric. The verbal outrage and false tears are for themselves. They act out in such ways to falsely convey upon their fellow hypocrites and charlatans that they are good and true people, because they are endowed with the ability to empathize with the downtrodden and those who are subjected to the whimsical brutality and victimization of those without such societal concerns for their fellow man and woman." Harris shook his head in disgust. "What these thespians fail to admit, a fact that their brethren will never raise for fear of exposing themselves for the selfish liars they are, is that they were never personally invested or familiar with the unfortunate person in the first place, and therefore cannot truly feel the pain for which they proselytize cries of injustice. We, as people, can undoubtedly attest that whatever the situation in question is can indeed be labeled as a tragedy, call the whole thing unfortunate, even sympathize with the person or persons, but we can never become emotionally shattered by the incident because we are just not that connected or invested with a stranger on any real emotional level that could ever cause such catastrophic results."

"So altruism is a bunch of garbage as far as you're concerned, is that your position?" Miller asked sarcastically.

"For all intent and purposes, absolutely," Harris replied. "No one does anything for another without some sort of personal benefit. It's human nature to be concerned only for oneself, and nothing will ever alter man's motivation for action or inaction."

"So what's your motivation to catch these animals, if I may ask, if you have not a care in the world about anyone?" Miller asked. "After all, you said it yourself, man only cares about his own agenda. So what's yours?"

"Why, my dear lieutenant, it's the chase and apprehension of someone who thought they were smarter than me," Harris replied.

"So it's nothing more than ego for you?" Miller asked.

"That, and the fact that I am instrumental in maintaining a balance in my world," Harris replied.

"Don't you mean our world?" Miller prodded, wanting the man to clarify the meaning behind the words.

Harris tapped his head with an index finger. "No, I mean my world," he said. "You see, I live in my own head and perceive things in the abstract, far removed from how you may see it. Everything in life is fluid. There is no right or wrong. There just is. If you disagree with me, that is your prerogative. Although I think our victim would agree with everything I just said. Bad things happen to good people, because it just is."

"I'm sorry, Detective, but I just can't be so …" Miller began, and then he paused as he searched for the right word.

"Misanthropic," Harris finished for him, sighing as he shook his head in disappointment. He had just started to enjoy the exchange of words, daring to hope that the man would not naively reach out for the nonsensically intangible. He then decided to withdraw from the conversation when it became abundantly clear that the man was more of a mystic than a cerebral realist.

"I was going to say cynical, even pessimistic," Miller said. "I'd like to believe it's okay to have faith in people, that they will do the right thing."

"And that is what will always serve as your Achilles heel, my friend," Harris said, looking at the clock on the wall. "My credo is, no hope, no disappointment."

"That sounds like one hellava lonely way to go through life," Miller said, shaking his head and pressing his lips together. "I don't think I could go through life like that, at least not without it ending with me putting a shotgun in my mouth."

"We all have our crosses to bear, Lieutenant," Harris said. "I just choose to tote mine alone and on my terms. Suicide is always the inevitable conclusion, be it quick and painless with a shotgun or slow and painful by trudging on through life until society usurps everything a person once was in his youth, when he was filled with hopes and dreams that would never come to fruition in later years, leaving nothing but an empty husk of skin and bone. Death is the ultimate release from misery."

Miller stared at him in stunned silence. If he hadn't thought the man completely insane before, little doubt was now left as far as he was concerned. "I, uh," he stammered uncomfortably.

"Didn't you have a medical appointment to keep, Lieutenant?" Harris asked, tilting his head to the side, curious as to why the man had suddenly become so obviously distressed.

Thankful for the reminder, feigning concern that he had inadvertently forgotten about it, Miller exhaled a breath of relief for the excuse to distance himself from the detective. "Yeah, that's right," he said, peering down at his watch. "It's still a little early, but it's a bit of a drive."

"Then I guess you better get going," Harris said in a tone of voice that denoted a complete lack of interest.

"What are you going to do?" Miller asked, curious. "Are you going to stay here by yourself?"

"Why do you ask?" Harris asked.

"Just interested, that's all," Miller replied. "We're still going to work the case together, a sort of combined effort, right?"

"That's my intent," Harris said. "We can call it a friendly collaboration, if you will." He then walked over and began to gather up the evidentiary items in order to secure them in a locked closet. "I still have some interviews to conduct, so I will probably return to the hotel and see if the missing employee has returned to work. The couple of them I spoke with were complete morons and were of little help. Evidently, according to most of the staff, this Billy Preston character is a hard worker and actually has a brain. So I would like to find him as soon as possible. He may possess some important information. At the moment we have nothing more than a few theories. We need something else, anything that might help to provide a path to follow."

"Perhaps we'll catch a break and find something," Miller said. "Hopefully the information on the doll will offer some much-needed insight."

"Shouldn't you be getting on your way," Harris said, offering a crooked smile. "You're going to run late."

"Damn, you're right," Miller said. "I'll catch up to you a little later." He then walked out of the laboratory and disappeared around the corner.

Harris watched the man exit the area and shook his head in annoyance. *Idiot*, he thought.

After spending well over an hour meticulously cleaning up and sterilizing the tables and equipment, taking careful measures to wipe down everything he may have touched, he went to the sink and thoroughly scrubbed his hands with a hospital-grade liquid disinfectant soap until the skin was red. While drying them off he looked about the room to make certain each and every item had been returned to the same place in which he had found it. The last thing he wanted to happen was for one of the paranoid technicians to find something out of order or missing and file a written report to the department of internal affairs that could invite an investigation revolving around the possibility of evidence tampering or contamination. Many of the crime labs across the county were already under close scrutiny for evidence corruption, and the teams who worked in them would not hesitate to report just about any disturbance for the purpose of protecting themselves from being accused of incompetency or manipulation of the evidence.

Satisfied that everything was in proper order, Detective Harris shoved his hands into his pockets and left the laboratory.

By the time Harris stepped out of the building and into the cool air outside, the lip of the sun was just beginning to emerge from the distant horizon. He stopped on the painted line that ran down the sidewalk and squinted his eyes against the unexpected brightness. When that maneuver failed to clear his blurred vision, he began to rub the palms of his hands into them in an attempt to rectify the bothersome predicament.

He yawned widely.

Although there was no doubt in his mind that he would never have fallen asleep last night, he still wished he could've at least caught an hour or two of rest. He was beginning to feel the effects of staying awake for over thirty hours, and the new day had just barely started. *It's going to be a long one,* he thought as he yawned again. Tears sprang from his eyes. *Might as well get started. After all, the case isn't going to solve itself.*

He yawned a third time and stepped down off the curb, when he heard a familiar voice call out his name from somewhere behind him.

"Bob," a voice said. "Bobby Harris, is that you?"

Harris groaned inwardly and slowly turned around to see who had called out to him. "Yes, I'm Bob ..." He began, and then he fell silent when he recognized the woman who had called him by his first name. Lost for words, thinking back to the time when they'd last spoke, he stared at her for several seconds before speaking. "Sasha, Sasha Driver, is that you?" He stood motionless, disbelieving his own eyes.

"Oh, my God," Sasha breathed, giddy. "As I live and breathe, it is you, isn't it?" She smiled brightly, beaming like a schoolgirl. "How long has it been, ten, maybe twelve years?"

Harris blinked stupidly for several seconds before answering. "Uh, yes, at least ten years," he replied, nervous. In spite of the number of years that had passed, Sasha Driver still had the same effect on him as she did when they had first met in class. "You look great." His heart felt as if it would explode and burst from his chest at any given second.

Sasha blushed a deep red and smiled from embarrassment. It was the first time he had ever paid her such an openly verbal compliment. "Thank you, Bobby," she said demurely. She then opened her arms and moved toward him. "Well, don't just stand there gawking at me. Get over here and give me a big hug."

Harris merely stood still and stared at her as if he'd not heard a single word. It wasn't until she had actually wrapped her arms around him that he felt muscle control return to his limbs. Gently, almost overly cautious so as not to hurt the one woman with whom he had secretly had a crush on since grade school, Harris hugged her in return. Suddenly he felt himself catapulted back into the distant past, to a time when he was still innocent and full of hope that life could be a happy and fulfilling experience. He thought back to the night when he had first kissed her beneath the strobe lights of the prom.

"Oh, Bobby, I've missed you," Sasha said, rocking back and forth, tightening her grip around him.

Harris struggled to fight back the tears that were pushing forward from his eyes. Although more than ten years had passed since he had last heard her voice or touched her, a fact which would undoubtedly feel like an easy decade to her, practically a lifetime ago, it seemed like only yesterday to him. He still remembered every tiny line on her face, the way a dimple formed on her cheek every time she smiled. He wanted nothing more than to tell her that he still carried a torch for her, that nothing had changed for him because he was forever stuck living in the past, a brief moment in time when all felt as it should for a young man in love. Instead, opting to take the cowardly route in order to avoid humiliating himself, he kept those profound feelings hidden.

"I've missed you, too, Sasha," he said in a hushed tone of voice.

Hearing the whispered words spoken by the man who had always been notoriously quiet ever since she'd known him, Sasha broke the embrace and looked into the face of the boy she had met through her older brother so long ago, years before he'd been killed by a drunk driver on the way to work. "I believe you really mean that, Bobby," Sasha said, placing a single hand on his chest. Even though it was slightly shadowed by the accumulation of life experiences and disappointments, she could still see the boy she had known behind the eyes that had always looked upon her with adoration.

"Of course, I mean it," Harris said. He smiled weakly and took a firm hold of her hand. It felt just as he remembered it.

"So how have you been?" Sasha asked.

"I've been all right, I suppose," Harris replied. "And you, how have you been?"

"I can't complain," Sasha said. "Life's been, well, more or less like everyone else's in the world. You know, ups and downs."

"I heard you got married," Harris said.

Sasha smiled crookedly, half wondering how he had come to know about Marty. "Yeah, that's right," she said. "We got divorced about three years ago."

"Oh, I'm sorry to hear that," Harris said. "I didn't know."

Sasha waved the words off with a mild sweep of the hand. "Don't be; I'm not," Sasha said. "It was no one's fault, not really. We just grew apart." She paused. "I suppose we were always growing apart, at least since the marriage. I guess we were always two different kinds of people."

"Children?" Harris asked.

"No," Sasha replied. "Marty didn't want any. I suppose that's what caused the first rift between us. I wanted kids. He didn't." She shrugged her shoulders. "Now it's simply a footnote in life. On the bright side, we're still friends, so that's something."

"That's too bad, Sashay," Harris said.

She smiled. "No one has called me that in eons," Sasha said. "God, but those were some good days."

"They were at that," Harris agreed. "The best in my life."

"Well, enough about me, silly," Sasha said. "How about you? Are you married?"

"No, I never got married," Harris replied.

"Girlfriend?" Sasha asked, furrowing her brow.

"No, Sashay, no girlfriend," Harris replied. "No kids, either."

"Gay?" Sasha asked.

Harris chuckled under his breath and shook his head. "It's nice to know that you still speak your mind," Harris said. "No, I'm not gay." He smiled at her. "Are you?"

She laughed aloud. "And it's nice to see that your comebacks still suck," Sasha said, struggling to stifle an outburst. "So what are you doing with yourself these days?" She craned her head around and looked at the building. "I hope you're not in any trouble."

"Huh?" Harris asked, stunned by the implication. "Why would you think ..." His voice then trailed off when it suddenly dawned on him how standing in front of the police department could be construed. "Oh, of course." He shook his head from his own clumsiness. "No, I'm not in trouble. Actually, I'm a cop, a detective in fact."

Sasha stepped back and carefully measured her old friend. "Really," Sasha said. "Funny, I never would have pegged you for a cop."

"Why is that?" Harris asked, curious as to why she would ever think of him being anything different.

"You always seemed too normal," Sasha said.

Harris smiled and shook his head side to side. "Me?" He stated. "You think I was always too normal?"

"You always were when around me," Sasha said. "So how do you like being a detective? It must have its fascinating moments."

Harris shifted his feet uncomfortably. One of the things he truly detested about his job was answering civilian questions related to it. Although he thoroughly enjoyed the hunt the job required, there were several downsides to it. Unless the person making the unwelcome query had ever been awakened in the early hours of the morning and summoned to an alleyway for the purpose of fishing out some poor woman from a filthy dump site, no one would ever understand the inner machinations of being a professional police detective, particularly one in the homicide division of the department. People thought his job was similar to the sanitized version of the popular police dramas on television, when in fact it wasn't anything even remotely close.

Normally, he would have just ignored the question and shrugged his shoulders in silence, but it was Sasha Driver who had showed interest in what he did for a living. And he'd never been able to ignore her, no matter how much sarcasm she would happily toss in his direction. "It has its ups and downs, Sashay," Harris replied. "What can I say? I love my job for the most part, but there are aspects to it that are less than savory."

"Like what?" Sasha asked.

"What?" Harris asked, perplexed.

"Like what's the unsavory stuff?" Sasha asked again, her voice a little more forceful and laced with a touch of mischief.

"You haven't changed one bit," Harris said. "You're still the little troublemaking instigator, aren't you? Do you realize how much trouble you got me into when we were kids? My dad actually got tendinitis from beating my ass so much. You were always talking me into doing some of the stupidest things, some of them landing me in the hospital."

Sasha punched him in the arm and laughed. "Oh, stop it, you big baby," she said. "You didn't do anything you didn't want to do. You loved every minute of it. I can still remember how my parents would chase you out of the backyard in the middle of the night. I used to just laugh and watch you jump back over the fence."

"Yeah, I remember that, too," Harris said. "I also remember that dumb dog of yours biting me on the leg." He smiled from the memory. "God, your dad really hated my guts. Do you remember when he bounced that baseball off my head?"

Sasha bent over at the waist and broke out in hysterics, the reminder of the time striking her like a bolt of lightning. "God, yes, I remember that," she said through a stream of tears. "You were hung up on the fence when he plunked you in the head and knocked you off the top of the fence." She punched him in the arm again. "You know, he really loved you." She wiped at her eyes with the back of her hand.

"Who did?" Harris asked, confused.

"My dad," Sasha replied. "He talked about you years later with such a fondness that I was almost jealous. In fact, you are one of the reasons he never warmed up to Marty. Even though he said it only once, my dad said I married the wrong man, and that no one would ever love me the way you did." She looked at him with warm eyes, pursing her lips. "Now that I've seen you again, he was right."

Stunned beyond belief, Harris stared at her with his mouth agape. Of all the things he could've imagined that she might say to him, none of them would have been on his list of dreams. "You're kidding," Harris murmured. "I thought he hated my guts."

"No, Bobby, not even close," Sasha said. "He just had the best time chasing you around and trying to keep you away from me because it was fun for him to watch all the crazy things you would do to see me. You were like a son to him."

Harris frowned. "Were?" Harris stated.

"Yeah, Bobby," Sasha said. "Daddy died about five years ago. It was strange. The doctors didn't know why. I think he just died of a broken heart. You see, my mom died the year before and he was never the same. I think he just lost the will to live without her. They knew each other their whole lives. Daddy just wanted to be with her, so I think he just let go to join her in the afterlife. Wherever he is, Bobby, I know he's happy because he's with Mom."

"I'm sorry for bringing up such a painful memory, Sasha," Harris whispered morosely. "I didn't have a clue. Some detective, huh?"

"It was a long time ago," Sasha said. "I've made my peace with it."

"Regardless, I'm sorry," Harris said. "If there is ever anything I can do for you, please don't hesitate to ask."

"Do you mean that?" Sasha asked.

"You know that I always say what I mean and do what I say," Harris said. "I never pull any punches."

"If you actually mean it, then have dinner with me tonight," Sasha said, jutting out her delicate chin.

"Tonight?" Harris asked in a surprised tone of voice.

"Yes, absolutely tonight," Sasha said. "Why not, unless you're just a big chicken and don't eat dinner."

"Of course I eat dinner," Harris said. He looked down at his watch to check the time.

"What are you clock watching for?" Sasha asked teasingly. "You got a hot date or something?" She poked him in the stomach. "Should I be jealous?"

"No, it's nothing like that," Harris replied. "I have a couple of errands to run and am just trying to orchestrate some mental time management."

"I thought I smelled burning rags," Sasha said, giggling. "Just like in the old days."

"I remember how you were always one big pain in the ass," Harris said, smiling in spite of the accusation he had just flung her way.

"Oh, you loved every minute of that, too, you big goof," Sasha teased. "So is it a date, or are you going to make me eat alone?"

Harris had to use every ounce of self-control to stop himself from acting like a foolish schoolboy with a childhood crush the moment he heard Sasha mouth the "date" word. He straightened himself up and nodded his head in a methodically slow manner. "I'd like that, Sasha," he replied. He felt a nest of butterflies in his stomach suddenly awaken and flutter wildly like a cave full of angry bats in search of the intruder who had dared to enter their private domain. "No," he smiled brightly, "I'd love it."

"Great," Sasha said happily. "Shall we say around eight?" She removed a pen and a small piece of paper from her purse.

"That sounds good," Harris said, craning his head so he could get a look at what she was scribbling down on the paper. "What are you doing?"

She dropped the pen back into her purse and handed the piece of paper out to him. "You're going to need my address, silly," Sasha said.

Confused, Harris furrowed his brow and looked at the piece of paper as if it was some sort of bizarre mystery. "For?" He asked. His voice cracked from nervousness. The only women he had visited at home for the past ten years were limited to the victims of an enraged boyfriend or husband on a jealous warpath.

"You're really bad at this, aren't you, Bobby?" Sasha said. "A little out of practice, are you?"

Harris heard the words, even measured them against the panoply of smooth lines that had bounced around in his head for years, but all he could manage to do was stare at her and nod his head, numb. Finally, he took the piece of paper and looked at the writing.

"That's my home address and phone number," Sasha said. "I think you'll need both of them if you're going to come over later, don't you? You know, after you take care of the things on your to-do list. I realize you could probably just look the information up on your cop computer, but I prefer to do it this way."

Harris looked up with a quizzical expression. "Your house?" he asked, blinking dumbly several times. The tone of his voice was a mixture of awe and trepidation.

"Jeez, Bobby, for a detective you don't detect very much, do you?" Sasha asked. "I'm going to cook you dinner, stupid."

"Yeah," Harris mumbled under his breath. "You're going to cook for me?"

"That's the plan," Sasha replied. "I hope you like hamburgers because I'm not much of a cook."

"I love them," Harris replied.

"Perfect," Sasha said. She looked at her watch. "Well, Bobby, I better get going so I can get to work." She leaned over and kissed him on the cheek. "I'll see you tonight, okay?"

"Yes, tonight," Harris breathed. The warmth of her lips catapulted him back to the time when he had first kissed her.

Lost in thought as the merging past and present collided, holding the paper clutched in a closed fist, Harris watched the only person he had ever loved stroll across the pavement of the parking lot. In spite of the misanthropic views he harbored for the entire planet, he was unable to deny the effect the woman had on him. She was the only person on the globe who provided a challenge to his beliefs, the only one who gave pause for him to consider the idea of having faith in the decency of mankind.

She epitomized perfection, always had, and always would. The only one that made him feel normal and not some sort of freak.

Chapter 8

Smiling with the brilliant excitement of a small child on Christmas morning that had just discovered an abundance of miracles surrounding the immaculately decorated tree downstairs, Jillian reached out and pressed the button that operated a hidden trapdoor in the center of the room. Biting down on her lip in anticipation while jumping up and down, she began to clap her hands happily when she heard the familiar hum of the motor that opened the sliding doors in the floor. While she stood back, never growing weary of watching the enormous, professionally handcrafted dollhouse emerge from below the highly polished floorboards that lined the immense room, Jillian opened her mouth in awe and exhaled deeply from the majesty of it all. Everything was just so perfect, like heaven on earth, an Eden for her babies.

Seconds later a second hum came from overheard.

The splendor of it all never ceased to amaze her as she tilted her eyes upward just in time to watch dozens of sliding doors in the ceiling open, which allowed streams of confetti to rain down like a Technicolor rainbow of the most exquisite colors. She screamed out in jubilation, dancing about like a twirling pixie, and slowly made her way across the room, where hundreds of dolls sat on shelves watching their beloved mother joyously celebrate the upcoming nuptials of one of their sisters.

"Isn't it beautiful, girls?" Jillian asked, holding her hands overhead and spinning around in circles. "It just takes your breath away, doesn't it? It certainly does mine. All you need to do is appreciate what we have."

The soft sound of gears grinding came from a nearby wall just as a hidden panel slid open like a tiny garage door. A small electric car the color of a ruby that looked like a miniature version of a Corvette was revealed and was pushed from out of the cubicle on a horizontal escalator. Music burst from unseen speakers and filled the area with the rhythmic wonder that accentuated everything else in the room.

"Yea!" Jillian screamed as she ran over to the car and got behind the wheel.

She sped off across the floor and drove around the impressive structure situated in the center of her world. "Who wants the first ride with Mommy?" She laughed hysterically when the voices of all her children echoed in her ears, begging to be chosen first. Momentarily indecisive because of the vast enthusiasm in the mass of cheers, Jillian looked over at the shelves when she rounded the dollhouse and yelled in delight at the sight of all her daughters standing up, happily jumping up and down, and wildly waving their hands in the air to get their mother's undivided attention to be the first one picked. The boisterous words of "pick me, Mommy, pick me," resounded in her ears with crystal clarity as she raced toward her girls. "Who wants to get married the mostest?"

The dolls continued to jump up and down excitedly, waving frantically to be picked, and screamed, "I do; I do!"

"Who's been a good girl?" Jillian called out.

"I have, I have," the dolls declared in unison. "Pick me, Mommy, pick me. I love you, Mommy!"

"Who wants a husband?" Jillian cried out, shaking her hair about wildly. She made a sharp left-hand turn and headed back around the dollhouse. The small tires squeaked as they gripped the floor.

"I do, I do!" the dolls yelled.

"Who needs a husband?" Jillian asked as she circled the structure.

"Not me, not me!" The dolls yelled even louder.

"What is sex?" Jillian called out as she rounded the house in the little car.

"Filthy, filthy!" the dolls screamed angrily. "Sex is filthy, men are filthy, and penises are even filthier." They clenched their fists together and began to stomp their feet in mutual disgust for the male species. "Filthy. Dirty. Unclean. Rapists. Destroyers of innocence in the female spirit!"

"What will we never do?" Jillian asked.

"Have sex!" the dolls shouted.

"What do we think about sex?" Jillian asked.

"Ewww," the dolls replied. "It's icky."

Jillian yelled in delight and raced over toward the shelves where her children waited in hope of being selected, beeping the horn that alerted all of them that she had indeed made a choice as to whom would be the next bride.

All fell silent when she slowed the car at the right end of the shelf and began to coast down the length of it. The sound of disappointed sighs touched her ears as she passed by without comment. Some would hold their breath when they saw her slowly approach, while others bit down on their lip in hope of attaining the ultimate goal of being preferred over all others.

Although Jillian wished she could pick all of them at the same time, filled with sympathy for the plight of being passed over yet again when she saw the hungry expressions on each of their faces transform itself into a sadness, the immutable fact was there could be only one wedding held at a time. Halfway down the path she stopped the car, smiled widely, and looked over to her right. Not more than a foot away stood a stunning brunette with piercing brown eyes.

The doll tilted her head and smiled at her loving mother. "Me, Mommy, is it really my turn?" the doll asked in an accented voice.

"That's right, Dorothy," Jillian breathed softly. "It's your turn to leave the nest and get married." She reached out and gently took Dorothy from off the shelf. She could feel her baby girl tremble from happiness in her hand.

"Dorothy, Dorothy, Dorothy!" The dolls chanted, ecstatic over their beloved sister's fortunate change of events.

Jillian pulled Dorothy against her chest and hugged her with every ounce of love she held in her heart. "I love you so much, Dottie," she said. Tears ran down her cheeks.

"I love you, too, Mommy," Dorothy said.

Jillian looked up at her daughters with tear-streaked eyes, smiling at her beloved creations with the most profound demonstration of motherly love, and waved happily to each of them. "Mommy loves all of you very, very much," she said tenderly. She then set Dorothy in a tiny, custom-made seat on the passenger side of the car and safely buckled her in it.

The impressive army of female dolls jumped up and down in jubilation, moving in a synchronized wave of bodies and hands, and cried out ecstatically at the top of their lungs. "We love you, too, Mommy!" the voices decreed enthusiastically. "Mommy … Mommy … Mommy!" They stomped their tiny feet in perfect unison.

Licking her lips in response to the loving declarations of the multitude, Jillian stomped on the accelerator and sent the miniature vehicle screeching forward at an amazing rate of speed.

"Weeeee!" Jillian screamed as the car rapidly approached the dollhouse. "Hang on, Dorothy, we're going in!" Jillian jerked the wheel to the right and then to the left in order to steer the car around the house at near breakneck speed. The car tilted up on two wheels. She averted her vision from the path and laughed when she saw that Dorothy had thrown her hands over her eyes to blind herself from the reckless maneuver. Jillian sped around the house several times before finally bringing the car to a halt. She then removed the seat belt that held Dorothy firmly in the seat and snatched her up with delicate grace.

All fell dead quiet.

When she lifted her gaze to the family of bedazzled spectators, who had openly expressed their love by cheering the duo on with great exuberance only minutes earlier, each and every one of the human miniatures had resumed their former position of sitting down atop the shelves while silently observing the mother and child with a fixated attention that only mesmerized eyes could produce.

Frowning slightly, Jillian stepped out of the car and looked on with narrowed eyes across the room to where her children sat like dormant sentinels waging judgment from a distance. She placed Dorothy on the expansive front yard of the dollhouse, without taking her eyes off the other children. *Why, you little brats,* she thought. *Don't you dare be jealous of your sister.* She closed her eyes, while whispering pleas of forgiveness under her breath if she had inadvertently hurt any of the others' feelings, and shook her head. "Don't be like that, you little stinkers." When she reopened them, to her immense pleasure, she found that the fruit of her many labors were systematically leaping from off the shelves and running toward her with their small arms held out for acceptance, screaming in delight for their mother to hold them and for her to never let go.

Jillian dropped down to the floor on a single knee and frantically urged them forward by waving a hand for them to hurry so they could all play together. She laughed deliriously when she saw their tiny legs and arms pump furiously in competition as each of them struggled against the crowded bodies of the feminine masses. Each of the elegant dresses that covered their perfectly sculpted forms floated about their legs and the floor in a giant, colorful tide of shimmering silk and satin. And the dazzling diamonds that adorned their wrists, necks, and hair sparkled with the glittering brilliance of countless stars in the night sky.

The more the distance decreased between them and the woman who gave them life, the more it appeared that they were nearly climbing over one another to reach her with each subsequent step. The click-clack of high-heel shoes striking against the floor reverberated throughout the room like a thousand excited tap dancers showing off for an audience of millions.

"Come on, girls, come on!" Jillian shrieked wildly. "You can do it. Faster, sweeties. I'm right here waiting." She laughed even louder.

"Mommy, Mommy!" they cried out in unison, holding their arms out toward her, opening and closing their tiny fingers in anticipation, as if performing some sort of hand exercise with them.

Blonde, brunette, and red hair swirled and twisted about wildly in the air. Eyes were ablaze with fiery need.

They came within fifteen feet of their mother's arms.

"Come on, sweethearts!" Jillian urged excitedly. "Come to your mommy, my little angels."

Vivian and Tanya were out in front, leading the group of competitive siblings.

Ten feet.

"Hurry!" Jillian said. She felt as if she could almost touch their beautiful faces. "Mommy is right here."

Five feet.

Tanya had just leaped into the air like an impala seeking escape from the maw of a hungry cheetah when the cell phone Jillian had attached to her belt suddenly sprang into life, startling her enough to force a small yelp to slip from her lips. She shifted her eyes to the noisy disruption and reached down to pluck the rectangular device from its harness. Annoyed from being so rudely disturbed in her inner sanctum, Jillian flipped the phone open. When she raised her eyes to search for her offspring, a single tear coursed down her cheek. She found that all of them had returned to the shelves in utter silence.

"This had better be damn important, Brad," Jillian warned in a hard tone of voice. "You of all people should know and understand how I do not like being interrupted during personal, family time."

I deeply apologize for the intrusion, Miss Hanson," Brad said, his voice soft and sincere, "but I'm afraid it is completely necessary, albeit regrettable." He paused for several seconds. "If I could have somehow avoided—"

"Enough, Brad," Jillian interrupted. "I neither have the time nor the inclination to listen to a panoply of doltish prattle that leads absolutely nowhere, so why don't you just spill the proverbial beans and tell me the problem?"

"Of course, Miss Hanson," Brad said uneasily. "'I'm sorry."

Jillian exhaled deeply, quickly growing irritated. "Just get on with it," Jillian said impatiently, slowly shaking her head side to side.

"Uh ... well, yes, of course, Miss Hanson," Brad stammered. "You see, a detective just entered my office and asked to personally speak with you on a matter that he described as extremely important.

"Why didn't you ask him to leave before you decided to pester me?" Jillian asked. The tone of her voice denoted a degree of dissatisfaction. It took little effort for her to recognize the immutable fact that Brad was using his uncanny ability to select and incorporate specific words into the conversation.

"I don't understand," Brad mumbled nearly incoherently.

"Shall I elaborate?" Jillian asked in a voice that held no amusement whatsoever. "I'm incredibly busy."

"That shall not be necessary," Brad said.

"He's standing right in front of you, isn't he?" Jillian asked. Her voice was overflowing with confidence.

"Yes, he is," Brad replied evenly. "But how did you ..."

Jillian chuckled into the phone piece. "Haven't you learned by now that I know absolutely everything, my dear Bradley," Jillian interrupted. "You might as well refer to me as the Great Oracle of Delphi." When no response was forthcoming, Jillian sighed in resignation because of the man's utter lack of sense of humor. "That was a joke."

"Oh, sorry," Brad said.

"You really need to get a girlfriend," Jillian said.

"I said I was sorry," Brad said. "There's no reason to bag on me."

"Whatever," Jillian said. "So what does the mindless Bolshevik want with me?"

"He wishes to have a few moments of your time, to speak with you, Miss Hanson," Brad replied.

"I know that much," Jillian shot back. "I meant, what does he want to talk about with me?"

"I'm uncertain," Brad replied, embarrassed. "He refused to disclose the reason for the requested audience."

"I see," Jillian said. She looked over to where her family watched her with stoic patience, their eyes never wavering from her. "I am a little busy today, Brad, so how long does he expect all of this to take?"

"He assured me that it would not take very long, Miss Hanson," Brad replied.

"Dare I bother to query as to whether he has a warrant?" Jillian asked.

"No, Miss Hanson," Brad replied. "That was the first question I asked of him." There was a pause. "He said he could obtain one, though."

Jillian laughed out loud. "Unlikely, Brad," Jillian said. "It's a vacuous threat all of those knuckle-dragging apes throw at those who are either too frightened or intimidated by cops to simply tell them to pound sand." Jillian sighed audibly. "So tell me, what is this detective's name and division?"

He looked at the detective and smiled cruelly. "Bob Harris," Brad replied in a monotone voice. "Evidently, if you opt to believe him, he is currently assigned to the homicide division of the local police department."

"Homicide, huh?" Jillian mumbled under her breath, smiling into the receiver. "Now that's a little more interesting, don't you think? Tell me, is our sleuthing genius alone or does he have one of those storm-trooping sidekicks with him, and in close tow?"

"Yes ..." Brad replied.

"Yes, what?"

"He appears to be all by his lonesome," Brad said, his voice taking on a curious note. "Should I tell him to scram and try to get a warrant?"

"Hang on for just a second, Brad," Jillian said in a cryptic tone of voice. Without offering any explanation to the paralegal as to why she was placing their conversation in abeyance, Jillian walked over to a computer terminal that rested on a large mahogany desk and quickly typed in the detective's name for the purpose of conducting a quick but very comprehensive background check on the man to familiarize herself with all the necessary facts that defined Mr. Bob

Harris—not only as a professional homicide detective but also as a human being.

Seconds after she ran the program, information began to stream across the large display screen. "So, who are you, my dear detective?" Rapidly reading each and every syllable as she scrolled down at an incredible rate of speed while the lines flashed in front of her eyes, Jillian's mind greedily gobbled up every shred of relevant data until there was nothing left to search.

Contrary to the personal history, usually finding their lives nothing more than a mundane and pointless existence, Robert Harris, the only son of Agatha and Harold Harris, seemed to be a little more of a curious mystery. *Why would someone with such a high aptitude ever settle for limiting himself to functioning as a mere government employee, particularly a lowly cop?* she wondered, finding the intellectual puzzle fascinating. She was certain that something had to be missing. And whatever it was, she knew there was no possible way for her not to discover the elusive answer, so she shut down the program and brought the cell phone up to her ear. "Hello, Brad."

"Yes, Miss Hanson, I'm still here," Brad said.

"Please tell Detective Harris that I shall be right down to speak with him," Jillian said in a flat voice.

"Are you certain?" Brad asked, unable to hide the surprise in his voice.

"Yes," Jillian replied.

"Should I notify one of the lawyers to—" Brad began.

"No," Jillian interrupted. "That will not be necessary."

"I don't recommend a private meeting," Brad said.

"I agree," Jillian said.

"Then I shall be present?" Brad stated.

"Yes," Jillian replied. She snapped the phone shut and looked at her girls. "Mommy's on the hunt again, girls, so you be good, and we'll finish our little slumber party a little later, okay?"

Silence.

"Fine, be like that, you bad girls," Jillian said, glaring at them with pained eyes as she picked up a handbag. She then grabbed

Dorothy and placed her inside. "You're coming with me, Dorothy, and I don't want to hear any lip." She huffed. "Your sisters are being little brats. They must realize that Mommy has to go to work. After all, money doesn't grow on trees, you know."

When she stepped out of the oversized playroom and into the main office on the top floor of the massive structure, Jillian didn't waste any time admiring the beautiful swimming pool or any of the other amenities that most men would have killed to have in their homes. Instead, indifferent to her immediate surroundings, she locked the padlock that was hanging precariously from the door and headed for another door that led to a sterile room, which was the last one before entering the hallway.

Unaware that their employer was leaving the floor, the two uniformed guards who were posted on either side of the elevator door stepped away from the wall and looked at her with concern filling their eyes when they saw Jillian come walking from around the corner at a hurried pace. The men immediately waved to the third man, stationed down the hall, who moved with haste in their direction the moment they had gotten his attention. Surprised by the unannounced situation, though fully prepared for anything and anyone, the man rested a palm on the butt of his gun when he saw Jillian come striding toward them. The two men moved toward Jillian and allowed for her to pass between them, each drawing their weapon and holding it at the ready.

"Please excuse me, but is everything all right, Miss Hanson?" the third man, dressed in a suit, asked, his eyes dancing about in search of an interloper. He slowly slid the gun free of its holster and held it down at his side.

Momentarily confused by the peculiar question, Jillian looked at him strangely. "What was that?" she asked, tightening her grip on the handbag. She cringed back just enough for the movement to be noticeable.

"I apologize, Miss Hanson, but we were not expecting you," the man said. "You did not notify us of your intent to depart, so I'm concerned as to whether you are all right."

"Oh ... Of course, Mr. Pashka," she stammered. "It's my fault for causing alarm." Jillian placed a hand against her chest. "In my haste to attend a meeting, I forgot to signal you and your men with foreknowledge. I do hope that I didn't cause too much of a problem."

"Not at all, Miss Hanson," the man said, waving for the other two guards to return to their posts. "Our only concern is for your safety and well-being."

"That is very kind of you to say," Jillian said. "You and your men never cease to impress me with your staunch professionalism."

The two uniformed guards returned to standing on either side of the elevator doors and were once again staring forward, into a world where nothing existed but the parameters of their duty to protect Jillian Hanson.

"Thank you very much, Miss Hanson," Mr. Pashka said. "It's our duty to protect you at all cost." He looked at his men and nodded approvingly. "Shall I press the button?"

"Yes, please, Mr. Pashka," Jillian replied.

A few seconds later the doors opened and Jillian stepped inside. "I shall see you a little later today, Mr. Pashka," Jillian said.

The man looked at her with an expressionless face. "Always a pleasure, Miss Hanson," he said, tilting his head forward ever so slightly as a demonstration of respect.

The doors closed.

Brad Renfro, devoted protégé and loyal employee of Hanson & Hanson, was waiting by the elevator doors the moment they opened and Jillian stepped out onto the floor.

Although curious as to why Jillian would be visiting the floor where most of the lawyers of the firm conducted their daily business, no one dared to look her way for fear of gaining unwanted attention. Choosing a more prudent course of action, most of them simply lowered their heads and picked up the pace of their feet in order to put as much distance as possible between themselves and the unpredictable she-devil and her pernicious cabana boy.

"Good morning, Miss Hanson," Brad greeted. A smile was

plastered across his face. "Once again, I apologize for such a bothersome little man interfering with your daily itinerary, but he was quite persistent."

"Please don't blame yourself, Brad," Jillian said softly, smiling. "I shall deal with this swiftly." She looked about the floor with mild curiosity. "So, where is our leisure-suited sleuth?"

Brad chuckled softly and shook his head. He had always appreciated Jillian's wicked sense of humor and innate knack for hurling insults at an undesirable. "I thought it best to have him wait in Miss Lasko's vacant office, Miss Hanson," he replied. He held an open hand to the side of his mouth as if conveying a state secret. "I didn't want him aimlessly wandering about the floor bothering everyone with whatever seems to be swimming around in that bulbous head of his."

"That was wise," Jillian said, nodding her head. "Mental infection is definitely a possibility." She paused and licked her lips. "So what do you think of him? I've always believed you a superb judge of character."

Brad rubbed his chin, deep in thought, and methodically contemplated the question. "Actually, Miss Hanson," he began, biting down on his lip, "I ... I find him to be slightly unusual, even strange."

"How so?" Jillian asked, furrowing her brow.

"Well, for one thing, it's his vocabulary," Brad replied. "He doesn't speak like the normal type of cop. His language is far more polished, as are his mannerisms."

"A police officer who speaks well, is that correct?" Jillian giggled. "How grotesquely quaint." She smiled at Brad and lifted a single eyebrow. "Now I must really meet this person, if only for amusement's sake, so please lead the way to our loquacious fascist."

Always the tenacious investigator, thorough in every forensic way, Detective Harris knew that people in positions of excessive power liked to play games with those who were summarily deemed as genetic inferiors. Fortunately, to his immense credit, he had been one of learned and cultivated patience when dealing with such arrogant overachievers. It was a quality that had actually served in helping him to discover that the Hanson woman had been to the hotel around the time Samuel Smith had been killed. Luckily for him, even though no one had bothered to ask any of the employees who worked in maintenance, the janitor had a far better memory than any of those who dealt directly with the public.

Oversights were all too common. And despite being generally unemotional, he was still more than a little irritated that Billy Preston had yet to show up for work, and that was compounded when he discovered that the young man was little more than a typical drifter who rarely stayed in one area for very long. Discouraged by the prospect that the kid may have already left town permanently, desperately hoping the high-powered attorney might be able to offer some sort of information to liven up the rapidly fading path of potential evidence, Harris decided to take a risk by dropping by the prestigious law firm without an appointment on the chance that Jillian Hanson would agree to meet with him for the purpose of answering a few questions germane to the ongoing investigation. He knew it was a long shot, but the fact remained that the case was beginning to grow ice cold, and there would be no thawing out the trail once it turned arctic. The idea that the whole case rested solely on the opinion of a senior citizen who may or may not be a qualified expert on handcrafted dolls was utterly repugnant to him. There was no doubt in his mind that the grand jury would opt to indict him for professional stupidity if he were to take what he had to it.

Those who worked on the floor fell silent the moment they saw Brad escorting Jillian Hanson across the area in what appeared to them as some sort of serious business exercise for which none of them were privy. Not that any of them expected to be kept in the inner loop of their boss's work schedule. But the unexpected news of Heather Lasko's meteoric rise in the firm as the first appointed junior partner had sent shock waves through everyone who worked beneath the mysteriously powerful Hanson woman.

Harold Piper and Nathanial Brooks found it nearly impossible to believe when they received the memorandum that announced the young woman's promotion to a position second only to Jillian's. At first they had thought it had to be nothing more than some sort of in-house prank on the associates, but then both of them had heard the firm's spokesperson inform the legal community about the unprecedented elevation of Heather Lasko as the first and only junior partner in the history of the prestigious law firm of Hanson & Hanson. Harold had inadvertently dropped the cup of coffee from which he was sipping when the news break interrupted his favorite soap opera.

Within ten minutes of the public announcement, while in absentia, Heather Lasko's personal effects were removed from the office and summarily relocated upstairs by men no one had ever seen before. The personnel who remained downstairs could do nothing but assume the young woman was joining their boss on a floor where none of them had ever had the privilege of paying a visit. Once the former office of Heather Lasko was emptied of all personal property, leaving only the firm's furniture behind, many of the associates began to scurry about, drafting their own memorandums in an attempt to jockey for senior position to take the office as their own.

When Jillian and Brad arrived to the door of Heather's former office, it was Brad who gracefully opened the door and stood to one side to allow her to pass unencumbered. Jillian tilted her head and entered without delay. Brad immediately followed her inside and shut the door. Without speaking a single word, Jillian walked around behind the desk located directly in front of a huge window, set the handbag that held Dorothy safely inside on the top of it, and sat down. She paid no attention to the detective, who stood up in respect the moment she walked into the room. Brad moved over to the left side of the desk and crossed his arms over his chest. He gazed upon the detective, as if he were little more than an unwelcome parasite intruding into their immaculate world.

Harris studied the man for several seconds in an attempt to profile his character, weighing the depth of his relationship with the woman, and then shifted his eyes over to the woman who sat behind the desk with features that gave less than nothing away. He quickly concluded that the situation was going to prove far more intriguing than he had first anticipated. He smiled ever so slightly from the prospect of facing an interesting challenge. It was abundantly clear to him that Jillian Hanson was far from the usual woman. She was a person who wielded the power of her position without fault or mercy, and the man standing to her right was no doubt loyal to the one he served.

Jillian folded her hands together and leveled a steady gaze at the detective. "Do you find something amusing, Detective Harris?" She asked in a flat voice, her face like hard granite. "I assure you that I am far too busy for childish antics."

Harris didn't answer immediately. Instead, using tactics honed over the years, he looked about the office and wondered why there was not even a single piece of personal property in the room that might offer even the slightest sentiment of comfort or warmth from home. The lack of a hospitable environment spoke volumes to him. "My name is ..." he began.

"I know exactly who you are, Detective," Jillian interrupted in the same cold voice. She then grinned knowingly and licked her lips. "If you are trying to extrapolate some sort of psychological profile from the lack of hominess in the room, Detective, then you should know that such would be premised on a faulty assumption, and thus a futile exercise."

"And what would lead you to think that I was attempting to do such a deliberate act?" Harris asked.

"Because that is exactly what I would do," Jillian replied.

"Could it be that you somehow feel guilty over something you may have done in the past, Miss Hanson?" Harris asked. He knew he was taking a huge chance by dishing out an implied accusation, but it was necessary for him to determine the depth of the woman's ability to control her emotions and body language.

He was not disappointed. She gave away nothing. The woman was made of ice.

Brad lowered his arms and glowered at the detective. He started to move forward, but Jillian tapped him on the arm with a single finger, which caused him to stop where he was and lift his arms back to their previous position.

"I am quite certain that I've never felt guilty over a single thing in my life, Detective Harris," Jillian replied. "What I am not certain about is the reason for your visit to my firm." She exhaled deeply. "So tell me, what is it that you want—Bobby?"

The sound of Jillian using the pet name that less than four people had ever called him caught the detective slightly off guard. It came completely unexpected and caused him to momentarily lose his train of thought, something that almost never happened. "Wh … what did you say?" Harris asked, narrowing his eyes.

"Miss Hanson wants to know what you want, Bob … beee," Brad teased, his voice exceedingly patronizing.

Jillian giggled into her hand. She then slapped Brad on the arm. "Be nice, Bradley," she said. "I'm quite sure the detective is here for a very valid reason and would not be using his position as a police officer to waste our time." She peered up at the detective and smiled cruelly. "Isn't that correct, Detective Harris?" The smile quickly vanished from her face. "I mean, if I were to feel that the whole pretense of this interview was nothing more than some form of unwarranted harassment, I suppose I would have no choice but to file a formal complaint with the mayor and demand reparations in which to appease me enough to resist the urge to sue the city for damages."

Harris cursed himself for not doing more research on the woman. He had underestimated her in nearly every possible way. She was not only intelligent, but also vicious. "Miss Hanson, I assure you that there is no reason to threaten me," he said. "I'm just trying to—"

"Oh, contraire, my dear detective, that was not a threat, neither overt nor implied," Jillian interrupted. "It was a solemn promise." She leaned forward and leered at the detective with the eyes of a shark. "I'm here speaking with you only as a professional courtesy, nothing more, so don't think for even a glimmer of a nanosecond that you or that pathetic rabble of genetic misfits in your corrupt department can frighten or intimidate me even in the least. I do not recognize your supposed authority over me, or those in my employ. Everyone here at Hanson & Hanson is my family, and I am extremely protective over each and every one of them." She looked at her watch.

Unperturbed by the woman's obvious aggression toward authority figures in general, not entirely disagreeing with her opinion about most of his colleagues, Harris removed a pad of paper and a pen from the pocket of his shirt. "Perhaps, Miss Hanson, I should just get to the point as to why I've come here to speak with you," he said.

"Perhaps you should," Brad said. He then pulled a small recording device from his pants pocket and set it on the desk. "Do you object if we opt to record this interrogation?" He smiled, watching the detective for any negative sign.

Harris eyed the man, curious. *Damn lawyers,* he thought, shaking his head slowly. "No, I don't mind one bit," he began. "I'm sorry, I didn't get your name."

"That's because I didn't give all of it," Brad said. "It's Brad, Brad Renfro, Detective, and I don't care for cops."

"Brad it is, then," Harris said calmly, not taking the bait. "And I don't care for cops much either." He then scribbled the name down on the pad of paper. "Actually, Brad, I prefer recordings." He waved the pad of paper in the air. "Tape removes the possibility of misconstruing words. But I just can't seem to shake using the classics. I like the personal touch that comes with writing things down in my own hand. Also, it helps me to remember the conversation." He then tapped the pen against the side of his head.

"How retro of you, Detective," Brad said, his voice dripping with sarcasm. He depressed the play button on the tape recorder. "We're hot."

Jillian nodded her head. "You may begin the interrogation, Detective, whenever you're ready," she said, leaning back in the chair.

"Interrogation is a rather harsh kind of word, don't you think,

Miss Hanson?" Harris asked in a friendly tone of voice. "Wouldn't interview be more appropriate?"

"Semantics, Detective," Jillian said. "I'm an extremely busy woman, so let's move forward, shall we?"

"Yes, of course," Harris said. "Are you familiar with the hotel on East and Pine, Miss Hanson?"

"Which hotel are you referring to, Detective?" Jillian asked. "There are four of them in that immediate area."

"I apologize for the ambiguity," Harris said. "Are you familiar with the Hilton that is located in that area?"

"Yes," Jillian replied.

"How so?" Harris asked.

"Numerous reasons, Detective," Jillian replied. "I've held conferences there. I've dined there, and have often held private meetings with clients who do not wish to be seen. Hell, I've even stayed there overnight when I just needed to get away from things." She shrugged her shoulders. "Like I said, numerous reasons."

"So the staff knows you by sight?" Harris asked.

"Perhaps some of them do," Jillian replied. "However, most probably do not. It's not as if I make it a habit to fraternize with the help at the hotel, Detective."

"No, of course not, Miss Hanson," Harris said. "I didn't mean to imply that you would ever do any such thing."

"I'd hope not," Jillian said. She sighed deeply and looked at her watch. "Perhaps things would go a little faster if you just cut to the chase and disposed of the tiresome cat and mouse nonsense, Detective. Either I will answer your questions or I will not. Besides, we both know this is about the murder of that man in the hotel room."

Harris tapped the tip of the pen against the pad of paper. "Oh, so you know about that heinous crime, do you?" he asked, watching her facial expression closely in hope that she might reveal at least a hint of guilty knowledge.

Nothing.

"Of course I know about that awful event, Detective," Jillian replied coolly. "The whole city knows about it because the story was splattered all over the front page like some sort of ghastly advertisement for the new opening of a local haunted house on Halloween night." She looked over at Brad and shook her head. "What I don't know is whether you are questioning me as a potential suspect, a person of interest, or a witness."

"Quite honestly, Miss Hanson, I would have to say none of the above, while at the same time all of the above," Harris said. "I'm simply investigating a terrible murder that happened to a family man."

"It sounds more like a fishing expedition to me, Detective, and you've dropped your line in a dry lake," Jillian said, her face stoic. "May I offer you a friendly piece of advice?"

"Sure," Harris replied, "as long as it's free. I'm afraid to admit that my meager salary cannot afford your hourly rate."

In spite of the seriousness of the situation, Jillian chuckled audibly and nodded her head. "I suggest you drop your hook and bait in another body of water, Detective Harris, because you will only find piranha in this one," she said. She then motioned for the two men who were dressed in black uniforms standing outside the office to enter. "It was a true pleasure speaking with you, but I have a busy schedule and must adhere to it."

Even though the detective still had several additional questions he wished to ask the woman, it became abundantly clear to him that he'd been summarily dismissed from her presence in a subtle manner not so dissimilar to that of a queen dismissing a serf who had taken up enough of her majesty's precious time and resources. He considered the idea of taking another risk by asking just one more question but then decided against it out of concern that failure to recognize her superior position could result in total estrangement from the opportunity to ask future questions. The lack of emotion on Jillian's face left no doubt whatsoever that she expected to be obeyed without delay or question.

He offered a slight smile and tilted his head in a manner that conveyed understanding that the conversation had been terminated.

"Of course, Miss Hanson," Harris said. "I assure you that I completely understand you are an extremely busy woman." He placed an open palm against his chest. "On behalf of the department and myself, I thank you for seeing me with no notice." He turned and shifted his vision to Brad. "And I shall take your advice to heart."

The two guards entered the office and stood unmoving just inside the threshold. Neither man said a single word, only stared at Jillian with severe expressions across their icy faces.

Brad grinned without a hint of humor. "Would you like an escort to the front door, Detective Harris?" Brad asked in a flat tone. "I'm sure these gentlemen would make certain you reach your car safely, without incident."

Jillian remained absolutely silent. It was her world, and everyone merely lived in it by her benevolent leave.

Harris prided himself on his innate ability to recognize dangerous men. When he turned to face the two who had just stepped into the office, there was no doubt in his mind that both guards were professional killers for hire, who merely disguised themselves as security personnel. He suspected each was probably lured away from some sort of unnamed government agency by sums of money that only a huge conglomerate could afford to pay. Corporate mercenaries came to mind as he committed each face to memory. Somehow, intuitively, perhaps for survival's sake, he knew it was important to remember them.

Jillian watched the silent, visual exchange between the three men with acute interest. It was at that moment when she knew the detective was no fool, but a worthy adversary to be reckoned with on a much higher intellectual level.

Satisfied, Harris then brought his full attention back to Brad. "I appreciate the offer, Brad, but I can find my own way out of the building," he replied belatedly.

"As you wish, Detective," Brad said. He then jerked his head at the two men, motioning for them to escort the man out of the room.

"Once again, Miss Hanson, thank you for your time and patience with me," he said politely. "Both of you have a pleasant day."

"Good day, Detective," Jillian said.

"Yes, Detective, have a very good day," Brad said. He then smiled. "By all means, drive safely."

"I will, thank you," Harris said. Without saying anything further, he moved past the two men and walked toward the elevators.

The two guards followed close behind him.

After Harris had left the room and faded down the corridor that led to the metal doors, Brad walked around to the front of the desk and looked down at Jillian in absolute fealty. He licked his dry lips nervously.

"So what do you think of our illustrious detective?" Jillian asked. She rested two hands on her chest and then intertwined her fingers.

"Not much," Brad replied simply. "Nevertheless, he's not a dummy. I don't believe a man such as himself would be just digging around without some sort of reason or agenda, Miss Hanson. No. Whatever the purpose for him coming here today, believe me, there was no doubt a definite reason, even if it is misplaced."

Jillian nodded. "I agree with you," she said, rising from the chair. "I want you to see what he's up to, Brad, so have him followed around the clock."

"Of course, Miss Hanson," Brad said. He turned to leave.

"And Brad," Jillian said, before he got to the door.

He turned and looked at her with a curious expression. "Yes, Miss Hanson," Brad stated.

"I want the surveillance to be invisible," Jillian said, her voice dead serious. "Do I make myself clear?"

"Crystal," Brad replied. He then left Heather Lasko's former office and headed for his own on another floor.

Jillian gently opened the purse that was lying on the top of the desk and looked into it with the loving smile of a mother admiring her beloved daughter. "Sssh, girl, I know," Jillian said soothingly. "That Mr. Harris was just an awful faker, wasn't he, Dorothy?" She giggled. "Yeah, I agree, sweetheart. Nothing but a big, old phony baloney." Jillian nodded her head emphatically. "Yes, don't worry.

I'll take care of it. Yes. I promise. Yes. Soon. Real soon." She then zipped the purse and left the office. Her schedule had just gotten a little more congested.

While Jillian was making the necessary arrangements for her next conquest, Brad was sitting back behind his desk and busily punching in the emergency number on his private cell phone. He had to wait only two seconds before his call was answered by the person on the other end.

"Code?" the voice asked.

"Eternal sentinel," Brad replied.

"Number?" the voice asked.

"All prime, except for five," Brad replied.

"Hello, Bradley," the voice greeted. "What can I do for you?"

"We have a slight problem that needs to be rectified effective yesterday," Brad said, his voice dire.

"Very well," the voice said. "You know where and when. I shall be waiting for your arrival."

The line went dead.

Brad clicked the phone off. *No loose ends, ever,* he thought. He then retrieved a small hammer from the top drawer of the desk and smashed the phone to pieces. *Ever!* No matter what the consequences to be paid, Brad Renfro would fulfill the promise he had given so many years ago. No amount of sacrifice was too much.

Chapter 9

B one tired after walking the streets in search of his best friend for over a dozen consecutive hours, the arches throbbing as if the bottom of his feet had been continuously spanked with a board by a Turkish prison guard, Petie was beginning to wonder if he'd ever find Billy. The first place he had checked for him was at his apartment in hope that he was just laid up in bed from the flu.

When that proved fruitless, his hopes once again dashed, he asked a few of the neighbors if any of them had seen Billy. But the answer was always the same. No one had heard from or seen any sign of the young man. Never one to be easily discouraged, especially since it concerned one of the only people who had ever treated him with any respect and friendship, Petie took to the streets and swore to the gods that he would not give up until he found him.

He first directed his attention on the few places Billy was known to frequent, several of which he had gone to with Billy to have a good time and share a couple of much-needed laughs. However, to his chagrin and ever increasing worry for the welfare of his friend and colleague, no one who knew Billy had seen him since the bicycle messenger had delivered the piece of paper with the small notation written across it. It was beginning to appear that he was one of the last people to see Billy. Somehow, contrary to what Jeb had said to him earlier, Petie knew something was wrong, definitely wrong, and he was afraid for his friend. He could feel it deep down in his bones.

Although he was tempted to call the police and report his worries about his missing friend, not that he actually believed they would be of much help, if any at all, Petie thought it best to wait until a little more time had passed before utilizing such a dramatic tactic. The last thing Billy would appreciate is him overreacting by sending the cops without first knowing whether he was doing something that was not exactly within the boundaries of the law. Even though Petie was fairly certain that Billy didn't use drugs, there was actually no guessing what he might be doing with the mysterious woman, who had obviously taken a shine to his friend. He may not have seen the woman's face as clearly as he would have liked, but even at such a distance there was no denying the fact that she was indeed quite beautiful. And Petie knew that women who possess such physical qualities could get a man to do just about anything with just a few flutters of an eyelash.

No man, at least not one he had ever met or read about, was immune from the sexual wiles of a woman who showered him with compliments and flattery on his masculine prowess. Petie was no different, and neither was Billy. Deep down, if actually honest with themselves, men were generally weak and easily manipulated into doing some of the stupidest things on the planet in the name of either love or the bastardized version of it that qualified animal lust as little more than a momentary horny infatuation.

While Petie mentally juggled the differential between love and lust, his thoughts returned to the night before and the desires that ran through his own mind when he remembered how pretty Harriot had looked, still wishing she would not have left before he could've summoned up the courage to ask her to dance. *Stupid Jeb and his scumbag friends,* Petie thought. *Those maggots ruined everything for me. Now she probably thinks I'm just like them. Not that I'd blame her one bit,* he thought.

While Petie was still obsessing over the image of Harriot and busy cursing Jeb and the unholy crew of party crashers under his breath, his mind straying from the mission to find Billy, he rounded a corner and stopped dead in his tracks when he saw a major disturbance occurring just down the street.

Dozens of people were standing around in a small congregation of multiple groups just outside a long strip of yellow police tape and watching whatever was taking place inside an alley. Several police cruisers were parked haphazardly alongside the curbs on both sides of the street. Seven or eight uniformed officers stood just inside the tape to keep the curious onlookers outside the area that had been cordoned off from the public. There were a few men and women dressed in plain clothes who were busy moving in and out of the alleyway that ran between two large buildings. Each of their faces was drawn tight and was somber in appearance.

Unable to resist human nature for the macabre, in spite of the exhaustion threatening to overtake him at any given second, Petie walked up to an elderly woman who stood closest to him and gently tapped her on the shoulder. "What's going on?" he asked, craning his head around to try and get a better look at what everyone had found so fascinating.

Irritated that she had been rudely distracted, and unwilling to pull her eyes away from the scene for fear of missing something juicy, the woman turned her face only a few inches to the left. "I'm not real sure, but someone said they found a dead body in the alley about a half an hour or so ago," the woman said from out of the corner of her mouth. "I got here only about five minutes ago. The cops aren't saying anything at all. One of them puked a few minutes ago, so it must be kind of bad."

"Are you serious?" Petie asked.

"Yep," the woman said. "Puked up everything."

Petie's throat suddenly closed up on him. He licked his lips nervously, his eyes darting back and forth. "Is ... is it a guy about my age?" Petie stammered, his voice cracking. His eyes began to water. Oh, God, no, not Billy, Petie prayed in silence.

"I don't ..." The woman began, but she failed to finish the sentence when she turned and saw the agonized expression on the young man's face. She bit down on her lip, trying to find something sensitive to say. The boy's pain was obvious. "I'm sorry, but I don't know anything else." She looked at him with sympathetic eyes.

"Are you looking for someone, son?" She placed a tender hand on his shoulder.

Numb, barely hearing her words, Petie nodded his head.

"A friend?" she asked.

Petie nodded again.

"Come on, son," the woman said. "Maybe one of the policemen can help you." She draped a single arm over his shoulders and guided him over to where a uniformed officer stood just inside the crime scene tape.

Those who stood between them quickly parted to allow a clear path for the two people to pass unencumbered when they saw the tearful anguish on the young man's face. Many lowered their head in respect for what was obviously a personal loss of a loved one.

When the officer saw the woman approach with the distraught man held closely against her side he held up a single hand and shook his head. "Sorry, ma'am, but you will have to stay behind the tape," the officer said sternly.

"Excuse me, Officer, but you don't understand," the woman said.

"No, you don't understand, ma'am, I have orders to keep everyone out of the area," the officer said.

"Look, Officer," the woman said in a firm and unyielding voice, squeezing Petie's shoulders reassuringly, "this young man might know the person in the alley. He's been looking for his friend and well ... you can probably guess the rest."

The officer looked at Petie, his features softening, almost tender. "Is this true, sir?" He asked. "Are you missing a friend?"

Petie nodded his head and wiped at his eyes with the back of his hand. "Yeah, since last night," Petie croaked out. "Can you tell me who it is?"

"I'm sorry, sir, but I'm not at liberty to discuss that particular detail," the officer said. "However, if you'll wait here for just a minute, I'll get my lieutenant for you. He's in charge of the investigation and crime scene."

"So someone was killed in the alley, right?" the woman stated.

"Um ...yes, ma'am," the officer said. He held his palms outward as if to ward them off. "If you'll just stay here for a minute, I'll get my lieutenant."

After the woman nodded her understanding, the officer quickly jogged off and disappeared down the alleyway. A few seconds later he emerged from the narrow corridor.

Lieutenant Miller was only two feet behind him, walking with distinct purpose in their direction, and immediately slowed down when he recognized the young man from the hotel.

"Excuse me, Lieutenant, this is ..." the officer began.

Miller furrowed his brow, confused by the man's disheveled appearance. "Mr. Robinson, Mr. Peter Robinson," he finished. He rubbed his chin. "From the hotel, am I right? Everyone calls you Petie?"

Petie nodded his head. "Yeah, that's right," he said. "You talked to me and my friends at work."

The officer shifted his gaze back and forth, wondering if he was somehow missing something. "So the two of you already know each other?" the officer asked.

"Uh, yes, Danny, sort of," Miller replied awkwardly. He then waved a hand nonchalantly. "Thank you for coming to get me, but you can leave us now. I'll speak to Mr. Robinson alone."

The officer bit down on the inside of his cheek. "Sure thing, Lieutenant," he said. "If you need anything, just give a holler." Without saying anything further, the officer walked along the perimeter of the crime scene tape.

Petie looked at Miller with a pained expression. "Is it m ... m ... my friend Billy?" Petie stammered. "It's Billy, isn't it? He's dead, isn't he?"

Miller ran a hand over his head and thought of the best possible way to break such terrible news. It was one of the few aspects of the job that he utterly loathed. In order to spare the young man from prying eyes and ears, he lifted up the tape and motioned for Petie to duck beneath it and join him on the other side. "Come on, son, follow me," he said. "I'd prefer to speak with you in private, away from all the busybodies out here."

Petie looked up into the face of the elderly woman, who was now crying softly, and kissed her on the cheek. "Thank you for your help," Petie said.

"You're welcome," she said. "I'm really sorry to hear about your friend."

"Me, too," Petie said. He then moved underneath the tape and followed the lieutenant over to where an ambulance was parked up on a curb, passing the entrance of the alley. He tried to look down its path but was unable to see much of anything, except for several technicians and plainclothes personnel moving about the area.

The lieutenant climbed into the back of the ambulance without hesitation and quickly motioned for Petie to join him. He looked about the street several times, wondering why none of his questions had been answered; stepped up on the oversized bumper of the vehicle; and then took a seat on an opposite side.

Miller stared at Petie in silence for several seconds before speaking to the unexpected guest. "Mr. Robinson ..." he began.

"Please, just call me Petie," he interrupted. "That's all I've ever been called since I can remember."

"Okay, whatever you like," Miller said, folding both hands in his lap. "What are you doing down here, Petie?"

Petie sniffed back tears. "I came looking for my friend Billy," he replied. "He never came back to work. I went to his apartment to see if he was there. But he wasn't there either. I started to get scared for him."

"But how is it that you came down here, to this street, to this neighborhood?" Miller asked. "It just seems to be a little off the beaten path for you."

"Yeah, I guess it is," Petie admitted, "but I already checked everywhere else. I just thought I'd keep walking around until I found him. I wasn't going to any place special, just around."

Miller's face softened considerably, studying the man's features and seeing only genuine concern for his friend. "So the two of you are pretty close, huh?" he asked. "You're real good buddies?"

"Yeah, Billy treats me better than everyone else," Petie replied, shrugging his shoulders weakly. "He doesn't make fun of me for not being as smart as everyone else at work." He smiled. "He sticks up for me when people start to pick on me for being dumb."

"He sounds like a pretty good guy," Miller said.

"Yeah, he's cool and my best friend," Petie said. "He also watches out for me."

"How long have you been walking around the city looking for him?" Miller asked, curious as to the length of the young man's devotion to his friend.

"Since I left Jeb's stupid, pervert party last night," Petie replied, wrinkling his nose in distaste from the memory of the local bag whore.

"And when was that?" Miller asked.

Petie looked at the watch Billy had given to him on his last birthday. "A little after nine o'clock, I guess," he replied. "I was worried about Billy because no one had seen him, so I decided to leave and find him. I tried to get that worthless Jeb to help, but all he wanted to do was screw some gross drug addict. He didn't care a lick about Billy."

"So you've been wandering around the entire city for over twelve hours in search of your friend, is that about right?" Miller asked, his eyes wide open, impressed with the degree of commitment demonstrated.

"Yeah, I guess it's been that long," Petie replied.

"You know Billy pretty good, don't you?" Miller asked.

"Better than I know myself," Petie replied, nodding his head to emphasize the point. "Like I said, he sticks up for me."

"Petie, do you think Billy would ever hurt anyone, even if it was somehow just an accident?" Miller asked, choosing his words ever so carefully to avoid an unnecessary confrontation with his only potential witness.

Petie shook his head adamantly. "No, sir, Billy would never hurt anyone, ever, for any reason," he replied, his voice rising in pitch. "He's not like that."

"Are you sure?" Miller asked.

"Yeah," Petie replied.

"Are you absolutely positive?" Miller asked.

Petie bobbed his head up and down in fervor. "Yes, absolutely, I know Billy," he replied. "He's a great guy. Never does nothin' wrong." He began to fidget on the thin mattress of the gurney. He bit down on his lip. "So can I see Billy now, to say good-bye to him?" He made to stand up and leave the back of the ambulance when Miller placed one hand on his leg and gently pushed him back down.

"Just one thing you should know before you leave, Petie," Miller said, his voice taking on a much softer tone. "Billy isn't the one who died last night. We still have no idea as to where he might be, whether he's missing or hiding out."

Confused by the unexpected information, Petie wrinkled up his face and looked at Miller with a perplexed expression that denoted a complete lack of understanding of what was being conveyed to him. He blinked several times, his jaw becoming slack. "Huh?" he mumbled incoherently. "I thought you said my friend ..." The words trailed off.

Miller shook his head, searching for the best way to break news that he was certain would upset the boy. "No, kid, I think you may have misunderstood what I was saying to you," he said.

"No, I didn't," Billy muttered. "You said Billy ..."

Miller held up a hand to interrupt the much younger person. "I never said anything about it being Billy," he said.

"Then I don't know what you're trying to say to me," Petie said. His hands started to tremble, a physical manifestation whenever he became frustrated.

Miller leaned forward and placed his hands over Billy's. "I didn't mean that it was your friend Billy," he said. "Um ... you see, there was a carjacking sometime last night, maybe around eight or so. We're guessing that it was a couple of gangbangers with guns who did it."

"Okay," Petie mumbled, slowly nodding his head to show that he was following the conversation. "Some gang members stole a car last night." He paused to allow the information to sink in. "So whose car was it?"

Miller inhaled, then exhaled, his eyes never wavering from the man's face. "I believe you know the driver of the car," he said.

"I do?" Petie stated, furrowing his brow in concentration. "I can't think of anyone who it would be down here."

"Yeah, kid, you do," Miller said, his voice just above a whisper. "The driver of the car was a girl by the name of Harriot Mills."

Petie blinked stupidly several times as his slow-witted mind absorbed the information. "Someone stole Harriot's car," he mumbled almost incoherently. "That doesn't make any sense. Why would anyone want to steal Harriot's junker?" He leaned forward and looked out the back of the ambulance. "Is she here? Can I talk to her, you know, to see if she is okay and not too scared?"

Miller cringed inwardly when he realized the young man's feelings for the girl went well beyond a simple friendship at the workplace. He reached out and rested a firm hand on Petie's right shoulder. "No, Petie, I'm sorry," he said, forcing himself to contain his own emotions. "That won't be possible."

"Where is she?" Petie asked, growing alarmed by the police officer's demeanor. He was well aware of the fact that cops were nice only when something bad had happened to the person they were talking to.

Miller slowly shook his head back and forth. "I'm sorry, Petie, but Harriot's dead," he replied. "She was shot and killed during the robbery." He didn't dare provide any additional details.

Petie slapped the lieutenant's hand from off his shoulder and stood up. "Harriot's not dead, you liar," he spat, his facial features drawn tight, the veins protruding from the temples of his head. "I just saw her last night, and she was beautiful. We were going to dance." He narrowed his eyes in hatred. "Liar! You're just trying to trick me into saying something bad about Billy. Everyone is always trying to trick me."

"I wouldn't do that, kid," Miller said. "Please sit back down, so we can talk and maybe find out who did this terrible thing."

"Yes, you would!" Petie spat angrily. "You're a lousy cop, and Jeb says that all of you lie, cheat, steal, and kill people like us because no one cares if we go to prison, get beat up, or even killed."

Miller shook his head, saddened by the words being flung at him because they were not entirely untrue, and stood up. "That's not true, Petie," he said.

"Yes, it is," Petie snapped. "I'm just a friggin' retard, so why not trick me. No one gives a crap about some idiot."

"Come on, kid, please sit back down," Miller said in a sympathetic tone of voice. "I want to catch the people who hurt your friend and make them pay for it." He reached out to comfort the young man, who was close to the point of collapsing to the ground.

"No!" Petie shouted, yanking his arm away from the man's reach. "Shut up, you lying bastard!" He then jumped out of the ambulance and ran toward the entrance of the alley, ignoring the pleas of the lieutenant calling for him to please come back.

Several of the officers who were gathered around the area looked up at their superior officer and started to mobilize themselves to form a barricade against the man running toward them, but then opened a human gateway after they were signaled by Miller that everything was perfectly fine and to let the frantic man pass.

The moment Petie entered the alleyway, catching sight of several people who didn't look anything like police officers, he slowed his pace to a mere walk that was no faster than an infant's crawl. Trepidation filled him to the point of overtaking his senses. His heart pounded inside his chest like a chieftain's drum. Even though everyone wearing the same type of jacket appeared to be shuffling about and extremely busy doing whatever it was they were doing with instruments Petie had never seen before, and obviously noticed the stranger who did not belong as he continued to walk deeper into the belly of the filthy corridor, no one bothered to offer him a second glance or question his inappropriate appearance. At most, the men and women would look up, silently nod their heads, and then focus their full attention back on the task at hand. Petie had never felt so out of place in all his life.

At the far end of the narrow path, just in front of a pair of trash bins, two people dressed in a similar type of coat were kneeling down on the ground. Each of their backs was turned to him, making it impossible for him to see past either of them, so Petie continued to move forward, even though every fiber in his being was screaming out for him to stop, to turn around, and to just walk back the way he had come. There's nothing for you to see here, boy, nothing you want to see, the voice inside his head warned. Enormous mounds of garbage littered the roadway, which only increased as he stepped farther into the bowels of discarded refuse. The stench was overwhelming. However, in spite of the mental warning and the putrescent assault, combined with the chill that coursed down his spine, Petie could not bring himself to stop. He had to know the truth, to prove that Jeb was right that the cop was nothing more than a damn liar like everyone else in the world, and to see with his own eyes in order to confirm that there had been a mistake, and that Harriot was safe at home. No one ever told the truth, unless it was either convenient or suited the person's immediate needs. Everyone lies, except Harriot. She always tells the truth, no matter how much it might hurt.

The sound of something brittle snapping caused the two members of the forensic team to turn around, which inadvertently opened a clear view of the young woman's mutilated, naked body.

Petie gasped in horror from the sight. His chin quivered uncontrollably. Tears streamed down his face. The two people looked at one another, then back at the man who appeared to be on the verge of a nervous breakdown.

Bruised and battered, with a single gunshot wound in the forehead, it was obvious to any observer that each of the woman's limbs had been broken at the joint. Her once beautiful face and breasts were now covered with circular burn marks that could have come only from a burning cigar. The gaping wound that traversed the circumference of her neck was angled up at him, as if offering some sort of a hideous, red smile. Petie felt his knees grow weak. There was no doubt in his mind that the mangled human form he was slowly backing away from was Harriot Mills, the same wonderful woman he had worshipped from afar. Horrified by the ghastly scene that would not go away, wondering what kind of monster could possibly do such an evil thing to such a wonderful, special person, Petie fell to his knees on the heavily soiled ground. He placed his face in his trembling hands and began to weep uncontrollably. She was forever lost to him.

The two men who were processing the cadaver looked at each other for several seconds, completely dumbfounded. Neither one of them knew what to do.

"Excuse me, sir, but I don't think you are supposed to be here," the man on the left said. "This is a crime scene and ..." His words trailed off when a familiar face moved within eyesight, held up a hand in a common gesture that let them know everything was under control and for them to ignore the distraught person.

Lieutenant Miller moved in behind Petie and helped the devastated man to his feet. "It's okay, fellas, he's with me," he said to the team members. He then gently patted Petie on the back. "I'm really sorry you had to see that, son. I wish you would have just believed me and not run over here."

"Did you see what they did to her?" Petie asked, now weeping softly.

"Yes, son, I did," Miller replied.

"I ... I don't understand," Petie moaned miserably, his whole body convulsing. "Who would do such a horrible thing to Harriot? She was such a nice and caring person. She never hurt no one."

Miller looked down at the girl's body and gritted his teeth angrily. Hatred for those who had murdered the young woman welled within him like the lava of an active volcano, erupting into a burning need for justice. "I don't know, son, but I do have a few pretty good ideas as to who's responsible for this," he spat, his tone both hard and cold. He tasted the distinct flavor of bile at the back of his throat. "No matter what, son, I promise to get every one of the bastards and make them pay." Miller shifted his vision away from Harriot.

Petie turned and faced him. "And kill them, right?" Petie asked, his voice a hiss. "Kill them like they killed Harriot."

Miller stared at the younger man with a shocked expression covering his face. The last thing he expected was murderous solicitation. "Well, no, son," he said. "I mean that I'll arrest them and make them pay by sending them to prison for the rest of their lives. I can't just kill someone because they broke the law. Whoever did this will stand trial in a court of law and be prosecuted."

"That's not good enough," Petie said, wiping his eyes.

"It will be," Miller said. "I will—"

"Oh, so you're not going to do nothing," Petie snapped angrily. He then spit on the ground. "That's because people like us just don't matter to people like you. Because you think you're so much better than me and Harriot."

Miller studied the much younger man's face with an inquisitive and knowing eye. He was well aware of what hunger for revenge looked like, and the eyes peering back at him were filled with unrelenting rage. "You shouldn't be thinking about such things, son, not while you're so mad," he said softly. "You should—"

"What, walk it off and everything's gonna be all right?" Petie interrupted, flailing his arms around in anger. "You know what? Jeb was right about all of you. The only justice Harriot can get is what I get for her."

"You don't want to do anything stupid," Miller said.

"How do you know?" Petie hollered. He smacked himself on the side of the head. "I'm a big stupid head and always do stupid things."

"You're not stupid," Miller said.

"Yes, I am," Petie said. "Everyone says so."

"Listen, son, I know you're upset," Miller said soothingly, "but don't go and do something that's going to get you into a bunch of trouble."

"Why, because you'll arrest me, too," Petie snapped. He shook his head. "You know what, screw you." He then looked down to where the object of his affection for the past two years lay in a pile of decomposing trash and squeezed his hands into tight fists. *It's not fair*, he thought. *Nothing is ever fair or right. Don't you worry none,*

Harriot, I'll get 'em back for you. I'll get all of them. I'll kill every single one of them. He looked up at the lieutenant with tear filled eyes. The pain of losing her was more than any one person should ever be asked to bear. "Why don't you go arrest someone, cop." Without saying another word, Petie turned and walked toward the street.

Utterly helpless to reach out and convince Petie that nothing good had ever come from anyone taking the law into his own hands by becoming a vigilante, while wondering if the young man was in the process of adding his name to a long list of statistics, Lieutenant Miller could do absolutely nothing but watch the distraught man disappear around the corner and vanish from sight. Compounding his concern for what might occur next, Petie never bothered to look back, a sign denoting that his mind had been made up and nothing could change it. Miller shook his head in defeat, lowering it.

"Not that it's any of my business, lieutenant, and you can tell me to shut the hell up," the forensic man on the left said, "but that boy is definitely going to kill somebody, maybe even a whole bunch of them."

Miller looked down at him and frowned. "I really hope you're wrong on that," he said in a distant voice.

The man on the right stood up and brushed off the front of his pants. "That's one pissed-off kid, man," he said. "I've got the strangest feeling that we're not done with the body count." He shrugged his shoulders. "I sure wouldn't want to be the guys who raped and killed his little girlfriend."

"Gee, ya think, Gus?" Miller said sarcastically, rolling his eyes. "Thanks for telling me something I already knew, bonehead." He wondered if his day was going to take an even sharper turn for the worse when he looked back to the street and saw the unsmiling detective walking toward him at a relatively quick pace. *Now what?* he wondered, wishing he'd never gotten out of bed.

"I see you're still trying to make friends with people who want no part of you, Lieutenant," Harris said as he approached the three men. He pointed a thumb over his shoulder. "So what was that all about? Are you making the neighborhood children cry? The kid ran out of here so fast that I barely got a look at him. He did look familiar, though, sort of like that simpleton at the hotel. You know, the real dumb ass."

Miller sighed tiredly. The last thing he felt like doing was verbally fencing with the most pompous man he had ever met. "That's because it was him," he said. He looked over at the two forensic men and motioned for them to get back to work on processing the rest of the evidence.

"No kidding?" Harris asked in half a grunt. "Well, that explains why he looked so familiar, doesn't it?" He lowered his eyes to the dead, naked body of the girl, furrowed his brow, and then raised them to look at the lieutenant. "Isn't that the young girl from the hotel, the one who worked the desk?"

"Yes, detective," Miller replied. "Her name is Harriot Mills."

"What was she doing way over here?" Harris asked.

"I'm not sure that she was," Miller said.

"It looks like the body was dumped," Harris said. "Look at the lividity, and there is no way all of that damage was done here." He walked closer to the body and kneeled down next to it. "I don't see any signs of splatter trace or secondary evidence around the girl." Craning his head up and down the length of the body in a slow, methodical fashion, Harris studied each and every wound for the purpose of extrapolating the story the trauma had to tell. "Do you know if someone reported hearing a gunshot?"

"No, I don't believe so," Miller replied, "but it's still early in the investigation, and we're still taking statements."

"I didn't think so," Harris said. "I don't think you will find anyone who heard anything at all. Who found the body?"

"I believe it was discovered by a couple of kids who come into the alley to play," Miller replied evenly. "I'm pretty sure they live just down the street in some rundown hotel with their mothers."

"That makes perfect sense under the circumstances," Harris said in a distant voice. "I would say that you are looking for at least three, maybe four, perpetrators." He removed a pair of latex gloves from his pocket and snapped them on.

"What are you doing here, Detective?" Harris asked. He was quickly becoming annoyed with the man, who seemed to be taking over his investigation without offering the slightest glimmer of professional courtesy.

Harris licked his lips and inhaled the familiar scent of death resting before him. It was absolutely intoxicating to his olfactory, causing him to shudder. Allowing his mind to sail across a sea of puzzles and riddles that coursed through his mind, ignoring the obtuse and irrelevant words of the lieutenant, Harris exhaled deeply and searched the depths of his mind in order to better connect with the tragic fate of the young woman who stared upward with milky eyes. It was the most wondrous aspect of his job, solving the chain of past events.

He then looked up at Miller with unblinking eyes. "Whoever did this to the girl either lives in or frequents this area," he said in a firm and confident voice. "She was raped, but not here, not this morning. Wherever their paths crossed, it was an area more familiar to her than to them, a place where she would have felt relatively safe from being attacked."

"It was a carjacking just a few blocks away from her house," Miller admitted reluctantly. Even though he didn't want to do or say anything that might further fuel the man's arrogance, finding the woman's killer took priority over his own wounded pride. "We got a call last night from some of the neighbors, who witnessed the whole thing, but the car and those who stole it just seemed to have vanished into thin air."

Harris stood up and stretched his back. "Nothing vanishes, Lieutenant, at least not entirely," he said as he removed the gloves and tossed them to the forensic members.

"Where was she prior to being snatched by the ghetto scum?" Harris asked.

"I was getting to that when my witness got upset and ran away," Miller said, unsuccessfully veiling the contempt in his voice. "From what I've gathered so far, Mr. Robinson, that's the kid from the hotel, saw her last night. He alluded to something of a dance at Jeb's."

Harris glared at him. "And you just let the kid run off before you were finished questioning him?" he asked, incredulous.

"No, I just told you that he ran away," Miller said angrily. "He was extremely upset over the death of the girl."

"Oh, I just bet he was," Harris said. "Did it occur to you that he might be involved in the girl's death?" He shook his head, amazed by the total lack of competence.

"There is no way in hell that kid is involved," Miller said venomously, squeezing his hands into fists. "No damn way!"

"Well, that's about the most idiotic assertion I've ever heard," Harris said. "You don't actually know that, but merely hope that it's an accurate assumption."

Miller stepped closer to Harris and lifted his lip into a curl. "You might want to ease back on the tone, Detective," he said. "You may get away with treating everyone else like a bunch of second-class citizens and morons, but I won't put up with such disrespect. I'm good at my job."

Harris offered a patronizing grin and shook his head. "Easy, tough guy," he said. "You shouldn't let your mouth write checks your ass can't cash." His eyes suddenly turned cold and vicious.

"Is that a threat?" Miller asked, narrowing his eyes.

"It's whatever you opt it to be," Harris said, stoic. He then clucked his tongue. "Do you feel better now that you could beat at your chest?"

"Why don't both of you get the hell out of here and let us do our damn job," Gus spat. "I can barely hear myself think with the two of you chattering on like a couple of magpies. Shit, either get to fighting or shut the hell up!"

"Amen, brother," the forensic man on the left said. "How about a little respect for the victim, jerk-offs? I'm rather certain that she doesn't want to listen to the two of you yammer on any more than we do about a bunch of nonsense. Grow the hell up!"

Miller unclenched his hands and relaxed his shoulders. He looked down at the two men, who were shaking their heads in a mixture of disgust and disappointment over their behavior, and felt the enveloping fingers of shame grip him for acting like an egocentric teenager. "Look, Detective, I don't want to fight or argue with you," he said. He ran a single hand over his head. "I just want to get the animals that did this."

"Agreed," Harris said.

"You never did say what you're doing here," Miller said. "How did you know where to find me?"

"I was pulling out of the parking lot of that Hanson law firm when I heard the call over the radio," Harris said. "I called in to learn who was on the scene, and dispatch told me you were the investigating officer."

"So you thought you'd just drive on down for a little visit, huh?" Miller asked. "Don't trust me to do my job right?"

"Sort of, I guess," Harris replied, shrugging his shoulders with indifference. "It's nothing personal."

"Oh, of course not," Miller said. "So what were you doing at the Hanson firm?"

"Nothing much," Harris replied. "Just following a potential lead. I interviewed the Hanson woman. She was a little unusual."

"You actually spoke to Jillian Hanson in person?" Miller asked, grimacing slightly, perplexed. "Are you friggin' nuts?" He shook his head. "I hope you didn't say anything even remotely offensive to her."

"Of course not," Harris said. "What do you take me for, a complete miscreant?"

"I can't believe she gave you the time of time," Miller said. "She never speaks to anyone outside the office, and everyone who has ever talked to her says she's a nightmare to deal with if she gets mad. I remember talking to that gargoyle by the name of Brad. Now that was one creepy dude."

"I sensed no such thing from either of them," Harris said. "I found her to be an extremely interesting person, even if she was a little standoffish. But then again, what attorney isn't, am I correct?" He smiled widely. "Nonetheless, I did get the distinct feeling that she was hiding something. She plays extremely close to the vest."

"Was she helpful at all?" Miller asked, his curiosity rising.

"Yes and no, I suppose," Harris replied. "It depends on your definition of helpful."

Miller looked at him with a quizzical expression masking his face. "And exactly what does that mean?" he asked. "What did she say?"

"It's not what she said so much as what she didn't say," Harris replied. "And I found her associate just a little too protective over his boss." He shrugged his shoulders. "Let's just say that I got a strange vibe, and leave it at that for now."

Miller held up his hands in mock surrender and smiled playfully. "Hey, I'm on your side," he teased. "I'm just saying that you should be careful about poking around that woman and her friends. I've heard a few things here and there about how she knows some very dangerous people, who owe her and the Hanson family big time. Even though it was before my time, I've heard stories that her dead old man was a real bad dude, and that he had killed several members of the board right in front of the rest. And there's a hellava lot more."

"I'm sure most of the stories you've heard have been greatly exaggerated over the years, Lieutenant," Harris said. "It's a very rare thing for most of those impugned postmortem by those still alive, who were too afraid to confront the person before death, to have been an actual tyrant. It's just the actions of typical cowards."

"I don't know, maybe," Miller said, unconvinced.

"So how did the dental appointment go?" Harris asked, smiling knowingly. "No cavities, I take it."

"Wh ... what?" Miller stammered. He then remembered the lie he told the detective to keep the man away from his mother's house. "It went okay. You know, just the usual stuff."

"I see," Harris said, eyeing the man carefully. "And did you have a chance to show your mother a picture of the doll and speak with her about its possible origin?"

"As a matter of fact, I did," Miller replied. He scratched his head. "Unfortunately, she was of little assistance. All she could say for certain was that it was Scandinavian. Nothing else. I'm really sorry she couldn't have been of more help. I really thought she would be able to narrow it down a lot more."

"Yes, that is too bad," Harris said with raillery. "The peninsula of Northern Europe is a rather expansive piece of property to go hunting for a single doll maker." He smiled crookedly. "Hey, it was worth a shot, even if we both knew it would be an extremely long one. All we lost was a little time."

Miller looked down at the two men, who were still gathering evidence from the body. "Do you know how much longer this is going to take, Gus?" he asked.

Gus suddenly stopped scraping underneath the girl's fingernails for trace evidence and released her hand. Grumbling under his breath, the man craned his head with a note of irritation. "Why, are we keeping you from a hot date or something?" he snapped heatedly. "You really are becoming an insensitive prick, you know that?" He jutted his chin at Harris. "It's probably due to the company you seem to be keeping these days."

"Relax, buddy, I was just asking," Miller said. He ran his tongue over his lips. "I didn't mean any disrespect."

"Yeah, well, we don't need you hovering over our shoulders and telling us what to do while we do our job, so why don't you just beat it until we're finished," Gus hissed. "One of us will contact you when we're ready to seal the girl's body."

"If that's what you prefer," Miller said uneasily. He disliked leaving the immediate scene of any crime until the body had been placed in a body bag and securely zipped up.

"It is," the other man piped up. "You're doing nothing but delaying and distracting us from finishing."

"Are you sure?" Miller asked, hesitant.

"Yes, leave," Gus replied. "Now!" He then returned his attention to the girl and resumed working on her.

Harris chuckled loud enough for everyone to hear. "Well, you heard the man," he said.

"What's so damn funny?" Miller asked, not remotely amused by being undermined in front of his subordinates.

"Nothing, nothing at all, Lieutenant," Harris replied, grinning widely. "Are you up for a little field trip?"

"What, now?" Miller asked.

"Right now," Harris replied.

"You can't be serious," Miller said.

"I'm dead serious," Harris said.

"But I have to maintain the integrity of the crime scene," Miller said, shifting his feet uneasily. The prospect of leaving was repugnant to him.

Harris peered down at the two busy men. "You got things covered, don't you, Gus?" He asked in a dry tone.

"Yes," Gus replied without averting his eyes.

"Then you won't mind if I borrow your lieutenant?" Harris asked, though he already knew the answer to the question.

"Take him," Gus said flatly.

"See, no one needs you here," Harris said mildly. "So now are you game for a short trip?"

Miller exhaled deeply. He was really beginning to despise the detective with extreme prejudice. "To where?" he asked, showing very little interest in the other man's supposed whims.

"I thought you might be interested in accompanying me to the local jail," Harris said. "You did say you wanted to work as an equal partner on the Smith case, correct?"

Miller perked up when he heard the invitational words. "Well, yeah, that's the plan," he replied. "But why the jail?"

Harris looked down at the girl and then frowned. "Well, it appears that nearly everyone connected with the hotel murder is either dead or missing in action, even if only temporarily, so I thought it prudent to speak with the only person who is still alive and whose location is still known," he replied.

"And who would that be?" Miller asked.

"Why, that would be a Mr. Jeb Cartwright," Harris replied. "Evidently, according to my source, he was arrested last night for drug possession."

"How convenient for you," Miller said snidely.

Harris wagged a finger in the air. "No, my dear lieutenant," he said. "How convenient for us. Now I'm certain he will drop the attitude and be more than willing to talk to us. Arrest and the prospect of spending well over twenty years in prison have a way of loosening a convict's lips. It's all in the presentation of how you sell a deal."

"And if he still refuses to talk?" Miller asked.

"He won't," Harris said with conviction. "They never refuse to help themselves, not if they have at least a modicum of common sense. I have the distinct feeling the Jebster will be more than accommodating with helping the investigation by answering any and all questions we ask of him. Actually, I guarantee it." He smiled. "Would you care to make a wager on it?"

Miller shook his head. He knew better than to ever bet on a convict's ability to keep his mouth shut. "Naw, I'll pass," he mumbled.

"Smart man," Harris said. He then turned and started to walk away at a brisk pace.

Chapter 10

It was exactly 4:00 p.m., when Brad pulled the small outboard boat up to the dilapidated dock that appeared to be made entirely of puckered driftwood, which was haphazardly nailed together by what could be described only as a dyslexic madman. The tainted water, shimmering with a sickly greenish layer of film that skimmed across the top of the swamp, caressing the sides of the hull with gentle ripples, disappeared beneath the planks just as the boat banged against two decomposing tires that had been attached to the side of the dock to serve as rubber bumpers. Several small schools of fish swam about the murkiness in search of food. The deep croaks of frogs belching out objections to the intrusive noise of the machine echoed across the vast marshland. Somewhere in the distance, hidden deep in the trees and reeds, the distinct sound of wildlife much larger than the plump amphibians that sat upon floating perches could be heard splashing around in the primitive wetland.

The sun had just descended below the tree line, so the creeping shadows of inevitable nightfall were slowly laying claim to the landscape that had not changed for thousands of years, and would ultimately remain as such long after man had vanished from the earth.

Seconds after Brad shut off the engine that was precariously affixed to the back of the tiny craft with little more than a few long strips of duct tape and chicken wire, the creatures of the wild fell completely silent. Even the breeze that was blowing through the trees, rattling the drooping branches that reached down to the cool water below, ceased to exist.

Content that no one else was present within miles, except for the one man he trusted well beyond anyone else on the planet, Brad retrieved a short rope from the bottom of the boat and used it to secure the boat to the dock.

As he stepped out from the boat and onto the dock, the faint sound of ancient wood creaking beneath the weight of his body, Brad wondered if it was truly necessary to go to such extreme measures for a meeting that should take no longer than thirty minutes. He could appreciate the fact that his contact wanted to remain completely anonymous, free from ever being discovered by anyone outside the two of them and their secret alliance, but he was beginning to wonder if the man he had known for years was now drifting over the precipice of sanity that most fanatics negotiated on a near daily basis. There was a delicate balance that inevitably tilted in favor of psychosis, which eventually caused the overwhelmed to be sent spiraling down into the black abyss of madness, from where there would never be a scintilla of hope for return.

Satisfied that the only form of transportation off the small island was securely fastened, Brad craned his head around and looked up the serpentine path that wound its way through a series of trees and bushes until it ended directly at the front door of a wooden cabin resting atop a heavily forested hill several hundred yards away. Unaccustomed to such a rustic environment, preferring the comforts offered by modem conveniences in the city, Brad groaned inwardly. He shoved his hands down into the pockets of his pants and began the arduous trek up the dirt road to the agreed-upon destination.

While holding a pair of high-powered binoculars up to his face, chuckling under his breath because of the sweat-covered expression on Brad's face, Ferguson rotated in a controlled arc and searched the land below for any sign of intruders who may have followed the man to the private sanctuary. A sniper rifle rested on a nearby table as insurance to make certain that no unwanted party would breach the perimeter. The last people who had set foot on the shore had each taken a perfectly placed bullet to the head and were subsequently tossed into the bayou as a healthy snack for the indigenous alligators. He had lost count as to how many unwary victims had been converted to food for the local wildlife by Zachariah when the man used to have those people who would not be missed by anyone summarily snatched from off the street and brought to the island as prey for a personal hunt.

Brad had just emerged from the foliage and walked into the clearing that encircled the wooden domicile when Ferguson lowered the binoculars and let the instrument dangle from the cord that was looped around his neck. The man appeared to be soaked from head to toe in sweat, his clothes sticking to him.

Ferguson lifted a single hand and waved to the gasping paralegal, grinning from the sight. "You really should start to get some exercise, Brad," he said. "You're sweating like a stuck pig, and I could hear you wheezing from a hundred yards away."

Brad stopped walking toward the modest porch of the cabin, still panting heavily, and stared up at the much-older man. "Do you think I'm unaware of my lack of physical fitness?" He asked sarcastically.

"I can't say that I do," Ferguson replied.

"Then you will simply have to please excuse my less than stellar condition," Brad said. He then began to move forward again. "I do, after all, spend at least fourteen hours a day working in a stuffy office."

"All I hear is an excuse, not a solution," Ferguson said. He removed the binoculars that hung around his neck and set the pair on the table next to the weapon. "It's nice to see you again, old friend." Ferguson walked down the four steps of the porch and held his hand out in proper greeting and friendship. "How have you been?"

Brad accepted the man's hand with a firm grip and shook it. "I've been quite well, Ferguson," he replied. He noticed that the older man was looking over his shoulder. "There is no reason for you to worry if I was somehow followed. I took the necessary precautions to make certain that it was impossible." He smiled broadly. "After all, I learned from the best." He looked down at the sidearm on Ferguson's right leg. "What's with the additional artillery? Are you expecting some sort of a war?"

Ferguson looked down at his hip and smiled. "No, not at all," he replied. "I'm just taking proper security measures to ensure safety. I would rather be overprepared rather than not at all." He then stepped aside and motioned for Brad to enter the cabin.

Brad nodded his head and did as requested.

Ferguson took a last look around the area to check and see if there was any hint of unwanted visitors.

There was nothing to be seen or heard except the sound of the natural environment and its inhabitants.

Content that he and Brad were completely alone, at least for the moment, Ferguson picked up the rifle and the pair of binoculars and entered the structure Zachariah had built with his own hands nearly thirty years ago.

Brad was already standing behind a wet bar and helping himself to a glass of bourbon when Ferguson walked into the main room. It was the same routine every time the two men agreed to meet on the secluded island, after one of them came across critical information and thought there was a possible threat to Jillian and the Hanson legacy.

While Brad quickly downed a glass of the expensive elixir, Ferguson set the equipment on a table and walked over to the bar. He rapped his knuckles on the hard surface several times. Brad retrieved a second glass from behind the back of the cabinet, refilled his glass up to the rim, and then poured a healthy shot for the his secret cohort, who gratefully accepted the drink. Ferguson brought the glass to his lips, took a couple of small sips, closed his eyes, and then smiled from the exquisite flavor as he expertly swished it around in his mouth. He then swallowed the remaining liquid in a single gulp and set the glass back down on the bar. He tapped the rim with an index finger to signal for a second.

"Thank you for agreeing to meet so quickly," Brad said. He guzzled the second glass of alcohol and rolled the empty glass in his hands.

Ferguson watched him carefully over the top of the glass as he took another sip. He smiled to try to help Brad relax because it was obvious that something was genuinely bothering the younger man. "There is no real reason to thank me," he said, lowering his own glass onto the wooden surface. "It's my pleasure." He paused. Ferguson had known Brad Renfro nearly all his life and could easily identify even the smallest nuance that evidenced something had definitely rattled him. Like many men his age and younger, they lacked the personal skill to maintain absolute control over their emotions. Although the man had proved to be an exceptional student under his personal tutelage for years thus far, Brad still allowed himself to become emotionally invested each time a perceived threat against Jillian arose. He'd lost count as to the number of times he had warned his protégé how harboring personal feelings for someone or something adversely affects professional performance and creates an inescapable atmosphere for amateurish sloppiness. "So, how have you really been, my dear boy?"

Brad poured himself a third glass. "I've been well," Brad replied. He started to lift the glass to his lips but was prevented from completing the maneuver by Ferguson, who laid a hand on his wrist and pushed his hand back down onto the wet bar.

"You might want to slow down on the imbibing, son," Ferguson said, his voice tender. "I'm in no hurry to leave." He took his glass of bourbon and walked over to a small couch on the other side of an enormous Kodiak bear rug that covered the center of the room. He sat down and crossed his legs. "So, how is Jillian?"

"She seems to be well, but ..." Brad began, losing his train of thought.

"But what?" Ferguson asked, prodding him to finish the sentence. "You mentioned that there was the possibility of a problem, or something to that effect, did you not?"

"Yes, I think there is a definite problem that needs to be

rectified immediately," Brad said. "But I think there's a little more involved."

"For instance," Ferguson said, unperturbed as he took a sip from the glass, eyes unwavering.

"I think she's a top suspect in a current homicide investigation," Brad replied.

"And," Ferguson pressed.

"And I think the detective in charge is going to come after her," Brad continued. "I didn't like the implications being made during the interrogation he conducted with Jillian. The man genuinely believes he's on the correct path, even if there is no evidence to support his suspicions. And he seems to be competent."

Ferguson waved a single hand in the air. "I'm unconcerned," he said. "Whatever his intelligence, if any at all, is inconsequential. My only concern is for Jillian's happiness and welfare. All else can fall by the wayside. The earth itself can perish for all I care."

"I agree," Brad said. "However, I must inform you that my opinion is that she is having a few more mood swings that appear to be more apparent. I'm becoming a little more concerned over her mental state of mind. Cleaning up is getting more difficult. And the crooks in Congress are pushing for more money to stay in line."

"How so?" Ferguson queried. He took another sip.

"Well, for one thing, you are aware that she recently promoted Heather Lasko to junior partner in the firm, aren't you?" Brad asked. He picked up the glass and walked over to a chair that was situated opposite the couch.

"Yes, I know about it," Ferguson replied. "In fact, Jillian consulted with me on that particular course of action."

Brad sat down and looked at his mentor with curious eyes. "And you didn't object to the maneuver?" he asked, perplexed.

"Of course not," Ferguson replied calmly. "She was lonely and wanted some company to share in the daily business of her life, someone who could fill the shoes of being sort of like a sister to her. I suspect she is yearning for the unity of family as she gets older. It's an inevitable curse that claims all of us as we age. Even the most outcast of family members wants to rejoin the fold when time begins to run out."

Angered by the unexpected revelation provided by Ferguson, Brad stood up from the chair and glared at him. "She already has a family," he said.

Ferguson narrowed his eyes at the man as a signal of warning. "You will never speak of that!" He growled deeply. "She must never know."

"But I'm her family, Ferguson, her only true living relative," Brad said. "Everyone else related by blood is dead."

Ferguson stood up from the couch. "You must leave the past where it belongs," he said. "We have already spoken on this and reached an agreement that no one is ever to know."

"Things change," Brad said.

"Not this, not ever," Ferguson said.

"But I'm her brother," Brad pleaded. "I love her and will do anything necessary for her. She's my blood."

"I know you will, Brad," Ferguson said, his features softening when he saw the pain that crossed the man's face, "but do you really want to tell Jillian that your mother was pregnant with you when your father had her hidden away in that asylum, and that I killed every living threat so that you would be safe and allowed to live? I promised your mother that I would keep the two of you safe, before you were surgically removed from her body and smuggled out of the hospital under the cover of night. I've had to live with the fact that I had to kill the attending nurse and support staff to hide the information that you ever existed, which is a guilt that I am more than happy to bear. I loved your mother like no other in the world and would have promised to do anything for her if she asked. Well, she did, and I shall keep my promise to her, as you will to me." Ferguson suddenly felt the full mileage of his age, sighing deeply, and sat back down. He was exhausted. "I won't risk ever having Jillian look at me as if I was some sort of grotesque monster that lied to her all her life."

"I don't think you could ever do anything to cause her to look at you with anything but loving eyes," Brad said. "And I doubt you could ever do any wrong in her eyes. The manner in which she speaks about you is one only of love and friendship. She has even referred to you as Dad on several occasions."

"Are you serious?" Ferguson asked, blinking back tears that began to fill his eyes. "She talks about me to you?" Just the idea of Jillian telling another person that she considered him a father figure brought a sincere smile to his face.

"Yes, quite fondly," Brad replied. "Ferguson, if there was one person other than her mother that she truly loves, it would be you." Brad smiled from the memory of all the stories she had told to him over the years when they were alone in her office. "She has told me about all the presents you gave to her on the sly as a little girl, and how you thought she didn't know you were watching over her during the nights when she was afraid."

"She knows?" Ferguson asked, bewildered.

"Of course she knows," Brad replied. "Very little escapes that one. She used to hear the creak of the old rocking chair when you sat in it after you sneaked into the room to guard her against nightmares and the monsters in the world."

Ferguson slumped back on the couch and grimaced in shame. "I'm afraid that I failed to protect her from the worst monster of them all," he said miserably, guilt enveloping him.

"You do realize that it wasn't your fault, don't you?" Brad asked. "You couldn't have known."

"But I should have," Ferguson said.

"Why?" Brad asked. "No one would have ever guessed that her father was nothing more than the worst kind of pedophile."

"Because I knew the man was pure evil," Ferguson replied.

"You do know that she doesn't blame you for what Zachariah did to her and our mother, don't you?" Brad asked.

"How can you be so sure that somewhere deep down in her subconscious she doesn't hold me at least a little responsible for the hell she suffered?" Ferguson asked. "I mean, if there—"

"Because she has told me as much," Brad interrupted. "There is only one person she blames, and it is not you."

Ferguson offered a weak grin. "Then that is all the more reason why the two of us must protect her no matter what the cost," he said. "The unanswered variable is, what degree of threat do you believe this detective is to our Jillian?"

"I would say it's palpable," Brad replied. "He's a definite threat to her."

"Then we have only one option," Ferguson said. He stood up from the couch and stretched.

"Which is?" Brad asked, though he was already fairly certain about the remedy.

"The detective and anyone else directly connected to the investigation must be killed," Ferguson replied. "It's the only way to guarantee absolute closure." He looked over at Brad. "That is, unless you have an alternate solution."

Brad thought about any other possibility short of committing cold-blooded murder, mulling every scenario and option over in his mind, and concluded that there was only one avenue to take.

He reluctantly shook his head. "I agree," Brad said. "The only way to be certain is to remove the threat."

Ferguson eyed the man curiously because the tone of Brad's voice actually seemed to denote a hint of regret. "Does our agreed-upon solution bother you?" he asked. "You appear to be a little disappointed."

"I wouldn't say disappointed, at least not exactly," Brad replied. "The detective was kind of an interesting sort of man. There was something about him that was intriguing. He had a lot more nerve than I'm accustomed to, I suppose. It's a shame to kill someone who is not a complete waste of skin, especially since the world seems to be overflowing with such obsolete people."

"Killing the man is not going to be a problem for you, is it?" Ferguson asked, his tone dead serious. "If you have any reservations, then tell me now so I can formulate a plan to eradicate him alone."

Brad looked him directly in the eye with a stoic expression. "No, I assure you there is no problem whatsoever," he replied. "I'll do what I always do."

"Excellent," Ferguson said. "Now that we have resolved that bit of business, I suggest we go to the armory and select the most suitable tools for this particular endeavor." He turned to walk into the next room. "Do you have any opinions on the matter? After all, you have an advantage over me because you've already met the man."

"I recommend minimal collateral damage," Brad said as Ferguson disappeared into the adjoining room. "It will have to be an inner city removal, so I suggest the one-shot one-kill approach for the intended target or targets."

"That sounds acceptable," Ferguson said from inside the next room. "Hurry up and get in here so we can begin."

The soft sound of gears came from inside the room that Ferguson had just entered, and reverberated throughout the cabin.

When Brad walked through the open doorway and into the section of the cabin that was used as a small game room, the pool table located in the center of the room was tilted on one side, revealing a hidden trapdoor that led beneath the wooden domicile and into a secret chamber that lay underground. The top of Ferguson's head disappeared from sight just as Brad made his way into the room.

A set of pool cues rested firmly in a rack that was inexpertly nailed to the wall. A folded-up Ping-Pong table was leaning against the wall, and a Budweiser light that had not experienced the flow of electricity for over ten years hung in a lopsided fashion on the opposite wall. Overhead, like a pair of flickering glow sticks, two dust-covered florescent lights ran parallel across the ceiling from one wall to the other.

Brad couldn't help but wonder how much longer they would last before the final spark of life was forever extinguished. The sound of footsteps echoing up from the chamber as Ferguson's feet stepped deeper into the shelter dulled to a low pitch until they faded altogether. A bright light suddenly shot out of the entrance.

"Are you coming down?" Ferguson called out. The sound of his voice was deep and throaty. "I don't have all day. Jillian will be trying to reach me before the end of the day, and I would prefer to be somewhere on the main premises when she does."

"I'm coming," Brad replied. "You are really starting to become impatient with each passing year." He walked around to the side of the pool table and made his journey down the thirty feet of steps. The intensity of the light grew fiercer with every step.

Unlike the rustic atmosphere of the cabin aboveground, the entire area of the shelter that stretched out to the length of twenty five yards in every direction was originally constructed to function as a nuclear fallout bunker. A dozen surveillance screens were located at a station situated in a corner cubicle. Metal gun racks filled with every make and caliber of semiautomatic, automatic, and sniper rifle lined three of the walls. Hanging from the fourth wall was an eclectic collection of military explosive devises, ranging from basic dynamite to rocket-propelled grenades and polished mortars.

Ferguson looked up from the table he was working on when Brad finally made his appearance downstairs. A pair of bifocals rested on the tip of his nose. "So the prodigal son finally decided to join me," Ferguson said. He offered a crooked smile and then lowered his head back down to the worktable and the sniper rifle that was resting across it.

"What are you doing?" Brad asked. He slowly made his way over to the table and studied the weapon of choice.

"Taking your advice," Ferguson said. "I'm going to take him out from a distance."

"What's the range of that rifle?" Brad asked. "You're going to want to be far enough to hide the trajectory, at least until the team is called in to evaluate the variables involved."

"I can hit him with this without breaking a sweat from at least one mile," Ferguson replied. "I'm more interested in adjusting the pressure of pull required for the trigger; I'm expecting more than one target, so I want as light a touch as possible for an easy double or triple tap." He picked up the gun and tested it for balance. "I don't expect any problems. It will be a hit and move. You will be armed with a sister rifle as a secondary resort to tap any target if I either miss completely, which has never happened in my life, or somehow botch the kill shot. You'll maintain a constant vigil on the target through the scope and fire only if it is evident that I didn't put the hostile down with the first shot."

"No offense to your tactics, Ferguson, but why don't we do something a little quieter, covert, like a home hit?" Brad asked. "Wouldn't it be better if the man simply showed up on a carton of milk?" He chuckled from the thought of seeing the detective's face on the side of a half gallon of milk with the question "Have you seen me?" written beneath the picture in large, bold letters.

"None taken," Ferguson said. "I would prefer to avoid a mishap. He's a professional detective and has a different type of survival instinct than the everyday civilian. I would also like to avoid unnecessary collateral damage."

"We could just snatch him off the street," Brad said.

Ferguson walked over to a neighboring table and picked up the second rifle. He checked it carefully before bringing it over to his work station. "Too many unpredictable variables," he replied. "I don't want to risk being seen by someone, who would have to be dealt with in a similar fashion."

"Why not poison him the same way we did the last target?" Brad asked. "It was easy. I'll just get into his house and lace the coffee filters with a high concentrate."

"And what if he doesn't drink coffee?" Ferguson asked, lilting a single eyebrow. "That's what I mean by variables."

"All cops drink coffee," Brad replied simply, shrugging his shoulders.

"Perhaps," Ferguson said, "but I don't want to wait any longer than necessary to terminate the potential problem. The longer we wait the higher the possibility that more people will be made privy to the information. The murder of a police detective will raise more than enough attention, so I want to keep the numbers at a minimum."

"I understand," Brad said. He picked up the second rifle and gently glided his finger over the cool length of the barrel. "Excellent weapon of choice." He then brought the rifle up and rested the butt of the stock against his shoulder. He peeked through the lens of the high-powered scope and imitated the sound of a shot being fired.

Ferguson moved toward an open metal locker and removed a box of ammunition. Each of the bullets had been personally loaded by him so that he could increase the grain for optimum effect, a modification often referred to as hot loads. He walked back over to the table and set the box down, ignoring the other man, who was pretending to fire the gun.

"So, where do you want to take him out?" Brad asked. "Have you made any decision regarding location?"

"No, not yet," Ferguson replied. "I don't have enough intelligence to make such a decision. Do you have an opinion?" He put the box of ammunition into a small backpack and then began to disassemble the rifle into three separate parts so that it could be stashed away in a custom-made case. "Have you finished inspecting the second rifle? I gave it a quick perusal, but not a thorough check on the pin."

Brad nodded his head. "Yeah, I gave it a good once-over and it's good to go," Brad replied. He began to follow Ferguson's lead by first twisting the scope a quarter and snapping it free from the bridge. "You do realize that Jillian is going to hear about the death of the detective, don't you?"

Ferguson closed up the case and looked over at his colleague. "Yes, of course," he replied. "What's your point?"

"You don't think she'll have questions?" Brad asked.

"About what?" Ferguson asked.

"You can't be serious, Ferguson," Brad said. "She's going to be curious as to why the same detective who came to ask her questions is suddenly found with a bullet hole the size of a silver dollar in his chest."

Ferguson offered the man a condescending smile. "I think you are overestimating the level of Jillian's concern for people in general," he said. "She may find the whole chain of events curious, even suspicious, but she won't make a query because the murder of some detective is about as inconsequential to her as either you or me stomping on the head of a dead gopher." He shouldered the backpack and picked up the rifle that was securely hidden away inside the thick case.

"What if I'm questioned about it?" Brad asked. "I don't want to lie to my sister."

Ferguson looked at him with tired eyes and sighed heavily. "Why, you've basically been lying to her for years," he said. "Whatever you do, Brad, don't go and try to develop some sort of misguided conscience. It will only bring you pain and regret. Trust me, I know about such things. People like us are better off without a moral center." When he saw a forlorn expression cover Brad's face, the same one he'd seen in the mirror the day he had learned of their mother's death, Ferguson shook his head in deep sadness. He set the items on the table. "What's the matter?"

Brad placed the separate parts of the weapon in a bag and quickly zipped it up. "Nothing," he replied glumly.

"Well, there must be something bothering you," Ferguson said. "I've never seen you act so peculiar. Whatever is bugging you, I want you to tell me now or forever drop it." He looked at the watch fastened around his wrist. "We still have a little time to talk. I don't want you going mentally sideways on me in the middle of our project."

"I swear to you that nothing is going to interfere or distract me from what we have to do to protect Jillian," Brad said.

"I'm aware of that," Ferguson said softly, "but sometime things get into people's heads and they don't realize that it's affecting far more than they believe. So, whatever is on your mind I want you to tell me. We are not leaving until you do."

"I want to tell Jillian the truth about me and her," Brad said. "I want her to know that she has a brother."

"Why?" Ferguson asked in a raw tone of voice. "What do you hope to accomplish by telling her?"

"So she'll know that she is not alone in this world and that she can trust me as her younger brother," Brad replied.

"She already knows that she isn't alone, Brad," Ferguson said. "And she already trusts you with everything." He paused. "Are you so certain the reason you want to tell her isn't based more on your own selfish motive rather than for her happiness, so much that you are willing to risk estranging her for the rest of your life? You know as well as I do that Jillian does not forgive or forget those who have wronged her ... ever."

"But she would eventually come to understand, don't you think?" Brad asked, desperately trying to elicit the answer that would please him most.

"No, Brad, she wouldn't," Ferguson replied. "I love your sister as if she were my own daughter, and I would destroy the entire world for her without batting an eye, but there are things that have happened in her life that you are unaware of, things that molded her into the person she is today, most of which were extremely horrible. I only know such things because I was present during those years and most since. There is now a very dark side to your sister that you do not want to know, a side that was instilled by your father through acts of ..." His voice trailed off.

Brad narrowed his eyes. "Dark side, like what?" Brad asked.

"That is not for me to say," Ferguson said.

"Why not?" Brad asked. He moved closer to Ferguson and took the man by the arm. "And what other evil acts did my father commit?"'

Ferguson lowered his gaze to the hand that held tightly to his arm, gently shaking his head side to side, and pursed his lips. Understanding the man's concern over what had just been insinuated, and careful so as not to be interpreted as threatening, he pushed Brad's hand away from his arm. "I understand how being kept in the dark for so many years could be so upsetting, but I will never disclose the hideous details of what only I and Jillian know to be true. I apologize if this upsets you, but it's not my story to tell. I only wish I could somehow forget. You shouldn't dwell on things you cannot know or change. Trust me, some things are best left in the shadows of history, never to be revealed. There is nothing to be gained by digging out skeletons of a closet that is best left closed forever."

"That's one opinion," Brad stated.

"Yes, it is," Ferguson said. "And it is the only one that matters in this lifetime, I assure you."

Brad looked at the older man with deadly serious eyes. "And if I choose to not heed your advice?" he asked in a hushed tone, well aware that he may be treading into potentially dangerous territory.

Ferguson shrugged his shoulders nonchalantly, expertly disguising his true feelings. "I would be greatly disappointed in you," he replied simply. "Of course, as is related to Hanson matters, second only to Jillian herself, the final decision does rest within your discretion, regardless of how great I would object to it." He sighed deeply. "Just remember, Bradley, if she somehow learns of your sibling connection it would most likely destroy her completely. There are things about your sister that you should remain totally unaware of. Things that are not entirely conducive to the supposed family setting, and I shall do whatever is necessary to protect her from harm. I failed her once before, and I shall never do so again." He stared at Brad. "You do understand my position, correct?"

Brad licked his lips nervously. "Yes, I do," Brad replied.

"There is nothing I would not do for her," Ferguson said, "so please do not test the length or the depth of the depravity to which I will sink to protect her."

"Of course, Ferguson," Brad said, swallowing with slight difficulty.

Ferguson smiled. "Perfect," he said. He then picked up everything and headed for the stairs that led up to the cabin.

Intrigued by the unexpected mysterious conduct of the man, though slightly unnerved and annoyed that he continued to be so cryptic, Brad picked up his own stuff and followed Ferguson. He had made only a couple of steps up the staircase when the lights suddenly went out in the underground bunker. The sound of the older man's booted steps ascending the steps resounded throughout the area with crystal clarity.

Ferguson was standing over by the pool cue rack with a remote control held in his hand when Brad finally emerged from the depths below the terrain.

Seconds after Brad was clear of the heavy pool table, Ferguson pressed the red button in the center of the small device that electronically sent the gears back into full motion. Both men watched until everything had returned to its former position. A loud snap sounded as the locks fastened the heavy door firmly onto the floor. Never leaving anything to chance, Ferguson quickly made an inspection of the rectangular outline to make certain any residual evidence that might show disturbance was effectively covered up.

Silent, Brad watched him, never ceasing to be impressed with the man's infallible eye for even the tiniest detail. "You sure are one anal-retentive man, Ferguson," Brad commented, a hint of humor touching his voice. "Nothing at all ever gets past you, does it?"

"Everything that is of any consequence in life rests within the details, Bradley," Ferguson said dryly. "You might he surprised by how many men have fallen from grace because they took something for granted or simply got careless through laziness. One never knows when his life may come to depend on learning a shred of information or the discovery of the slightest overlooked detail."

"I suppose that's a fair enough statement," Brad said. "Although, I think you are being a little overly—"

"Don't suppose," Ferguson snapped hotly, interrupting Brad. He dusted himself off. "Know that it is fact. Nothing exceeds like excess. If you act as though someone is always hunting you, always watching you, waiting to kill you while asleep, full awareness of your surroundings becomes an innate habit, including cognizance for covering all potential tracks. Just remember, my young protégé, that the enemy need defeat you only once, as to where you must never lose or risk being lost forever."

"I heard you," Brad said irritably. He didn't like being treated as if he were a child. He slid his right arm through the loops of a duffel bag and pulled it over his shoulder. "We've been through this many times before, Ferguson, and I don't need to be reminded on a daily basis. I'm not an idiot."

Ferguson ignored the smarmy retort, instead opting to focus on the important aspect of the topic. "But did you listen and understand?" he asked, narrowing his eyes. "There is a rather large difference between hearing, listening, and actually understanding the subject matter."

"Yes, I understand," Brad replied evenly, growing angry. His face began to turn to a deep red.

"Are you certain?" Ferguson pressed. He hoisted his own bag over his shoulder, grunting heavily in response to the shift in weight and the stress it placed on the muscles of his back.

"Yes," Brad replied impatiently. "I don't need a refresher course."

Ferguson nodded appreciatively, pride filling him. "Excellent," he said. "Now if we can just get you to fully control your emotions more efficiently, we'll be all set. You allow yourself to become upset far too easily. You must learn to channel all hostile feelings."

"I'll work on it," Brad said.

"I have no doubt you will," Ferguson said, grinning. "Are you all ready to head back to the mainland?"

"Yes," Brad said, exhaling from relief. He then moved to take the lead, but Ferguson stopped him in his tracks when he stepped directly in his intended path.

Brad pulled up short and wrinkled his brow. "Is there something wrong?" he asked, curious.

"Where do you think you're going?" Ferguson asked.

"I was going to take us to the boat I used to get here," Brad replied. "I moored it off that broken-down dock."

"That won't be necessary," Ferguson said. He walked out of the game room, strolled across the main room, and then opened the front door of the cabin, where he stood for several seconds before stepping outside, onto the rustic porch.

Following closely behind, Brad was right on his heels.

"Why not?" Brad asked, "It's a piece of junk but floats well enough to get us off the island."

Ferguson turned and faced his young apprentice. He wagged a single finger in the air. "Never return the same way you came," he said. "Such a grievous error might facilitate an ambush by an unknown intruder."

"But there is no one else here," Brad said, somewhat exasperated.

"Are you certain of that position?" Ferguson asked, eyeing the younger man with a glint of amusement.

Brad waved an arm through the air. "Just look around, Ferguson," he said. "We're the only ones on this friggin' island, probably the only people around for at least ten miles as the bird flies."

"Are you so certain that you would be willing to bet your life on it?" Ferguson asked, in a voice flat and dead serious. "Would you bet Jillian's life on what you suspect but do not factually know?"

Brad hesitated momentarily as he weighed the gravity of the question and the consequences attached. He then shook his head. "Uh, well, no, I guess I wouldn't go that far," Brad replied finally, reluctant.

"No, I didn't suppose you would," Ferguson said. "So if you wouldn't risk life or limb, why would you take the chance at all?"

"I'm not sure," Brad mumbled.

"Always remember that anything left to chance is a fool's decision," Ferguson said. "Either you know something to be fact or you don't. Anything less than absolute is nothing more than silly conjecture and speculation. And the results of such reckless behavior usually end in death ... or an effective form of suicide."

"So how did you get here?" Brad asked.

"Seaplane," Ferguson replied.

"Well, wouldn't returning back to it be the same sort of scenario?" Brad asked, smirking slightly.

"Of course, it would," Ferguson replied. "In fact, it would be exactly the same thing, which is why we are not returning to it."

"I don't understand," Brad said. "If we can't use the barnacle barge I drifted in on, or the means you used, then how are we to get off the island?"

"By airboat," Ferguson replied. "I had it delivered over a month ago."

Without further explanation, he then walked down the wooden steps, oblivious to the sharp snaps and dull creaks underfoot, and took a left turn.

Brad readjusted the straps on the bag, eyeing the older man curiously, and trailed after his mentor.

"What airboat?" Brad asked, calling out just as his right foot touched the dirt. "I didn't see anything resembling a boat."

Ferguson chuckled under his breath. "That, my dear Bradley, is sort of the point for making alternative scenarios for escape," he chided. "Never allow yourself to be boxed in, with no trapdoors." He paused. "Now do hurry up and come along, young man. We have a great deal to get accomplished and not a whole lot of time in which to finish." He then disappeared around the side of the cabin.

Brad began to slow his pace as he approached the far end of the left side of the wood structure, then stopped dead in his tracks. Trepidation filled him. One of his greatest pet peeves was for someone to keep him in the dark. He considered the idea of turning around and just walking back the same way he had come, back to where he had docked the crude craft, firmly believing that Ferguson was being overly paranoid, because he was almost positive that there was no one else anywhere near their position, but then decided against it. The last thing he wanted to do was act impetuously and estrange the only man who had treated him like a son since the day he'd mysteriously appeared from out of nowhere and rescued him from an abusive orphanage so many years earlier.

Jerking his shoulders upward to manipulate the straps that were painfully digging into his collarbone, Brad lifted his chin and looked up to the clear sky. He let out a small breath of awed relief at the sight of an eagle flying majestically overhead, all the while the words uttered by Ferguson about Jillian having some sort a dark side haunting his thoughts for some macabre reason. Although she was his sister and he loved her dearly, there was a great deal of her life for which he was completely ignorant. In the past, perhaps against his better judgment, he had made several attempts to learn more about her childhood and the man only he and Ferguson knew to be his father, but her demeanor would change instantly at the mention of Zachariah, which was immediately followed by a sinister scowl clouding her face. Whatever the underlying reason for such a physical transformation, it was abundantly clear she harbored no desire whatsoever to unburden herself from the hidden skeletons dangling in the Hanson closet by discussing memories, be they good or bad, or the secret of family business from past history. Adding to Brad's ever increasing frustration, Ferguson was equally tight-lipped over the relationship between father and daughter. Oddly enough, the mother seemed to be little more than a footnote in the family chronicles.

Ferguson suddenly appeared from around the corner of the cabin and glared angrily at Brad with cold eyes. A note of impatience covered his face. "Well, are you coming along or not?" he asked in a husky tone of voice that denoted a certain degree of displeasure with his cohort. "I do not wish to remain here any longer than is absolutely necessary. I suggest, if you prefer to lollygag around all day long, that you do it on your own time, not mine." He looked down at the watch strapped to his wrist. "It's getting late."

Shaken from his reverie, Brad shook his head a couple of times as if clearing the troublesome thoughts, and offered a lopsided grin of apology. "I'm sorry, Ferguson. I was just watching the bird and thinking about some things," he said.

"How very quaint," Ferguson commented sarcastically. His face held no humor at all. "As much as I wish I could join you in your mental meandering on pointless matters, what do you say about moving your feet, while attempting to solve the world's problem with cold fusion at a later date?" He rolled his eyes in utter annoyance. "Is that at all doable?"

"You know, Ferguson, for a man who prides himself on the time-honored tradition of being a gentleman's gentleman, you sure do seem to carry a severe mean streak in you," Brad said. "I mean, sometimes you are just a downright scary, dude." Brad held up a single hand. "Of course, I mean to cause no umbrage." He smiled.

Ferguson grinned cruelly. "Naturally," he said, tilting his head slightly to the right. "None taken, I assure you, even though there have been many moments in time when the ever flexible parameters of my service to those with whom I owe absolute fealty required the implementation of professionally acquired skills beyond the enumeration of my orthodox duties."

"I am quite certain you have been an asset to the Hanson legacy," Brad said, "an invaluable one." He paused. "And that was a mouthful."

"And you would be quite right, of course," Ferguson said. His facial features softened ever so slightly. "So, are you joining me?"

"You cut me deep, Fergo," Brad replied, placing a hand over his chest to feign a heartache, "because you know I am. Did you ever doubt my allegiance to our family or to your duty in protecting it?"

"Not even when you complain the most," Ferguson replied. He waved for Brad to come along and then quickly disappeared around the corner yet once again. The soft sound of rustling bushes soon followed.

Still feeling the physical exertion of traveling up the hillside on foot, already sore due to being unaccustomed to exercise in any form, Brad hefted the bag higher up on his back and walked in the same direction Ferguson had gone just moments ago.

After he rounded the far end of the cabin, a sense of dread filled him when he found no apparent trail to safely traverse down the mountain. He walked to where there appeared to be a ledge of sorts and stared down with widened eyes. Thick foliage covered the entire area. The sound of breaking branches below could be heard as he desperately searched for a marked path to use to help with the descent.

There was nothing to be found.

In the distance, barely visible in the deep brush that surrounded him, Ferguson was standing in a tiny clearing a quarter of the way down the hillside and waving him onward. *This is friggin' ridiculous,* Brad thought with dismay, biting down on his lip as he imagined himself tumbling down the mountain and hitting every stray rock and stick until there was nothing left of his carcass but a bloody pulp. *Oh, come on, Fergo, I'm not a damn mountain goat. I'm going to break my stupid neck.* He waved back to Ferguson and mouthed the words for hello.

Ferguson, who was not remotely amused by the other man's foolish antics, placed both hands on his hips and glared menacingly at Brad. A few seconds later he waved angrily for Brad to hurry up and stop playing around. He then tapped at his wrist to demonstrate his concern about the time.

In an almost effeminate manner, Brad reluctantly stepped off the small precipice, half expecting to trip and hear the distinct sound of his neck being snapped like so many of the scattered twigs lying about the dirt, and slowly made his way down the hill. Although his feet slipped several times, causing his heart to leap up into his throat multiple times, he managed to keep his footing and join Ferguson on the barren mound, who impatiently continued to wait for him in the clearing.

"You climb like a little girl," Ferguson commented when Brad finally moved beside him.

"Screw you, Fergo," Brad said, panting heavily. He bent over at the waist. "I work in a law office for a living, not the wild kingdom."

Ferguson patted him on the back and belted out a genuine laugh. "That's the problem with you kids these days," he said jokingly. "None of you enjoy the great outdoors anymore. You're all getting soft as marshmallows, because all any of you do is lie around and eat fatty trash."

"I hate nature," Brad muttered through gasps.

Ferguson laughed again. "Apparently she's none too fond of you either," he said happily, genuinely enjoying himself at the expense of the much-younger man. He lowered his face next to Brad's and grunted mockingly. "You're not going to retch, are you?" He began to rub the man's back to help comfort him.

Brad craned his head upward to meet Ferguson's eyes and grimaced. "I might," he replied. "I'm not used to physical activity like this."

"Well, suck it up, Bradley, because we must get moving," Ferguson said. "Do you want me to carry your pack for you?"

"Oh, you'd just love that, wouldn't you?" Brad shot back. "I'd never hear the end of it if I let you do that, would I?"

"Probably not," Ferguson replied, smiling broadly.

"Then forget it," Brad said. "I can carry my own weight." He held out a hand. "Just help me stand up."

"As you wish," Ferguson said, standing upright and assisting the man, who sounded as if he were having a coronary.

"So, how much farther is the airboat?" Brad asked, slowing regaining his wind.

"Not far," Ferguson replied.

"How far is not far?" Brad asked.

"Maybe a mile, perhaps two at most," Ferguson replied, smiling. He then patted Brad on the back one final time when he heard him groan miserably. "Come on, it will be over before you know it." He then stepped out of the clearing and continued down the steep slope.

After Brad had finished stretching out his back, he watched the man disappear back into the deep brush. The sound of boots smashing down on dry kindling could be heard. *God, I hate my life sometimes,* he thought, shaking his head. He then pulled the bag back up on his shoulder and headed off into the wilds of the expansive wilderness that lay before him.

Chapter 11

Since the first choice of husband for her daughter Dorothy was unacceptably busy chasing down criminals of the most foul, soon concluding that he was just one more man to have his priorities askew, Jillian felt vexed by such behavior. All he had done since leaving the alleyway, where the unfortunate girl had met a tragically violent end, was to carouse around town with someone who appeared to be his new best friend. Jillian finally decided to give up on waiting for the man meant for her little girl. Instead, exercising a mother's prerogative to make decisions that involve the family unit, she placed Dorothy's upcoming nuptials in abeyance and opted to move Agatha to the top of the list, which was not an easy matter because Dorothy had openly voiced her objections to being passed over in favor of her younger sister. It wasn't until she accused her mother of loving Agatha more than her that Jillian had put her foot down and told her to be silent, or she would call off the wedding altogether. She then leered at Dorothy with narrowed eyes to show that she was not joking, causing the young beauty to avert her eyes and look down at the floor in shame.

The stupid man was messing up everything.

Jillian had just run her tongue along the salt that laced the rim of her first margarita when an attractive middle-aged man took a seat on the stool next to her own. At first she didn't acknowledge his appearance, choosing rather to play the perfected art of seduction she used every time she was attempting to lure a male away from the herd of those too intimidated to approach a woman as beautiful as she, or the silent attention he showered on her as she continued to lick the side of the glass with expert ability.

He couldn't help but envy the glass.

Aware of the man's eyes watching every move she made, wondering if he would prove worthy of her daughter's devotion and love, Jillian darted her tongue in and out of the pink liquid to see if she could get some sort of response from him.

She was not disappointed.

He exhaled in a manner that reminded her of a lover sighing from unabashed lust. It was not so different from the man she'd met in the hotel room earlier in the week. She smiled inwardly and took a seductive sip from the glass, looking at the man from out of the corner of her eye. Then she winked at him.

Accepting the provocative move as one of subtle introduction, the man made a quarter turn on the stool and smiled at her. He had not seen such an attractive woman in more years than he cared to count. She was about as physically flawless as a female could be, and the effect of her sensual proportions caused an immediate reaction in his lower extremities.

"Hello," he said, flashing that same toothy grin. "I'm Eryk Severson. That's Eryk with a y." He rested a single elbow on top of the bar and leaned on it, in a move to seem far more suave and masculine.

Jillian set the glass down on the bar and smiled back at him. "Hello, Eryk with a y," she said in a sultry tone of voice, batting her long eyelashes. "My name is Scarlett Burkett. It's a pleasure to make your acquaintance." She offered one delicate hand to the man.

Half disbelieving his good luck, questioning the reality of the situation and whether he was asleep at home and dreaming, Eryk reached out and excitedly accepted the woman's hand. The texture of her skin felt soft and supple, causing him to blush when she teased him by gently running the tips of her fingers against the palm of his hand as she slowly slid it from between his. "Trust me, Miss Burkett, the pleasure is all mine, I assure you," Eryk said, forcing himself to give off the false persona that he was calm, cool, and collected in her presence, immune from her feminine wiles, which encircled him like a pheromonal tornado.

Jillian ran her thumb and forefinger up and down the stem of the glass and glided her tongue over the top of her lower lip with sexual precision. "Please, Eryk, we're now friends, so call me Scarlett," she breathed. "All my friends call me Scarlett."

"Like the character in the book?" Eryk asked, trying his best to play along with the dance of erotic temptation.

"Exactly," Jillian said, smiling devilishly. "So you are aware of her antics, am I correct, Eryk?"

Mesmerized by the woman's busy hand as it caressed the elongated neck of the glass, Eryk nodded his head and cleared his throat nervously. "Uh, yes, I'm familiar with the basic story line," he mumbled.

He had no idea as to whether the woman he'd just met was trying to sexually entice him either consciously or subconsciously, not that it actually mattered all that much to him as long as the end result proved fruitful. But he was almost certain that she was attempting to dominate him with her womanly prowess. He shifted his eyes downward, allowing them to drink in the shapely contours of her physically fit body until they came to rest on the muscularity of her perfectly formed legs. He wondered what it would feel like to have them wrapped around his waist. Eryk licked his lips at the thought of having sex with such a breathtaking woman, one that was so far out of his league that to do such was equivalent to the unattainable sexual aspirations of an adolescent boy harboring a crush on his teacher.

When he lifted his eyes back to her face, flustered, feeling the warmth in his cheeks rise when she shifted the position of her thighs in response to his obvious ogling, Eryk found that she was staring at him with a knowing smile creased across her lips. Desperate not to lose her company, though embarrassed of being caught red-handed, he hoped to salvage such an awkward moment. He searched for some sort of way to apologize to her for acting like a typical bar drone buzzing aimlessly around in hope of pollinating the nearest willing flower, but there was nothing to say without sounding completely ridiculous. Whatever could be said would only make the situation worse.

Although Eryk was just slightly older than Jillian would have preferred to have as a husband for Agatha, it occurred to her that a more mature man might a be wiser choice because he would undoubtedly be more patient with her daughter's seemingly incurable mood swings and petulant antics, which unexpectedly sprang up at the most inopportune times. Perhaps he might be a positive influence on her, she thought, and teach her the proper manners expected from someone in such an affluent station. Always the incorrigible recalcitrant, Agatha had refused to obey her mother years ago, incessantly complaining about every single decision that did not end in her favor, and often proved rebellious and mean to her tolerant sisters. She also had a propensity for acting crass and uncouth at the worst possible times, often embarrassing the entire family.

"May I get you another drink, Scarlett?" Eryk asked, making certain to avoid staring at her physical attributes. He opened his mouth to say something else but then closed it in fear of ruining the moment by uttering something really stupid or, even more disastrous, weird, to her.

Jillian didn't answer him right away. Instead, using the situation to her advantage to measure the man's inner strength and confidence within himself, she just stared at him with her piercing green eyes and then smiled warmly when she saw a few beads of perspiration break out across his forehead. It was then when she knew Eryk was someone she would be able to easily maneuver into doing anything if she asked. She reached out and laid a perfectly manicured hand on top of his hand.

"Yes, Eryk, I would like that very much," Jillian replied softly, squeezing gently.

"So, what are you drinking?" Eryk asked. "It looks like it might be a margarita."

"That's right," Jillian replied, "but mine is still almost full. I'm not a real connoisseur of potent potables."

Eryk smiled. "Neither am I," he teased playfully, feeling his confidence heighten. "So I guess we'll just have to drink a little faster."

"I guess we will," Jillian said. She then brought the drink up to her mouth and took several deep swallows. She then turned the glass in her hands. "To us."

"Absolutely," Eryk said.

"Now, you wouldn't be trying to get me drunk, would you?" Jillian asked, raising the glass yet again.

"I might be," Eryk replied.

"I must warn you that I can't be held responsible for my actions while under the influence of alcohol," Jillian said. "Inhibitions go right out the window."

"Let's hope so," Eryk said.

"To the future," Jillian said.

"Yes, the future," Eryk reiterated. He then lifted his hand into the air to signal the bartender, who was standing at the opposite end of the bar and shamelessly flirting with a young brunette abusing her liver by consuming far too much alcohol.

Indifferent to the patron's wishes to be assisted, the bartender merely raised a single hand to show his lack of interest, while rudely nodding his head up and down a couple of times, and continued to talk to the giggling girl. In an act of even greater rudeness, he leaned over the bar and whispered a few faint words into the drunk's ears.

She laughed out loud.

Jillian shifted her head to the left and then to the right.

Eryk snapped his fingers. "Excuse me," he said, waving his hand around in the air, "but I'd like to order a ..."

The bartender turned around and glared hatefully at Eryk. "I'll be there in a minute, pal," he barked. "Just wait your turn. You're nothing special." He then turned back around and started to talk to the girl again.

Jillian continued to watch the scenario unfold with increasing curiosity, wondering how far Eryk would go to try and impress her with his ability to dominate another man in some archaic demonstration of misplaced chivalry.

Eryk looked at her with an uncomfortable expression on his face. It was abundantly clear to even the casual observer that he was indecisive as to what he should do.

She neither spoke nor looked away from him.

Eryk rapped his knuckles on the surface of the wood several times. "Hey, can I get some service over here?" he asked.

The bartender looked over his shoulder with a note of irritation. "I said I'd get to you in a minute, pal," he said. "You'll just have to wait your turn."

Angered by the situation and the miscreant creating it, Eryk slammed a fist down on the bar. "I waited a minute—two, in fact," he spat. "Now I said I wanted some service, so get your lazy, worthless ass down here and pour my friend and me a couple of drinks!"

The bartender spun on his heels and stared at the customer with absolute disdain. The girl was no longer in his thoughts, only the man who had just yelled at him. He pulled a towel from off his shoulder and tossed it to the side. "You should be a little more careful about who you try to treat like some sort of bitch, dude," he said. "It's not going to do you one bit of good to try and impress your slut of a girlfriend by running your mouth and getting your ass kicked in front of her." He began to walk toward Eryk. "I've sodomized tougher-looking punks in prison than you."

Eryk shifted his eyes back and forth between Jillian and the bartender. Even though the fear was welling up in him like a volcano about to erupt, a certain amount of excitement was rushing through him that he could not deny. His heart was racing a thousand beats a second. Breath was difficult. And he loved it. The woman he knew as Scarlett only looked at him with the same bland expression. If not for the blinking of her long lashes, it would have been easy to confuse her for one of those mannequins used in the widows of major department stores.

He then straightened and looked the man directly in the eye. "I guess that makes your mother extremely proud," he said, smirking. "Did you do the same thing to her as well? After all, isn't everyone in prison a butt bandit?"

The bartender's features tightened as he clenched his jaw. The sound of grinding teeth could be heard. He stepped up to the bar and pressed his face forward, glowering at the man. "What did you just say to me, punk?" he asked, spittle flying from his mouth.

"You heard me," Eryk replied. "I didn't stutter." He lifted his chin in defiance to show that he was standing by the words and was unafraid.

"Yeah, I guess I did," he said.

Without saying anything further, he drew back his arm and threw a short, wicked punch into Eryk's jaw, sending him tumbling backward on unsteady feet.

Surprised from actually being assaulted by the man, a barely audible yelp escaping from his lips, the pain that rushed through him was white hot. Eryk had never been involved with a physical altercation, so the dizziness that laid claim to his head and threatened to send him into the nether regions of unconsciousness was something he'd never before encountered. He felt a dull throb in the center of his back. In the background, somewhere in the deep recesses of his sense of hearing, the sound of a slight scuffle of feet and a couple brief mewls of some sort could be heard.

And then everything fell eerily quiet.

When Eryk opened his eyes, slowly fluttering several times at first, he groaned aloud. Confused, his vision clouded by a kaleidoscope of colors dancing within his small field of vision, he furrowed his brow the moment he came to realize that he was lying on his back and staring up at ceiling lights, which was curiously puzzling, since he retained no memory of falling down. He attempted to raise his hands to his head but felt something take a firm hold on his wrist.

A tender voice followed.

"Just lie still for a few minutes," Jillian said in a tender, caring voice.

"What happened?" Eryk croaked, grimacing from the pain that came from speaking. He slowly turned his head and smiled when he saw the woman of his dreams next to him and looking down with genuine concern filling her eyes.

"Nothing much," Jillian replied simply. "You sort of got into a fight."

"I've never been in a fight before," Eryk said.

Jillian smiled broadly. "That was rather clear," she said.

"So how did I do?" Eryk asked.

"Not too good," Jillian replied, shrugging her shoulders. She went to stand up when Eryk reached out and grabbed her by the ankle.

"Where are you going?" Eryk asked.

She looked down at him and smiled. "Don't worry, I'm going to call for some help," Jillian replied. "Just stay here for a minute. I'll be right back. You lost consciousness, so we should call a doctor. You might have a concussion."

Eryk nodded in understanding.

Content that the man she had just met would do as instructed, Jillian stood up and walked over to the front door and securely locked it. She then went over to the window, turned the Closed sign around, and shut the Venetian blinds.

"What happened?" Eryk asked. "Did it just get darker in here?"

"Yes," Jillian replied. "I closed the blinds to avoid direct sunlight on your eyes until the doctor checks you out."

"Oh, thank you," Eryk said. "I didn't know the sun could be bad."

Jillian moved over to the stool where she was sitting just moments ago and picked up the bag she had set on the floor. She looped the strap over her shoulder and walked over to where Eryk obediently remained on the floor. "Let's get you up and in the back so we can get some ice on your head until the doctor arrives," she said.

"You already called him?" Eryk asked. He was slowly regaining his senses.

"Of course," Jillian replied.

"When?" Eryk asked, curious.

"Just now," Jillian replied. She then bent down and pulled his arm around her neck. "Now let's get you up on your feet."

Confused even more, Eryk furrowed his brow. "Huh?" he muttered.

"That's what I said," Jillian offered. "Remember, you hit your head pretty hard and passed out."

"I did?" Eryk mumbled, his vision blurring.

"Yep," Jillian said.

Amazed by the level of strength from such a petite woman, Eryk felt himself nearly lifted up to his feet. With nearly the same amount of ease, Jillian helped carry him around the end of the bar and into the back. She then helped him to sit down on a small stool located just to the right of the door that led into a walk-in refrigerator.

He swayed to and fro, his head still swimming from the blow he had sustained, and moaned in response to a dull throb that emanated from behind his eyes. Jillian corrected him and pressed him flush against the wall. Once she was certain that he was relatively stationary, keeping a free hand ready to right him if he started to tilt to either side, she let the bag slip from her arm and fall to the ground.

She quickly unzipped the bag and withdrew a syringe filled with several units of ketamine hydrochloride.

Eryk shook his head. "Hey, where did the bartender and his little tramp go?" he asked.

"Away," Jillian replied.

"What do you mean, away?" Eryk asked, groggily. He blinked his eyes slowly several times and twisted his neck as if stretching it out.

"I mean away," Jillian said. "We didn't need those two interfering with our plans today, don't you agree?"

"What plans?" Eryk asked.

"Why, your wedding, you silly goose," Jillian replied. "You know, you and Agatha tying the knot for all eternity."

"Huh?" Eryk groaned.

"You're getting married today," Jillian chirped happily.

"What in the hell are you talking ..." Eryk began, and then he felt the rest of the words stick in his throat when he saw the woman turn around with a large hypodermic needle held in her hand. He opened his mouth to scream out, his eyes widening in horror, and then abjectly cringed just before she sank the needle into the thick muscle of his trapezius.

"Don't be afraid," Jillian cooed softly. "Trust me, this won't take long. And you will be a much happier and fulfilled man because of it." She smiled brightly. "You are just going to love Agatha." She bobbed her head up and down. "Of course, she can be a handful, but I have faith that you are up to the job." Jillian dropped the empty syringe into the bag.

The effect of the drug was almost instantaneous.

Eryk stared at her with unblinking eyes, wondering what she had injected into him, and felt every muscle in his body go limp. Heart racing and pounding in his chest, tears welling in his eyes, he slowly sagged forward, as if someone had surgically removed his spine without his knowledge, and collapsed onto the floor in a paralyzed heap. He tried to open his mouth in an attempt to speak to her, to beg for his life, for her not to hurt him, but found that he could not utter a single word even though he was conscious and fully aware of his surroundings. And he could still hear the woman talk about his wedding to someone named Agatha.

Jillian bent over and stared down into Eryk's unmoving face, smiling like a giddy schoolgirl. "Would you like to meet your new girlfriend?" she asked, her head dancing about on her neck in jubilation. "The soon to be Mrs. Severson." She placed her right hand against her ear. "Was that a yes?" She then threw a shadow punch of victory into the air. "Good for you, Eryk. You go ahead and take control of your new family. If she's a naughty girl, then I assume you will paddle her little behind." She winked at him. "Hang on, I'll get her, even though the groom shouldn't see the bride on the day of her wedding."

Eryk could hear her digging through something. He tried to turn his head and look out of the corner of his eye to see what she was doing, but to no avail. Whatever she was doing, it was out of his field of vision.

A few seconds later Jillian reappeared. She held Agatha in her hands and was making her dance over Eryk by shaking her pride and joy with zestful enthusiasm. Jillian playfully walked the doll over the palm of her hand, then up her arm and onto her shoulders.

"Isn't she lovely?" Jillian asked. "You're a very lucky man, Mr. Severson. She is as pure as the new-driven snow." She suddenly fell silent and looked at Agatha. "What was that, sweetheart?" She brought Agatha up to her ear, and then she nodded her head approvingly.

She looked down at Eryk.

"She says she's the lucky one, and the two of you are going to be so happy together." Jillian said. Tears began to pool in her eyes. "God, in and through the true church and holy doctrines, has ordained your blessed union with his unconditional love, provided ablution in accordance to the law is executed."

Rendered utterly helpless, Eryk looked up into the beautiful face and eyes of a madwoman, who was clearly far more deranged beyond anything he could have ever dreamed remotely possible. And even though the situation was one of lunacy, there was no doubt in his mind that she genuinely held real affection for him. Her hypnotically piercing catlike eyes called to him, drawing him to her like the mythical Sirens from ancient times had cried out to those unwary mariners who had the misfortune of inadvertently sailing near their island stronghold.

She began to twirl the doll in circles on the palm of her hand like a performing ballerina.

He listened to her proselytize about the irreconcilable schism being created by the false prophets of right-wing fanatics and their unholy brethren sinisterly seated on the left of iniquity's bosom.

And then Jillian suddenly stopped the perversely disturbing pomp.

She pulled Agatha away and playfully hid her behind her back. She did nothing else for several seconds but stare down at him with a strange glint in her eyes. Eryk imagined himself getting up from the unsanitary floor and running as fast and as far away from the insane woman as humanly possible. Instead, with every scintilla of hope for escape now fading to black like so many boyhood aspirations from yesteryear, a chattel of subjugation to serve her most bizarre caprice, all he could do was helplessly lie there on the cold surface of an obscure bar he had never visited before that day, in a town that resembled a pillaged demilitarized zone, and wait for the end.

"Well, I think that's enough entertainment for the groom," Jillian chirped happily, rocking side to side on the balls of her feet. "The rest shall have to wait until the wedding night." She looked at the clock on the wall and clucked her tongue. "Oh, dear, it is getting late, isn't it? And I still have so much to do. I have to get you ready for the big moment and still get Agatha in her gown."

Eryk tried once again to open his mouth to plead for mercy and to be let go, but the muscles in his jaw refused to move, leaving him to continue to lie on his back in a conscious trance.

Jillian stepped back to where she had left the bag. She carefully set Agatha back inside and withdrew a second syringe that was filled with the paralytic drug. Then she looked down when she heard Agatha mumble some sort of incoherent complaint. "What was that, Aggie?" She asked. "I didn't hear you. Sorry."

"Why can't I put on my dress now, Mother?" Agatha asked in a petulant tone. "I want to be beautiful for my new husband."

"I know, sweetheart, but Mommy has a lot to do first," Jillian replied gently. "I have to be a good hostess and inform our guests and help prepare Eryk. You know how men are helpless to do things right. They have no sense of romance and would be completely happy just sitting on the couch in their underwear, drinking that awful-tasting beer all day long and watching stupid sports on the television."

"I know they're hairy beasts, but you never pay any attention to me," Agatha complained. "It's my special day, and I want to be treated with love." Agatha turned her face toward her mother and frowned. "I don't know any of the guests. They're icky, and the girl smells funny. Where are my sisters? They should be here."

Jillian held the hypodermic needle up to the light to check for any sign of air bubbles. She then set it on a nearby table when she was satisfied that all was perfect. "I agree, Aggie, but sometimes one must make do," she said. "We all need to make sacrifices for the good of the whole."

"But I would prefer to marry Brad," Agatha said. "I love him, Mother."

"I thought you said you were a lucky woman to marry Eryk," Jillian said, furrowing her brow. "I thought—"

"I know what I said, Mother, but I would rather marry Bradley," Agatha interrupted. "He's so yummy."

"That's not possible," Jillian said, her voice growing tight. "I cannot permit that to ever happen."

"Why not?" Agatha asked.

"Because I said so, that's why," Jillian shot back.

"But that's not an answer!" Agatha said. "I want to know why."

"It's forbidden," Jillian said. "Now stop acting like a spoiled baby. You will marry Eryk, and that's the end of the conversation, so drop it."

"But I'm in love with Brad," Agatha said, adamant.

"No, you're not," Jillian said. "You can't be. It's not a natural love."

"How do you know?" Agatha asked angrily.

"Because there is no such thing," Jillian replied. "Love with the idea of sex involved is a lie, an abomination of nature, and it is an affront to all that is pure in the eyes of our one true God." Jillian paused as she looked into the disgruntled orbs of her stubborn child, sighing defeatedly. She dreaded the thought of shattering Agatha's innocence of believing in romantic love; however, it would be even worse to send her beloved daughter out into the real world with unrealistic expectations of life shared with a man. "Like most women who erroneously believe they're in love, Aggie, they are only in love with the fictitious concept of being in love. Women are generally romantic fools and dreamers for an ideal that is just not real." She reached down and stroked her daughter's hair.

"Then why marry them?" Agatha asked, tears beginning to well in her eyes. "Why, Mommy, why?"

"Because we need to save them from themselves and their own self-destructive behavior," Jillian replied. "We must help cleanse them for God. We must sacrifice, no matter the pain we must endure."

Agatha nodded her head up and down. "I understand, Mommy," Agatha said, choking back tears. "I'm sorry. I didn't realize how important it was for women to be the rational half of marriage."

"It's all right, baby," Jillian said, smiling weakly.

"Thank you for telling me the truth," Agatha said.

"You're welcome, sweetheart," Jillian said. "I promise that I will never lie or deceive you or any of your sisters. I love all of you very much."

"I love you, too, Mommy," Agatha said softly, closing her eyes.

Jillian picked up the bag and walked down a small corridor that led to two large storage rooms in the back of the bar. A door was located on either side of the hallway. Focused solely on the multiple tasks that were in dire need of her immediate attention, Jillian pushed the door on the left open and walked into the smaller room. She set the bag and needle on a small table located just inside the room, on the right side of the door. She then shook her head with a small mixture of disgust and disappointment. The atmosphere was far from ideal but would have to suffice on such short notice.

The decor in the larger of the two rooms, an enclosed area that looked as if housekeeping had taken a vacation for the past ten years, consisted of several racks that held glass bottles of alcohol. Cases of beer from a number of lesser-known countries were stacked high in two of the corners. In a third corner, on the left, duct taped to a matching pair of swivel chairs with chins resting on their chests, the bartender and drunken harlot, who he had been tirelessly trying to convince to have sex with him in the back in exchange for free drinks, sat in macabre silence. Each throat had been efficiently slit with professional precision. The front of their shirts and pants were thickly stained with blood.

Exhaling her exasperation, Jillian looked over at the two guests and critically shook her head at them.

"And just what do the two of you think you are doing?" Jillian asked. She walked over to where they sat and lifted their heads up so she could see their faces. "I swear, the two of you are unbelievable. If you are not going to help, the least you can do is appear interested in the blessed event. There will be no sleeping on my watch. No siree, you two." She reached up to the nearest wine rack and removed a thick roll of gray tape. She pulled off several long strips and used it to provide the necessary support for their heads. She stepped back and took a long look at her work. "Now, that's a lot better." She clapped her hands together happily, then set to tidying up as much as time would allow because there were still so many other things left to complete.

Silently praying to God to save him from the maniac, a ray of hope beamed through Eryk when he felt the first sign of sensation return to his body. How long he had been lying unconscious on the floor he had no clue. He guessed a few hours, and that the drug was starting to wear off.

Although it was exceedingly difficult, he was finally able to wiggle a finger just a little. His jaw loosened just enough to move it side to side. He was able to generate a small, gasping mewl from his throat. *I'm going to make it,* he thought. *I'm going to live through this hell.* He worked his jaw further, a rush of joy coursing through him when he felt it continue to break free from its drug-induced shackles. He then moved his feet. Just a little more, come on. He closed his eyes to concentrate on moving his legs.

"Now you didn't think I forgot about the groom, did you?" Jillian asked. She held a single hand against her chest as if horrified by just the mere thought. "Good heavens, Eryk, I would never do such an insensitive thing to my soon to be son-in-law." She shook her head. "I had preparations. I'm sure you understand."

When Eryk opened his eyes and found that she was hovering directly over him with a large smile formed across her full lips, he moved his mouth in a feeble attempt to beg for her not to hurt him. Other than an incoherent whisper, nothing helpful came from his lips. The woman produced another syringe filled with liquid and pumped another dose into the same area as the first.

Seconds later his entire body returned to its pharmacological paralysis.

Jillian giggled aloud. "I do hope you don't weigh too much," she said jokingly as she took a firm hold on his ankles, "but it's time to get married. Agatha can be a very impatient girl and doesn't take disappointment very well. So, come along." She turned her back to him and manipulated his legs so she could put his feet under her arms and drag him across the floor with relative ease. She still had a hard time swallowing the fact that her guests were so selfishly lazy.

Having been rendered completely inert and impotent to fight off the woman, Eryk could do nothing but stare up at a ceiling, which had not been washed in years, as he slid across the ground. The florescent tubes provided a desolate ambiance to the already dismal situation, glowing with an eerie luminescence. From the angle by which he involuntarily made his way down the poorly lit corridor, the scene overhead reminded him of one of those old horror movies, where a man believed to be dead while lying on a hospital gurney was being carted toward the morgue for an autopsy.

Grunting from the exertion of dragging a grown man around the end of the bar and down the stretch of hallway that led to the wedding party, Jillian pulled Eryk's cumbersome frame around the corner of the storage room and dragged him over to the far end of the room, where she quickly propped him up against the wall.

"It may not be the Ritz, Eryk, but it will have to suffice for now," Jillian said as she stood up and stretched her arms skyward. "The two of you have the rest of your lives together and shall share far better." She then looked at him and wagged her finger at him teasingly. "You have gained some weight. I'm quite certain Agatha will put an end to all your late-night snacking. She does like a fit man." She looked over at the two guests and winked at them with a hint of mischief.

Eryk stared at her with unmoving eyes.

Several candles had been spread throughout the area and were burning brightly. The scent of jasmine filled the air.

Jillian straightened out the wrinkles of her dress, wriggling her hips as she did so. "Well, I guess we're all prepared for the big moment," she said. She looked down at him with a look of affection. "You're going to be amazed by how beautiful your bride-to-be is when you see her with your own eyes."

Eryk continued to stare at her, utterly helpless to stop the madness unfolding before him.

Jillian turned and walked over to where she had placed the bag. She reached into it, humming melodically to herself, and carefully removed Agatha, who was dressed in an immaculate gown of pure white silk. Jillian held her out at arm's length as if to present her as the newly born queen of the people. "Isn't she breathtaking, Eryk?" She asked, admiring the glitter of diamond dust that had been sprinkled in her hair. "She is one in a million, maybe a billion."

Eryk made a guttural noise from the back of his throat.

Jillian reached back down into the bag with her left hand and removed a small chair that had been specially made for the event. She set the tiny structure down on a small table and sat Agatha comfortably in it, careful so as not to ruin the expertly tailored dress. "Now you wait right there, sweetheart, and don't move," she said as she reached back into the bag and removed three glass jars. "Mommy just has one more thing to do before we can begin."

Eryk remained still, watching her with the same frozen stare that never wavered.

Jillian then removed a large scalpel from the bag. She held it up to the overhead light, twisting the blade into a slow circle, and smiled in appreciation from the way it glittered off the stainless-steel blade. Almost sensually, she glided her finger over the side of the immaculately sharpened blade, while maintaining a watchful eye on Eryk, and smiled cruelly. "I know what you're thinking, Mr. Severson, but this is necessary to purify the matrimonial ceremony," she said in a hushed tone. "And you will be a better husband for it, a better man. Had Adam protected Eve in the garden none of this would have come to pass. Man has been violating women with his pernicious tool of fornication, and I must remove the evil serpent and all other physical attributes that cause lust to be born in your heart and mind so that your vows may be sanctified in the eyes of God."

A deep groan came from deep within Eryk's throat. His eyes turned to ones of glassy terror as he watched her walk toward him with the surgical instrument held tightly in her right hand. *Please, God, help me!* Eryk thought as he mentally struggled to move away from the demented female, who continued to look upon him with deadly intent. He tried to open his mouth to speak, but no audible words slipped from his lips.

Jillian kneeled next to him and lovingly ran her hand over his head. "Please do not be scared, dear," she whispered. "This is the most treasured part of life, one that you will remember for all the days you are together." She leaned over and kissed him on the forehead. "I shall release you from all sin."

Seated in a form of suspended animation, Eryk looked at Jillian from out of the corner of his eye. He tried to cry out in one final attempt to beg for his life but only managed a weak croak of sorts.

Jillian placed the handle of the scalpel between her teeth and kneeled next to him. She looked at him with kind eyes. "Now don't fight me on this, because I don't want it to be any more difficult than necessary," she said, ignoring the muffled mewling sounds coming from the man. She then reached out and placed both of her hands on his mouth, and pried it open with relative ease. "That's a good boy." With a craftsman's skill, lowering her head to peer into Eryk's open orifice, she took the instrument and severed his tongue with one clean sweep of the blade. A thick stream of blood poured from his mouth and ran down his chin like a dark oil spill from the hull of a ruptured super tanker.

Eryk watched in frozen horror as the woman held the bloody

pulp of meat for him to see, dangling it from the tips of her fingers as if it was some sort of treat being held out for a dog, and then discarded it by placing the crimson refuse into one of the jars. It hit the bottom of the glass with a sickly wet sound. The pain that coursed through his mouth was far more excruciating than anything he'd ever experienced. Tears ran down his cheeks.

Jillian wiped the bloodstained blade on the sleeve of his shirt. "That is for the false witness man bears," she said in a monotone tone of voice, "and the evil for which the tongue speaks." She then pushed on the chin to close his mouth. She looked over to where Agatha sat patiently and smiled lovingly at her.

"Finish, Mommy," Agatha urged, bobbing her head up and down. "Make him clean for me."

Offering an appreciative smile in response, silent, Jillian returned the scalpel between her teeth, turned her head back around, and began to unbuckle Eryk's pants.

Eryk, in mute abhorrence, shuddered uncontrollably inside as a voice screamed out in his head. He began to pray when the woman took a firm hold on his genitals with her left hand and pulled on them until they would not stretch any farther.

Stoic, narrowing her eyes as if studying an interesting specimen, her face completely devoid of any emotion, Jillian removed the scalpel from her mouth and severed the organ with one slicing stroke of the hand.

Several heavy streams of crimson pumped into the air like a miniature geyser, spurting over three feet across the floor, and then quickly slowed to a steady flow that pooled on the ground.

Indifferent to the man's suffering, ignoring the faint choking sounds emanating from the back of his throat and the rolling of his eyes, Jillian furrowed her brow and held the trophy high enough for him to see clearly. She passed the wet sack back and forth in her hands as if juggling a deflated ball, and then she dropped the trophy into a second jar. She quickly sealed the top for preservation.

It took only a few seconds before Eryk started to feel the effect of massive blood loss.

Consciousness fading away into the abyss of the afterworld, feeling the strength that once surged though his veins begin to wane, Eryk stared forward with the knowledge that he would soon be dead. The pain that had mercilessly shot through his body had now diminished to little more than a dull throb, as if it too had surrendered to fate. The pounding that had reverberated with a near deafening vengeance in his ears from the life of his own heart, a rhythmic scream crying out in terror, was now barely audible. He felt so tired, so very drained of energy, far more exhausted than he had ever felt before, and all he wanted was to find somewhere to rest his head so he could melt into a deep slumber, away from the dizziness that was quickly claiming his mind. Everything will be better in the morning, Eryk told himself. It has to be.

"Almost done, handsome," Jillian said, her head dancing up and down. "Just one more little pesky chore to be done to complete the purification process of ablution." Without the slightest hesitation, renewing the melodic hum of the Seven Dwarves, which Ferguson had sung to her as a child, she dug the scalpel into each of Eryk's eye sockets and cut the optic nerves with practiced skill. She removed them and plopped both of the deceased man's eyes into the third jar. "Now you're worthy of my daughter." She stood up, pulled him away from the wall to maneuver the body into a prone position, and looked down at her handiwork with total satisfaction.

"Is it time, Mommy? Is it really time?" Agatha asked impatiently. "Am I going to be a big girl now?"

Jillian looked over her shoulder, wiping a single tear from her eye as she realized another one of her children was leaving the nest, and smiled brightly. "Yes, sweetheart, you are about to enter the realm of womanhood," she replied. She then shifted her gaze over to the two guests. "Well, you're part of all this wonderful celebration has come, you silly geese, so stop looking so glum." She walked over and pushed each of the chairs on either side of Eryk's body. She then retrieved the bag and removed a wedding band from a tiny black box. "You, mister bartender, are the best man." She placed the ring in the palm of his hand. She then focused her attention on the girl as she reached back into the bag and withdrew a handful of rose petals. "And you, little miss barfly, though admittedly not my first choice, are the flower girl." She set them on the woman's lap. "I am, of course, the maid of honor." Jillian took several steps back, placed her hands on her hips, and quickly surveyed the room to make certain everything and everyone was in proper place for the ceremony.

"Is everyone ready yet, Mommy?" Agatha asked, hopeful.

Content, tears of joy streaming down her cheeks in large rivulets, Jillian slowly nodded her head. "I believe we are, sweetheart," she replied. "I believe we are all good to go." She sniffed back tears. "Oh, but the time passes so fast."

"Yeah!" Agatha cried out in happiness. "Let's get hitched. Let's get this girl married off to my man."

Jillian smiled proudly when she turned around and found Agatha standing up from the chair and holding her arms out to her mother, her fingers opening and closing in anticipation of the biggest moment of her life. "Although, I understand your excitement, Aggie, please remember that it is not ladylike to appear too anxious," she said, wagging a single finger in the air. "What have I always taught my girls about proper etiquette?"

"That it's proper to look more dignified by feigning aloofness," Agatha replied, slightly pouting. "I'm sorry, Mother."

Jillian walked over to where her daughter waited with her hand lovingly held toward Agatha and tenderly picked her up. "It's okay, baby, I forgive you," she whispered softly. "We all make mistakes, even me."

"Even you, Mommy?" Agatha asked, gasping in total disbelief. "I don't believe you could ever make a boo-boo."

"Yes, sweetheart, even me," Jillian replied, swooning when she felt Agatha wrap her arms around her hands and hug them tightly. Tears began to well anew in her eyes as she taped Agatha to Eryk's chest. She adjusted the doll's arms to give the impression to anyone who might disturb them, man or woman, that any attempt to try and tear the matrimonial bond asunder would fail because the holy embrace signified an eternal union between man and wife that was ordained by the one true God. "Farewell, my beloved daughter, I shall miss and always love you."

Agatha lifted her face from off Eryk's chest, turned her head so she could look at the woman who had given her life, who had protected her from all the evils of the world, and who had provided all that she needed for all the years of her life, for what would be the last time, and offered a perfect smile that only a daughter could ever give a mother. "Thank you, Mother," Agatha said. "Thank you for everything you've done for me, even though I acted horribly to you some days and didn't deserve your love most of the time." She paused. "I love you, Mommy."

Jillian wiped her eyes with the back of her hand. "I know, baby," she croaked. "I love you, too, Aggie, more than you may ever know." She picked up the bag containing a clean set of clothes, sniffing back tears, and headed toward the door so that she could wash away the blood and change in the tiny bathroom of the bar.

"Now you and Eryk go out into that big, crazy world and have the kind of life my father denied me. I want you to be happy and to live free, Agatha." She craned her head around and smiled weakly just before she rounded the corner. "Live for both of us."

When she was finished with washing the blood from her body, having soaked the wig and stained clothes in alcohol before setting them ablaze in the sink, she retrieved the large coat and hat she had asked the bartender to tuck away behind the bar, put them on, and walked out the front door without a care in the world. Her last responsibility as a mother to Agatha had been completed. And her spirits were higher than they had been since the last wedding.

To her great relief, it was still fairly warm and sunny when she stepped out onto the sidewalk. She looked at the position of the sun. It had already started to make its descent in the sky for the day. She looked to the left and then to the right. She knew either Brad or Ferguson would soon begin to search for her if she didn't check in at home or the office soon. In spite of the downtrodden neighborhood, the first signs of the late afternoon rush hour began to raise its busy head, as those who held jobs returned home after work. She pulled the collar of the coat up to her ears and headed over to the nearest bus stop, the exact place where she had gotten off the bus hours earlier.

When Jillian arrived at the wooden bench built alongside the curb she found an elderly woman sitting alone, holding a stack of newspapers on her lap. It was clear the woman, who was dressed in raggedy clothes, was just one of the many homeless in the city who had been summarily ostracized by a society that cared nothing for their famished plight. At first the woman pulled the refuse against her chest when the stranger approached. And then the woman relaxed when she saw the person draped in a heavy coat was another woman.

Jillian smiled brightly and held her hands out to show she was harmless.

The woman reciprocated in kind. She tried to get a better look at the stranger, but her hat was pulled down so far on her head that it shadowed most of what must have been a lovely face.

"May I have a seat?" Jillian asked politely, pulling the collar higher up when she noticed the woman studying her a little too closely for comfort.

"Why, yes, of course," the woman replied in a friendly tone of voice. "You can sit right next to me." She scooted over to allow more room for the stranger to take a seat on the bench.

"Thank you," Jillian said. "I really appreciate it."

She took a seat.

"Excuse me, miss, not to be rude or anything, but do I know you?" The woman asked, eyeing her curiously. "You seem so familiar, like we've met before, maybe seen you before."

Jillian shook her head, pursing her lips. She thought about getting up and walking away, but decided that such an action would only draw more attention to herself. "No, I don't think so," she replied calmly. "I'm fairly new to the area and don't know many people."

"So where are you from?" the woman asked.

"Everywhere … somewhere … nowhere," Jillian replied in a stammer, feigning a defeatist demeanor.

"Yeah, me too," the woman agreed, shrugging her arthritic shoulders. "I have no place, either." She held out a tattered gloved hand. "I'm Maude, Maude Clemens. All my friends call me Ma."

Jillian accepted the hand and shook it. "I'm Scarlet Burkett," she said. "It's nice to meet you, Ma."

The bus suddenly appeared from around the corner and stopped in front of the bench, followed by a loud swishing sound of the brakes. The driver opened the door and waved for the two women to hurry up and get on.

"I think your ride is here," Maude said. "How sad; we were just getting to know each other."

"I think you're right," Jillian said. She stood up and smiled at the woman. "Once again, Ma, it's a pleasure to have met you." She then stepped onto the bus and disappeared behind the door, which quickly closed behind her.

Still unconvinced that she had not met the woman before, Maude stared after the bus as it rolled down the street, searching her memory for the answer as to the identity of the woman who was so familiar to her. Baffled by her inability to recall the woman's face, angry with herself for getting so old and mentally withered, Maude flipped the newspapers over and began to read the front page.

The headline read that the powerful law firm of Hanson & Hanson had just promoted Attorney Heather Lasko to the unprecedented position of junior partner. A picture of two women with their arms draped over one another, smiling into the cameras, was plastered directly below the bold letters. Maude lifted her face back up and looked at the corner the bus had just rounded and whistled aloud. *I knew I knew her,* Maude thought, pleased to know that her mind was not entirely gone.

Chapter 12

C ompletely alone and obsessively committed to avenging the senseless murder of Harriot, the girl he'd loved with every ounce of his being, particularly since all of his friends were now either missing or dead, Petie knew it would take money to set things somewhat right. So he decided to stop by the bank shortly after he'd left the lieutenant in the alleyway and withdraw every cent he had saved for the past six years, effectively closing it. He stuffed every bill into a brown paper sack.

When the teller asked him if he was certain that he wanted to end his business with the bank, all Petie did was nod his head and sign the slip of paper she had pushed across the counter. He knew the police would do very little to investigate the murder of a girl from the wrong side of town, contrary to what the lieutenant had told him in the back of the ambulance, because no one cared about people like them. The only justice any of them would ever get was the kind they took by force.

At most, the news of Harriot's murder would be listed at the bottom of page thirty in the newspaper and would be little more than a blip over the television right before the station went to a commercial break. She would be considered just another statistic in a long line of those better left forgotten in an obscure cold file. When weighed against the more prominent and popular news, such as the divorce of a well-known movie star or rock legend, the death of a single street urchin who worked behind a desk in a hotel just didn't rate at all. She meant nothing in life, so it stood to reason that she was even less significant to the icy indifference of a society that was concerned with only instant gratification and the next floating rumor of someone deemed to be important enough to have a show on television each week.

Tossing the brown paper bag full of cash on the passenger's seat, Petie looked at his reflection in the rearview mirror. *Well, I care, damn it!* Petie thought. *And I don't give a crap about what anybody thinks, even that lying cop. I'm gonna make things right, Harriot, and get the bastards who killed you. I swear it!* He opened his wallet and looked at the only picture he had of her. Unbearable pain. He then pulled out a single piece of paper Jeb had given to him over a year ago.

Written down on it was the name and address of a man who could provide just about anything if the price was right. Petie had forgotten all about it, until it dawned on him that not only was he alone, but didn't personally know any real criminals. Jeb had always been the one to score the party favors for the group and stolen goods for a far cheaper price than the stores could ever offer. Before handing the slip of paper over to him, Jeb had warned Petie that the man and his gang were extremely dangerous and should be contacted only if it was a real emergency. Although he had initially shook his head, assuring Jeb that nothing could ever happen that would cause him to go so far as to even think about enlisting the help of a gang of violent criminals, eventually he succumbed to the bland expression and penetrating eyes that quietly accused him of being a big sissy and reluctantly accepted the folded-up note. Feeling a little uncomfortable with carrying the information of a known gangster, Petie looked around in paranoia and surreptitiously tucked it safely away in his wallet.

He slid the picture of Harriot back into the plastic sheath for safekeeping and lifted his gaze back up to the mirror. He was grateful that Jeb wasn't around to tease him about being right. Petie just wished he would have had better luck in finding Billy. There was no doubt he could certainly use Billy's assistance in devising a good plan.

Petie took one more look at the piece of paper before putting it back into his wallet. Even though he wasn't familiar with the actual street, he was well aware of the part of town where the notorious Matt Fleming, also known as Bloodstone, lived and ruled with a murderous fist. It was a part of town that only those outsiders who were partial to a violent carjacking and forced sodomy dared to go. It was heavily rumored that most people never returned. Even the local police avoided the area like the plague, openly admitting that law and order weren't part of the program in "Honeysuckle Heights." *Well, a man's gotta do what a man's gotta do,* Petie thought as he drove out of the parking lot of the bank and steered the car in the direction most people with even a glimmer of brain power and common sense stayed away from.

Almost to the minute when Petie turned off the freeway and entered the sixteen-block neighborhood often referred to as the "Funeral Parlor" the atmosphere immediately changed from the warmth of everyday busy life to a chilly morgue-like one that would appeal only to the most mangled, graveyard dead cadavers that didn't have enough sense to stay in the ground. Wrinkling his nose and tasting the faint flavor of bile at the back of his throat, there was a palpable stench in the air that reminded him of fifth-grade science class, when the students were forced by the faculty to dissect pinned-down frogs and then callously place each of their green, eviscerated bodies in a glass beaker of clear solution.

People dressed in torn and long-faded clothes sat on the dilapidated porches of tiny structures covered in graffiti by an artist long dead from a drive-by shooting years earlier for deliberately tagging the wrong street with gang signs. Like those too afraid to venture outside and who stared out of the cracked windows from inside each rotting hovel, the sentinels who were either suicidal or insanely brave enough to sit outdoors with guns resting on their laps watched the foreigner with eyes that sparkled with about as much life as those of a raggedy doll. No one had a clue as to what business the stranger might have in their neck of the woods, not that any of them actually cared, but all were relatively certain that he would not be returning from where he was driving toward. It was only on a rare occasion when anyone who was stupid enough to enter what those who lived in the vicinity called the "Forbidden Zone" of the neighborhood was ever seen again. The local scuttlebutt was that several undercover officers had disappeared in the zone a few months ago, including their cars and everything inside of them. Most likely the driver would disappear, and parts of the car would magically show up and be summarily sold at the next swap meet by one of Bloodstone's band of murderous cohorts. Such was the circle of life in the lawless region of Honeysuckle Heights.

It wasn't until Petie began to slow the car as he approached a stop sign, which sat atop a steel post that was embedded in a concrete tire and rested in the middle of the street, that he saw the first signs of actual life walking toward him along the sidewalk on either side of the car. He brought the car to a complete stop and swallowed with difficulty when two more men suddenly appeared in front of him, each carrying a large gun in their hands, and looked at him with the dead eyes of zombies. When Petie craned his head around to search for any avenue of escape, five more heavily armed men appeared directly behind him. He then looked to his left, then right.

Trapped!

Fifteen more stepped into view.

The people who had been sitting on the porches only moments ago silently stood up and walked into their ramshackle homes. Those who were staring out of the broken windows moved back into the shadows of their desolate lives and pulled the sheets that hung like curtains closed to what was sure to happen to the unlucky outsider, who had probably just made an unfortunate turn onto a wrong street. It wouldn't be the first time a traveler paid handsomely for such an error in navigational judgment.

Nervous from the unexpected siege on his car, Petie licked his lips. He weighed every option at his disposal. Nothing of magnitude came to mind. He thought about just dropping the clutch and racing off to flee for his life, but quickly dismissed the idea for fear of being gunned down by the arsenal being carried by the men who were closing in on his position. None of them looked as if they would hesitate to open fire on him.

Instead, remembering the advice Jeb had given to him when he passed the piece of paper over, Petie stood his ground and waited in the middle of the street for the man on his left to step up to the side of the car. He put on a face of courage and confidence, for which he definitely did not feel.

When the man was no more than a foot away from the window he placed his hands on the door and leaned over. The man's knife-scarred face was close enough for Petie to get a good whiff of his rancid breath. "Are you lost or what, homeboy?" he asked in a husky voice that had been assaulted by far too many cigarettes.

The other men now completely surrounded the automobile and were standing no more than five feet away in all directions. All held guns trained on the driver of the car.

"No," Petie said, shaking his head. "At least, not exactly."

The man smiled malevolently. "What does that mean?" he asked. "You mean that you meant to invade our territory, is that what you're saying to me?" He rested the weapon on top of the door and eyed Petie with a hint of curiosity.

"Yeah, I guess I did," Petie replied.

"Now why would anyone be stupid enough to do some dumb shit like that?" he asked. He looked over at a man who was standing near the opposite door. "Did you hear the stupid shit this guy just said to me, Jackal?"

Jackal shook his head, smiling crookedly. "Yeah, I heard him, Crank," he replied, chuckling under his breath.

Crank shifted his sleepy gaze back on Petie. "Didn't anyone ever tell you that no one is allowed in the zone?" he asked. "I thought it was common knowledge on the streets."

"No," Petie replied, somewhat under his breath, shaking his head. "Not exactly. I've just heard a few rumors. I'm not from around here."

The man smiled viciously and then sucked back on his lower lip. "What does that mean, homey?" he asked, slowly opening and closing his eyes as if bored with the conversation.

"Nothing," Petie replied. "Just that I've heard a few things here and there."

"Maybe we should just cut off his friggin' head and stick it on the back of my bike, Crank," Jackal said. "Now that would be sweet."

"We could do that, all right," Crank said. He then looked back at Petie. "What do you think about that idea?"

Petie shook his head. "No, thank you," he replied. "I kind of like my head right where it is, on my scrawny-ass neck."

Crank broke out in a morbid type of laughter that made Petie's skin crawl, because it had an unnatural sound to it, like he laughed only when he was either torturing or killing another human being. Petie did everything he could not to show the level of revulsion that tugged at him. He was beginning to think he'd made the biggest mistake of his life by coming to a place where he had little chance of leaving alive.

The other armed men broke out in a similar kind of laughter.

"So, does this mean we're not going to cut his foolish head off?" Jackal asked. The disappointment crossing his face was unmistakable. He lowered his weapon.

"Yeah, at least for now," Crank replied.

"Then can we gang rape him?" Jackal asked, lifting the gun and pointing directly at Petie's head. "He looks kind of juicy. After all, there's no greater joy than a fat butt boy."

Petie noticeably cringed back in the seat from just the mere thought of being raped by a group of men, shuddering. Jeb had never mentioned anything about forced homosexual rape.

Crank raised his eyes and shook his head in disapproval. "No!" Crank replied evenly. "Man, dude, you really need to get a girlfriend. I'm really getting tired of all your idiotic sex talk about screwing butts and such. It just ain't right." He looked over at the other men, who were standing nearby. "What do you guys think? Are you getting as sick of hearing all the weird stuff coming out of his mouth?"

All of them shook their heads.

Hog shifted his eyes and looked at Jackal. "He's right, dude," he said. "At first it was kinda funny, but now we're starting to wonder about you."

Jackal lowered the weapon in his hand and glared at Hog. "You know what, screw you guys," he mumbled. "I'm just kidding." He then walked off, leaving the others behind to laugh at his humiliation.

"Well, that was fun," Crank said humorlessly. "So, what are you doing here, dude? And what do you want?"

Petie pulled out the piece of paper and held it up for Crank to see. "Jeb said you guys had certain connections to get things I need," he said. "See? He said I should get in touch with some guy called Bloodstone."

Crank snatched the piece of paper out of his hand and quickly read it. "You mean Cartwright?" he asked suspiciously.

"Yeah, Jeb Cartwright," Petie replied.

Crank narrowed his eyes. "So, how do you know the Jebster?" he asked.

"We're friends," Petie replied.

"I asked how you knew him, not that you were friends," Crank said, his tone dead serious.

"Oh, sorry," Petie said. "We work together at the hotel."

Crank prided himself on his ability to measure a man's honesty. He methodically studied the stranger's face for any sign of deceit, knowing that he would simply kill the man where he sat if he recognized anything resembling a lie. After several seconds, clucking his tongue as was his habit when trying to read the veracity of another man's words, he decided the man was telling the truth, even after the man moved uncomfortably beneath his penetrating stare.

"Is something wrong?" Petie asked nervously.

Crank smiled in a friendly type of manner that only made his features appear even creepier. "Naw," he replied, lifting the gun from off the door. "I'm just making sure I didn't hafta shoot you in the head." He placed the index finger of his free hand to the side of his head and cocked his thumb. He then motioned to the other men still standing around that all was clear and that they could leave.

One by one, with the similar stealth they had used to appear in open view, each of the men slowly mobilized and faded back into the background, disappearing the same way they had come. No one said a single word.

Fascinated by the control the man obviously wielded over the group, Petie watched in a strange sort of awe, grateful that the gang of thugs was gone.

"Contrary to popular belief among the guys, I really don't care for shooting people all that much," Crank said. "It gets kind of messy, a real pain to clean up."

Petie chuckled uneasily when he saw no hint of kidding emanating from the man.

"So, what's your name, homeboy?" Crank asked.

"Pete," he replied. "Everyone calls me Petie."

Crank slid a hand through the open window in an unexpected form of introduction. "Everyone calls me Crank, short for Crankshaft," he said, shaking the other man's hand. "So, what can we do for you?"

"I need to buy a gun," Petie said, "and information on some guys." He picked up the paper bag that contained his life savings and opened it wide enough for Crank to get a clear view of the cash. "I have money and can pay what you want."

"Is that right?" Crank asked, eyeing the man. He had difficulty believing anyone could be so naive as to show someone such as himself a bag of money before checking on the merchandise meant to be purchased. He shook his head. "Put that away." He studied the man. "No offense, but you don't seem to be the kind of guy to carry one."

"Why do you say that?" Petie asked, furrowing his brow.

"You kind of seem like a video game sort of dude, not a gangster," Crank said. "Playing *Grand Theft Auto* isn't real. You know that, right?"

"Yeah, and I still need a gun," Petie said firmly.

"All right, homeboy," Crank said, shrugging. "What kind of gun do you have in mind, and how much do you have?"

"What do you mean by kind?" Petie asked.

Crank smiled. "Man, you really are new at this, aren't you?" he half teased. "What brand and caliber?"

"What would you say is best?" Petie asked.

Crank rubbed his forehead, quickly growing impatient with the whole conversation. "That depends on what you want one for," he said. "There are all sorts of reasons why someone might want a gun, but usually it's to shoot someone."

"Okay, let's say it's to shoot someone, maybe even a bunch of someones," Petie said. "What would you say then?"

"I'd say that's your business," Crank replied.

"And don't forget, I need some information," Petie said. "I can pay." He put the paper bag of money on his lap.

"Information about what?" Crank asked, and then he realized the question would elicit a series of answers he would prefer not to hear. Annoyed and tired, he threw his hands up into the air in frustration. "Never mind." He reached for the handle and opened the car door. "You know what, this is getting a lot more complicated than it's supposed to be. You should talk to Bloodstone about all this stuff. I don't feel comfortable about giving you a gun to go on a killing spree." He moved to the side. "Come on, I'll take you to him." He paused. "And bring your money."

Although still a little apprehensive, keeping a watchful eye out for the guy everyone called Jackal, Petie grabbed the bag and stepped out of the car. Crank was already walking away and down the street at a fairly quick pace in the same direction he had come, demonstrating no concern as to whether the visitor was going to follow him or not. He was humming to himself, a strange behavior that seemed incongruent to the man's predatory personality. The whole situation and change of ambiance was surreal.

Petie looked around the street and noticed that people were starting to come out of their homes and retake their positions on the porch chairs. Those who remained indoors pressed their faces against the glass of the cracked windows.

Evidently all had returned to normal in the life of Honeysuckle Heights.

When Petie rounded the corner at the end of the block, he found Crank standing just outside a pair of storm doors that led to a cellar hidden below a large house, which would have been incredibly impressive in its day, long before the neighborhood had been abandoned by the once affluent population well over fifty years earlier.

All that was now left of a once prominent town were the crumbling edifices that were little more than a skeletal memory. And the tiny shanties that had been erected after the economic collapse in a feeble attempt to hide the shameful past failures of greed and oppression only added to the demilitarized appearance.

Surprised to find the man waiting with his arms crossed over his chest, the gun dangling dangerously from the tips of his fingers, Petie clutched the bag against his body. He wondered if he was about to be shot, robbed, and tossed down the man-made hole of wood and concrete. He took two steps back.

Crank rolled his eyes, "Relax, Petie," he said soothingly. "Trust me, if I was going to steal your money, I wouldn't have walked all the way over here to do it. I would've killed your ass and taken it back at the car."

Petie licked his lips, hoping he didn't insult the man. "I didn't mean to act like ..." Petie began, but the words trailed off.

Crank waved him off and opened the heavy doors. "Don't worry about it," he said. "I have a pretty thick skin."

Several of the men who had been at the car walked around from behind a half-burned-out house from across the street and took seats on a small collection of chairs that were scattered about the front of the dirt-covered yard.

"What are they doing?" Petie asked, pointing in the direction where the half dozen men sat like stone gargoyles.

"Security," Crank replied, tapping his hand on one of the wooden doors. "Ignore them. They're just doing what Matt instructs them to do."

Petie furrowed his brow. "Don't you mean Bloodstone?" he asked.

"Same difference," Crank said, shrugging his shoulders. "We grew up together, so he's always been Matt to me."

"And what if they don't do what he says?" Petie asked, looking in Crank's direction.

"He'll kill them," Crank replied simply. "A lot of what he'd do would depend on his mood at the time."

"That's insane," Petie said.

"Maybe," Crank said, shrugging his shoulders. "It's not my call." He paused. "Well, enough chatter. If you still want that gun and the other stuff, you better come on down before I change my mind." Without saying anything further, he walked down the steps that led beneath the house.

Undecided, still harboring a tinge of trepidation over possibly walking into a den of lethal vipers that were hiding in the shadows ready to strike their innocent prey down, Petie remained aboveground for several seconds. He listened to the faint sound of shoes scraping across the concrete steps until they faded away. He then thought of Harriot and what the animals had done to her. The image of what he saw in the alleyway and the once-life-filled eyes that were now vacant and milky burned into his consciousness with the fiery heat of hell itself, haunting him as if he were still standing over her, crying from the loss of such a wonderful girl. He looked back across the street, where the soldiers of a man he had never met sat unmoving. *In for a penny, in for a pound,* he thought. He stepped through the doors, tossing all fear of the unknown aside, uncertain as to whether he would ever see the beauty of the sky again.

Crank was waiting at the bottom of the steps when Petie arrived at the bottom.

To Petie's surprise, the cellar was much larger than he would have ever believed. It was at least the size of an Olympic-size swimming pool and was illuminated by dozens of lamps, overhead lights, and other assorted electrical equipment. The entire area of the expansive room was beautifully furnished with contemporary, high-quality furniture of every make and design. An enormous plasma television was situated at the far end of the room. Different stereo systems and speakers were spread out along walls that were covered in abstract art. Two dangerous-looking men that wore shoulder holsters sat in front of a wide-screen, mindlessly watching a program Petie didn't recognize. Four women dressed in the shortest skirts he had ever seen in his life, each holding a drink that was no doubt alcohol, stood off to the side and giddily talked about something indecipherable. Sitting in the far left corner behind a desk, apparently oblivious to the presence of everyone downstairs, a man who looked to be the size of a grizzly bear was busy scribbling something down on a stack of papers. He didn't bother to look up when Crank and Petie showed up unannounced.

Petie craned his head around and peered up the stairway, wondering if it was too late to change his mind and leave. Whatever he was expecting to find, none of what he saw was part of it.

Crank leaned over and nudged Petie on the shoulder. "You might want to stay here while I go talk to Matt," he said. "He gets a little grouchy when someone bugs him when he's doing his taxes. I think it's the math that pisses him off."

Petie opened his eyes wide in shock. "He pays taxes?" he asked, astonished that a known criminal would actually bother to file.

"Well, duh," Crank replied. "We all pay them. The last thing we want is for the IRS to do an audit. They're a bunch of greedy Nazis who want to get paid. We have stocks and bonds, and own quite a bit of property. You have heard of property taxes, haven't you? If you make sure they get their cut, they leave you alone." He smiled crookedly. "We have two basic rules. Don't screw with the IRS or the mailman."

"I take it that killing people isn't a rule of what not to do because it's a bad thing," Petie said with a hint of sarcasm.

Crank laughed under his breath. "Not so far," he said, amused by the other man's obvious distaste for their logic. "Matt says killing is an honest business because there's no deceit. You get the guy who wronged you and kill him. No fuss, no muss. It's a straightforward act that most who get it did something to deserve it."

"That's a hellaya credo, don't you think?" Petie asked, grimacing slightly.

"I guess it depends on how you look at it," Crank replied. "For our line of work, it's functional. Anyway, you stay here, so I can clear you."

Petie held up his hands in innocence. "I'm not going anywhere," he said. "You go do your thing and I'll try not to get myself dead while I wait."

Crank slapped him on the back. "See, that's the spirit," he joked. "You keep that positive attitude." He then walked over to where Bloodstone was hunched over the desk with a firm look of concentration covering his face as he continued to read through each separate document that made up the stack.

The young women, who were happily chatting only moments ago, suddenly grew somberly quiet and looked at the stranger with a peculiar sense of morbid curiosity. It was unusual for anyone outside the immediate family to be brought down into their home, especially by Crankshaft.

Petie did everything he could to avoid their questioning stares, not wanting to inadvertently create a situation that might get him shot, and maintained a constant vigil on his escort as he approached the huge man's desk.

Crank stood in front of the desk only a couple of seconds before the man known as Bloodstone stopped his busy writing and looked up from the stack of papers. He said something that Petie was too far away to overhear, and then he looked over to where Petie stood nervously biting down on his lower lip with the paper bag held tightly in his hands. Crank turned his head around, nodded, and then waved for him to come over.

The two men who were mindlessly watching the television a few minutes ago were now kneeling on the couch and watching the stranger with clouded expressions.

The women remained dead quiet, barely moving.

Increasing Petie's anxiety, the sound of footsteps suddenly echoed from above the stairway, getting louder as they grew closer. And then there was an armed man standing not more than a few feet away. He looked at Petie and offered a chilling smile. Petie was almost certain that he was only seconds away from being murdered by a gang of maniacs. He looked over and sighed in relief when he saw Crank was still motioning for him to come on over. Preferring to distance himself from the man who continued to smile at him for no apparent reason, he did as requested by the only man who might not want to slit his throat, and walked over to where the two men remained waiting for him.

"Petie, this is Bloodstone," Crank announced. "He's the one who can help you with your little problem. I explained what I know about what you want, so the rest is up to you."

Petie held out a single hand of introduction. "Hello, I'm Petie," he said in a friendly voice, then quickly withdrew the offered hand when the monster of a man merely looked at it emotionless.

"No offense, kid, but I don't shake hands," Bloodstone said in a voice that was completely incongruent to what one would expect from such a giant. "You know, disease and all. The last thing I want is to be taken out by something I can't see."

"I guess that makes sense," Petie responded uncomfortably. "I can't say that I've really given it much thought at all."

"Yeah, well, you should," Bloodstone said in a serious tone of voice. "Hell, even though you look clean enough, I have no idea as to where your dick beaters have been. So, why in the world would I want them touching any part of my body?"

Petie grimaced from the insinuation that his hands were little more than tools for compulsive masturbation and looked down at them with utter distaste, wondering how many men's hands he had shaken over the years that had just finished the self-gratifying deed on themselves. Crank did the same and then conspicuously wiped the palms of his hands over the front of his pants. Deeply amused for the first time in weeks, chuckling under his breath, Bloodstone smiled at the two men and leaned back in the chair. It squeaked in protest to the amount of weight.

Still a little freaked out over the possibility of coming directly in contact with some sort of malignant disease, Crank continued to stare at his hands for several silent seconds after wiping them off. He would've sworn on a stack of Bibles that he could actually see minuscule creatures scurrying across the skin, spreading their plague as they nibbled at will. The purpose for the visit to the main house had escaped him until Petie nudged him in the side to get his attention.

"Are you going to tell him or what?" Petie asked impatiently. He looked down at his watch to check the time. It was getting late.

"Relax, killer, I'm getting to it," Crank replied, rolling his eyes in annoyance. He then turned his focus on Bloodstone. "Dude wants a gun, Matt."

Bloodstone cocked a single eyebrow and looked appraisingly at the youthful stranger. "Him?" he asked astonishingly, pointing a freakishly large finger at Petie. "You've got to be kidding. He looks like he should be in school or something, not running around with a damn gun."

Crank snickered.

"What's so damn funny, Darren?" Bloodstone asked, irritated enough to use his best friend's birth name.

Crank waved the question off as innocent. "Nothing," he replied. "It's just that I thought the same thing when he first asked me. I actually thought he might be some sort of new, geeky, undercover cop."

Both men chuckled.

"Hey," Petie interrupted, offended by the blatant implication. He stepped forward two paces. "Can you not talk about me as if I wasn't standing right here? Everyone does that to me, and I hate it."

Crank placed a reassuring hand on the man's shoulder to calm him down before he did or said something stupid. "Easy, tough guy," he said, squeezing. He was tired. The last thing he wanted to do on such a pleasant day was to go back out to the foul-smelling city dump and dig another hole for a guy who angered the most dangerous man he'd ever known. "We're just funnin' around, that's all."

Bloodstone nodded approvingly at the smaller man's unexpected moxie, though his facial features showed absolutely no emotion whatsoever. One of the things about a man he admired most was courage, genuine bravery, not the type that was often confused for cowardice. In his opinion, real courage came from when a man would enter into a fight even though he was afraid and knew he would take a severe beating, maybe even die at the hands of the opponent. It took nothing to fight when the outcome was deemed as a foregone conclusion. Such was the epitome of a coward.

"You've got guts, kid, I'll give you that," Bloodstone said evenly. "I truly admire that quality in people." He paused and shifted his bodyweight in the chair. He then placed two catcher-glove-size hands on his massive chest and steepled eight fingers. "However, and let me be very clear on this aspect, Petie. If you ever get mouthy with me again, I promise"—he held a single hand up—"I swear that I'll cut out your tongue and throw it into a blender to drink when I make my next protein shake." Bloodstone offered a wicked grin that held no humor, denoting that he was dead serious about doing exactly as stated.

Petie stared at the man, horrified.

"Do you know how I came to be called Bloodstone?" he asked.

Petie shook his head.

"My favorite choice of makeshift weapon is to put large stones in a sock and beat people to death," Bloodstone said in a cold voice. "I like to watch and hear how bones break."

Petie swallowed hard.

"Do I make myself clear, young man?" Bloodstone asked. "You seem like a decent enough guy, and I would prefer not to kill you."

Petie nodded his head up and down numbly. "Yesss, I understand," Petie replied obediently.

"Excellent," Bloodstone said. "So now that we understand one another, what do you want the gun for?"

Petie wrinkled his brow. "Does it matter?" Petie asked.

Bloodstone smiled crookedly. "It might," he replied. "After all, you might want to shoot me, maybe even my good friend here." He leaned forward. "You seem like a fairly smart kid, so I'm sure you can see the potential for a conflict of interest in providing a weapon to someone who intends harm to me or one of my people."

"Why would I want to do that?" Petie asked, confused. "I don't know any of you."

"Maybe you're a sleeper sent here to kill me," Bloodstone said. "Stranger things have happened, right?"

"But that's just ..." Petie began, letting the words trail off.

"What, crazy?" Bloodstone finished. "Hey, people do crazy things all the time." He paused for effect. "I'm just saying, how can I know?"

"I swear that my beef is not with any of you," Petie said. "I only found out who you were because Jeb gave me your name and number a while back. He said you had a way of getting things regular people can't."

"And that would be Jeb Cartwright?" Bloodstone asked, lifting a curious eyebrow. "Is that right?"

"Yeah, Jeb," Petie replied.

Bloodstone shifted his eyes over to Crank. "Is this what you were telling me about?" he asked.

"Yeah, Matt," Crank replied simply. "It's why I decided to bring him over to you." He handed the note over to the giant. "I checked the writing before I brought him. There's no doubt that it's the Jebster's."

Bloodstone quickly perused the familiar scribbling and ran an open hand over his lantern jaw. "I see," he said, tossing the piece of paper on the desk. "J. C. must really like and trust you, kid, because he damn well knows that I'd cut out his liver and eat it if he sent someone to me who was less than acceptable." He studied the visitor with newfound curiosity.

"So you know Jeb?" Petie asked.

Crank laughed out loud.

"Of course, dummy," Bloodstone replied, smiling. "We all know the little pain in the ass. We've known him for what seems like forever."

"If you don't mind me asking, how do you know him?" Petie asked.

"He never told you anything about me?" Bloodstone asked, a

hint of surprise filling his voice. "Never opened that idiotic mouth of his to brag?"

"No, not a word," Petie replied. "I just got the paper; that's it."

Bloodstone and Crank exchanged entertained glances. Jeb never ceased to amaze them.

"He's my little brother," Bloodstone replied. "My screwy little brother who seems to get into constant trouble because he lacks any semblance of common sense or self-control, which is why I let him sit in jail overnight. I thought he could use some time to think about the stupid crap he's been up to. He thinks he's slick, but I know exactly what he'd been doing." He looked at the clock on the wall.

"Jeb's in jail?" Petie asked, shocked.

"Yeah, he got busted for some dope with some nasty skank," Bloodstone replied, shaking his head in disappointment. "I don't know why the little idiot can't stop using that garbage. I swear to God that our mother killed our father and then herself just so neither one of them had to deal with his nonsense anymore." He rolled his eyes. "Damn it, but I envy them because he's a complete pain in the ass who doesn't learn a damn thing, no matter how many times I try to knock it into him." He cocked a thumb at Crank. "Darren thinks his brain is fried from taking too much of that crap."

Crank nodded.

"Aren't you going to get him out?" Petie asked, perplexed that he would not have bailed his own brother out of jail the very minute he learned of the arrest. "He could get hurt in there by one of those violent guys."

"Yeah, I'll get his sorry ass out, but not until after we're finished here," Bloodstone said. He leaned back, exhaled, and folded his fingers behind his head. "So, what kind of gun do you want, and what do you want it for?"

"Something big and fast enough to kill a bunch of gang members," Petie replied matter-of-fact. "I want to make sure it is powerful enough to kill with one shot."

Bloodstone cocked a single eyebrow and looked at Crank with a peculiar expression. The vehemence in which the younger man spoke had caught him by surprise. He had seen the desire to murder in many men's eyes, especially his own, and knew exactly what it looked like. It was that which gleamed in the man's eyes who stood not more than a few feet away, clutching a paper bag in his hands. "Is he for real, Darren?" Bloodstone asked, untangling his fingers and moving forward in the chair.

Crank moved his eyes to Petie, measured him carefully, and then turned back to his longtime friend. "Yeah, I think he's dead serious, brother," he said. "He has the glint in his eye."

Petie took a step forward and set the paper bag filled with money on the top of the desk. "It's all I have in the world," he said. "And it's all yours if you just give me what I need to set things right."

Bloodstone tilted the bag upside down and spilled several large stacks of cash that were bundled together by rubber bands. He whistled softly. "I think you're a little out of touch with what things cost, kid," he said. "There's at least five thousand dollars here, way more than you need for a gun. Don't get me wrong, I have no problem with keeping your money, but I'm a businessman, not a rip-off artist. I deal with people fairly."

Petie shook his head. "I don't care about the money, not anymore," Petie said. "I just want to make things right for her, and I can't do it without your help."

Bloodstone stuffed the money back in the bag and folded the top over. When he looked up there was a shock of surprise on his face because tears were forming in Petie's eyes. In spite of the streak of cruelty that ran down to his core, Bloodstone had a difficult time dealing with anyone who cried. He didn't understand the reason behind the alien reaction. But tears had a tendency to fluster him. He looked over to Crank for some sort of help, but all Crank could muster was a baffled shrug of his shoulders in answer because he was equally mystified.

"Will you please help me," Petie pleaded. "I have nowhere else to go to get what I need so she can rest in peace."

Although Bloodstone knew better than to get personally involved on any emotional level with the purpose of another's motive to purchase anything from him, there was a certain credibility in the man that went far beyond just wanting a gun to shoot someone. He could not deny the curiosity that accompanied the need to know exactly what it entailed. "Who is she?" he asked softly.

"Huh?" Petie mumbled, blinking back tears.

"Who's the girl?" Bloodstone asked in an almost hushed tone of voice.

Petie wiped at his eyes. "Will you sell me a gun?" he asked.

Bloodstone nodded. "Whatever you need," he said.

"She was going to be my girl," Petie replied. "She was so perfect, almost too perfect. I loved Harriot like no other, and those animals killed her."

"Did this just happen?" Bloodstone asked, placing his elbows on the desk. He leaned farther forward.

Petie nodded his head silently.

Bloodstone shifted his eyes and offered Crank a knowing look, then brought them back to Petie. "Was it the young girl in the alley?" he asked sympathetically.

"Yes, that's her," Petie replied.

Bloodstone was lost for words. Neither he nor Crank knew what to say to a man who had lost the girl he loved. "I'm sorry, kid," he said softly. "That was a terrible thing to happen for such a young girl."

"Yeah … it ain't right," Petie muttered. "The cops said they'll get the guys who did it, but I know they won't do anything because Harriot was just a regular type of person, like me, and they don't care about people like us."

"Do the cops know who did it yet?" Bloodstone asked.

"No, not really," Petie replied. "They just said it was a gang who stole her car and hurt her real bad."

"So I take it that's the kind of information you were hoping to get, right?" Bloodstone asked. "You're hoping I either know who did it or can find out?"

"Yeah," Petie replied. "Like I said, I can pay." He pointed at the bag of money. "You can keep all of it; I don't care no more."

"I now understand," Bloodstone said. "If you'll just give me a minute to talk to my guy in private, I'll let you know. You're not asking something so simple. There are catches for getting involved with someone else's business." He pointed a finger at a chair that was ten feet away. "Go ahead and have a seat. This won't take but a minute."

Petie pulled his head down into his shoulders and did as requested.

"What's your opinion, Darren?" Bloodstone asked.

"Are you sure you want my input?" Crank asked. "I mean, it's your call. Whatever you say, I got your back."

"I know, brother," Bloodstone said. "You know who raped and killed the girl, don't you? I've about had it with their grotesque antics."

"Yeah, it's that group of dirtballs that hangs out over on Seventy-Fourth Street," Crank said. "I don't even remember what they call themselves. Who gives a damn? They're nothing but little turds wearing jackboots. And I hate rapists. I've always thought we should have gotten rid of that whole crew a long time ago because they're stinking up the whole city."

"I agree, but we're not cops," Bloodstone said. "I mean, hell, my hypocrisy does have limits, brother. After all, it's not as if we're running a Kool-Aid stand here."

"No," Crank conceded, "but we also don't force our will on anyone and don't hurt innocent civilians." He paused. "What they did was wrong, Matt, even by our low standards."

"So you think we should help him?" Bloodstone asked.

"Honestly, yeah, I do," Crank replied. "We should at least give him what he wants so he can try to do what he thinks is right. Who are we not to help him kill the animals who did that to his girl?"

"Where do you think the boys will sit on this?" Bloodstone asked.

"Wherever you tell them, brother," Crank replied. "We trust you to do what's right for all of us. But most of all, we know you'll do what's right. You always do."

"And you think it's right to give him what he needs?" Bloodstone asked.

"Yeah, I do," Crank replied, shrugging his shoulders. "I think he's going to go after them no matter what we decide to do. If we don't help him at all, he won't last ten seconds with those guys." Crank looked to where Petie sat bent over with his face held in his hands, weeping softly. "What those animals did ain't right, Matt, and you know it. We should've killed the whole bunch of them back when they beat up Jeb."

"So, what are you saying, that it's my fault?" Bloodstone asked. "That the girl was raped and killed because I didn't give the order to wipe out Felix's sick-ass crew?"

"No, of course not," Crank replied, shaking his head side to side slowly. "I'm just saying that some people need to be killed, that's all." He paused as he searched for the next string of words. "Come on, Matt, you know they need to die."

"You do remember that Jeb did actually owe them money for that junk, right?" Bloodstone asked. "He had a beating coming. It was business, nothing personal."

"I know," Crank said. "And we agreed with your decision for not retaliating against them for just wanting their money. However, brother, this is different. That crew is different. We're different. Nothing like them. You know what they're doing every damn day. They're hurting innocent people, and we can stop them."

"Don't differentiate ourselves from them too much, Darren," Bloodstone said. "That can be an impossible balancing act. Just remember that we're not avengers or vigilantes."

"I know what we are," Crank said.

"Hell, I've done worse things than any of them have done," Bloodstone said.

"Not rape and not anything against anyone who was not a willing participant in this type of lifestyle," Crank reminded him.

"Yeah, that's true enough," Bloodstone mumbled. "So you think we should just kill them off for the guy?"

Crank shook his head. "No," he replied evenly. "It would

look unjustified to the other factions. I say we use this kid to our advantage to get rid of a damn blight on the city once and for all. At the minimum, he'll probably get several of them before he's taken down, if we arm him for it. Besides, I doubt the cops will give much of a damn if all of them end up on a slab of cement."

"Always business, huh?" Bloodstone asked with a note of cynicism. "Just exploit the man's pain."

"Hey, I know the look," Crank said, "and that kid's gonna do it whether we help or not. At least we can help him get some of them."

"How well do you want to arm him?" Bloodstone asked. "The kid can cover most anything with the amount of money he brought."

"To the nines," Crank replied. "Fully automatic and body armor, maybe toss in a couple grenades to help him get the jump."

Bloodstone ran a thick hand over his head and nodded, thinking deeply. "Okay," he said. "Go into storage and grab everything you think the kid should have to get the job done."

"You serious?" Crank asked, eyes widening, anxious. He was surprised the man would agree with him so readily.

"Yeah, sure, why not?" Bloodstone replied, yawning slightly. He smacked his lips together. "To tell you the truth, I kind of like the kid. He has guts, and I admire a guy who wants to kill the men who hurt his woman. It seems that most of the men anymore are just a bunch of pussies, who call the lousy cops for everything. You know the scenario. I heard something in the bushes. That guy punched me in the nose. I'm a punk, so save my family because I can't. It's kind of nice to meet someone who wants to handle his own business, to hell with the stinking system of proverbial injustice, and do things how they're supposed to be done, like they were done in the past."

"You're doing the right thing," Crank said.

"I think you mean that we're doing the right thing," Bloodstone said. "I'm following your advice."

"You won't be sorry," Crank said.

Bloodstone waved off the words. "I never am," he said. He pushed the bag of money across the desk. "Take this and put it in the safe. Get the hardware for the kid and bring it to me. I want to speak with the kid alone."

"I'll be back in about a half an hour," Crank said. He started to turn to leave but then stopped and studied the huge man sitting behind the desk. "Whatever happens to the kid, you do know that it won't be your fault, don't you?"

Bloodstone smiled. "I haven't gone that soft yet," he said. "Regardless, old friend, thank you." He snapped his fingers. "Now get the hell out of here and get the kid some real firepower."

Crank clapped his hands together loud enough to get the attention of the men who were watching television. After they stood up and turned around, he motioned for them to follow him down into the armory that rested below the cellar.

The women returned to their excited banter.

The moment Petie looked up from the sound, he wondered if he'd done something to cause Crank to order the other two men to follow him. The man apparently infamous for beating people to death with bags of rocks sat stoic, doing nothing but watching him with the eyes of a cold-blooded killer. The only shred of comfort came from the women who had resumed their conversation. *He won't kill me in front of women,* he thought. He licked his lips nervously and then swallowed hard when the man waved for him to come over to the desk.

Half expecting to be viciously murdered within the next couple of seconds, Petie stood up and walked over to where the man who stood nearly seven feet tall and easily weighed over three hundred pounds waited. It was the longest ten feet he had ever walked in his life.

Chapter 13

Nearly six hours later, the sun had just dropped below the horizon when Detective Harris and Lieutenant Miller drove into the parking lot of the local jail, where Jeb Cartwright had been brought by the arresting officers early that morning. Miller had been constantly checking the time during the entire trip, growing angrier with each passing minute because the detective made continuous stops on the way as a supposed aspect of the ongoing investigation for which they were alleged to be partners. But when Miller made a query as to the reason for each delay all Harris would do was mumble under his breath. Nothing had been said about stopping anywhere on the way to the jail, and the lieutenant was quickly growing tired of being treated like a third wheel.

The final straw that had served to test what remained of his depleted patience, an insulting insinuation that basically accused him of professional incompetence for failing to obtain the necessary information, which had caused a palpable rift between the two men, was when Harris demanded to speak with his mother for the purpose of picking her brain about anything that might have been overlooked about the history of the doll, a small detail that might be of some sort of use in finding the killer. He was certain there would be another murder in the very near future.

In spite of Miller's assurances that another bout of questions would prove futile, Harris refused to listen and followed his gut instinct. The next two hours were spent at her house, while Harris nearly pummeled her with every question imaginable.

Following the fruitless verbal badgering of the elderly woman who loved to collect dolls, Miller now considered to be more voluntary hostage than partner, Harris drove over sixty miles to the law firm of Hanson & Hanson in hope of finding any sign that Jillian was inside the building.

There was none.

The only evidence that anyone was still at work was a few domestic cars far more modest in price to anything he believed the enormously rich woman would ever be caught dead driving.

Miller had posited several questions while they drove aimlessly around the parking lot for twenty minutes as to why he'd bothered to drive back to the law firm, but Harris only offered the same rude mumble in response before finally steering the car back onto the main road.

Ten minutes later they were on the freeway, heading to the original destination. The tension between the two was thick. And neither man uttered a single word until the car was parked in a reserved space for some unknown staff member of questionable rank in the police department.

Miller cleared his throat. "You do know that the guy whose space you're violating will probably have your car towed if he shows up, don't you?" he asked in a tired voice.

Harris sighed deeply and craned his head around to look at the man seated to his right. "You sure do complain a lot," he said in a huff, rolling his eyes. "You don't like to drive any distance. You didn't like the way I talked to your mom. You got to pee." He shook his head. "You do realize that we're trying to stop a serial killer, right? And if someone's feelings get hurt, then so be it."

"You are about the most pompous asshole I've ever met," Miller said. "What in the hell does a parking spot have to do with a serial killer?"

"You don't know?" Harris asked, raising an eyebrow.

"No," Miller replied. "What possible correlation could there be?"

Harris removed the keys from the ignition and smiled. "None," he replied. He opened the door. "Are you ready to go interrogate this sack of shit?"

"Yeah, I guess," Miller replied lamely. He followed the man he was growing to detest to the front doors of the local jail.

At the sound of the doors slamming shut, the desk sergeant, who appeared to have never missed a single meal for the past fifty years, lifted his poorly aging features with little interest. The folds of sagging flesh that ran alongside his face seemed to stretch like pockmarked taffy that had been tugged on far too many times. The eyes that peered through scratched bifocals were black and beady, not unlike those of a pig. The patches of gray hair pathetically splattered over the top of his scalp had all the earmarks of a failed comb-over. And when Harris and Miller got within five feet of the desk, the smell of cheap, rancid booze assaulted their sense of smell so strenuously that it caused Miller to nearly retch.

"Yeah, what can I do for you?" the sergeant asked in a gritty voice.

Both men flashed their badges at the cantankerous man, who appeared to have at least one foot in the grave, the other not far behind.

"Okay, so you're cops," he growled. "Aren't we all? That still doesn't tell me what the two of you want."

Harris put his badge away. "We're here to question a suspect," he said. "I was told he's in your custody."

The sergeant pulled out a clipboard that had a stack of papers attached to it and dropped it on the desk. "What's the name?" he asked.

"Jeb Cartwright," Harris said. "He might be listed as Jebediah."

"When was he arrested?" the sergeant asked in the same disinterested voice.

"My information was that it was last night," Harris replied.

The sergeant began to thumb through the stack of papers,

shaking his head as he reached the end. "Nope," he said. "There's no Jeb Cartwright in our custody." He put the clipboard back under the desk and stared at the men with lazy eyes.

Miller stepped up and placed his hands on the desk. "But that can't be," he said. "He was taken into custody last night."

"I didn't say he wasn't arrested," the sergeant said with a note of arrogance. "I said he wasn't in our custody."

"What the hell does that mean?" Harris asked.

"It means, Mr. Wizard, that he was bailed out," the sergeant replied. He looked at the clock on the wall. "According to the log, he was released about an hour or so ago."

"What do you mean he bailed out?" Harris asked angrily.

The sergeant folded his sausage-like fingers together and leaned forward. "Well, you see, Detective, it works like this," the sergeant said. "A guy gets arrested, someone puts up a chunk of money to get his sorry ass out of a cell, and he goes away."

"How much was the bail?" Harris asked.

The sergeant sighed again and retrieved the stack of documents. He flipped through it, stopping on the correct date. "Hmmm, let's see," he mumbled. "It reads at fifty thousand."

"No friggin' way," Harris spat. "That kid doesn't have two fake nickels to rub together, so how did he come up with that kind of money?"

The sergeant let the pages fall back into place and shoved the documents back under the desk, nearly slamming them into the shelf. "Whatever," he griped, looking at the two men with a sour expression. "I'm not the lowlife's damn accountant, so I don't give a rat's ass about his financial status. The book says he was bailed out on fifty thousand dollars by a local bondsman, and that's all I know and care about."

"Which one?" Harris asked heatedly. He looked at the name tag on the man's breast pocket.

"Which one what?" the sergeant asked, exhaling.

"Which bondsman, Sergeant Peters?" Harris asked. He was quickly becoming agitated over the man's obtuse intellect.

"The same one most of those people use," Peters replied."Freddie's Friendly Family Bail Bonds."

"That's off Avon, isn't it?" Harris asked as he took a pen and scrap of paper out of the pocket of his shirt.

Peters groaned aloud. "What, now I'm a damn travel agent," he moaned miserably. "Look, you two, I just work the desk. You're the detective, so why don't you go out there and detect some damn thing and leave me alone." He shifted his beady eyes over to Harris and winked one of them. "Hell, you even have a lieutenant to back you up, so why are you hounding me? I don't know anything, and I don't want to know."

"Well, that's obvious," Miller snapped.

Peter flipped him a chunky finger. "Sit on it and rotate, you puke," he said. "I got nothin' to say."

Harris shook his head in unadulterated disgust. "You're a real credit to the department, Sergeant," he snarled, scribbling down the name of the bondsman. "If only we had a hundred more like you, then I could retire knowing the whole world is going to hell in a handbasket." He turned on his heel and walked back out the way he had come.

Miller stared at the desk sergeant with a menacing expression, wishing he could just reach across the counter and strangle the worthless piece of trash dressed in blue until he coughed up what remained of his pathetic life, and shook his head in shame. It was officers such as the illustriously lazy sergeant that made the public distrustful of everyone in authority.

"What?" Peters asked in a belligerent tone of voice, narrowing his eyes until they were little more than two small marbles. "You got a problem with me, boy? If so, then talk to my union rep. I have only six months left until retirement and don't give a wart on a bullfrog's ass what you or your girlfriend think."

"Yeah, you've made certain to make that crystal clear, Sergeant," Miller said. "Enjoy your retirement, asshole. I hope you get hit by a big truck on the same day so we can go out and detect the smear on the pavement. I'll try not to piss on your crushed head." Without saying anything further, certain that he was only moments away from punching the irritant in the face, Miller turned and followed Harris out the door.

"Hey, screw you, buddy," Peters yelled from the top of his lungs, after them. "I put my time in, so you can't judge me." He slammed a meaty hand down on the desk. Veins of outrage broke out in his neck. "You can both just go straight to hell. I'm a vet, for Christ's sake, a bona fide hero."

Harris was already at the car and leaning against the door on the driver's side when Miller walked alongside the opposite side. He was furious. The cords on the side of his neck stood out like two thick cables. His head pounded from a headache that had been brought on by a massive increase in blood pressure. Miller, finding the sergeant's unprofessional conduct inexplicably vile and entirely inexcusable, slammed a closed fist down on the roof of the car with an impressive thump.

Startled by the unexpected assault against metal, Harris jumped away from the side of the automobile and drew his weapon with incredible speed. He turned and pointed the gun at the source of the noise, then glared at the man standing on the other side of the car when he realized it was nothing but the lieutenant throwing some sort of ridiculous adolescent tantrum.

"What in the hell is the matter with you?" Harris asked angrily, putting the gun back into the holster. "I damn near shot you. What's with the conniption? You almost gave me a heart attack."

"How can you be so calm?" Miller asked, perplexed by the man's stoic attitude. "Didn't that moron's bullshit make you mad?"

"No, not angry—exactly," Harris replied, stammering, then finished, "just annoyed. No one can make you mad. You can only allow yourself to become such." He laid his arms over the top of the car. "What can I say about the man, Lieutenant, that he's a fat, lazy, worthless boob? Why else do you think he has almost thirty years on the force and is still a lowly third-watch desk sergeant? You don't need to be a nuclear physicist to figure that one out, because it takes a special type of village miscreant to accomplish that little feat of magic."

"Yeah, well, they should've shit canned that lousy specimen in blue years ago," Miller said, curling his hands into fists in preparation to strike the hood again.

"Please stop beating on my car," Harris said in a soft voice. "I can't afford to have dents repaired."

Miller relaxed his hands. "I just want to wait for him out here and beat the snot out of his worthless hide," he said.

"And what will that accomplish, other than an internal investigation from IA?" Harris asked mildly.

"I'll feel a lot better," Miller replied.

"For a minute," Harris replied evenly, "and then regret will set in."

"Just one in the nose. What do you say?" Miller asked, grinning widely at the thought. His voice was less severe.

Harris drummed his hands on the car. "Ah, just forget it," he said, waving a hand as if none of it mattered one iota to him. "You take things far too personal. Besides, in spite of the man's acute laziness, we did get what we came for, right? At least sort of." He plucked the piece of paper from his pocket and held it up in the air.

"So you really think the kid knows something?" Miller asked in a tone that denoted new-found hope. He was already beginning to calm down from the prospect of narrowing down the identity of the murder suspect.

"I do," Harris replied. "He just might not be aware of it yet." He paused and scratched his chin. "It just occurred to me, lieutenant. If the killer is as brilliant as I believe, Jeb may be next on the list. I highly doubt such a loose string will go unnoticed for long, which makes it all the more curious as to who shelled out fifty grand for the kid. Somehow I just don't see him running around in a crowd with that sort of money."

"Yeah, that is an interesting development," Miller admitted, nodding his head. "Do you think the killer could've bailed him out to get to him?"

"It is a distinct possibility," Harris said, hesitating, "but I think the killer would have used some sort of buffer as a shield to avoid exposure." He replaced the piece of paper.

"Pursue the lead?" Miller asked.

Harris nodded in response. "I guess we'll just have to pay a short visit to friendly Freddy and see what ..." Harris began, but he stopped in midsentence at the sound of his cell phone ringing in his pocket, leaving Miller to stare at him in anticipation to hear the rest of what the man had to say while he answered it. "Yeah, this is Harris." His face went blank in less than three seconds. "Wh ... what?"

Miller's back went rigid when he heard the grave tone in the detective's voice.

"I said we have another murder, Detective," the unknown voice over the phone announced.

"Oh, no," Harris muttered miserably. "Okay, how bad is it?"

"It's pretty bad, Detective," the voice replied. "I've never actually seen anything like it. It really freaked me out. Everyone is having a real hard time over here, Detective, because of ..." The voice trailed off.

"Pull yourself together," Harris ordered.

"Yes, sir," the voice croaked.

"How many victims?" Harris asked. In spite of the reassuring confidence in his voice, he dreaded the answer.

"We count three, sir," the voice said.

"I ... I see," Harris said, stumbling for words while ignoring the inquisitive expression covering Miller's face. "What's your name?"

The owner of the voice cleared his throat. "Jarmel, Detective. Officer Sam Jarmel," he replied.

"Where are you, Sam?" Harris asked.

"Down in the low-rent part of the city, at a bar called The Watery Pelican," Sam replied. "It's one of the local dives on the strip."

"I want you to do me a favor, Officer," Harris said. "I want you to remain there until I arrive, do you hear me?"

"Yes, of course, sir," Sam replied.

"I don't care who might try and order you away," Harris said forcefully. "But I don't want you to move. If anyone tries to pressure you, I want you to tell them to go to hell because you're acting as

Detective Harris's liaison to the scene. If you leave for any reason whatsoever, I'll make your career spin in the circular file. Do you understand what I'm telling you, Officer Jarmel?"

The officer swallowed in reaction to the not so subtle threat. "Yes, sir, I understand," he replied nervously. "I won't move. I promise."

"Good man," Harris said. "I'll be there as soon as I can, Officer." He then paused. "One more thing, Officer."

"Yes, Detective," Sam said when nothing followed after several silent seconds. He wondered if the man hadn't already terminated the call.

"Was there a doll at the scene?" Harris asked in a pinched, almost hushed tone of voice. He was almost afraid to hear the answer certain to come.

Always one who prided himself on his intelligence and unmatched ability to deduce by means of reason, considering himself truly gifted, Harris felt a definite tremor in the once impenetrable armor that was his ego and unshakable confidence in outsmarting even the wiliest of criminals. With wounded pride, Harris found it difficult to admit the indisputable fact that he was getting beat by a killer who seemed to ply the trade of murder with absolute impunity. Although he had several plausible theories, none of which were supported by any empirical evidence, the bottom line was that he was no closer to catching the person.

"Uh, yeah, Detective, there was," Sam replied uneasily. "That's what has a lot of us completely freaked out. The way everything was laid out is almost like a—"

The line went dead in Sam's hand.

Well aware as to how the officer's sentence was going to end, Harris clicked off the phone and slid it back into his pocket. He looked up at Miller with grim features. Things were not going well with the investigation. And he scolded himself silently for being outmaneuvered yet again, quietly chastising his own myopic techniques, which had caused him to be easily beaten with the distraction of chasing a kid who may or may not know anything. Harris growled audibly. It was then when he fully grasped the true gravity of the circumstances, that he was on the trail of an ultimate predator, a killer who had defeated him with relative ease. The pain was obvious to Miller, unlike the flood of mixed emotions swimming through Harris's mind. For perhaps the first time in his life, there were tangible doubts possessed by him as to whether he could actually catch the person responsible. Even worse, it was just a matter of time before the newspapers caught a whiff of the series of murders and ultimately connected the dots. Soon to follow would be the media circus, and then the embarrassment that their department was helpless to stop the string of murders taking place throughout the city.

"There's been another murder," Harris said bitterly.

Mistaking the man's anguish for one of sympathy for the victim, Miller frowned in sorrow. "Is it our killer?" he asked, grimacing from the thought of having to deal with another grisly scene. The one of the young girl in the alleyway was still fresh in his mind. *What is wrong with people these days?* he wondered, knowing very well that there would never be an acceptable answer to explain how one human being could treat another with such unspeakable savagery.

"It sure sounds like it," Harris replied. "The same MO."

"Then he's getting bolder," Miller said.

"Hmmm," Harris mumbled, biting down on his lower lip.

"What?" Miller asked.

"You said he," Harris said.

"Well ... uh, yes, I did," Miller stammered uneasily, knitting his brow.

"Why did you say he?" Harris asked, curious.

"I guess it's because I just assumed the killer's a man," Miller replied. "All serial killers are men."

"But that's not entirely accurate," Harris corrected in a methodical tone of voice. "Although it is rare for women to join the ranks of a serial—I grant you that—but it is not entirely unheard of, Lieutenant. Women can actually be far more vicious than any man."

"What are you saying?" Miller asked.

"I'm not saying anything, Lieutenant," Harris replied, monotone. He was thinking.

"Well, you must be implying something," Miller said. "Even though I haven't known you long, I kind of figure you for a guy who doesn't just ramble on about a bunch of nothing. So there must be a reason."

Harris started to answer but thought it more prudent to keep the alternative theory to himself, at least for the time being, so as not to create a secondary puzzle that may only convolute the situation more than necessary. His thoughts drifted over to the Hanson woman and those in her employ.

He then opened the car door and started to get in.

"Aren't you going to answer me?" Miller asked, somewhat offended by being completely ignored by the man.

Harris paused, mentally weighed the options at hand, and looked at the lieutenant with a blank expression. "Not yet," Harris replied. "Come on; get in."

"Where are we going?" Miller asked.

"Where do you think?" Harris shot back. "We're going to some dive called The Watery Pelican, so we can catch a not so very nice person." He ducked out of view.

"Oh, that's just great," Miller commented as he got into the passenger side of the car. "I could've gone without seeing another dead body this week."

"Bodies," Harris corrected.

"Plural, as in more than one?" Miller asked gravely.

"Yes. I thought I mentioned that," Harris replied.

"No, you didn't," Miller replied miserably, shaking his head.

"Are you sure?" Harris asked.

"Yeah, I'm sure I would've remembered," Miller replied.

"Huh," Harris huffed. "I thought I'd mentioned that fact." He shrugged his shoulders. "Anyway, there are three dead, two men and a woman."

Miller groaned.

Harris turned the ignition and headed to the bar where he had broken up several drunken brawls during his short time working as a beat cop.

Not so surprising, Harris found little had changed in the rundown neighborhood since he had last walked the streets, when they arrived twenty minutes later. It may have gotten worse. Trash littered the sidewalks that lined the pothole-covered roadways. The small businesses, at least those still open, offered no welcome. Wooden planks had been nailed over most of the broken windows. The colorful paint that had once splashed and brightened the edifices in the area decades earlier was chipped and faded to a deathly gray, appearing more like the tattered residuals of a ghost town abandoned after the final firebombing of an unfriendly nation. Homeless people of all ages and ethnic backgrounds were either standing around and watching the curious spectacle taking place by the bar or lying on the ground with cardboard and discarded rags wrapped around their bodies as they attempted to sleep off the effects of the previous night's alcohol-induced bender. Several members of the semiconscious audience craned their heads around at the sound of a car pulling up against the curb to park.

Miller looked out the window and frowned in response to the numerous eyes that stared at them from under dirty eyebrows that had never been trimmed. Several were leaning on shopping carts to guard their most prize possessions. Those who remained unconscious on the ground didn't budge at all.

Although Miller was fully aware of the ignored section of the city, had even spent hours working in local soup kitchens to help make amends for past sins of guilt that were destined to occur in his line of work, he didn't remember the numbers being so high. More than a half dozen children were huddled together in the doorway of a burned-out shoe store. And not so mysteriously fewer in numbers, two uniformed officers stood two doors down the street talking on a set of concrete steps.

"Are you sure you got the name correct, Harris?" Miller asked, apprehensive. "I mean, there's no one here."

Harris turned off the engine and leaned down so he could look up through the windshield to see the sign that dangled haphazardly on a single chain that was suspended from the overhang on the bar. "Yes, this is the place," he replied. "The officer said it was The Watery Pelican."

Miller shifted his gaze from one end of the street to the other. "Man, this place is a dump," he said distastefully. "A lot worse than I remember it to be. If this is where the killer has struck, then I'd have to say it's a major shift in MO, wouldn't you?"

"Not necessarily," Harris replied, finding the change in atmosphere morbidly interesting. "The location can be altered while the method remains the same."

"How can that be?" Miller asked, bewildered.

"Let's go and see," Harris said. He opened the door and stepped out of the car with a deliberate slowness so that he could maintain a vigilant eye on his surroundings.

Miller got out of the car next and looked toward the two officers, who continued to stand and chatter on. "I guess we're early, huh?" he asked. He then looked around in search of additional squad cars, finding none.

"What makes you think that?" Harris asked.

"I see only two cops and two cars," Miller replied simply. "There should be more officers on scene."

"Why?" Harris asked.

Miller's features pinched. "Why?" He repeated, astonished. "It's a triple murder, that's why."

Harris smiled, amused, and shook his head. "That's rich," he chuckled as if just told a good joke. "A few more may show up a little later, if the story gets leaked to the press, but no one really cares about these poor souls, and you damn well know it."

"I know no such thing," Miller said heatedly.

"Then all the more pity because you should," Harris said. "People will say a lot of platitudes, Lieutenant, but in truth no one really cares about these people. The only time the homeless actually become an issue for the news is when some slick politician is running for office and it's the flavor of the month, ripe for exploitation, not unlike saving some whale or squirrel in the wild. I find it all so very tiresome, but the public seems to buy the lies and false promises year after year." He pointed a finger at the cluster of children huddled together. "Meanwhile, those unable to fend for themselves starve to death because those same manipulators continue to send billions overseas to countries that hate us and want to kill everyone who lives here."

"Aren't you just a joy to be around," Miller said without a note of humor.

"That's why they pay me the big bucks," Harris said. He then shut the door of the car. "Come on; let's go see how bad the damage is." He started to walk toward the bar, while paying no attention to the frightened eyes of those who didn't trust the police and watched his every move as he went past each of them.

Reluctant, deeply dreading just the idea of viewing another murdered woman so close in time to the last one, Miller thought about what the boy had said to him about no one caring about people like him and his little friend in the alleyway. He couldn't help but wonder if the young man might not have been correct. The lack of officers at the scene certainly didn't support his position that people cared one iota about the poor and disenfranchised. A sense of guilt suddenly gripped him when he realized that he couldn't remember either of their names. He knew the girl's names started with an H, the boy's with a P.

Sensing that the lieutenant wasn't following him, Harris turned around. "Aren't you coming?" he asked, half growling as he placed his hands on either hip. "I thought you wanted to be a part of this investigation."

"Yeah, I know what I said," Miller said. "I was just thinking about the girl from earlier and how young she was."

"You mean Harriot?" Harris said. "What about her?"

Miller shrank back from the shame that the detective, who was not actually assigned to the case, had remembered the name of the girl when he couldn't recall it all. "Yeah, her and the boyfriend," he said, testing the man's memory.

"Petie," Harris offered. "What about them?"

"You actually remembered their names?" Miller asked, somewhat astonished. "But I thought you were indifferent to such things."

"Look, Lieutenant," Harris breathed. "This is not the time or place to be engaged in a philosophical debate. I don't have to carry any personal feelings for a victim to do what's right by them, to get them fair and proper justice. I didn't know either of them, so there's no true foundation, not if I am actually honest with myself and their memory, to base any personal feelings about the boy or girl. I can sympathize, even empathize, with what atrocities were incurred by both, especially for the girl, but to say that I am swayed by anything that resembles a derivative of some antiquated sense of love or like would be false."

"So you don't care at all?" Miller asked.

"Personally?" Harris parried.

"Yeah," Miller shot back.

"No, I don't," Harris replied. "But that doesn't mean I won't do right by the girl."

"You're a strange man, Harris," Miller said. "An odd duck and a half."

"I shall accept that as a compliment, Lieutenant," Harris said, grinning mildly. "So, if you're finished with querying my psychological profile, can we get back to work?"

"Lead the way," Miller said. He shut the door and followed Harris.

The two officers stopped their conversation when they noticed the two men approach. The man on the right moved forward and held up a single hand.

"Stop right there, buddy," the officer warned. "This establishment is closed. Police business." He pointed back at the car. "If you'll please step back."

Harris removed the gold shield from his pocket and held it out for the officer to see. "I'm aware of that fact, Officer," he said dryly. "The man coming up behind me is Lieutenant Miller."

"Uh, yeah, sorry, Detective," the officer stammered. "We've been expecting you, sir." He studied the lieutenant and his mannerisms as he approached. "I'm sorry, but we weren't aware that a lieutenant would be with you."

"Well, now you do," Harris said. "I'm looking for an Officer Sam Jarmel. Do you know where he is?"

"Uh, yes, sir," the officer replied awkwardly. "He's inside, in the far back of the bar last time we checked, but that was over ten or fifteen minutes ago. Sam's been guarding the place like some sort of pit bull."

Harris smiled as he walked past the two men without saying anything further. Miller was right on his tail, eyeballing the two officers as he followed him through the front door.

Seated at one of the small tables in the center of the bar was a young officer who seemed to be no older than twenty years old. Unexpectedly, there was an elderly woman sitting at the same table, located opposite him. She was sipping at a coke through a small straw. Harris walked up to the table and peered down at the young officer. The woman looked up and offered a friendly smile. Miller quickly joined them.

"Hello," Maude said. "My name's Maude. Everyone calls me Ma."

Harris silently tilted his head in polite greeting and then turned his attention to the officer who had just stood up. "I'm Detective Harris," he introduced. "This is Lieutenant Miller."

Harris held out an open hand. "Are you Jarmel?"

"Yes, sir," he replied. He gladly accepted the proffered hand and shook it. "I've preserved the scene as you requested. There are a couple members of the forensic team gathering evidence."

Harris stepped to the side. "Lieutenant Miller and I will be working jointly on this case," he said. He looked over at the woman. "And who is this?"

"I told you already," Maude replied, somewhat hurt. "I'm Maude."

"What I meant to say is what are you doing here?" Harris asked diplomatically.

"She's a possible witness," the officer replied.

"Have you questioned her about anything, Officer?" Harris asked critically. "Did you take a statement?"

The officer licked his lips nervously, hoping he had not committed any form of dereliction. "Um, no, sir," he replied uneasily. "I thought it best to wait for homicide to get here. Besides, she wouldn't speak to me. She said it was too important, and that it was very interesting information, something we would definitely need to know about what happened. However, she said she would talk only to the main guy in charge of everything. I didn't push the issue."

Miller stepped forward. "How so?" he asked. "Did she actually see the perpetrator?"

"I … I'm not …" he stuttered beneath the lieutenant's hard stare.

Harris rested a hand on Miller's shoulder and eased him back. "We'll get to that, Lieutenant," he said, interrupting. "First things first." He nodded his head. "You did well, Sam." He looked down at the woman and grinned warmly. "You don't mind waiting, beautiful, do you?"

Maude shrugged her hunched shoulders. "Ma has nowhere else to go," she replied, grinning ear to ear. "I don't mind waiting, not one bit if it helps."

"It may be a few, dear," Harris said softly.

"That's okay," Maude said. "It's nice and warm in here. My old bones start to ache when I'm outside too long."

"Are you hungry?" Harris asked.

Maude downcast her eyes, ashamed to admit that she hadn't eaten all day, and pulled her tattered shawl tighter around her emaciated body. She had passed out most of the money the young man had given to her at the bus stop to several of her homeless friends, keeping only enough to buy herself a couple of sandwiches and a coke, most of which she had also shared with those who were hungry. "If it's not too much trouble, I could use a bite to eat and maybe a little something to drink with it," she replied in half a mumble.

Harris removed his wallet and pulled out a twenty-dollar bill, then handed it over to Sam. "Give this to one of the officers and tell him to get Ma something to eat," he said. "Get whatever she wants."

"You're a kind man," Ma said, tears welling in her eyes. "Thank you. Most people wouldn't even care enough to bother to wonder if someone like me was hungry or not. No one cares anymore."

"You're welcome, dear," Harris said.

The words the boy had said rang in the lieutenant's head yet again.

Sam took the money and turned his attention to Ma. "What would you like to eat, dear?" he asked.

"How about a hamburger, fries, and a coke?" Ma asked brightly, rubbing her stomach like an anxious child. "I love hamburgers."

"Like the detective said, whatever you want," he said, winking at her. He then headed toward the door.

Shocked by the genuine affection displayed by the man toward the homeless woman, Miller stared at him in complete confusion. He wondered how a seemingly misanthropic man, who treated everyone and everything around him with undiluted contempt, could be capable of bestowing the level of benevolence he'd just witnessed. The behavior was undeniably a blatant contradiction. Detective Harris was truly an enigma, and Miller was determined to learn the finer details as to what made the man tick.

Although Detective Harris had researched hundreds of homicide cases over the past few years, none of the previous crime scenes even remotely compared to what he found waiting for him in the back of the bar. Miller gasped in total revulsion when he rounded the corner and came face to face with the most disturbing display of murderous aftermath he had ever heard tell of.

The sight of the doll resting atop the corpse of a man close to his own age forced him to avert his eyes. The two team members who were standing in the far corner held up rags to their faces. They merely waved in their direction as they struggled against the reflexive action to vomit violently.

"My God," Miller breathed aloud, feeling the slight taste of bile at the back of his throat. "What kind of monster are we dealing with?"

"Not a monster, Lieutenant, but a perfectionist," Harris replied in a faint whisper. He walked over to the deceased, kneeled beside him, and began to study the wounds. "This is absolutely amazing." He retrieved a pen from his shirt pocket and used it as a pointer. "Can you see how precise everything is? Every small detail?"

"What are you talking about?" Miller asked wildly. "These people were butchered in here."

"And your point, Lieutenant?" Harris asked, unperturbed.

"That is my point," Miller snapped. "You're viewing this slaughter through the eyes of a damn ghoul."

"That is merely an opinion rather than demonstrable reality," Harris said. "You're ignoring the skill the killer possesses, the efficiency. Just look at the position of the doll and the delicate care exercised to set her on a lover's chest."

Miller craned his head over to where the two people taped to the chairs sat. "And what are they, witnesses to the perversity?" Miller asked disgustedly.

Harris smiled. "That's exactly what they are," he said as he rose to his feet. "This was a marriage between man and woman." It suddenly became crystal clear to him. "In fact, all of them are matrimonial unions." He pointed at the two bound people. "Do you see how they were erected to keep their eyes forward? They weren't securely fastened to keep them immobilized in the chair, but to keep the event within each of their field of vision."

"What?" Miller cried out wildly, unconsciously backed away from the man. "That's totally insane! And you're as crazy as the person doing this for thinking in such an insane way. You need help, and I mean deep psychological therapy."

The two forensic team members moved toward the door, grimacing in response to what the detective was implying. Neither scientist wanted to hear anymore of the man's deductions, for both did in fact have a foundation, though eerie and extremely disturbing, on which to premise the twisted conclusion.

"Perhaps, but that doesn't mean I'm incorrect," Harris replied, barely listening. "Hmmm, I wonder." His features took on a faraway look.

"We'll be back when the two of you are finished with whatever it is you're doing," the older of the two members said as he pulled his colleague out of the room with him.

"Now what's gotten into that head of yours?" Miller asked, though he wasn't certain he actually wanted to know.

Harris walked toward the door and waved for the lieutenant to follow. "Come on; I need to speak with the old woman," he said. He stopped just inside the door and turned around to see if Miller was doing as requested.

"Why?" Miller asked.

"To see how smart I am," Harris replied sarcastically. "Just come with me and don't argue."

Miller cocked his head toward the cadavers. "What about them?" he asked, shaking his head.

"What about them?" Harris shot back. "They're dead and won't be going anywhere, ever, so they'll keep for now. I have better things to do at the moment, like question the old woman." He took a deep breath. "If it makes you feel any better, send the two flunkies back in here to keep them company."

Maude had just sat down to enjoy the meal Sam had brought her when Harris and Miller emerged from the rear area of the bar. She smiled through ketchup- and mustard-covered lips when she saw the man who had made it possible for her to fill the empty space of her stomach. Harris offered a sincere look of genuine affection and kneeled beside her. Miller was as baffled as ever by how the man's emotional state of mind could shift from one side of the psychological spectrum to the other so inexplicably fast.

"Excuse me, Ma, but did you have some information that might help us to catch the person who did this?" Harris asked.

Maude nodded her head silently.

"What are you doing?" Miller asked, perplexed. "You can't believe she actually saw anything that could help."

Harris craned his head around and glared at the other man. "Shut up!" he snapped. "I know she can help."

Maude sneered at the lieutenant and then used a napkin to

daintily dab at her mouth. It was important to her to be both prim and proper in front of the detective, who had treated her so ladylike.

Miller rolled his eyes in annoyed silence.

Sam continued to remain silent as he studiously observed the subtle interrogation from a nearby table, fascinated by the tactics being utilized by the detective.

Harris brought his attention back to the elderly woman. "Did you see the murders?" He asked, almost too softly to hear.

Maude shook her head.

"Did you see a man who you think killed the people here?" Harris asked.

Maude shook her head again.

"You see, this is a waste of time," Miller stated angrily. "We should be getting back to work."

"Quiet," Harris said, furrowing his brow. "Do you know there were people killed in here?" he asked.

"Yes, I know," Maude replied in a barely audible whisper. "It's just terrible how people treat one another these days."

"I agree, dear," Harris said. "But how did you know?"

"I heard a woman scream inside here and saw her run out a few seconds later," Maude said. "I got curious and came inside. That's when I found those poor people in that room, dead."

Tears began to pool in her eyes. "I've never seen anything like that before, so I called the police."

"Do you know the woman who ran out of here?" Harris asked softly.

"No, I've never seen her before," Maude replied. "But she was sure scared. She went in and came out screaming a few minutes later."

Harris turned to Miller. "Check the employee records, Lieutenant," he said. "The woman probably works here as a barmaid or something of that nature. That would explain why she went in the back."

"I just knew something was askew when I saw that woman at the bus stop," Maude said to no one in particular. "It just didn't make sense that someone like that would be slumming around in our neck of our woods. It's unnatural for people like that to associate with us lower types."

All three men turned their undivided attention on Maude.

"I'm sorry, dear, but did you say something?" Harris asked.

Maude nodded. "Yes," she replied. "I knew something was out of whack when I saw that woman on the bench. She just didn't belong. I knew I'd seen her from somewhere but couldn't remember where, and then I saw her picture."

"Whose picture?" Harris asked, growing more curious with each passing second. "What woman?"

"Why, the superrich woman," Maude replied. She then reached into her pocket and withdrew a wrinkled page of a newspaper. She unfolded it and held it out for the men to see. "This woman."

"Holy shit," Sam muttered. "That's Jillian Hanson."

Miller gasped audibly. "Do you realize who she has just implicated, Detective?" he asked.

"Of course I do," Harris snapped. "This brave woman has just confirmed my suspicions, because I knew something was awry."

"So you think Jillian Hanson is the killer?" he asked crazily. "Are you insane?"

"If not her, then it's someone very close to her," Harris replied. "And she's protecting him or her. Like Ma here just said, why would she be down here at all?" He paused to take a breath. "Don't you find that at all curious?"

"Curious?" Miller repeated. "Yeah, I find it more than just a little interesting, more than enough to pursue, but her presence down here isn't evidence connecting her to the murders. It could be one of those bizarre coincidences."

Harris eyed him critically. "Are you trying to tell me you're not willing to ruffle a few feathers?" he asked bitterly.

"That's not what I'm saying at all," Miller replied. "I'm saying we have to be smart about this, and cover our asses each way to Sunday, or we'll get shut down before we get started." He paused when he saw a sour expression cloud Harris's face, before continuing.

"Look—I understand you're about the best in the forensic science type stuff to chase these people down, but the real world, particularly in something like this, doesn't work like that."

"But if we could get a warrant to—" he began.

"With what?" Miller interrupted. "Our good looks? The bottom line is we got nothing to show probable cause, reasonable suspicion, or anything else. We got jackshit! And you want to pester a judge? He'll laugh in our faces and have us thrown out of his chambers. Keep in mind, we'll get one shot at it."

Harris let out a heavy sigh of frustration. As much as he loathed to admit it, the man was right. They could jeopardize everything if they made a mistake by jumping the gun. "So, what do you suggest, partner?" he asked, willing to swallow his pride for the benefit of the case.

Miller smiled. He knew it must have galled Harris to admit that he didn't know everything, especially to him. "Partners, huh?" He jabbed playfully to add some levity to the situation.

"Oh, jeez," Harris moaned. "Don't make me say it again!"

"Never," Miller promised. He then turned serious, all joking tabled for the moment.

"You really do think it's the Hanson woman, don't you?"

"Yes, in my gut I do," Harris replied evenly. "And I admit that it's going to be next to impossible to ever make her stand trial for it. However, I do think it's worth a shot, sort of like tackling Goliath and coming out of the fray without a scratch."

"You can't be serious," Miller said. "She will destroy you, if you don't have an ironclad case."

"All the more of a challenge," Harris said, adamant. "Are you in?"

While Lieutenant Miller contemplated the prospect of committing both professional and political suicide, trying to reciprocate the interested gleam in the detective's eyes but failing terribly in the attempt, he was startled when the cell phone in his pocket sprang to life. Grateful for the unexpected distraction, he turned around and answered the call. A few seconds later the blood drained from his face. "I'll be right there, Sergeant," he said, exhaling a deep sigh. Numb from receiving even more bad news, he terminated the conversation and turned to the detective. His face was deathly pale.

"Everything all right, Lieutenant?" Harris asked offhandedly. His attention was focused on Maude.

"I have to go," Miller mumbled, blinking slowly. He wasn't sure as to how much more he could take. Everything—the world, people, even his life—was coming apart at the seams. "I ... um, have a serious situation and have to go." He looked around the room in a sort of daze. "I'll have to talk to you about this a little later."

Harris waved him off. "I understand," he said, his tone noncommittal. "Go take care of your business. I'll give you a call later. Sam and I can handle this, right, Officer Jarmel?" He turned to the younger man and nodded his head, coaxing him to agree.

"Uh ... yeah, sure, I got your back," Sam replied. "No sweat."

Miller looked at Harris with a bland expression. "Are you sure?" he asked. "I can stay if you really need me."

"Yes, go," Harris replied. "I'll brief you later."

"Thank you," Miller said. He then left the bar with his shoulders slumped down.

After Miller had left the building, Harris switched knees. He smiled in the friendliest manner possible. "Okay, where were we?" he asked politely. "And, by all means, please tell me all about the Hanson woman."

Thoroughly enjoying the attention being showered upon her, secretly wishing it would last forever, Maude smiled brightly and pulled a fry from the bag. It was nice to have people wanting to hear what she had to say.

Chapter 14

T ime was of the greatest essence, an immutable fact that Heather Lasko unquestionably knew was in extreme short supply, and any unnecessary delay would unequivocally cause immeasurable damage to her objective.

An absolute first, at least to the best of her limited knowledge, both Jillian and Brad had been mysteriously absent from the firm for well over six hours. Regardless of the time, weekday or weekend, one or both of them were always present somewhere in the building, even if no one employed by the firm knew exactly where. She had made several surreptitious queries among several of the lawyers whose forte was to conduct legal research and brief cases during the hours when the courthouses were closed for the day, but none of them could provide any answers. Most of them were completely unaware of Jillian Hanson's coming and going because they were constantly locked away in some obscure room updating case law so the attorneys who actually practiced in a courtroom would have all the recent decisional law at their disposal to do battle with the opposing side.

Completely frustrated and fed up with the seemingly limitless ignorance of those indentured by the powerful Hanson woman after wasting an hour on fruitless inquiries, roaming from one sparsely populated floor to another, effectively making a circuitous path across each so that no one was accidentally overlooked, Heather decided to take the elevator and head up to the main offices upstairs. She had squandered enough time on a pointless endeavor.

As was standard operating procedure pertaining to the strict security measures applied uniformly within the immense building, Heather was met by two heavily armed security guards when the elevator doors parted. No matter how many times she repeated the same process, the two men who stood unsmiling front and center gave her the creeps. They made her skin crawl from head to toe. The man who always remained just down the hall, though he had never actually done anything remotely scary, was by far worse than the two waiting robotically for her to exit so she could be inspected for unacceptable contraband that was disallowed on the floor.

None of the men had ever been seen to break a smile.

The guard on the right, the only one who ever uttered a single word, stepped forward with the same handheld device he used each time when conducting a search of her person. "Hello, Miss Lasko," he said mechanically, in a tone that held zero warmth or feeling. "Please step out so we can conduct a noninvasive search of your person." He turned the device on with the push of a button.

Heather smiled and lifted an eyebrow. "I bet you say that to all the girls, don't you?" She asked playfully, attempting to add a little levity to the situation to assuage her own frayed nerves. But the man only stared at her with dead eyes.

"I'm quite certain I don't understand your point, Miss Lasko," the guard said. "Please step out of the elevator so we can do our job as instructed."

Heather looked over at the man down the hall and frowned when she noticed him slowly slide a hand underneath his coat. She couldn't imagine ever growing accustomed to being treated in such a harsh manner. It felt as if she were some sort of common criminal. Reluctant to comply, the thought of backing away entered her mind. She wondered if she had made a severe error in judgment when she accepted the job, and then she moved forward and held up her arms. The humiliation of having her personal space invaded yet again had not diminished in the slightest as the man ran the infernal machine over her body.

"She's clean," the guard announced dryly. He then turned his head and nodded at the man, who remained eerily unmoving down the hall to convey his conclusion, which was immediately reciprocated in order to give acknowledgment that clearance was granted for the woman to be released from detainment.

The two guards resumed their former positions without delay. They stood on either side of the doors as if reattached against the wall by steel bolts.

Heather went to walk left and was immediately snatched by an arm, causing her to wince and cry out more from surprise than actual pain.

The man did not speak or blink, but merely stared at her profile as if she were snared prey. She tried to wrench her arm free, but the man's grip was like iron. He turned her around and looked at her with vacant eyes. The other guard moved beside her and took a firm hold on the other arm, curling his lip in a snarl.

"Where are you going, Miss Lasko?" the guard on the right asked harshly. "Your office is down the other way. Have you become confused?"

"I'm well aware of the location of my office, mister," Heather snapped. "So you don't have to remind me of that fact."

Mr. Pashka approached the three people, with a gun hanging loosely from a hand, and narrowed his eyes at the newest recruit to the floor. "Excuse me, but may I inquire as to what's going on here?" he asked, his voice severe.

"Yes, you may," Heather said angrily. "One of your gorillas hurt my arm and is refusing to let me take care of firm business personally entrusted to me by Jillian herself." She tugged against the men's hold on her again. "I have never been treated so shabbily in all my life."

"Is that a fact, Miss Lasko?" Pashka said as he gently slid the gun back into the holster. "I don't know anything about that or whether you were personally sent up here by Miss Hanson."

"Well, that's not my problem," Heather snapped, still struggling. "I have important work to do, and this man has injured me. Just ask him, why don't you?"

"I can't do that, Miss Lasko," Pashka replied evenly.

"And why not?" Heather asked, outraged.

"Because he cannot answer me, due to the fact that he doesn't have a tongue," Pashka replied. He looked at the man. "Show the woman, Zeke."

Zeke moved his face closer to Heather's and opened his mouth as wide as possible, exposing a cavernous area where his tongue used to be before it was savagely cut out and thrown to a pack of rats.

Heather gasped in horror and averted her eyes from the hideous sight, praying that she would never have to see anything like it again.

"It's an old war injury," Pashka said, amused by the manner the woman squirmed away from his deformed colleague. "It was a penalty for refusing to cooperate with an enemy of this great country." He offered a lopsided grin. "Of course, as is required as recompense, those responsible paid with their lives—eventually."

"Please tell your men to release me immediately, or I shall be forced to inform Miss Hanson of how you and your men mistreated a partner of this firm," Heather said firmly, leveling her eyes at him.

"Junior partner," Pashka corrected.

"But a partner nonetheless, sir," Heather said with a note of authority. "I highly doubt she would appreciate the fact that her attorney has been victimized by one of her own employees, wouldn't you agree?"

Pashka carefully weighed what the woman had just said to him. "Perhaps," he admitted, pausing momentarily, "but that still doesn't explain why you were heading in the opposite direction of your office, does it? The only office located on the left is Miss Hanson's, and no one is supposed to be allowed in that area."

"I really don't have to explain anything to you," Heather said, glaring at him. "But there are some files in her office I need for a case she assigned to me when I was first promoted, if you really must know."

"What case?" Pashka asked. The tone of his voice was losing its edge. "Do I know this client?"

"That is not how it works," Heather replied evenly. "Because that information is protected by both confidentiality and privilege. If you want to know, then you will just have to ask Miss Hanson. However, I surmise that she will more than likely tell you to mind your own business and security matters within the parameters under your purview."

Acquiescing, Pashka motioned for the men to release her. "I apologize for any delay or discomfort you may have incurred, Miss Lasko, but Miss Hanson is most adamant regarding all security concerns—as is Mr. Renfro," he said. He then jerked his head to give a silent order for the men to stand aside. "May I assist you with obtaining the files?"

Baffled by the man's rapid change in demeanor, Heather rubbed her sore arm and looked at it with a befuddled expression masking her face. *Is everyone who works here completely insane?* she wondered, shaking her head. There was nothing she wanted more at that moment than to put as much distance as possible between herself and the three goons. "No, that will not be necessary," she replied in as calm a voice as she could muster. The man frightened her down to the core. "No offense, but you wouldn't know what to look for in the system. And besides, if I know Miss Hanson half as well as I believe, I suspect there will be a number of coded files that will need to be deciphered."

Pashka peered at the watch attached to his wrist. "How long do you think it will take to complete retrieval of the documents?" he asked, pinching his eyebrows together.

"I understand your trepidation, but the work is critical to our boss," Heather stated. "And it would be reckless of me to give an exact time."

"I just don't feel entirely comfortable with granting you access to Miss Hanson's personal office without her prior approval, Miss Lasko," Pashka said uneasily. "Will it take long for you to get what you need?"

Heather exhaled tiredly. "I wish I could say, give you a specific time," she replied, "but it depends on the complexity of the program.

I'm not a computer major. In fact, I may not even be able to log onto her system, or whatever they call it when you get into someone's machine."

"Yeah, I'm not too fond of this so-called technological era myself," Pashka offered, shrugging a single shoulder. "I'm more of an outdated version of doing it the old-fashioned way by using pen and paper. It's a lot more personal and helps the memory."

"I'm a book girl myself," Heather added. "I prefer to feel something tangible in my hands when I'm reading or whatnot." She paused, studying the man's body language. "So am I clear to go?"

"Do you have your security card?" Pashka asked.

Heather removed a gold piece of rectangular plastic and held it up for him to see. "I do, indeed," she replied. "I never leave home without it."

"Then you're all clear, I suppose," Pashka said, tilting his head politely to the right. He took a step back.

"Thank you," Heather said. She turned to walk away when Pashka called out to her. She slowly spun around. "Yes, was there something else?"

Pashka cleared his throat, embarrassed that he was going to ask the woman they had just harassed a favor. "Miss Lasko, would it be possible for us to keep this unsavory incident just between the four of us?" he asked softly. "I would prefer to—"

"What incident?" Heather asked feigning innocence, interrupting the man. She then smiled in a friendly manner.

"Thank you," Pashka said sincerely. "I appreciate it." He offered a weak smile. "I owe you one."

She nodded her head in silence and then turned and disappeared around the nearest corner a few seconds later, humming happily to herself.

The minute Heather vanished from sight, Pashka turned to the men and twisted his index finger in a circular motion. "Lock down the building and don't let anything in or out unless clearance is beyond reproach," he ordered, his eyes cold and deadly serious. "Do I make myself clear?"

"Yes, sir," the man capable of speech replied, while the other man mutely nodded his head in understanding.

"Excellent," Pashka said. He peered down at his watch to check the exact time. "I'll signal you by emitting two taps; now go and do as ordered." He held up a hand of warning. "I urge you not to disappoint me."

"Yes, sir," the man said obediently. "We'll take care of everything, so don't concern yourself."

"Dismissed," Pashka said.

The two men entered the elevator.

While walking down the desolate corridor that led to Jillian's office, using all her skills and training to maintain a purposeful stride that exuded a demonstrable quality in her demeanor that she was acting in an authorized capacity just in case she was being monitored by hidden cameras, Heather was still trying to get her saliva glands to wash away the dryness that claimed her throat during the confrontation.

When she came to the door that led to the powerful woman's inner sanctum, she looked up and down the hallway to check for any sign of prying eyes. Although she had not heard or seen anything remotely suspicious or out of the ordinary, something was bothering her. Everything was going almost too easily. Heather trusted many things, but simple was not among those on the list. The silence was incredibly unnerving. Finally, convinced that she was indeed alone after several moments, she slid the security card home and entered the room where only a single desk and phone system rested.

The decor was exactly the same from when she had been initially summoned by Brad to speak with his boss. Without hesitating, she used the card to gain access to the adjoining room behind the door on the left, which opened with no problem. She then entered the splendor that was Jillian's secret world, a universe that was distinct and apart from the ravaged sickness of society that existed outside the protection of the firm's walls. She allowed her eyes to drink in the environment that never ceased to impress her senses, scanning the entire area from left to right, until her visual acuity came to focus on the door that was strangely adorned with a crude padlock, and was in direct contrast to everything else in the room. Heather withdrew a set of lock picks that had been constructed from a composite of annealed clay from the bun that held her hair off the shoulders and moved toward the door. She continued to search the room for any sign of surveillance equipment.

There was none at all as far as she could determine.

Growing more confident that her mission was going to go off without a single glitch, she slid the picks into the keyhole and expertly manipulated the tumblers until the familiar sound of the lock clicking open reverberated in her ears. She quickly removed them from the clasp, carefully opened the door, half expecting some hidden gargoyle to leap out from somewhere on the other side and tackle her to the ground, and stepped past the threshold. She then exhaled with childhood awe as she marveled at the magnificent sight that would be the answer to every young girl's Christmas wish.

Streams of confetti blanketed the floor like waves of consolidated rainbows of every imaginable color. Situated in the center of the room, erected majestically before her, the most elaborate dollhouse she had ever seen stood in unobstructed view. Hundreds of dolls sat upon shelves that lined the walls from one end to the other. It was like nothing Heather had ever dared to imagine. The fact that the room even existed in the building made her wonder all the more what happened behind closed doors, within the secret confines of the most powerful law firm in the civilized world.

Still amazed by the sublime display of a young girl's fantasy, Heather shut the door behind her and then traveled across the paper-covered ground and over to another door that was located on the right side of the room. Not knowing what to expect, her breath was slowly becoming labored as she placed her hand on the knob. Bells and whistles of warning blared in her head, ringing loudly for her to get out, to run away as fast as her legs would carry her, and never come back, but she was compelled to finish the job for which she was assigned. It was her duty to complete the task given, and nothing would thwart her from accomplishing it.

She opened the door and entered yet another room.

Horrified, Heather opened her mouth in reaction to the abominable scene.

It took her several seconds to realize that it was her screams of horror echoing off the walls, and not those of someone else, like an innocent man who had been stealthily snatched from off the street and was now being mercilessly tortured to death by a talented sexual sadist in the throbbing green glow that illuminated the entire area that was spread out before her. An automated calliope suddenly sprang to life and began to play circus music at an incredibly high volume, the same familiar tune that made children stand up in the stands under the Big Top and cheer for the clowns running aimlessly around in circles.

Hanging from the ceiling on marionette strings like desiccated puppets, the eviscerated bodies of human males dangled limply like a collection of used, discarded condoms that had been left to bake under a hot afternoon sun for years. The skulls that had been left attached to the two dozen husks had been cleanly emptied of all contents, leaving the hollowed out eye sockets blank of any substance as they stared out from the abyss. Hundreds of large jars lined wooden shelves, each containing severed body parts consisting of tongues, eyes and male genitals which free-floated dreamily in a transparent, liquid solution. The air reeked of formaldehyde.

Now conscious that she had screamed aloud, that it wasn't just inside her head, Heather threw a hand over her own mouth and slowly backed away from the freakish display of carnage. *What in the name of God?* Heather wondered, unable to stop herself from trembling. She started to turn around when she felt a pair of strong hands grab her by the shoulders and throw her to the ground outside the room. She cried out in pain when she hit the floor, then shrank back when she looked up and found Mr. Pashka standing over her.

"Women," Pashka said in a monotone voice, shaking his head. "You really can't help yourselves, can you?"

"What do you think you're doing?" Heather asked, nearly hysterical. "Do you know what's in there?"

"You really should not have seen any of that," Pashka said. "I now regret that I let you past us."

"Have you any ..." Heather began as she looked over at the open door.

"Please, just be quiet. Miss Lasko," Pashka interrupted. "I'm extremely disappointed in you." He shook his head. "Do you realize the predicament you've created for yourself, including what you've done regarding me? I'm kind of in a real pickle here, no thanks to your nosey antics."

"What are you talking about?" Heather asked wildly. "There are parts of maybe hundreds of murdered people in there and—"

"Shut up!" Pashka yelled. "What, you don't think I know what has been going on for years? Is that what you think? If so, then you're a complete idiot."

"And what are you going to do about it?" Heather asked, eyes wide.

"About what?" Pashka asked. He looked down at her as if bored, eyes hooded.

"About your boss being a mass murderer, that's what?" Heather shot out.

Pashka smiled down at her. "Why, Miss Lasko, I'm going to do what I always do," Pashka replied. "I'm not going to do anything ... about her."

"I demand ..." Heather began.

"Miss Lasko, is the situation somehow unclear to you?" Pashka asked, watching her with a bland expression, indifferent to her ill-conceived orders. "You are in a position to demand nothing, and I am in a position to grant even less." He stepped over and quietly closed the door. "You see, Miss Lasko, Jillian Hanson is a great woman, brilliant beyond belief, and if she needs to dabble in a hobby that is generally frowned upon by the majority to relax, then the least I can do is provide a shield and a means so she can continue to lead us into a lucrative future." He then removed a small transceiver from his pocket and clicked the button twice to alert his men.

"What are you going to do?" Heather asked, scooting away from the man after he shut the door.

"I'm going to protect the woman who saved my life and the lives of my men and gave us a home," Pashka replied. "We were prisoners of war in a country you've most likely heard of and were awaiting execution by slow torture when Miss Hanson, our guardian angel, came from out of nowhere and paid the ruling authorities to release us. She paid five million dollars for three complete strangers. Of course, those evil bastards had already cut out Zeke's tongue, and our own government denied any knowledge of us, even referred to us as mercenaries of ill-repute, and were more than happy to just let those people murder us in some obscure town square for the unwashed locals who pummeled us with rocks when we were being dragged down the streets."

"But that doesn't excuse what she has done here," Heather said. "Surely you can see that?"

"My loyalties lie where they lie, Miss Lasko, and there is no deviation," Pashka replied. "So you might as well hold your breath. You have nothing to say that will change one damn thing!"

The two security guards showed up and stood at attention as they awaited their orders. Heather looked over at them and cringed away even farther.

"I hope you understand that this is a very unfortunate scenario that I deeply regret, Miss Lasko, but protocol must remain steadfast," Pashka said.

"Wh ... what are you going to do?" Heather asked, stammering.

Pashka exhaled tiredly. "I'm going to kill you," he replied, shrugging his shoulders. "You've given me no choice."

"But you can't just murder me," Heather said, tears beginning to pool in her eyes.

"I assure you that I can and will," Pashka said simply. "I've killed many people, and you will be no different."

"People know where I am," Heather said, desperate to save her own life. "There will be questions, and an investigation if I go missing."

"No, Miss Lasko, there won't be much of either," Pashka said with confidence. He shook his head again, as if he actually felt sorry for the woman's naïveté. "Our friends shall make certain the inquiries are kept at a bare minimum." He smiled apologetically. "I'm sorry to say, but you are simply not that important." He motioned to the two men with a simple snap of the fingers. "Get her up on her feet."

The uniformed men took her by the arms and lifted her up.

"You can't do this," Heather said. "I'm an FBI agent working undercover for the United States government and was personally selected by the attorney general to investigate violations of the Sherman Antitrust Act and the Clayton Act, nothing more." When the disclosed information didn't elicit the expected response, Heather stared at the man in total confusion. "Didn't you hear me? I am a government agent."

Pashka smiled broadly. "And you think that information comes as something unexpected, somehow?" he asked. He rubbed his chin. "Now that is funny. What I find even more humorous is that you think it will somehow change what I am compelled to do. This is nothing personal, Miss Lasko."

The color drained from Heather's face. "You knew I was a federal agent?" she asked, stunned by the revelation.

"Of course," Pashka replied. "How could you ever think a conglomeration of our magnitude wouldn't know everything about the people within the infrastructure?"

"But how?" Heather asked. "I was given the deepest—"

"By the same people who sent you in the first place," Pashka interrupted. "All governmental assets are expendable."

"If you already knew I was an agent, then why didn't you expose me immediately?" Heather asked, perplexed. "Why didn't you tell Jillian?"

"It was my decision to make," Pashka replied. "Miss Hanson really liked you, and I thought we had a chance of turning you to join our team. That is until you decided to poke your nose in places better left in the shadows. If it's any consolation, I was actually hoping you would pick the right team. I guess I was wrong."

The two men tightened their grip on her arms.

"Please, you don't have to do this," Heather pleaded, trying to pull away from the men. "I have information that will benefit the firm."

"I'm sure you do," Pashka said, "but it's too late to make amends." Ignoring the struggling woman, he turned his attention on the two men. "Take her and kill her. Make it look like an automobile accident." He paused and licked his lips. "And make it quick and painless. It's not her fault that she trusted a corrupt government."

"Yes, sir," the guard said. He then removed his grip and pushed her over to Zeke, who quickly coiled his arm around her neck and squeezed until he felt her go limp.

"She was a good little soldier, so treat her with respect," Pashka said.

"Of course, sir," the guard said, nodding his head. Without saying anything further, he offered a quick salute and walked away.

Zeke tossed her unconscious body over his shoulder with ease, turned, and walked in the same direction, never making even the slightest noise.

Pashka remained behind for several minutes as he thought about his next move. The circumstance of having to dispose of the Lasko woman was an unfortunate one. It was something he dreaded to tell Ferguson. But why Ferguson had insisted on allowing the girl into the family fold in the first place was a total mystery. But it wasn't his job to question reasons. It was one of action, and his position in the firm was to follow orders, not to second-guess them. Of course, Jillian was going to be extremely distraught over losing someone she genuinely liked, but Pashka was certain Ferguson would be able to make her understand why Heather had to be removed from the equation. No matter how long he lived, Pashka somehow knew he would never begin to understand why people inevitably got themselves into trouble by venturing into areas that are best left alone. In his opinion, nothing good ever came from curiosity.

When he heard the familiar sound of one of the other doors being shut, Pashka moved across the paper-covered floor to use the phone that was located atop the desk out in the sparsely decorated reception room. Although Ferguson had instructed him to maintain radio silence for twelve hours, Pashka believed the situation warranted a departure from that line of procedure, so he picked up the phone and dialed. When no answer came after thirty seconds he replaced the receiver. Content to wait until contacted, Pashka exited the area and headed in the direction of the elevator.

While Pashka waited to stop at one of the lower floors below Jillian's main office, the two men were busy shoving Heather into the trunk of a car that was parked in the underground parking lot beneath the enormous building. Even though both had killed dozens of people during the course of their military careers, neither derived any pleasure from murdering a woman in cold blood.

Unlike the amoral psychological makeup of their superior, the guard capable of speech sincerely regretted being the cause of ending any life prematurely. He understood that killing was often a necessary evil, but there was never a valid reason to murder innocent people, though he had done so more times than he would ever dare to admit. As the faces of his prior victims flashed across his memory, he peered down at the unconscious woman, whose hands and mouth were secured by strips of gray duct tape. Sometimes he hated his job. But there was little else he could do well enough to make a living. Regardless of his personal feelings about the government, it had trained him to be a perfect killing machine. *She is a pretty little thing*, he thought, pausing. *And far too young to die.* "Oh, well, such is the circle of life," he mumbled under his breath. "No one lives forever." He craned his head around when he heard the garbled noises emanating from Zeke and shrugged his shoulders when he found the man frowning at him. Self-conscious of how strangely alien the man sounded when attempting to speak, the only time his friend dared to try was when they were completely alone, with no chance of being overheard. "What?"

"Grrr," Zeke grumbled as he waved his hands around in the air. "Aaaarr."

"I know, I know," he said, then reached out and patted the man on the back. "I'm not going soft on you. I just don't like some of our chores, that's all."

"Grrr," the man continued. He pointed a finger at his own head.

"Relax, pal," he said. "I have no intention of avoiding our responsibility. I can still feel bad for having to kill the girl, don't you think?"

The man shook his head adamantly.

The guard slammed the trunk shut and offered the man a lopsided grin. "You're a cold man," he said. "I know you're still all pissed off about that dude cutting out your tongue so you can't talk to the girls with that onetime silver tongue, but you really got to move forward and put all that behind you."

"Grrr," the man growled, narrowing his eyes. "Arrr … Grrr … Ou …"

"Yeah, I know," the guard replied, even though he never actually understood a single grunt the man made, playfully shaking his head in a mocking way. "It's just not fair that women generally don't want to date a guy without a tongue. They should see the positive part about it, that it makes you a good listener." He chuckled lightly.

The man flipped him a middle finger in response. "Grrr, hooaao," Zeke grunted again.

"Nice way to communicate, buddy," the guard said, smiling. He then walked over to the driver side and got into the car. He rolled down the window and slapped the outside of the door. "Take her car and follow me out."

Zeke made a few disgruntled noises, removed a set of keys from his pocket, and then walked over to where Heather had parked her BMW earlier that day.

By the time the two men had secured the human cargo and drove out of the underground parking lot in tandem, Mr. Pashka was already down in the surveillance room studying the monitors that were receiving a direct feed from the hundreds of cameras that were installed throughout the entire structure. He walked up and down the long strip of carpet and scanned the screens that were mounted on the walls on both sides of the elongated room.

The technicians, who worked tirelessly on maintaining the sophisticated equipment, and the team members who kept a diligent watch for any sign of potential trouble paid no attention to the man who only spoke when demanding answers.

When Pashka came to the lead machine, still finding it impossible to shake the distinct feeling that something was awry, he tapped on the back of the lead programmer's head, who was sitting transfixed in front of the terminal, and motioned for him to get out of the chair.

"What in the ..." the man began as he turned around with an irritated expression on his face from being so rudely interrupted while doing his work. He then blanched when he saw who had disturbed him, all arrogance evaporating.

"I need to borrow your machine," Pashka said.

"Of course, Mr. Pashka," the man said, turning visibly nervous. The wire-frame glasses that decorated his face slid down to the tip of his nose when he adjusted his position. He quickly got up from the ergonomic chair and stepped aside. "Is there anything else I can do for you?"

Pashka pushed the chair to the side and moved up to the terminal. "Yes, you can go away for ten minutes," Pashka replied calmly. He began to strike the keyboard of the machine with dexterous fingers with amazing speed.

"Yes, sir," the man said. He started to walk away, grateful to put as much distance as possible between him and the man who scared the living hell out of him, but then stopped when called back. "Excuse me, sir?" He turned around.

Pashka craned his head around and looked at the man with dead eyes. "I asked you to get me a cup of coffee," he said. "Black."

"It would be my pleasure, Mr. Pashka," the man said. He then left in search of the dark, blended elixir.

As Pashka ran through the surveillance program in the system, triggering camera after camera on every floor in the building, conducting a physical profile search for Jillian, he was about to give up and notify the outside team members when she suddenly appeared on the monitor. She was alone and dressed in shabby-looking clothes. She was carrying something that resembled some sort of bag in her right hand, but he couldn't get a real clear picture of her or what she was doing because it was oddly dark. Curious, he tapped a key to identify her location because he didn't readily recognize the area, which completely surprised him. He had thought that there was not one section in the building he had not visited at least a hundred times. Unlike the vast majority of the population who worked for Hanson & Hanson, with the exception of perhaps five others, he held the highest clearance possible and could enter every section of the firm whenever the mood so moved him. Total access was an absolute necessity of the job, if control of the environment was to be expected from him.

A few seconds later the computer system designated her as being on the roof, in a utility closet where a gasoline pump that was often used to refill the firm's private helicopter was stationed. He leaned forward, nearly pressing his face against the glass. *What are you doing up there, Miss Hanson?* he wondered as he continued to stare intently at the screen. *You shouldn't be up there by yourself. It's far too dangerous.*

"Excuse me, Mr. Pashka, but I have your coffee," the man announced, holding out a cup of steaming, brown liquid.

Pashka turned and accepted it from him. "Thank you," he said. He then took a sip and smacked his lips to the flavor. "Hey, that's quite good. You're hired."

The man looked at the screen and furrowed his brow. "Is that Miss Hanson?" The man asked. "What's she doing?"

Pashka reached around and turned off the machine. "Nothing," he replied. "It's none of our business."

The man narrowed his eyes. "Then why are you spying on her?" he asked suspiciously. He placed his hands on his hips. "She has a right to privacy, and I don't think she would like that very much. I've heard she's a very secretive type of person and doesn't like to be watched at all."

"Is that right?" Pashka asked in a challenging tone of voice. "And how did you come across that little tidbit of knowledge?"

"Well ..." the man stammered, eyes darting back and forth, "I hear things here and there. You know what I mean, don't you?"

"No, I don't," Pashka said sharply, raising his voice loud enough so that the others in the room could overhear him. "Why don't you fill me in on these so-called things that are said about Jillian Hanson."

The man licked his lips, more nervous than he'd ever been in his life. Sweat broke out across his brow. "I ... I don't know," the man stuttered. He looked at the large handgun hanging from inside the man's jacket, half expecting to be shot to death for nothing more than a slip of tongue. "They're just rumors, Mr. Pashka. You know, workplace gossip, nothing more. I swear to you that it's all harmless."

"Is that right?" Pashka asked angrily. He glared at the man with scornful eyes, his lip curling into a slight snarl like a rabid dog preparing to attack. "From whom?" He clenched his teeth together and then clenched his hands into fists. "I want names, and I want them right now. If anyone has remotely slandered that wonderful woman's name, I swear to God I will cut out their heart and pin it to my dartboard."

In an almost synchronized order, cringing inwardly, the other employees, who were minding their own affairs and working diligently on the tasks at hand, got up from their chairs and exited the room with heads tucked down into their shoulders in single file line. No one wanted to be anywhere near the man suspected of being both insane and a personal hatchet man, possibly a professional killer for the firm. The rumor that circulated among those employees of lesser value within the firm was that those summarily discharged from their jobs were actually taken out back by Mr. Pashka and shot in the head. And the two men with whom he chose to keep company did nothing to dispel any heinous opinions about him. As far as they were concerned, certainly by unanimous consensus, Mr. Pashka was a freak of nature and even more diabolically creepier than Brad Renfro, a man no one, other than Jillian, liked or trusted any farther than he could be thrown.

The man strained to clear his throat after everyone had cleared out of the room. "You're not going to kill me, are you?" he asked through parched lips. "I didn't mean to say anything wrong."

"What?" Pashka asked, confused by the question.

"You know, rub me out, throw me in the river with cement shoes," the man said with a trembling lower lip.

Pashka broke out in laughter, nearly spilling the coffee, and shook his head. "You have watched far too much television, my friend," Pashka said, wiping tears from his eyes. "What do you take me for, the Mafia or something? You just made my whole day." He reached out and patted the man on the back. "What's your name?"

The man stared at him, stunned. He didn't believe the man was even capable of producing a smile, let alone outright laughter. "Um, Barney, Mr. Pashka, Barney Trabble," he replied uneasily. Somehow the visual of the man smiling gave him shivers because it looked unnatural, like how a venomous snake would look just before swallowing its stunned prey if it could show genuine joy.

"How long have you worked for the firm, Mr. Trabble?" Pashka asked.

"Nearly ten years, sir," Barney replied.

"And how do you like working here?" Pashka asked.

"I like it just fine, sir," Barney replied. "It's a great place to work, with nice people, and I enjoy my job a lot."

"That's good," Pashka said. "It's always a positive to like what one does for a living. In fact, the axiom that a man is truly blessed if he can do what he truly loves and also get paid for it is a favorite of mine."

"I've heard that before," Barney said. "Then I guess I'm a very lucky man."

"Are you married, Mr. Trabble?" Pashka asked.

Barney hesitated momentarily. The question about his personal life startled him just enough to cause him to contemplate whether he should try to lie. He quickly decided that it would be an extremely bad move if he did. "Yes, I'm married," he replied.

"Hmm," Pashka mumbled. "How long?"

"Twelve years, sir," Barney replied, growing more uneasy with the inappropriate line of questions.

"I haven't been so lucky," Pashka said. "Children?"

Barney cringed inwardly, wishing the man would just go away and leave him alone. "Excuse me, sir," he murmured. "I didn't hear—"

"Do you have any children?" Pashka asked.

"Uh, yes, I have a child, a little girl," Barney replied. "She turns three this April, on the tenth."

"That's great," Pashka said, grinning. "I've never been blessed with children—unfortunately—but I hope to have a whole brood of them one of these days. It must be a very fulfilling experience. Raising kids, that is."

Barney smiled at the thought of his daughter laughing and playing on the swings in the backyard of their home. "Yeah, there's nothing like it in the world," Barney replied. "I don't know where I'd be without her."

"I can only imagine the amount of joy and pride a father would experience raising and watching a child grow and develop into a woman," Pashka said softly. "It must truly be a beautiful part of a man's life, perhaps the most satisfying for a man." He sighed heavily, as if awed by the mere concept. And then the smile suddenly disappeared from his face, replaced by something else altogether, a look so malevolent that it made Barney's blood run cold. "But I can't imagine the pain one would feel if everything was to suddenly vanish from existence—just like that." He snapped his fingers together to accentuate the point. "Now that would have to be the ultimate nightmare, don't you think?"

Barney's chin quivered. "Wh … what do you mean?" He asked in a frightened stutter, near to tears.

"Mean?" Pashka asked, feigning innocence and failing. "I don't mean one thing, Mr. Trabble."

"Then what are you saying?" Barney asked. He curled his lower lip over the upper.

"I'm not saying anything, Mr. Trabble," Pashka replied, indifferent to the man's obvious emotional pain. "I was just making an abstract statement of how much it would hurt to lose such a treasure of the heart, nothing more."

"There is no need to threaten me, Mr. Pashka," Barney said in a barely audible whisper. "I would never ..."

Pashka stepped closer and rested a single hand on the man's back, then smiled to himself when he felt the man shudder beneath his touch. "I think you may have either misunderstood or mistakenly taken what I said out of context, Mr. Trabble," Pashka said calmly. "I wasn't threatening you. If you thought otherwise, then I apologize." He placed an insincere hand over his heart. "Trust me, if I was threatening you in any way, you would know it."

Barney swallowed with great difficulty. "Uh, yes, sir," he stammered. "I'm sorry if I insulted you in any way."

"Aw, come on, Mr. Trabble, we're all friends here at Hanson & Hanson, wouldn't you agree?" Pashka asked dryly.

"Um, yes, of course, Mr. Pashka," Barney replied nervously, half expecting the man to pull out a gun and shoot him in the head for no more reason than it might be fun.

"And you're my friend, right?" Pashka asked severely, draping his arm over the man's emaciated shoulders.

"Yes, Mr. Pashka, I'm your friend," Barney replied.

"That's perfect, Mr. Trabble," Pashka said, playfully slapping the man on the cheek. "May I call you Barney?"

"Sure, Mr. Pashka, whatever makes you feel most comfortable," Barney replied. "I'm a team player."

"I'm glad to hear that, Barney," Pashka said, nodding his head up and down. "We could use more good men like you at the firm." He reached out and retrieved the chair he had pushed away, and then he guided the man into it. "I want you to do me a favor, if that is all right with you." He sat the man down and patted him on the right shoulder. He leaned over and placed his mouth only inches away from his ear. "Can you do that for me, Barney?"

"Whatever you want," Barney replied.

Pashka reached over him and turned the monitor back on. Jillian was no longer on the screen. He depressed a few keys to adjust the camera's position, to no avail. "I want you to locate Miss Hanson for me," he said, carefully studying the picture for any sign of the woman.

Barney hunched his shoulders. "You want me to spy on Miss Hanson?" Barney asked apprehensively.

"No, not spy, locate her position," Pashka replied.

"Excuse me, sir, but this is highly irregular," Barney said. "Miss Hanson is the—"

"I'm well aware of Miss Hanson's station, Mr. Trabble," Pashka interrupted, "and I am responsible for her safety and protection."

Barney's eyes opened widely. "You think Miss Hanson could be in danger?" He asked, now growing alarmed.

"It's a distinct possibility, Mr. Trabble," Pashka replied. He looked around at all the expensive equipment that filled the room. "Can any of this equipment locate an intruder, someone who is not employed by the firm?"

Barney swiveled around in the chair and scratched his head, deep in thought, grasping desperately for an answer that would appease the man. "Well ..." he stammered, strenuously thinking, "I believe we could run a comprehensive facial recognition scan of everyone currently in the building; however, there is a major flaw because I cannot detect and cross-reference the physical features of someone if they're hiding from the cameras."

"Don't we possess some sort of thermal detection?" Pashka asked, running his eyes over the mass of electronics. "There must be something installed that locates body heat or something like that."

"Uh, no, sir, there's nothing like that here," Barney said, finding the man's line of query bizarre and extremely disturbing. "We would never have any need for anything like that because this is just a law firm, not the Pentagon."

"Well, we'll just have to remedy that little glitch, won't we?" Pashka grumbled under his breath as he straightened up. "Can you locate Miss Hanson and conduct the recognition program at the same time?"

"Yes, of course," Barney replied.

"Do you need anyone to help you run the surveillance?" Pashka asked.

"No, not really," Barney replied, furrowing his brow. "The program is pretty much an automated system." He rubbed at his eyes. "I don't understand. Is there some sort of reason why you don't want anyone else aware of what we're doing in here?"

"I prefer to minimize potential complications," Pashka replied evenly. "With more people involved, more errors arise. The proverbial standby of KISS, 'keep it simple stupid,' is my universal mantra. All I need to know is whether you can run everything simultaneous alone, without any assistance."

"Yes, I can do that," Barney replied confidently.

"Do it," Pashka ordered. He then walked over to a nearby desk and picked up a two-way radio. He set it on a workstation next to Barney.

"What's that for?" Barney asked.

"I want you to stay in constant contact with me and inform me the moment you locate Miss Hanson or discover an intruder," Pashka said.

"But where are you going?" Barney asked.

"I'm going to search the building on foot," Pashka replied.

"Every floor?" Barney asked, opening his eyes in disbelief. "That would take you forever."

"Not if you do your job right," Pashka said.

"I'll do everything I can, Mr. Pashka," Barney said.

"I'm sure you will, Barney," Pashka said with assurance. "If it helps to motivate you, I can guarantee a promotion and pay raise if you pull this off."

"Are you serious?" Barney asked.

"Deadly," Pashka replied. He then walked toward the door and turned his head around just as he opened it. "I'm going to send the rest of the team home and lock this door. You know, to minimize problems."

"I understand, sir," Barney said. He then spun around in the chair, barely hearing the sound of the locks being triggered.

Chapter 15

The rush of crystal meth coursed through Petie's body like an unstoppable freight train, filling him with an almost overwhelming surge of euphoria and belief that nothing and no one could stand in his way or prevent him from fulfilling the postmortem promise he had made to Harriot. Although it had taken every ounce of self-control and discipline to remain patient and hidden away in the shadows for hours, he had taken Bloodstone's advice to wait until just before sunup to make his strike against the ruthless gang that had raped and murdered the girl he loved.

Bloodstone had explained to him that the police used a similar tactic when they were executing a warrant on a dangerous crime organization and that the element of surprise was the most effective weapon in one's arsenal to overcome an opponent with minimal risk to life and limb. After listening to the man describe the most efficient strategy to implement if he wanted any chance to prevail over the men who would not hesitate to kill him, completely understanding that he would get only one opportunity to set things right, Petie accepted the fact that he had no choice but to follow the man's instructions to the letter. It was common knowledge among all players that even the most hard-core partiers were either long gone or passed out on the floor before dawn.

Petie pressed the button on the Indiglo watch that was fastened around his thin wrist. It was just past 5:00 a.m., one hour before the sun would start to make its appearance from behind the horizon. He rolled across the carpeted floor of a van he'd stolen just a few hours earlier and looked out a tinted window in the shape of a heart on the side of the vehicle. Everything was exactly how it had been for the past three hours—dead quiet and dark. Luckily for him, and extremely welcome under the particular circumstances, most of the streetlights had been broken by the neighborhood children, who loved to throw rocks at them. The sound of shattering glass was a local favorite among most juvenile delinquents.

Five more minutes, and he would move to fulfill his destiny.

In an attempt to help pass what might very well be the last moments of his life, Petie removed a small penlight from a pocket in the body armor and the picture of Harriot he carried with him always. He studied her face, with the tiny smile lines that were already beginning to form around her pouty mouth, and smiled broadly. She was so beautiful, so understanding and compassionate, nothing like how he had last seen her, after those monsters had destroyed everything that had made her so very special. He pressed his lips against what remained of her and then affectionately tucked it away in the same pocket. I'll make them pay, Harriot, he swore. I'll kill every damn one of them. He checked the laces on the boots he'd gotten from Bloodstone as part of the purchase and fastened the military mesh belt around his waist that held several hand grenades and magazines tooled to fit the modified HK-91. The 79 mm grenade launcher that was attached beneath the barrel was oiled and ready for immediate use, as was the Starlight scope that was mounted atop the bridge of the weapon. The weight of the night-vision goggles pulled at his thin neck.

As instructed by Bloodstone, he gave a quick inspection of the assault rifle, the .45 Colt that was holstered on his right hip, and the fourteen-inch K-bar knife that was strapped to the other leg. Everything was in perfect working order. He looked at his watch again.

Two minutes to go.

Petie listened the soft ticking of the second hand as it moved around the face of the watch, forcing himself to remain as calm as possible, controlling his breathing, and wondered if there was any chance of surviving such a feat.

According to the man called Crankshaft, the rival gang was comprised of a collection of violent sadists who had respect for nothing. There was nothing any of them would not do, be it robbery, drug dealing, murder, even rape, most of which he could plan on personally experiencing for hours if he allowed them to capture him alive. It didn't matter that he was a man, because each of the thirteen members would take turns sodomizing him until they grew bored and simply killed him, if they were feeling benevolent enough to spare him further humiliation and torture.

Petie shivered from the thought of being gang-raped by a group of degenerates for no more reason than fun and games, followed by a physical puckering of his sphincter muscle. Such a fate left no doubt in his mind that falling into the hands of the enemy was not remotely an acceptable option.

He couldn't be certain as he pulled at the neckline of the heavy armor, but it seemed to be growing uncomfortably hot inside the van.

The chime of the alarm from the watch alerted him that time was up.

He reached over and set the detonator that was attached to four sticks of dynamite for one hour. The click of the device being activated just as the red LED light burst into life signaled Petie that the moment of truth was upon him and that the time had finally arrived to exact deadly revenge for what the evil crew had done. So Petie opened the side door and slid out from the vehicle. There was no going back, for he had willfully passed the point of no return, not that he would take a single step back if he could. Careful so as not to inadvertently awaken anyone in the downtrodden neighborhood, he slowly closed the door.

Prepared for just about anything, Petie moved across a gravel-covered yard of the house he'd parked the van in front of and stepped into the darkest of shadows, taking painstaking measures to stay out of the direct line of moonlight. Even though the residence where the gang members lived was around the corner, at least half a block away, Bloodstone had made it abundantly clear to him that there would more than likely be a guard posted somewhere along the streets, possibly on some roof of a neighbor's home, and any detection of movement in the area would result in an immediate response.

Once stealthily tucked away in the background of a row of hedges that served as adequate camouflage, Petie stopped moving and listened intently for any sign that he'd been discovered. He placed the goggles on his face and methodically searched the streets. All was deathly quiet. The only evidence that any form of life existed at all in the area was the sporadic sound of dogs barking in the distance and a few squalling cats as they fought for territorial dominance.

Satisfied that his cover had not been blown, Petie unslung the rifle from his shoulder and silently moved alongside the adjoining houses. He kept as close as possible to the line of withering foliage that rested next to each tiny domicile as he rounded the corner at the end of the block, and then he stopped dead in his tracks when the house described in vivid detail by Bloodstone came into full view. He held his breath and moved to the left, just inside the bushes. The scenery was exactly as told to him. He kneeled down onto a single knee and studied the situation in front of him, weighing and measuring the best and most effective line of attack. Much of the information that had been shared with him now made far more sense. It was obvious that there would have to be surprise if he had any chance to prevail over such numbers. More than ever before, he wished Billy was with him. Even Jeb and his never-ending sarcasm would have been welcome to balance the odds and help with the predicament.

Three men were on the poorly illuminated porch of the house. One sat in what looked like an old rocking chair, drinking what was probably a beer, while the other two were walking back and forth and smoking cigarettes like a couple of coal-burning freight trains.

Petie quickly calculated the math and concluded that there were at least ten more men, not including any other people who might just be visiting the crew, inside the house. He guessed the distance to be approximately fifty yards, still a little too far for him to want to chance taking shots at the men. He wanted to get within twenty feet before all hell broke loose.

The man who was drinking from the bottle held it upside down and began to shake it. A few seconds later he waved for the two men to come over to where he sat. Each of the men stopped pacing and looked over at him. It appeared that there was some sort of conversation taking place among them, but they were too far away for Petie to hear anything, except for a couple of garbled complaints. The two men shook their heads at the man, moving their arms around in the air. The man who was seated unexpectedly jumped up from the chair, evidently angered by whatever had been exchanged between them, and pointed an accusatory finger at one, then the other. He then threw a hand with the thumb extended over his shoulder, at the house behind him. The two men flipped him middle fingers, flicked the cigarettes into the yard, and disappeared inside the house. The man who seemed to be in charge sat back down and took a pack of cigarettes from his shirt pocket. A few seconds later he was leaning back in the chair with his hands folded over his chest, the smoldering cigarette clenched between his teeth.

It was time to rock and roll.

Petie set the weapon to fire in semiautomatic fashion, gently raised the weapon and targeted the area just above the bridge of the nose. "Die, you evil son of a bitch," he whispered as he exhaled slowly and pulled the trigger.

The explosion shattered the silence of the neighborhood at the same instant the man toppled over with a bullet hole the size of a quarter through the exact spot Petie had brought into the crosshairs of the scope. Several lights in nearby houses sprang to life and then almost instantly went back out, as if those who dwelled inside the walls of their sanctuaries were signaling in domesticated Morse code to those who were bent on killing each other that they saw nothing and heard nothing.

Petie rose up to his feet, holding the weapon trained on the front door, and sprinted toward the house. "Come on, you bastards!" he screamed. He switched the weapon to fire as an automatic. "I'm gonna kill the whole damn bunch of you!" Tears welled in his eyes as he thought about what the monsters had done to Harriot.

One of the men who was pacing across the porch only moments ago stepped out from inside the house and leveled a handgun at him. Petie opened fire and laughed crazily when he saw the bullets pepper the man's chest, blood spraying the walls as he was being pushed back in the same direction from where he had just come by the impact of rounds. The second man leaped over the fallen body, started to shoot at Petie, and then fell forward as his head exploded into a mass of bone and tissue. The sound of glass shattering echoed in the night just as a flash of fire spat from inside the house. Petie felt a dull thump on his chest, but the bullet had no effect on the body armor. He adjusted his aim and opened fire at the broken window and laughed even louder when he heard someone cry out in pain from inside. Someone in the shadows inside the house began to bark out orders, screaming for everyone to get a gun and kill the bastards shooting at them.

"Jonny's dead!" a voice screamed.

"So is Magnum," another voice shouted.

"Jimbo's dead, too, boss," a third voice yelled, "and my main man Spooky took a bullet in the eye."

"I don't give a shit who's dead, you shit bags!" the man who was barking out orders shouted. "Kill the sons of bitches before they kill all of us!"

"Hey, boss, they killed Henny!" A voice cried out. "Henny's dead. Those sons of bitches killed my girl!"

A single gunshot sounded from inside the house.

"If I hear another one of you whine about some dead bitch, I'll shoot you, too," the voice said. "Now get the bastards!"

Petie had just reached the porch when a hail of gunfire erupted from inside the house, scoring several hits in his chest and abdomen. He grunted in pain and fell back from the steps.

"I hit his ass, boss," a voice cheered. "He's down and out!"

"I got him, too," another voice shouted. "Let's cut his damn balls off and feed them to the snake."

"Shut the hell up, you idiots!" the dominant voice ordered, waving for them to keep their voices down so he could hear. "Instead of talking shit, why don't you find out where the guy went? Where are his friends? Is the bastard alone?"

"Whatcha mean, boss?" A voice asked, the tone confused and oblivious to just the mere possibility that the man had somehow survived.

While keeping his shoulder pressed against a wall, he craned his head around and stole a peek out onto the front yard. "I don't see the dude anywhere," the boss said.

"That's because I killed his ass," a voice said happily. "Shot him right in the friggin' heart. Saw him fall off the porch, I did."

"Unless he's some kind of damn zombie, the man should be lying out there in the dirt if he was dead," the boss said.

"He probably just crawled off and died," the same voice said. "No one can get shot that much and not die."

"Then you should have no problem going out there and finding his body for me, right?" the boss asked, his voice dripping with sarcasm. "You know, since you're all so damn fired up sure he's all dead and shit."

"Why me, boss?" the man asked, licking his lips nervously. "I didn't do nothin' wrong at all."

The boss leveled a gun at him. "Because you're so sure he's dead and stinking, that's why," he replied. "And because I asked you nicely; don't make me ask you not so nicely. I promise you won't like it one bit."

"Man, this ain't fair, boss," the man complained, frowning. "I always get picked to be the lab rat in this crew. I go first on the crap no one wants to do and dead last on all the fun things."

"That's because you don't have enough sense to keep your trap shut," the boss said, growing impatient. He looked around at the heavy body count on the floor. "If it makes you feel any better, it appears you're going to move up in the ranks through process of elimination." He chuckled at his own sick joke.

"That's cold," the man said. "They were our brothers."

"Yeah," the boss said. "'Were' being the operative word. Now they're just in the way and attracting a bunch of flies." He pulled the hammer back on the gun.

"How about a vote?" the man asked, the tone of his voice denoting a hint of hope that their leader would agree. "This is America, after all. You know, home of the brave and all that democracy stuff." He tucked the gun behind his waistband.

"You want to vote on it?" the boss asked, smiling as if he'd just been told a riddle. "Are you friggin' serious?"

"Yeah, I do," the man replied, trying the mask the desperation he was feeling by putting on a brave face. "Why not, right? If one of us has to go out there, then there should be a vote. I think that's only fair, don't you?"

"Fine," the boss replied, rolling his eyes. He then turned to the others, who were standing nearby, and raised his hand into the air. "All those still alive raise your right hand if you vote for Squirrel to go outside and check on the crazy asshole in the yard."

The other five men raised their hands high, giggling loudly.

"Man, you guys suck big time," Squirrel said contemptuously. "How about two out of three?"

"It's unanimous, Squirrel," the boss said, adamant. He then leveled the gun he was holding at the man and used it to wave for him to go outside. "Time to do your job and flush out the man who shot our brothers."

Squirrel held up his hands. "Chill out, boss, I'm going," he said, glaring at the other men in the room. "There's no need to shoot me."

"I'm glad to hear it," the boss said, nodding his head. He turned to the others and smiled when he found that they were still trying to stifle the humor in the whole situation.

"If I get killed, then it's on all your heads," Squirrel said.

"I think we'll live," the boss said, "even if you don't."

Squirrel removed the gun from his pants and slid a fresh magazine into it. "Good looking out, homeboys," he said sarcastically, emphasizing the last word of the sentence, chambering a round with a loud snap of metal. "You just keep having a good time. I'll be back in a flash."

While the remaining gang members inside the house were forcing one of their own to venture outside the safety of the walls that separated them from the assassin and into unknown danger, Petie was lying on the ground with his body pressed up against the right side of the porch in an attempt to hide himself from the field of vision of those still inside the house. Although he couldn't quite make out everything being said between them, it was clear enough that one of them had been elected to go search for him. Grimacing in pain, fully aware that he'd been hit several times, Petie had run his hand over the areas that throbbed with a piercing white fire and drew away bloodstained hands. He had no way of knowing how badly he was shot but suspected that it wasn't life threatening, at least not immediately, because he didn't feel either weak or faint. In fact, in complete contradiction to what one might expect after being shot several times, he had never felt so alive, so strong and godlike. His thoughts returned to the girl he'd adored from afar for the past few years, and he momentarily wallowed in self-pity that he would never have the chance to tell Harriot exactly how deeply he felt, about how wonderful a person she was, and how utterly beautiful she was to him. Anger began to raise its vengeful head once again as the visual of what had been done to her resurfaced with unrelenting force, reinvigorating his need to set things right, to show the monsters of the world that she mattered, that there were people who loved her, and that there was a price to pay. He slid a new magazine into the rifle and plucked a grenade from the belt. *I'm trying, Harriot,* he thought as he closed his eyes to conjure up her image. *I'm doing my best.*

Filled with trepidation, holding the gun out in front of him with both hands, alert for even the slightest hint of danger, Squirrel negotiated his way around the dead body of his onetime associate, stepped across the threshold of the bullet-riddled front door, ignoring the third corpse, and moved onto the porch. He could still hear his so-called brothers in arms snickering behind him. Readjusting his grip on the gun, he moved toward the steps that led up to the porch and whipped the gun downward in expectation of finding the man on the other side. *What in the hell?* he wondered, pinching his eyebrows together. He bit down on his lower lip. *Where is he? Maybe the boss had a point.* The dude should've been right here. He looked at the dirt and smiled when he saw several small puddles of blood splatter.

"What do you see?" the boss asked from inside the house. "Do you see the bastard, Squirrel?"

"No, boss," Squirrel replied. "There's no sign of him, but there is blood out here, in the dirt. He was definitely hit a couple of times."

"How bad?" the boss asked.

"Not sure, boss, but he was hit," Squirrel replied. "It looks like he may have wiped the trail out with his hands. I don't know."

"Keep looking," the boss said. "We'll go out back and circle around. If that bastard is still alive, he won't be for much longer."

"Sure thing ...." Squirrel began, but then he felt his throat close shut when he turned just as Petie rose from behind the elevated porch with the HK-91 cradled in his arms. The opening of the barrel looked to be the size of a coffee can. His eyes grew wide as saucers when the flash of fire burned into them as if announcing that the wrath of perdition's flames were upon him. "... boss!"

Arms flailing wildly, the gun slipping from his hand, his body jerked and twisted violently like a dancing seizure victim as it was pelted with a volley of 7.62 mm hot loads. Blood spurted from every wound as he was blown backward until he tumbled off the other end of the porch and hit the dirt-covered ground with a dull thud. He was dead before his face was upturned to the dark skies overhead. A pool of blood rapidly surrounded his body like a maroon-colored outline at a crime scene.

Yelling wildly at the slain man as he tumbled out of sight, Petie pulled the pin of the grenade free with his teeth and threw it through an empty window. "I got something for you, too, you lousy bastards!" He called out as he dropped back down to the ground. He covered his ears with his hands and smiled in joyous expectation of wiping out the rest of the monstrous gang with one last act of vicious aggression.

"What in the hell was that?" a voice screamed out.

"All of you get out of here!" the voice of the boss shouted at the top of his lungs. "It's a bomb."

"Holy shit!" a voice screamed out. "Where did it go?"

"It doesn't matter!" the boss screamed. "Run!"

"But if I can ..." the voice began, but it was suddenly silenced.

The roar of the explosion was deafening, much louder than Petie would have expected, which was instantly followed by a second eruption that violently shook the ground, nearly ripping the roof off the house. Fire belched from each opening in the small home, igniting the plant life that surrounded the area into a thick blaze. The force of it blew what remained of the glass in the front windows across the desert yard, spraying him with tiny fragments of glass. The door was torn off the hinges, bouncing across the porch, and it flew out into the street. It crashed into the side of a car that was parked across the street in a fiery heap of splintered wood. The acrid smell of chemicals and black smoke filled the air.

Set aflame by the showering embers that drifted along the air current, Petie rolled across the dirt and slapped at the tiny flames that threatened to spread and engulf him in an inferno of death.

"Shit!" Petie yelled, surprised by its stubbornness to be snuffed out. The pain from the injuries he'd sustained during the assault caused him to wince as he continued to move about the ground. Once successful in snuffing out the last residuals of the fire, certain that his clothes would not spark back to life, he rose to his feet, groaning as he did so. He had never been so exhausted. The effects of the drugs were wearing off, and the weight of the armor that protected his body pulled down on him. While checking a throbbing wound on his shoulder he listened for any sign that anyone inside the house had survived the blast.

All was graveyard quiet.

Dozens of people were now looking out the windows of their homes, staring in amazement at the total destruction of the structure that housed the men who had tormented them for as long as anyone dared to remember, each silently thanking the stranger who had delivered their neighborhood from the whimsical horrors executed on a daily basis by the gang of murderous rapists. One by one, after nodding their heads and mouthing words that would never be heard by the savior, they shut the curtains to the windows and disappeared back into the shadows of their lives with a new sense of hope that freedom to go about their days unmolested was emerging from beyond the horizon like a phoenix from the ashes.

When the distinct sound of approaching sirens in the distance reached him, Petie dropped the spent rifle and goggles to the ground, then lowered his right hand and drew the handgun from the holster. He was running short on time because the sirens were growing louder with every passing second. He knew he had only a few minutes left to make certain he had finished what he'd come for, and nothing was going to be allowed to interfere with him eliminating every single man in the gang. The promise would be kept, no matter the cost to himself or anyone else.

The sound of the sirens was now only minutes away.

Wounded by bullets and second-degree burns, Petie hobbled around the porch on injured legs and lethargically limped up the steps that led to the front door of what he perceived to be his final act of desperation. Blood dripped from his arms, legs, and torso, leaving behind a crimson trail that told of his journey to see justice done. His left arm was beginning to grow numb, and his vision was slightly blurred. The amount of blood loss was quickly beginning to take its toll on him as he ascended each step with one driven purpose. *I'm trying, Harriot,* he thought as he felt the strength of his body failing him. *I won't let you down, not now. I'll make them all pay for what they did.* Tears began to well up in his eyes.

The sirens were nearly upon him.

Struggling to keep his balance as he stepped across the smoldering entrance of the destroyed residence, his head swimming in waves of dizziness, Petie squinted his eyes against the sting of smoke and chemical gas. The hydrogen chloride gas of what remained of the drug lab burned his throat as if someone had plunged a lit torch down it. Several bodies that looked more like charcoal briquettes were scattered across the war-torn floor. He couldn't tell if they belonged to men or women, not that it made a damn bit of difference to him. They had all been found guilty by him for just being in the den of iniquity and associating with such sinister creatures. The smell of ether touched his nostrils, which explained why the subsequent blast was immense enough to blow out most of the flames that spat out the windows, leaving only a few small traces of flickering patches across the floor and walls. Eyes stinging from the mixture of chemical residue and smoke, looking around and listening for any sign of human life, Petie walked across the floor and made a deep sigh of satisfaction when it appeared that he had fulfilled his promise to kill every one of them.

He then headed down a burned-out hallway and was about to enter one of the back bedrooms when he heard a faint cough from somewhere behind him. He stopped and turned around, his sense of hearing on high alert. He wobbled on weak legs, swaying ever so slightly, so he placed a hand against the wall to steady himself, and looked down the blackened aisle.

It came again.

Petie breathed in deep, grimacing as he struggled to stay conscious. "I hear you, you son of a bitch, and I'm coming to get you," he whispered, blinking his eyes in an attempt to wash away the wooziness that was threatening to overtake him. He took a step forward and stumbled, then quickly steadied himself by placing his hand against the wall again. *Come on, P-man,* he thought, urging himself on. *You can do it. It's not much farther, not much at all.* He growled loudly. "You can't hide from me, not now, not ever!"

The cough came again. It was closer now.

Petie stopped just outside a small closet, gun in hand, and listened for any sound coming from the other side of the shut door.

He pressed his ear against the scorched wood and smiled when the sound of labored wheezing was heard. "I got you," he breathed, "and no one can save you."

The sound of police cars converging on the neighborhood echoed in the house as the drivers slammed on the brakes to bring them to a stop just outside the house.

The sirens fell silent.

Seconds later someone identifying himself as a Sergeant Sanders of the police department was calling out from a bullhorn.

Petie tilted his head toward the sound and smiled. "You're too late, suckers," he whispered. "This one is mine, all mine."

"This is the police department," Sanders announced. "To anyone in the house, come out with your hands up."

Ignoring the man's order, Petie wrapped his blood-covered hand over the knob and pulled the door open with a single yank. "Got ya!" he said.

Bruised, battered, gunshot, and holding a tourniquet around a thigh that was missing the bottom half of his leg, the boss lifted a Smith & Wesson .38 and pointed it at Petie's head. "You got nothing, asshole," he said as trickles of blood ran from the corner of his mouth. He smiled just as Petie closed his eyes, and then he pulled the trigger.

Nothing. The firing pin struck an empty casing. Five more quick clicks sounded with no effect. All six cartridges in the cylinder were spent.

It was the sweetest sound Petie had ever heard. He slowly opened his eyes, still half wondering why his head was intact.

"Shit!" the boss said tiredly. He dropped the gun on the floor and then coughed up another wad of red phlegm. He looked at the man standing over him and shook his head. "I guess you got me, after all." He made a sickly chuckle, shaking as he was gripped by a convulsive seizure. "Go figure, huh?"

Petie lifted the gun and pointed it at the head of pure evil. "I was always going to get you, you piece of shit," he breathed. "You lose."

"Why?" The boss asked, curious as to why someone would go to such lengths to attack him and his brothers. "I don't even know you, do I?"

"No," Petie replied, "but I know you and the terrible things you did."

"Yeah," the boss said. "And what would that be?"

"You raped and killed my girl," Petie replied, feeling the taste of bile at the back of his throat from just speaking the words.

"Yeah," the boss said, showing absolutely no remorse at all. "Sorry to say, buddy, but I've raped and killed a lot of people, so you'll have to be a lot more specific." He shook his head again.

"She was driving home from work and ..." Petie began, stopping when the man started to chuckle through bloodstained lips.

"Now I remember," the boss said, smiling as if remembering a childhood memory. "She was a sweet piece of ass. All of us enjoyed that one. She was a real screamer." He studied the man with smiling eyes. "Are you telling me this is all over some dead bitch who had the time of her life?"

Petie fired two rounds into the man, the first into the crotch, the second through the right eye.

"Whoever is in the house, this is your last warning," Sanders proclaimed urgently. "You have three minutes to give yourself up before we open fire!"

Barely holding on to consciousness, Petie dropped to his knees and stared at the man who had brought so much pain and suffering. *What chain of events could possibly create a person like the man he'd just killed in cold blood?* he wondered, experiencing just a tinge of apprehension over his own grasp on sanity. He then looked around at all the destruction he had caused, all the death. *Was he now any different from those he had hunted?* He had just committed deliberate murder on a mass scale and felt nothing for the people he had slaughtered out of pure revenge.

"You have two minutes," Sanders said, his voice taking on a hint of aggression.

Nearly spent of all life energy, Petie let the gun slip from his hand and took out the treasured picture as he clumsily rose to his feet. "For you, my Harriot," he choked out in little more than a strangled whisper. "It was all for you. Rest in peace."

He then started to walk toward the door on wobbly legs that barely supported his weight, swaying drunkenly back and forth, where squads of uniformed men waited to gun him down like a rabid dog. There was very little left in him. His clothes were now saturated with blood, sticking to him like wet plaster. He unhooked the belt with a single hand and let it fall to the ground. Petie knew he was dying, that he had little time left on earth, but that was fine by him. Until today, contrary to what other people who knew him might say, his life had been a pointless existence, void of any true purpose. He wondered if there was life after death. He certainly hoped so. Just the idea of being able to see Harriot again brought a big smile to his face.

"One minute, or we open fire!" Sanders called out. "In the house, this is your last warning. We will shoot to kill."

"Go ahead and shoot," Petie mumbled, trudging forward. "I'm all done in here." He stumbled and fell to the ground. A cry of pain escaped his lips. *Not yet,* he thought, *and not in here.* He began to pull himself across the soot-covered floor.

When Lieutenant Miller steered his car around the corner of one of the worst neighborhoods in the city and saw the group of squad cars and police officers with guns drawn spread out in what appeared to be a siege on a residence, he stomped down on the accelerator and sent the car racing toward the house that was little more than a burned-out hovel. He honked the horn, forcing every officer who was either standing behind the side of a car or an open door to turn their attention on him. The sergeant holding the bullhorn held up his left hand and yelled for the man to stop where he was and come no closer, but the car kept coming.

Miller plucked the badge from his pocket and held it out the window so everyone could see that he was one of them, a cop.

"Who in the hell is that?" Sanders asked, directing the question to one of the men standing next to him. "Is he crazy or what?"

"I think I know him," the officer replied.

"From where?" Sanders asked.

"I think that's Lieutenant Miller," the officer replied.

Sanders brought the bullhorn up to his mouth again and rotated his body. "Men, hold your fire!" he ordered. "Do not fire unless ordered by me." He looked at the car that had just been brought to a screeching halt not more than thirty feet away. "Well, this should at least be a little interesting."

Miller shoved the door open and rushed over to where the man with chevrons on his arm stood. He kept the shield held high, gasping for air. "Who's in charge here?" he asked, his voice slightly louder than intended.

Sanders looked at the badge. "That would be me, Lieutenant," he replied. "We received an anonymous tip about an hour ago that there was going to be a gangland hit in the area." He paused. "Whoever it was refused to identify himself."

"So it was a man who made the call?" Miller asked.

"That's my understanding," Sanders replied evenly. "I didn't personally speak with the person."

"And you just got here?" Miller asked, incredulous. "What took so long for you to respond?"

"I'm not real sure, Lieutenant," Sanders replied uneasily. "It was just one of those things, you know. I think some wires got crossed. That, and no one in the department took it seriously."

Miller looked at the house and shook his head. "It looks pretty damn serious to me," he said. "Do you know if there are any survivors?"

Sergeant Sanders furrowed his brows. "I'm not sure, but there very well might be," he replied. "We heard two shots a few minutes ago from inside the house. It wasn't at us. At least, I'm fairly certain it wasn't. Everything has been dead quiet ever since, which is rather peculiar."

An elderly man holding a small dog in his arms passively stepped out of his house and looked at the dilapidated structure with a huge smile covering his wrinkled features. He hugged the hairy creature against his chest and unexpectedly burst out in laughter. The officers in the field stared at him as if he were completely nuts. His reaction was the last thing anyone would have expected. Other people—men, women, and children—began to slowly step out from locked doors. All were smiling brightly.

Completely flabbergasted by the spectacle of an almost giddy audience of spectators, Miller started to walk toward the old man but turned his attention back on the house when he heard someone shout out a warning that someone was coming out of the house. It took less than a second for him to recognize the young man from the alley. He moved forward and motioned for everyone to lower their weapons.

"I am Lieutenant Miller and am ordering every one of you to lower your weapons!" he yelled. "If any man fires a single shot, I will bring him up on charges."

The mass of officers lowered their weapons as ordered.

"Oh, kid, what did you do to yourself?" Miller breathed, shaking his head as he watched the boy he had interviewed in the back of the ambulance drag himself over the corpse of a body partially blocking the doorway. "Petie, you stupid, stupid kid." He slid the badge back into his pocket as tears coursed down his cheeks. "I should've known. You really loved that girl, didn't you?"

Sanders craned his head around and stared at Miller in surprise. "You know that guy?" he asked.

Miller nodded his head. "Yeah, I know him," Miller replied in a hushed tone of voice. "He's a good kid, just got wrapped up in loving someone far too much and got lost in its vacuum."

Awed by such an impossible feat, the people in the neighborhood focused their attention on the young man pulling himself across the porch, crawling toward the steps with blood-covered fingers. And then they did something that no one in a civilized world would have ever expected. Eternally grateful to the stranger for returning their neighborhood, they cheered and clapped for the man who did what none of them could ever hope to accomplish for themselves.

Shocked by the incongruent display of reverent behavior, the sergeant looked around at each happy face in amazement. "What in the hell are they so damn happy about?" Sanders asked. "It looks like a damn war took place."

"I think you're right, sergeant, and the boy is their hero for killing some very bad men," Miller replied. "I guess it is true that some people just need killing, if others want to live in peace with one another." He went to walk forward when the sergeant grabbed him by the arm to hold him back.

"Where do you think you're going?" Sanders asked.

Miller shook the man's hand free and looked at him with a less than friendly expression.

"I'm going to go see if I can help the kid," Miller said. "He's a victim, too."

"The suspect hasn't been secured, Lieutenant, and it's not safe," Sanders said. "You should wait—"

"For what?" Miller interrupted contemptuously. "The man is probably dying and doesn't deserve to die alone, not after he did our job for us."

"Look around, Lieutenant," Sanders said. "The kid's a damn killer."

"I know what the kid is, so don't you dare presume to tell me something you know nothing about," Miller spat.

"But," Sanders stammered. He didn't understand why the lieutenant had become so defensive.

"But nothing," Miller finished. "I'm in charge and am going over to the kid, so tell your men to make sure they stand down."

"Yes, sir," Sanders said obediently.

"Has anyone even bothered to call the paramedics?" Miller asked.

"Um, I think so," Sanders replied with uncertainty as he looked around at the other men.

"Well, why don't you get on that and see that it wasn't overlooked, too," Miller said irritably. He then walked toward the man whose clothes were still smoking.

The pain that wracked through Petie's body was nearly

unbearable, causing him to whimper as he dragged himself down the steps of the decimated house. Grunting with every slight movement, still clutching the picture of Harriot in his hand, he struggled desperately until he had successfully pushed himself up into in a sitting position on the bottom step.

The stars overhead were beginning to fade away as a new day slowly arrived. He looked out and across the street, to the east, and strenuously lifted his blood-crusted lips to form a smile when he felt the warmth of the sun caress his face. It was the second most beautiful thing he had ever seen in his life. He raised the picture and pointed the image toward the sunrise. At last he had finally found the courage to share a sunrise with the girl of his heart's desire. He had lost count of how many times he had dreamed of the moment when he would be holding Harriot in his arms. The only remaining thing he now regretted was that they would not be able to share its setting in the west just before nightfall.

"I can see everything so clearly now," Petie murmured as he began to slump forward. "All the love and meaning it holds." The picture then slipped from his fingers and drifted several feet on a current of wind before it came to rest on the dirt-covered pathway that lead out to the street. "So this is love?" With his last ounce of strength, eyes fluttering weakly, he smiled at the photograph and reached out for it just before he collapsed onto the ground with an inner peace that he had never known as he breathed his last.

Lieutenant Miller had just reached the curb when he watched the young man topple over and land on the ground in a lifeless heap. "No!" he shouted as he approached the fallen man. "Hang on, kid, it's going to be all right. Help is on the way."

The screeching sound of an ambulance's siren could be heard in the background.

Miller dropped down to his knees, emotionally moved by the boy's commitment to avenge the girl's senseless murder, and cradled Petie's head in his lap. He gently rocked him back and forth, doing everything he could to avoid looking into the blank stare of the eyes. "You stupid kid," he mumbled under his breath. "You didn't have to die. Why didn't you just let us deal with these people?" He then saw the picture that rested only a few feet away and picked it up with an almost loving grace. As much as he tried, silently praying for some sort of answer, there was no doubt in his mind that he would ever fathom any possible way how one person could love another so much. And in a strange way that he couldn't entirely comprehend, while gently laying the picture of the girl on Petie's chest, he also couldn't deny the fact that he was jealous of the boy and his capacity to love so profoundly.

Several of the neighborhood people who had seen death far more than anyone should ever have to witness during the course of a single lifetime began to weep from the loss of a boy clearly braver than any of them.

"It looks like you got all of them, Petie," Miller whispered. He was torn between the concepts that supposedly separate vigilantism from a society of law and order. He then respectfully ran the tips of his fingers over the eyelids to close them for the last time. *What a damn shame*, he thought, motioning for the sergeant to approach.

The deafening blare of the ambulance's siren was silenced the moment it was parked next to the sergeant's squad car. A pair of paramedics got out and looked at the scene in front of them. The man who had gotten out of the passenger side whistled in response to the amount of devastation, while the driver walked over and introduced himself to a man whose sleeves were marked with stripes.

"Excuse me, sergeant, but are you in charge of the crime scene?" the paramedic asked, finding the whole situation nearly unbelievable. He had never before seen such carnage in a neighborhood.

Sanders held up a hand to silence him and shook his head. He then turned his attention on an officer standing no more than eight feet away. "Myers, take some of the officers and check out the area to see if there are any survivors," he ordered. "But under no circumstances whatsoever are any of you to go inside the premises until the bomb squad has cleared the area. It looks like we may have to also notify the ATF."

"Yes, sir," Officer Myers replied. He then wandered off to select a handful of men to survey the area.

Sanders turned to the paramedic with narrowed eyes. "What took you guys so long?" he asked bitterly.

"Hey, me and my partner just got the call," the paramedic replied defensively. "We were told there was an incident involving a couple of possible victims; however, nothing was said over the radio about World War III. We got here as fast as we could, Sergeant." He looked at the scene and shook his head. "Lord almighty, what in the hell happened here? It looks like the place was carpet bombed."

"I'm not real sure," Sanders replied. "You'll have to ask the senior officer on duty." He pointed a finger at the lieutenant, who was still cradling Petie in his arms. "I don't know how, because he wasn't even here, but the lieutenant seems to have a better handle on things and what happened. What I do know is there was a massive explosion that literally blew the house apart."

"A bomb?" the paramedic mumbled uneasily, licking his lips nervously. "Are you serious?" He paused as he thought about the implications of a possible terrorist attack and looked around. "Do you know if anyone is still alive?"

"I doubt it," Sanders replied. "It looks like the only evidence that anyone survived the initial blast just died."

"How can you be so certain?" the paramedic asked.

The sergeant exhaled deeply, growing impatient with the man. "Because the lieutenant hasn't bothered to call you over, that's why," he snapped angrily.

"Hey, take it easy, pal," the paramedic said, taking a step back. "There's no reason to shoot the messenger. We're all on the same team here. I'm not the enemy."

"You're right, of course," Sanders breathed apologetically, lowering his eyes. "I'm sorry about the sour attitude. I just can't believe ..." Startled, the last words of the sentence trailing off, he turned at the sound of shouts.

"Officer down! Officer down!" a group of voices shouted at the top of their lungs, panic-stricken. The uniformed men and women scrambled to get out of the open clearing, away from the trajectory of additional rounds.

"Take cover and get down!" a young officer screamed, diving to the ground.

The neighborhood people, who had been mourning the death of the young man only moments ago, cried out and ducked for cover, some leaping to the ground. Others raced back into the safety behind closed doors.

"There's a sniper!" someone yelled. "Someone's shooting at us, and there's a man down. He's down. I repeat; he's down!"

"Who's hit?" another yelled out to anyone who might have seen what happened. When no one responded, he began to scan the area to find his own answer. He was about to repeat the question but then fell silent when his eyes came to rest on the near-headless lieutenant, whose body was now sprawled across the body of the boy. Rage filled him. He drew his weapon and searched for any sign of the gunman. "Where is he? Does anyone have a fix on the sniper's position?"

The other officers, who had regained their composure, were now holding their guns at the ready and studying the terrain. Each desperately struggled to find a visual target to shoot, but there was nothing to identify. Whoever had fired the lethal bullets was either waiting to kill another officer or had already fled the scene.

The sergeant leaned into his car and reached for the radio. "Dispatch, this is Sergeant Sanders," he announced, panting heavily. "We have an officer down and are in need of immediate backup. I repeat, we have an officer down and are in need of backup!"

The radio suddenly crackled to life.

"This is dispatch," the voice of a woman announced. "Where is your position, Sergeant Sanders?"

"Palisade Gardens, Birchwood Street," Sanders replied. "Please send a dozen units. We have a sniper. We're taking fire from an unknown."

"Acknowledged, sergeant," the woman confirmed. "Cars have already been sent to your position."

"Copy that, dispatch," Sanders said. He then tossed the radio on the seat and resumed his former position behind the car door.

While the team of officers remained sheltered behind barricades of safety, hidden away behind improvised bunkers for protection against an invisible shooter as they waited for additional personnel, Ferguson and Brad were climbing down from a water tower approximately three blocks away. With facial expressions of granite, neither man spoke a single word. Conversation was not necessary because they were forever united in a symbiotic relationship for the sole purpose of accomplishing a single mission, one specific objective, which was to insulate Jillian from all potential danger by eliminating the last vestigial threat to her and the Hanson legacy.

Chapter 16

Dozens of people were hurriedly exiting the building of Hanson & Hanson when Harris pulled into the large parking lot. Although it appeared uncharacteristic that so many would be leaving in such mass numbers, it was even more peculiar that no one seemed to be smiling or talking among one another as they spread throughout the area in search of their cars. The behavior is what most intrigued him.

Cautiously creeping through the hundreds of departing employees to avoid a collision with both flesh and metal, cursing those not bothering to watch where they were going before darting from between cars, he had to shield his eyes against the sun as he rounded an expensive Jaguar in search of anyone that might be willing to stop long enough to answer a few questions. If there was any reasonable chance to learn why an exodus was taking place during such early morning hours, he knew his best opportunity rested with asking an employee who was not an attorney. In spite of being designated as officers of the court, and with both a professional and ethical duty to uphold the law, it seemed to him that lawyers were the worst people to try and interrogate because they were seldom, if ever, remotely cooperative.

On a quest to find someone who would not immediately attempt to invoke an amendment to the Constitution, turning left when he came to the end of the long stretch of cars, it wasn't until he saw a man wearing a Windbreaker and baseball hat step out from the building and remove a pack of matches from one of the pockets to light a cigarette dangling from his mouth that Harris believed he had found his man. So, not wanting to miss his best chance to catch the modestly dressed man, he applied pressure to the accelerator and sped the car up so he could catch him before he set a single foot onto the tarmac. He removed the badge from his pocket and rolled down the driver's side window.

Bobby Picket could not have received better news when the announcement came from upstairs, issuing an order that all personnel were to take the rest of the day off with pay and exit the building immediately. He found it hilarious when everyone nearby looked around as if they had just been told that hell had truly frozen over and the world had come to an end, which was instantly followed by a series of panicked questions.

No one had answers.

When several members of the cleaning staff approached him to ask if he knew what was happening, quickly dismissing their obtuse concerns about a possible terrorist threat with a simple wave of the hand, Bobby merely shrugged his shoulders because he didn't understand why everyone was so resistant in refusing to simply enjoy a free day of fun in the sun at the expense of the powers that be. He could hardly wait to pay a visit to the local track and lay his last paycheck on a sure thing, which happened to also be the name of the horse that was destined to quadruple his money in just a matter of a few seconds. Bobby took a long drag on the cigarette and closed his eyes as the rich flavor filled his lungs to full capacity. *Now that's heaven,* he thought. And then he opened them at the sound of a car idling in front of him. *I knew it was too good to be true. Everyone always rains on my parade.* He flicked the cigarette into the parking lot.

"Excuse me," Harris began, palming the badge to hide it from clear view, "but can I speak with you for just a minute."

"What do you want, cop?" Bobby asked in a half growl.

Harris smiled. "What makes you think I'm a cop?" he asked, curious.

Bobby rolled his eyes. "I'm around friggin' lawyers all day long," he replied, the tone lacking any semblance of friendliness. "And cops are always somewhere around stinking up the place even more. You guys and lawyers have the same kind of stink. The only ones who smell worse are politicians. They're like a combination of both evils, a real gang of devils, like *Rosemary's Baby*."

In spite of the blatant insult flung by the man, who was probably some sort of janitor or maintenance worker, Harris laughed aloud. For some reason, unknown to him at the time, the comparison to one of the scariest movies ever made struck a funny bone. He dangled the badge from the tips of his fingers. "So I guess this wouldn't impress you in the least, huh?" he asked, even though he already knew the answer.

"Nope," Bobby replied, shaking his head,

"It wouldn't compel you to want to cooperate either?" Harris asked humorously, enjoying the exchange.

Bobby shook his head. "Nope," he replied. "Not in the least."

"No respect for the badge, is that it?" Harris asked.

"Oh, I have plenty of respect for what it's supposed to represent," Bobby said, "just not for the person who carries it." He smiled lopsidedly. "Nothing personal."

Harris tucked the badge back inside his pocket and nodded appreciatively. "I think that's about as honest an answer as I've ever heard," he said.

"I do my best, regardless of the overpaid people I have to clean up after," Bobby said. He took out another cigarette and slapped the butt against the back of his hand. "Are we about done here? I have a lot to do today."

"Will you answer me just one question?" Harris asked.

"Shoot," Bobby said. He lit the cigarette and took a heavy drag.

"Where is everyone going?" Harris asked.

"Home, I guess," Bobby replied, shrugging his shoulders. "Don't know why, but we were all given the day off—with pay." He waved to a few of his coworkers as they passed by on their way to their cars.

"I take it that such doesn't happen very often," Harris said.

"Try never," Bobby said. "Not that I'm complaining."

"So, everyone was sent home?" Harris asked.

"Yeah, as far as I know, buddy," Bobby replied. "I'm sure a few of those creepy dudes are staying because they never leave. But all of us regular people are gone." He took another heavy drag and exhaled a thick cloud of smoke.

"Thank you," Harris said. He then drove the car forward and parked in a reserved parking space that was vacant.

Bobby watched him for several seconds before stepping off the curb and walking over to where he had parked his rolling rust bucket of a car. *Pain in the ass cops,* he thought as he struggled to unlock the car door with a bent key. *All they ever do is pester people and ask stupid questions.*

Harris had walked no more than three steps away from his car when a woman immaculately dressed in an expensive power suit and carrying an attaché case approached him with a scowl covering her face. He tried to move around her in order to avoid any sort of time-consuming confrontation with a woman who was obviously an attorney with the firm, but she stepped in front of him and used the case to flank any attempt for an escape. He exhaled in exasperation.

"Excuse me," the woman said snidely, "but what do you think you are doing? These spaces are reserved for attorneys only, not visitors." She pointed at a sign with the name of the person for whom it was reserved. "Can't you read?"

"How do you know I'm not with the firm?" Harris asked.

"That hideous jacket told me," the woman said, intending to mock him. "Besides, Carolyn Bettingsworth has an office next to mine, and you're not her."

"I see," Harris said. He then retrieved his badge and held it up for her to inspect.

The woman sneered. "What, you think I care about that piece of tin?" She asked in a sarcastic tone. "It still doesn't change the fact that you can't park here, because it's reserved for employees."

"I'm on official police business," Harris said.

The woman snickered loud enough for him to hear. "I don't care if you're officially on a quest to find the Holy Grail," she spat. "It doesn't alter the fact that you cannot park here." She removed a cell phone from a jacket pocket and then smiled almost sadistically at him. "You can explain it to the tow truck driver."

Harris shook his head in annoyance. "I don't care," he mumbled. "Do whatever you want."

Without wasting any more time on the disgruntled woman, Harris maneuvered around her and headed toward the front entrance of the massive structure. *Pain in the ass lawyers,* he thought, shaking his head. *Miller is right to hate all of them.* He ignored the pompous woman standing in his wake, who was now waving her phone in the air and bragging about how his car was going to be dragged off to the city dump where it belonged.

The harried-looking secretary who was stationed at the main desk in the lobby appeared to be no friendlier than the woman in the parking lot when Harris walked up and displayed the gold shield that proved he was a detective of the police department. She pushed horn-rimmed glasses back up her nose and peered up with bloodshot eyes. She was still extremely displeased over being pressured by her superiors to work an additional shift after most of the support staff was allowed a free day with full pay because security was adamant over allowing no one on the premises who wasn't already inside the building.

"Good morning, Miss," Harris greeted. "I'm Detective Harris and am here to see Jillian Hanson."

"So what," she said, unimpressed with the man.

"Please call her and tell her that I'm demanding to speak with her," he said. "It's urgent police business."

The woman yawned. "And?" she asked.

"Did you hear me?" Harris asked, showing the first signs of growing angry. He knocked on the top of the desk with his knuckles.

"Of course, I heard you," she said tiredly. "You're standing right here." She paused. "We are experiencing some sort of security sweep, so I will please ask you to leave immediately. You were not supposed to have entered the building." She used a pen to point at the door. "Please leave before I call security."

"I'm not leaving until I speak with Jillian Hanson," Harris said. He then turned left and walked toward the elevator doors.

The secretary stood up from her chair and looked around for assistance. "Security, stop that man!" she yelled to no one in particular.

The last group of the employees who were heading out the door completely ignored her and continued on their way in anticipation of enjoying the day off from work. When no one seemed remotely inclined to help her stop the intruder, she picked up the phone on the desk and dialed a number that would connect her directly to the head of security.

Pashka was still searching for Jillian when the private line to his personal cell phone came to life. He pulled the miniature device from his pocket and flipped it open. "Yeah, who is this?" he answered in an annoyed tone of voice.

"This is Ruth Henderson, Mr. Pashka," she announced anxiously. She was deathly afraid of the man. "I work as the lobby secretary."

"What do you want?" Pashka asked, not bothering to hide the displeasure in his voice. "I'm a little busy."

Nervous over speaking with the man everyone in the firm had referred to as creepy, Ruth cleared her voice. "I apologize for the intrusion, but we have a breach in security," she announced softly, wishing she didn't have to speak with the man at all. There was a short pause on the other side of the line. "Hello?"

"Yes, I'm here, Ruth," Pashka replied. "Please explain."

"Yes, sir," Ruth said. "A detective was just here asking questions about Miss Hanson and was demanding to speak with her. I tried to stop him, but—"

"Was his name Harris?" Pashka asked, interrupting the woman.

"As a matter of fact, it was," Ruth answered uneasily. "I tried to stop him, but he refused to listen to me."

"It's okay, Ruth," Pashka said softly. "You did nothing wrong, so please just calm down and tell me where he is."

Ruth took a deep breath to calm her frayed nerves, only partially accomplishing the objective. "That's what I've been trying to tell you, sir," Ruth said, the stress in her voice rising yet once again. "He refused to leave the building, even after I threatened to call security. He then stomped off and sneaked into the elevator after the doors opened to let more employees who work upstairs off on the floor."

"So he's in the elevator, heading upstairs?" Pashka asked.

"Um, yes, sir," Ruth replied.

"Do you know where he was going?" Pashka asked.

"I'd say to find Miss Hanson," Ruth replied.

"No, I mean, do you know the floor?" Pashka asked.

"I'm sorry, but I have no idea," Ruth replied. "I called your private line the minute he walked away."

"There is no reason for you to apologize, Ruth," Pashka said. "You did the right thing in notifying me as soon as possible." He paused. "I would like you to do one more thing for me, okay?"

"Sure, whatever you want," Ruth said.

"I want you to make a general announcement that all personnel are to be out of the building within the next five minutes or face immediate discharge," Pashka said. "I don't want a single person left inside the firm, except the lone man in the surveillance room. Don't worry about him because I will personally contact him."

"Everyone, sir?" Ruth said uneasily.

"Yes, Ruth, and that includes you," Pashka said. "I want you to lock the front doors on your way out. Do you understand?"

"Uh ..." Ruth stammered.

"Do you understand, Miss Henderson?" Pashka repeated, his voice more aggressive.

"Yes, I understand," Ruth replied submissively.

"Good," Pashka said. "Now just follow my instructions to the letter." He snapped the phone shut and then retrieved the small two-way radio that was clipped to his belt and depressed the talk button. "Mr. Trabble, this is Mr. Pashka. Pick up."

Startled by the unexpected crackle over the speaker, nearly knocking the mobile keyboard from off the desk, Barney jumped in his seat and quickly reached for the radio that was in front of him. He then depressed the button on the right side of it. "Hello, this is Barney Trabble," he said.

"Have you located Miss Hanson?" Pashka asked.

"Yes, sir," Barney replied. "I've been maintaining a track on her ever since I detected her entering the elevator. It appears that she is heading back up to her office. As you know, Mr. Pashka, there is no surveillance beyond the elevator doors on the floor where her personal office is located."

"Shit," Pashka muttered through clenched teeth. He'd momentarily forgotten. "I knew that was going to come back and bite me on the ass."

"Excuse me, sir?" Barney said, praying that he didn't inadvertently do something to incur the man's wrath.

"Nothing," Pashka said. "There's going to be an announcement that everyone in the building is to evacuate effective immediately, but you are to ignore it. Under no circumstances are you to leave your post. Do you understand?"

"Uh, yeah, sure," Barney replied uneasily. "But why is everyone being ordered to leave the premises?"

"That's none of your concern, Mr. Trabble," Pashka snapped. "I have a new project for you to focus on."

"Is it legal?" Barney asked, trepidation filling his voice.

"Of course it is, you buffoon," Pashka growled angrily. "We have an intruder in an elevator, and I want him located as soon as possible."

"Do you know who it is?" Barney asked.

"Yeah, I do," Pashka replied severely. "It's someone who is not supposed to be in the building, a person I believe is a physical threat to Miss Hanson. The secretary, a Ruth Henderson, down in the lobby, tried to stop him, but he rushed past her and somehow got into one of the elevators and is now looking for Miss Hanson. I believe he means to kill her."

"God almighty," Barney breathed into the radio. "I had no idea the situation was so gravely serious. I'm so sorry." He paused, gathering his thoughts. "Did you say he slid into one of the elevators?"

"Yes," Pashka replied evenly. "Evidently, he dove into the one closest to the desk in the lobby. It happened only a few minutes ago."

"Do you have a physical description?" Barney asked.

"Yes," Pashka replied. "He's in his late twenties, maybe early thirties, brown hair, about 190 pounds and just under six feet tall."

"One moment, please," Barney said. He then set the radio down and began to madly type away at the keyboard. Less than ten seconds later the image of Detective Harris riding in the elevator showed up on the surveillance screens. "Gotcha, ya murderous bastard!" He picked up the radio, grinning from ear to ear. "He's still in the elevator, Mr. Pashka, going up."

"Is it possible for him to reach Miss Hanson's floor?" Pashka asked, growing more concerned by what he had heard.

"Normally, I would say no," Barney replied. "But nothing is normal today. I'm sure security on the floor will prevent him from ever getting off the elevator."

Remembering the task he had assigned to Zeke and his partner, Pashka gripped the device in an iron fist. "I want you to maintain constant surveillance on the man, do you hear me?" Pashka barked, his voice severe.

"Yes, sir," Barney replied. "Do you want me to notify outside security?"

"No," Pashka replied. "I will deal with this man personally, so do not contact anyone. In fact, I want you to shut down all outside communications." He paused, thinking. "And execute protocol thirteen."

Barney licked lips that suddenly went bone dry. "Are you sure you want to do that, sir?" He muttered uncomfortably. "That is reserved strictly for—"

"Just frickin' do what I say!" Pashka ordered, cutting the man off in midsentence. "I want all outgoing transmissions blocked. Do I make myself clear?"

"Maybe I should call the police," Barney said.

"No, Mr. Trabble, do not call the police," Pashka snapped. "If this man is some sort of terrorist, corporate or otherwise, the police will only get Miss Hanson killed."

"Uh, okay," Barney said, though still doubting the man's judgment to shut down the communications to the outside world. "Whatever you think is best and safest for Miss Hanson."

"Which is why I'm going to try and cut the man off before he finds her," Pashka added. "So keep a keen eye on him and contact me if something unusual occurs," Pashka said.

"I will," Barney promised. "I won't even blink."

"That's good to hear," Pashka said.

Satisfied that everything was somewhat under control and contained, at least for the moment, Pashka clicked off and reattached the radio to the belt. He then slid a handgun from the shoulder holster to begin the hunt for his intended prey. It had been several years since he'd last stalked a human being as game, something that had always proved to be an enjoyable sport, and was looking forward to mounting the detective's head on his mantle.

While Pashka was mentally calculating the best strategy to ambush and kill the man who had invaded the territorial boundaries of the law firm, Harris was staring at the flashing number on the panel inside the moving box as he continued to ascend to where he believed was his destination.

The sound of a tiny bell and the doors opening with a slight whoosh signaled that he had arrived at the end of the road. He stepped out of the elevator, which had stopped at the floor of Jillian's private domain, and looked around with a strange sense of curiosity. It was so quiet. Not a soul could be found.

Startled by the sound of the door closing, he placed his hand on the butt of his weapon and spun around on his heels as if expecting to be attacked from behind. And then he felt stupid for overreacting to nothing more than the mechanics of machinery.

After the sound of the descending elevator faded away, Harris turned back around. The hairs on the back of his neck stood on end. It was still so quiet. Too quiet. And it seemed that no one was anywhere to be found. He looked left, then right, and started to wonder if he had unintentionally gotten off on a vacant floor, when he heard what sounded like the playful voice of a child coming from somewhere down the hallway. *What in the world is going on?* Harris wondered. He then headed in the direction from where the giggles emanated.

"Attention, attention, by order of the head of security, all employees of Hanson & Hanson shall evacuate the building immediately," the voice of a woman thundered. "You have five minutes to leave the premises before the doors are locked. Anyone who is found inside the building after said lockdown shall be subject to dismissal from this firm. There will be no exceptions whatsoever. This is your first and last warning. Thank you."

The words announcing the order for evacuation by security did not sit well with Harris. Whatever was going on, there was no doubt that whoever was in charge was minimizing the risk of exposure. He removed a cell phone from his pocket and attempted to dial out to request backup and notify Miller that he had deviated from their original plan but received no signal. *What the hell?* he wondered, shaking the phone as if that would cure the problem with reception. It was quickly becoming abundantly clear to him that his narrow-minded arrogance and lone-wolf tactics had worked to his detriment, effectively isolating him in the belly of the beast. Cursing himself for being so reckless and stupid, he threw the phone to the ground in a fit of fury. His ego had finally trapped him.

The sound of a child giggling even louder than before caught his attention again.

Harris made a deep sigh. "Well, in for a penny, in for a pound," he muttered under his breath. He straightened up his shoulders and continued his journey down the corridor until he came to an ajar door with Jillian's name inscribed on an unpretentious plate.

The sound of giggling came again.

Slowly, quietly drawing his weapon, he pushed the door fully open and entered a near-barren reception room. He looked about the area, gun held at the ready, and exhaled with trepidation when he found nothing but just another door.

"Hello," Harris called out. "Miss Hanson? Miss Jillian Hanson? This is the police."

The sound of a child breaking out in a familiar lullaby came from the opposite side of the door.

"Anyone here?" Harris called out again. "This is the police."

When no one answered him, goose bumps rising on the flesh of his arm from the almost sinister sound of the child's voice, something in the tenor not quite right, Harris moved across the floor and opened the door.

In the blink of an eye, the truth had been exposed to the light, where only darkness dwells.

Gasping aloud, all sense of collective reasoning for rational contemplation vanquished, Harris looked down at the last thing imaginable. The image sent his analytical mind into turmoil, an intellectual chaos from which there was no escape. Nothing had been what it seemed on the surface.

Dressed in a fairy tale costume of Tinker Bell, holding a diamond-encrusted wand in one hand and Dorothy in the other, Jillian was sitting on the floor directly in front of the massive dollhouse when Harris entered the only sanctuary where she went to hide from the psychological ills of a deranged world. It was a special place, a home where she could live a childhood that was denied to her by a vicious father whose only interest in his daughter was to violate her on a daily basis to satiate his unnatural sexual desires. She danced the doll on stiff legs across the floor, while tapping herself on the top of her head with the jeweled end of the wand, giggling and singing happily in a voice of a young girl. Harris, his thoughts swirling about without intellectual end, could do nothing but stare at the image of one of the most powerful women in the world with incomprehension. Suddenly, like a collision of contradictory conundrums, everything and nothing made sense to him as he watched Jillian Hanson play with the doll in her hand while talking to the rows of others that lined the shelves. For the first time in his professional career, as

Jillian slowly craned her head around with a huge smile on her face to see who had come to visit her magic kingdom, Harris didn't know what to do or how to handle the situation.

And then Jillian's innocent smile was transformed into a heavy scowl.

Harris unconsciously took a step back, surprised by the level of savagery displayed. He lowered the gun.

Jillian lifted the hand holding the wand and pointed it at him. "You're a very bad man," she said in a young girl's voice, "and aren't s'pose to be in here. If you don't leave right now, you big stupid head, I'm gonna to tell." She pulled Dorothy against her chest and glared at Harris. "Dorothy doesn't like you anymore, either, so you can't marry her." She rose to her feet and walked over to the shelves that supported her children.

Harris stepped forward, smiling awkwardly, and held his arms outward with his hands open to show he was not hiding anything. "It's okay, Miss Hanson, I'm not here to hurt you," he said softly, continuing to move toward her.

"My name's not Miss Hanson, you big stupid," Jillian spat, moving away in fear. She looked around the room with wild eyes. "You better get out of before I tell on you. I swear I'll tell everyone what you did, how you hurt me bad. What you did to Momma." Tears began to course down her cheeks. "Go away!"

"Please, Miss Hanson—" Harris began.

"Stop calling me that!" Jillian shouted. "My name's not Miss Hanson."

"It's going to be all right," Harris said soothingly. "I'm here to help."

Jillian dropped to the ground and threw both hands over her ears. "You're a big, fat liar!" she screamed. "Get out! Get out! Get out!" She rolled up into a fetal position, clutching the doll against her chest while quivering violently, and began to cry uncontrollably. "You're a bad man. All men are bad. All men hurt. And everyone's a liar."

"But—" Harris tried again.

"No, Daddy, no!" Jillian screamed again, no longer hearing his words. "I'll tell Mommy. I swear I will. I'll tell Mr. Ferguson."

Harris started to take another step forward but then stopped when he noticed the hint of a shadow move across the floor. He went to raise his gun.

"Don't move a single muscle, Detective, or I swear I'll kill you where you stand," Pashka said, his tone chilling.

At the sound of the familiar voice, Jillian unfolded her body and looked up at the trusted face of the man holding a gun trained on the back of the interloper. She stood up and waved her hand at him. "Hello, Mr. Pashka," she greeted warmly, smiling like a schoolgirl.

"Hello, sweetheart," Pashka said gently. He returned her smile. "Are all of you okay?"

"We are now," Jillian replied, twisting her body around and hugging Dorothy. "We were so scared, Mr. Pashka."

"I can only imagine," Pashka said placatingly. "Mr. Harris is a very scary man, but you don't have to worry about that anymore because I'm here to protect you."

Harris turned his head around and looked at the man who held a gun pointed at his back. "What are you going to do, Mr. Pashka, shoot me in the back, in front of her?" he asked.

"If need be," Pashka replied in a whisper. "I'd prefer to handle our business in private." He looked over at Jillian and smiled warmly, pretending as if nothing was out of the ordinary. "I'm afraid Miss Hanson is having one of her more intense episodes."

"You do realize she needs help, don't you?" Harris challenged. "She's not well and should be in a hospital."

"Miss Hanson will be perfectly fine in a few hours," Pashka said. "You just don't understand the situation at all." He took a step back. "Now relinquish your weapon, using only your index finger and thumb, and hold it out at arm's length."

"You don't have to do this," Harris said. He did as instructed.

"But I do," Pashka said. He moved forward and snatched the weapon away, then stepped back again. "Now I want you to lift up your coat, then each pant leg, to show that you are not armed with a secondary firearm."

"If you'll just—" Harris began.

"Just shut up and do as ordered," Pashka said, interrupting the man. "I don't want to hear anything. None of us wanted this to happen. We meant you no harm, but you kept sticking your damn nose in places best left alone. Do you have any idea the level of inconvenience and annoyance you've caused with your nonsense? No. Of course not." He paused to take a breath and shake his head. "You should have kept your attention on just arresting the street trash and other unsavory people. You are so far out of your league, Detective, that it's not even remotely funny."

Harris continued to follow the man's instructions.

"You're smarter than you look, Detective," Pashka said, using the gun as an instrument to wave. "Now I want you to walk backwards and follow me out of the room. No fast movement. Do you understand?"

"Yes, I understand," Harris replied.

"If you try anything remotely funny, I will—" Pashka began.

"I know, I know, you'll shoot me," Harris finished. He began to step back.

"Where are you going, Mr. Pashka?" Jillian asked in a petulant tone of voice, pouting slightly.

"Don't worry, sweetheart, I'll be back in a little bit," Pashka said tenderly. "I'll tell Ferguson where you are when I find him, okay?"

Jillian smiled brightly at the thought of spending time with her surrogate father. "Okey dokey," she said. She held the doll up. "Me and Dorothy will be right here."

"Now you be a good girl," Pashka said, "and don't wander around and get into any mischief." He wagged a playful finger at her, causing her to giggle at his goofy antics.

"I will," Jillian replied. "Both of us will."

"Let's go, Detective," Pashka said. "Nice and slow. I really don't want to do anything that might make her current condition worse. She's been having some real difficulties as of late."

"You're making a very grave mistake," Harris said.

"Well, it wouldn't be the first time I did that," Pashka said without a hint of humor. "It's in my nature."

As the two men backed away, leaving the main room painstakingly slow, Pashka made certain the door was closed and securely locked before proceeding on to the next one.

Always a patient man, Harris waited for any opportunity that might present itself to lunge at his captor and disarm him. So far none had come. He knew he'd get one chance, if luck was with him. There was no doubt in his mind that the man planned to kill him once the two of them were alone, in one of the many private cubicles in the structure and safely out of earshot of Jillian. Summary execution would be carried out without delay.

"You do realize that I suspect Miss Hanson of murdering several innocent people, don't you?" Harris asked. He was desperate to drum up a discussion with the man in hope of creating some sort of distraction that might save his life. "I have a witness."

A pause.

"Is that right?" Pashka asked blandly, as if the implication meant nothing to him. "Well, isn't that just an awful thing to learn, Detective. It's a terrible world we live in these days, but everyone needs to dive headfirst into a hobby. I've heard it builds character."

"You think murdering people is a hobby?" Harris asked, shocked by the admission.

"Sure, why not?" Pashka stated, shrugging his shoulders. "After all, a hobby is basically just a preferred pastime."

"She may have killed many, possibly dozens," Harris said.

Although the man was about as cold-blooded as the worst serial killer he had ever researched, Harris couldn't help but be fascinated by the man's psychological makeup. Profiling such individuals was something he enjoyed immensely. It was his preferred pastime.

"And who hasn't, Detective," Pashka said. "None of us are exactly angels or saints, don't you agree? Besides, if we're to be brutally honest with one another, some people need killing. The world is better off without them in it." He paused as he stepped back into the barren reception room. "So, tell me, how many people have you killed?"

Harris was reticent about answering the question.

"What, cat got your tongue?" Pashka asked, taunting the man. "Now who's being coy about the job description? Admit it, Detective, you are an assassin who is sanctioned by the government to kill. Trust me, I know all about it."

"They were all criminals," Harris said flatly. "Real bad men."

"Of course they were," Pashka said condescendingly. "And they deserved everything they got, even if a trial had not yet been afforded, isn't that correct?"

"They were guilty," Harris said, adamant. "I was and am certain of that indisputable fact beyond any shadow of a doubt."

"And who made that determination?" Pashka asked. "You?"

"Yes," Harris replied evenly. "The evidence was crystal clear."

"It must be extremely liberating to be so certain of matters that result in the death of another person," Pashka said. "A little arrogant, don't you think?"

"Perhaps, to the untrained eye," Harris replied cautiously.

"And exactly who appointed you judge, jury, and executioner?" Pashka asked. "At least my hypocrisy goes only so far, Detective. I know what I am, what I was born to be."

"I'm pleased to know you've been disappointed in my sense of misplaced morality," Harris said sarcastically.

Pashka chuckled loud enough for Harris to hear. "So how many has it been?" Pashka asked. "I'm guessing it's an admirable number. Otherwise, you would not be so sensitive about the subject."

"A few, I suppose," Harris replied bitterly, somewhat evasively. His eyes darted back and forth when he suddenly realized they had just entered the last room, and the hallway was only one door away. Once they left the floor there was not a scintilla of doubt that his life would be forfeit. He was quickly running out of both time and opportunity.

"You suppose," Pashka said, chuckling softly, enjoying the moment. "What, you don't remember how many men you've killed in the line of so-called duty?" He backed out through the last door, holding the gun trained on the man in front of him, and backpedaled half a dozen steps down the hallway.

"I vividly remember each and every one of them," Harris replied, somewhat offended. "Why, don't you?"

"No, not really," Pashka replied, exhaling deeply to accentuate his level of indifference to another man's suffering. "There are too many to recall, not that I actually wasted any time thinking about it or them. Killing another man is no more a big deal to me than stepping on the head of a dead gopher."

"Then you're just a cold man," Harris said.

"I'm just an efficient and effective asset to my job," Pashka said. The tone of his voice was matter-of-fact. "It was good enough for Uncle Sam." He paused. "So tell me, do you care about or feel bad for any of the men or women you've killed?"

"Honestly?" Harris asked.

"No, I want you to lie to me," Pashka said facetiously. "Yes, honestly. Do you really care?"

Harris thought about the question for several seconds before answering. "No," he replied. "I don't feel anything for any of them one way or another. They were rotten to the core and died a violent and well-deserved death. It's all rather cut and dry." He backed up into the hallway, still searching for any means of possible escape.

Pashka chuckled mildly again. "You know what?" Pashka said. "I kind of like you. There's no lying with you, and I respect that in a man. Quite honestly, I kind of expected you to give me some lame song and dance, in some twisted version, of how killing a human being is a sin and morally reprehensible. You know, some sort of touchy, get in tune with your inner softness sort of nonsense. No one wants to admit that everyone has a killer inside just waiting for a reason to emerge from the depths of what is innately man's true nature."

"No, that's not me at all," Harris said. "I know exactly what I am and what I am capable of doing."

"That's good," Pashka said, grinning. "Every man should know who and what they are deep down. Perhaps, even more importantly, is for that same man to know what he isn't capable of doing."

"I completely agree," Harris said.

"You already know where the elevator is located, so get to walking," Pashka said. "Hands behind your head."

"You don't have to do this," Harris said. "Miss Hanson is obviously suffering from some sort of psychological problem and won't have to go to prison."

"It's a whole lot more complicated than that, pal, and you know it," Pashka said. "Stop talking and move."

The two men had just arrived at the elevator when the radio unexpectedly squawked to life, momentarily drawing Pashka's attention away from the prisoner. It was all the time Harris needed to spin around and bring a hand down in a chopping blow on Pashka's wrist, knocking the gun free. A look of surprise covered Pashka's face, which was instantly followed by a loud growl of anger. He ducked down to retrieve the gun that was lying near his feet. Seeing another opportunity, Harris sent a wicked blow to the side of his head, which rocked the man on his feet and caused his vision to blur for a couple of seconds. He saw the hired killer trying to reach for the weapon once again and threw another punch at him, this time just a glancing one off the top of his head. He knew if the man got control over the handgun, it wouldn't matter what floor they were on or who would hear the gunshot. He threw another blow, this one landing on the side of the man's face. The punch knocked Pashka slightly off balance. While attempting to manufacture a form of defense against the attack, stretching out one more time to snatch the gun from off the ground, he inadvertently overcompensated and stumbled forward, accidentally kicking the gun through the open doors of the elevator. The momentum of his weight caused him to fall forward and crash into Harris. Both men flew backward.

The elevator doors closed with a whoosh.

"Mr. Pashka, this is Barney Trabble," the panicked voice of the man crackled through the static of the small speaker. "What is going on? Do you need help? Should I call the police now? Please talk to me. I saw that man attack you. What is going on? Please, tell me what to do!"

The two men in the elevator ignored the panicked pleas coming from the communication device and continued to fight for their lives. Neither combatant was aware that the elevator was already moving down the shaft.

"Mr. Pashka, I need …" Barney began, but he then looked at the device with wide eyes when the sound of a gunshot rang out. Words failed him. All he could do was silently stare at the device and wait for directions as to what he should do next.

Winded and breathing heavily, Harris snatched the two-way radio and pressed the talk button. "This is Detective Harris," he announced calmly, doing everything possible to reduce the receiver's nervousness. "Who am I speaking to?"

"Um, my name is Barney Trabble," he said apprehensively. "How do I know you're not lying to me?"

"Where are you, Mr. Trabble?" Harris asked with a note of authority in his voice. "What is your job?"

"I'm in the surveillance room," Barney replied uneasily, unsure as to whether he should be telling the man anything at all. "I'm sort of a techno-security man."

"I want you to call the police," Harris said, the tone of his voice dead serious.

"Where is Mr. Pashka?" Barney asked. "I want to speak to him."

"He's dead," Harris replied evenly. "He was shot during a scuffle."

"You killed him, didn't you?" Barney asked, panting from a growing anxiety. He clutched at his chest. "You murdered him, didn't you?"

"Yes, I killed him!" Harris barked. "Now do your job and call the damn police. Call them right now!"

Barney craned his head around at the sound of the outside door being unlocked. Relief flooded through him. Just the thought of being rescued from such a nightmare caused his heart rate to slow. "Oh, thank God," he breathed through quivering lips.

"What is it?" Harris asked.

"I think someone already called the police," Barney replied. "Someone's already here, Detective Harris."

Harris gripped the radio tightly and moved his mouth closer to it. "Get..." he began, but the distinct eruption of gunfire cut him off. The entire world seemed to have fallen silent. "Barney, Barney, are you there?" He paused. "Mr. Trabble, please answer me." When no answer came from the other side, only the familiar sound of dead air, Harris dropped the radio on the ground and quickly checked the bloodstained gun.

The music that was playing inside the elevator only seconds ago fell quiet and was replaced by the squelch of a speaker in the far upper corner. A small video camera was located right next to it.

"This does not have to be painful, Detective Harris," a cold voice said. "Give yourself up. You cannot prevail or escape. Cooperate with my wishes, and I promise a quick death."

Harris peered up at the camera and flipped a middle finger at it. "Yeah, right, pal," he mumbled under his breath. "Like I'm just going to offer myself up on the altar of sacrifice."

"We really don't appreciate the unnecessarily rude gesture, Detective," the voice said. "There's never a reason to be disrespectful. Such antics are so, shall we say, pedestrian and, therefore, beneath you."

"Screw you!" Harris spat. "That's not cooperation; it's asinine suicide."

"Oh, that's just perfect manners," the voice said with a note of sarcasm. "Why don't you save us the trouble of pursuing you and just stick the barrel of the gun in your mouth. It would be greatly appreciated."

"Yeah, I bet it would," Harris said. "Why don't you come to me and try to stick it in my mouth for me?"

"You have less than sixty seconds to comply, Detective Harris," the voice warned, sighing audibly. "Please do not make this more difficult than need be. There is nowhere for you to go."

"Come and get me," Harris challenged.

"We are already on our way to rectify the unfortunate chain of events," the voice said. "You have really created a pickle with your infernal interference, and must now pay the consequences."

"The police will be here soon," Harris said.

"No, they won't," the voice corrected. "I'm afraid Mr. Trabble was unable to make that call before tragedy befell him. Of course, Barney was a beloved member of this firm and shall be missed. You should never have involved him. He had a family, friends, and a regular life many would envy."

"People know where I am," Harris said. "They'll come looking for me, asking all kinds of questions you won't like."

A dry chuckle.

"Nice try," the voice said humorously. "No one, not even your little partner, knows you're here. You don't even know who I am, and the two of you did help our predicament by keeping your suspicions between just the two of you. We really do appreciate that. Didn't want to risk sharing the credit, correct?"

"Glad to hear we could be of service," Harris snapped heatedly.

Another dry chuckle resounded over the speaker.

"The truth will be exposed," Harris said, "and justice will prevail."

"Whose?" the voice said mockingly. "Yours? That's rich, Detective, and awfully desperate for a man of your intelligence. Everything is fluid and open for interpretation, and I do hope you are not referring to your pathetic lieutenant friend. He is definitely incommunicado—rather permanently." A slight chuckle resounded over the speaker.

"So you murdered him, too," Harris said, distaste filling his voice. "He was good man, you evil bastard."

"Perhaps," the voice said. "'Was' being the operative word."

"Then why all this?" Harris asked, befuddled.

"I would destroy everything on the planet for Miss Hanson, Detective," the voice said. "She is the closest thing I have to family and shall protect her at all cost, even if it meant burning everything and everyone in the world." The voice paused. "I see you managed to get the best of Mr. Pashka. Congratulations on such a triumph. He was a very formidable opponent, not that defeating him has actually done anything to improve your precarious situation."

Harris looked down at the slain man and pointed an accusing finger. "That maniac tried to murder me," he said.

"I don't doubt it," the voice said calmly. "However, in all fairness, you shouldn't begrudge him for just trying to do his job, particularly since he failed so miserably. I can't tell you how much he disappointed me. Good help is really hard to find these days."

"The same thing doesn't have to happen to Miss Hanson," Harris pleaded. "I can go to the district attorney. I can speak on her behalf."

"We don't need anything from you," the voice said caustically. "Outsiders are not permitted to enter our inner circle."

"She's sick and in need of psychiatric help," Harris said.

"We can provide all that she needs," the voice said. "We have always taken care of her. She must be allowed to continue the work on behalf of the legacy. You are too small a man in intellect to even begin to grasp the fundamentals involved."

"You're insane!" Harris shouted.

The sound of men laughing echoed throughout the confines of the elevator. "Of course we are," the voice said humorously. "Who isn't, these days? We must protect our own, regardless of the means utilized. It is the way things have always been for those who carry the burden of excellence."

"You admit it?" Harris asked, incredulous.

"Why would we deny it?" the voice asked. "I know it's a trying time, even unsavory, but please conduct yourself with a modicum of dignity. If it serves as any form of consolation, I do regret removing an interesting person such as yourself from the earth."

"Go to hell!" Harris shouted. "You'll find that I'm not so easy to outmaneuver or kill, you sick bastard."

"I understand," the voice said, devoid of any emotion. "We shall test that theory, so please be prepared."

"I'll fight," Harris said vehemently. He held the gun trained on the elevator doors, methodically waiting for them to open.

"Five seconds," the voice said. "It has been a relative pleasure, Detective, but I must bid you adieu."

Without any warning whatsoever, the elevator suddenly stopped in between the fourth and fifth floors. Harris gripped the gun even tighter, taking a three-point stance. *Come on, you crazy bastard,* he thought, licking his lips. *I'm all ready for you, all of you.* He pressed his back against the back wall, firmly believing he was prepared for anyone and anything.

An odd hissing noise, like that of a snake, filled the elevator, which was immediately followed by a vapor that smelled of bitter almonds.

The effect of the cyanide gas that seeped into the sealed box was almost instantaneous.

The gun slipped from his hand and struck the floor with a loud clatter. Harris clutched at his own throat, squeezing his eyes shut against the excruciating pain that coursed through him as he struggled to breathe through seized lungs, and dropped to his knees. Lurching forward uncontrollably, his body wracked by a number of violent convulsions, spittle jetted from his mouth just as he fell facedown on the cold surface. He was dead less than ten seconds after inhaling the first tendrils of the chemical compound.

The sound of a vacuum began to hum softly, purifying the air by sucking away the deadly residue, just as the gears inside the shaft began to grind anew. Foot by foot, the thick cable raised the heavy weight attached to the end of its steel braided tether.

Both armed with automatic pistols, waiting for the familiar sound of the bell, Ferguson held the video transmitter out at arm's length so Brad could also see the deceased man on the screen.

"Are you sure he's dead?" Brad asked.

"Yes, Bradley, I'm quite certain," Ferguson replied. "No one could have survived the parts per square inch that were introduced into such a closed environment."

"Then why did you insist we remain armed and ready?" Brad asked.

"Because I never take any chances," Ferguson replied. "The key is to never take anything for granted or underestimate an adversary. Always remember that a wounded and dying animal is the most dangerous of all in the kingdom."

Ferguson pushed Brad over to the left side of the doors and then stepped to the right when it stopped on their floor. They made sure to move out of the line of fire. Ferguson pressed a single finger against his lips to signal his partner to remain silent.

The tiny bell rang. The doors opened.

Ferguson wasted no time to make certain that any potential threat was eliminated and the situation was secure. He swung his hand around the corner and pumped two rapid rounds into the head of each man. Startled by such a vicious assault on a corpse, Brad nearly dropped his own weapon. Ferguson then entered the elevator, pressed the gun against the detective's head and shot him one more time.

"What are you doing?" Brad asked, perplexed. "The man is dead as can be. You said so yourself."

Ferguson looked over at him and smiled cruelly. "Yes, he is," he said. "And now I'm most certain of it." He turned his attention back on Harris. "Never assume anything is ever what it appears."

"Understood," Brad said, watching the older man curiously. "So what should we do now?"

"I want you to go to the maintenance shack on the roof and grab some heavy-duty trash bags, so we can wrap up the bodies and prepare them for disposal," Ferguson ordered, sliding the gun back into its holster. "I also want you to get a bottle of disinfectant and muriatic acid to clean up this mess. We'll post a caution sign that the elevator is closed due to repairs."

"What are you going to do?" Brad asked.

"I'm going to go check on Miss Hanson," Ferguson replied. "Just bag up the bodies and clean the area, Bradley. And try to locate Mr. Pashka's men. None of them are in the building."

He stretched out his arms and yawned. "I'm quite certain Miss Hanson will want to be open for business as soon as possible. You know how obsessive she can be about the operation of the firm, and work."

"I'm more than aware of her compulsions," Brad said, smiling. "You can always depend on me." He nodded his head. "I'll never fail you or my sister."

"I never doubted that for even a second," Ferguson said admiringly, offering a fatherly smile of genuine affection for the man. "You're a Hanson, your mother's son, and are therefore incapable of failure." He then walked out of the elevator and toward the stairwell at the end of the hallway.

Jillian had just set Dorothy back on the shelf when she heard the faint sound of footsteps coming from behind her. She turned and gave a loving smile that nearly melted Ferguson's heart. Tears welled in his eyes.

Jillian pressed her lips together. Lines of worry creased her face. "What's the matter, Ferguson?" she asked. "Are you hurt?"

"No, Miss Hanson," Ferguson replied softly. "I'm just happy to see you, that's all."

"Well, isn't that about the sweetest thing you've ever said," Jillian said, smiling brightly. "You're just so good to me. I don't know what I'd ever do without you."

Ferguson walked over to her and hugged her tightly. "You never have to worry about that, Miss Hanson, because I will never leave you," he said sincerely. He then broke the embrace and looked at her with serious eyes. "I bet you're ready to conquer the world again, aren't you?"

Jillian placed both hands on her hips and smiled. "Now what would ever give you cause to think such a thing?" she asked playfully.

"Call it an educated guess," Ferguson replied. He then placed a hand against the side of his mouth as if preparing to convey a secret. "You see, I know these things."

Jillian giggled in response. "That's what I've heard," she said. She then held her arm out for him to take. "I will, of course, need a ride from my favorite dad."

"It would be my honor," Ferguson said, taking her by the arm. "Of course, we will have to take the maintenance elevator because the one for staff is under repair, which is why everyone was sent home."

"Everyone?" Jillian asked, showing a little surprise. "I hope they're still getting paid for the day."

"Whatever you want," Ferguson said happily, patting her on the hand. He then leaned over and kissed her on the cheek.

"What's gotten into you, Ferguson?" Jillian asked, experiencing the feelings of a daughter who was loved by her father. "It's unlike you to be so openly affectionate with anyone, especially me. What about protocol?"

"At least for the day," Ferguson began, "to the devil with it." He then made a hearty laugh. "I'm happy and with my little girl. Life is good."

"Should we tell Brad that we're leaving?" Jillian asked.

"Naw, I'm sure he's busy doing something, somewhere," Ferguson replied.

"Yep, that's Brad," Jillian said.

Wrapping Jillian's arm tightly inside of his own, leaving all evidence of the past events to be erased by Brad Renfro, the man who had sworn an oath to a woman he had loved more than life itself gladly guided her daughter toward the unwritten future.